A Step
TOO FAR

JOANNA NORTH

authorHOUSE®

AuthorHouse™ UK
1663 Liberty Drive
Bloomington, IN 47403 USA
www.authorhouse.co.uk
Phone: 0800 047 8203 (Domestic TFN)
       +44 1908 723714 (International)

Published by AuthorHouse 03/13/2020

ISBN: 978-1-7283-9994-2 (sc)
ISBN: 978-1-7283-9995-9 (hc)
ISBN: 978-1-7283-9993-5 (e)

Print information available on the last page.

Chapter 1

Survive by Facing Reality

There are many stories of love and hate in this world, old stories wherein the two emotions seem as inevitable as gravity itself. Gravity appears to both love us and hate us and we have never really fathomed why this is. None of us knows exactly why this force of nature supports us and holds us to her heart with intense power but also pulverises and grinds us to dust on deciding when our time is over. We are slaves to these forces and this is a story about two such enslaved beings – a story about how love can uplift us and set us free and how, just as often, an equal force of hate will attempt to destroy us. If we have one of these passions in our life, we cannot live without experiencing the other. This is the knowledge of those who have lived, loved and hated in equal measure.

Alicia Millward was not an easy victim for any persecutor, whatever their purpose or calling. Difficult her childhood may have been from her birth in 1953, but she had found ways to wrestle with this. Nobody, she had decided, would take her peace of mind away from her. She could face down all that existence can give in terms of challenge – the kind of challenges that we all must stand up to in this world: the bank manager, the weather, the clock, 'weight management', men who fell in love with her and men who fell out of love with her. Her decision, her vow to stay always and fight with an honest fist, had been made at around the age of ten when, in an empty classroom all on her own with no witness, she had accidentally knocked a bottle of ink – a whole new fresh bottle of ink – all over the desk of her French teacher. Black ink, particularly destructive on paper if unguided. After an initial panic she decided the best policy was to own up even though nobody had seen what had happened. She could have got away with it, but she sought out the teacher concerned, explained her accident and fortunately for her she was met not only with understanding but with praise for her honesty and a request that the child's explanation be repeated in French for good measure. The teacher would never know the lifelong consequences of her response to the child, although teachers should really realise the impact of their words. As a result, Alicia vowed always to tell the truth and face down threatening events. If only human beings understood the impact of their vows on their brains; they would understand themselves so much better. Alicia had not realised that, from that moment, she would be that person with that intention for the rest of her life through good and bad.

She had other good qualifications that might have helped with her competence – a degree in business management and a professional status in accountancy. Yes, that kind of qualification, but those certificates mean little really in terms of overcoming the challenges of life. As her family were poor both in their bank account and in group imagination, she worked her way through university without support. There then followed an apprenticeship during which she discovered another truth about life: 'Work hard and conscientiously at anything and you will get results, if only in terms of your pay packet.'

If you come from a working-class family, you learn either that hard work will set you free if you become accomplished or that it will keep you a slave for the rest of your life. Her working-class credentials ensured that she ticked two boxes relating to survival. First, the achievement of financial independence through hard work and diligence, and second, the attainment of some status through a good profession. Status and profession, she knew, were what make us think we are protected just a little from the ravages of real life. In fact, they are but fragile defences that would not protect her from the unimaginable events of her later life.

But, as a young woman, she had preparedness for the real challenges of life: the everyday challenges for which she had qualifications in what we might call emotional resilience, and her particular badge of honour was 'managing difficult people'. Yes, she could do this. This was not learned from a book but from experience and learned from a very early age, perhaps the cradle.

What does a baby do when a mother is hostile to their needs? They learn to keep quiet and wait. This can breed great anxiety or enormous patience depending on which way you look at the event. In her case, she had both – deep-seated and well disguised anxiety combined with an incredible ability to wait until she was old enough to look after herself so that no one ever again would be responsible for her needs except for her. There was little point in demonstrating too much anxiety, for as far as she was concerned those states all had to be kept under control. And what, then, does a toddler do when a parent wishes they would go away, just at a point when the child is most energetic and inquisitive and wants to explore their world? They become either naughty to gain attention or they learn to co-operate. In this case the girl learned to co-operate in order to gain the maximum approval from the scornful woman she was tied to for love, otherwise known as her mother.

You might have called her lucky, but Alicia Millward would have challenged you on this. She had a philosophical view of luck: 'You make your own luck in this world.' You can line up events so that they work in your favour and still something can come along when you don't notice and knock you down, and yet at the same time a chain of events may smooth your pathway to success. Was it God, she wondered, or a special event called luck? Or was hope what we are all really seeking rather than luck? Raised as a Catholic, there was definitely a God in place in her mind, but education got in the way of this and a module on evolution in her first-year options at university made her consider the idea that the whole of existence was up for grabs and had a will of its own that was not necessarily divine or benign, and this became one of the more anxiety-provoking realisations of her life. She concluded in the end, though, that she was open to the possibility that there may be a God.

The woman we find in this story is a woman willing to face reality, accept what life brings to her door and manage the unknown with the knowledge that one should be hopeful, while at the same time not surprised by the unexpected onslaught of difficulty. This position brought her strength and informed her reactions to life, and such was the state of her mind as she comes into our story at the age of thirty-seven, divorced, without children, in control and believing in prayer and hard work as being the major forces for coping. One may think that Alicia would be impossible to knock off her feet, but we will see how her strategy works out as she meets a challenge more unfair and unreasonable than anyone of her design should ever have to meet.

Or was it? Maybe she deserved what she got … Was it fate in the workings of her unconscious mind replicating the threat in the form of a young man who would want her dead? Or was it more likely due to the presence of the older man she was about to meet and fall in love with for the rest of her life?

Chapter 2

Survive by Avoiding Reality

If you want to understand the life philosophy of Charles Bradshaw, Alicia's second husband, then think of Mr Darcy …yes, Mr Darcy, the aloof romantic hero of Jane Austen's *Pride and Prejudice*. Like Charles Bradshaw he was a noble character at heart. Like Alicia, by the formative age of fourteen in 1956 Charles had made the vow that would carry him through life, and the vow was that he would behave as would a hero in all matters that came before him.

This idea was especially put to the test when the boys at school bullied him, often via boxing matches in the playground that usually ended up with Charles's nose being bloodied: a sign of the hero that he would one day become. 'Valiant' is the word, the word that describes our man with the intention to be the hero, to put things right, to get on in life by being jolly decent.

Luckily, our putative hero also had the good sense to keep secrets. The major secret that he kept from the bullies was that his favourite thing to do in the whole world was to go to the stables and help a stable girl with whom he was in love. His mother wondered where he was going after tea so quickly in the summer evenings. He had an unquestioning affinity with horses and the animals returned his connection to them with abiding obedience and understanding. He was never once thrown off a horse and they always stepped aside when he was mucking out their stables. This was where his Herculean intention in life was realised – he could be the genteel hero, and all was well in the world in the stables.

The smells uplifted him, the sweet musky hay, the soft oats, the smell of leather and polish. In addition to which, he was paid some very charming attention by this fourteen-year-old stable girl who was enormously sweet to him. She rather saw him as her little pet. She liked his soft horse-brown eyes that peered out at her from under his schoolboy fringe. He would do absolutely anything she asked of him – even the beastly jobs like wheel-barrowing horse dung down to the steaming dung heap in the heat of summer.

His faithful and unquestioning loyalty to her (loyalty being another of his heroic traits) was rewarded by smiles, soft gazes and more work to do. His world was complete. This was someone who showed him affection and was kind to him. And this girl's name? Alicia! The same name as that of his future partner. He would repeat it softly to himself as he walked to the stables and told himself he would never forget her. Alicia was scored into his brain and everything he did at that time was for her. Thinking of her even helped him to endure the beatings and humiliations at school.

Since he loved the stable and horses and Alicia so much you might understand why his future in the insurance industry did not immediately feel like home to him. But, being one to accept and settle, he soon made a good living from his work. Since he had loved Alicia the stable girl you might also wonder why he married June, who did not like horses and possibly did not even like Charles very much if she was honest. In fact, June was never honest with the most important person in her world, and that was herself.

But Charles was happy in the year that he met June. He had been travelling with his friends across Europe and Iran to India and Tibet, stopping to wonder at Everest and every day breathing in the elixir of just being alive. At the age of twenty-eight, in 1970, all his adventures came to an end when he returned home to England for a visit and was prompted by family and friends to think about settling down and getting married. This was his moment of truth with the call of the wild about to be taken from his hands. Would he stay, or would he go? Now, he was a fully-fledged adult, a man in his own right – quite tough but still quite tender – the man he wanted to be at this stage in his life. And so he stayed and re-established his role in insurance.

The adventure was over, and so the vivid and colourful pictures of his life of freedom – Tibet, Everest, Iran and India – gathered dust in the loft of the home that he bought with his wife June, as they began to raise their children. The colours of his life, his youth and his mythic dream were locked away in boxes in their loft. He would not find them again for years. The gold, lilac, saffron, and the brilliant sunshine of his travels, the pungent smells and the daily adventures were ended, and he resigned himself to marriage to someone he was not sure he loved and a career that he was not sure he enjoyed but at which he was at least prospering. Charles quietly forgot for nearly fifteen years until he met the woman who would bring the joy back to his life. Then, his endurance would be stretched much further than his early travels had demanded of him, and he would be forced to find that rarest of traits: the courage that rises in maturity out of the dream of adolescent heroism.

Chapter 3

Evolution of a Stepson – Freddie Bradshaw – Born, 1976

The problems with Freddie Bradshaw, son of Charles and June, were many years in the making. He was their long-awaited child, cherished and adored by his mother, yet eventually avoided and abandoned by his father. His was a personality forged on the fire of love and fear, just as his future stepmother, Alicia's, had been. Yet many facets to his being were the polar-opposite to hers, based more on privilege and over-indulgence than on deprivation.

The very great entitlement that this boy had in his life was that his mother had thought that he was a 'King', and he would remain a King in his own mind for his whole life as well as hers. As with most formative life experiences, as he grew older this mistaken projection of supremacy was a double-edged sword. He just could not understand why others did not think and realise he was also an entitled being, just as his mother had demonstrated to him every day of his life. So, long before Alicia Millward came on the scene as his stepmother there was a problem evolving. Freddie's construction was essentially tied to the personality traits of both his mother and his father, and we must go back to the relationship between the two of them to really understand the pathway and temperament of the child they raised together and to understand why he was not actually the person he had been led to believe he could be.

June had met Charles when he was twenty-eight and decided that he was the man for her. She was not by any means a good temperamental or even intellectual match for him. Her family were country people from the Somerset Levels living in the market town of Blessingham situated twenty miles from the county town of Taunton. The beautiful, rich and accessible land was subject to flooding due to its remarkably level terrain. Although at times disastrous to the generations who lived there, this ever-present hazard made the area uniquely fertile for farmland.

People had traded in the town with arable and animal agriculture – particularly wool, sheep, fruit and corn – for more than ten centuries and now Blessingham was a bustling market town with a population of around 30,000, hosting shops, offices, schools and amenities for the local community yet still surrounded by acres of flattened unspoiled landscape and endless waterways. The town was home to families across the social spectrum, with the unique status of serving many farming families, blue-collar workers, landed gentry and a smattering of the glitterati who escaped from London at weekends to their country retreats, as well as families living on social benefits and scraping together an existence. Much work was created by the farmers who inhabited the area. The Somerset Levels are just another example of the polarities of nature and the aforementioned forces of gravity, producing opportunity as well as great risk.

Charles had not chosen his own career and he had not really chosen his wife. She had chosen for him. He had wanted to farm and felt a deep affinity for the land, but he had been overruled by his father who threw him from public school into work in insurance. His marriage to June evolved in a similar fashion: she came along and pretty well threw him into wedlock with her. She had seemed nice enough but there was a fatal flaw in their chemistry, a fault line that would eventually crack, and this was the shocking differential in their deepest responses to being alive. Charles valued peace, quiet and the respectful gentlemanly pleasantries in life. He loved art and music and was deeply sensitive to others. Quite like his royal counterpart Prince Charles born the same year he was a sensitive gentleman, and perhaps his own parents had unconsciously named and therefore aligned him with the Prince as many parents do in Great Britain. Like Prince Charles, Charles Bradshaw was not happy at school and needed more love and affection in his life, whereas June was a sturdy character and made of altogether tougher material. She was both vivacious, pleasant enough and engaged enough with life to make her very appealing, but she was also limited by a mind that was unimaginative and which simply did not see far enough into the future. This difference accounted for many unreachable differences between them, especially in the raising of their child. If Charles argued that the child was being spoilt by doing and getting everything that he wanted, June would argue passionately that he was only young and did not fully understand things yet.

Charles's first real puzzlement and consternation with his child was when he, at the age of three, felt perfectly free to urinate behind the settee. All fair enough as a childish experiment and pushing of limits and boundaries, but guidance should have been given to get the behaviour on track. His mother, though, saw it as a creative act after which she was perfectly happy to clear up. By the age of five Freddie thought he could pee wherever he wanted, and could not understand why he was told off with great haste when demonstrating this at his school by urinating in the sink instead of the lavatory and encouraging his little classmates to do the same. Clearly a problem was emerging, and these were the early telltale signs that a child might have been affected by a mother's obsessive love and a father's ineffectiveness.

Initially, June was not without the capacity to enchant her man. She was petite, charismatic, and powerful in her self-belief, and in the early stages of their relationship her vibrancy and youthful enthusiasm were a panacea to Charles's natural tendency to despondency. She gave him hope, and in the early days of their relationship that was fatally attractive. As time went by the hope that she inspired was maladjusted to become a kind of prison in which he entombed himself. When baby Freddie was born they had already begun to establish this pattern of relating, with Charles relatively withdrawn into himself and June taking charge and running their family show.

Twelve years later these opposing forces would prove to be the catalyst for a divorce, throughout which June would never cease to battle for her right to keep her man, and by which means Charles just had to remove himself from the relationship, otherwise he felt he would quite literally hang himself. His parents could see this despair in his life and they wanted him to leave June as quickly as possible. Tough as they had been as parents in his childhood, they deeply loved their son and were more sensitive in their old age as they watched the story, and its inevitable outcome, unfold over the years. The coup de grâce was that June was an only child and had never really separated herself from her parental apron strings. Charles had been made to feel as if he lived in his home with her parents, to whom she remained invisibly bonded – they may as well have moved into Charles and June's home with them. As the iconic first wife of his royal counterpart, Prince Charles, had once declared to the world: 'There were three of us in this marriage,' Charles's quieter moments revealed to him that there were 'four of us in this marriage', the other three being his wife and her parents. They just would not distance themselves from June's life, and to prove this they moved to a cottage only one hundred yards down the road from their daughter so that they could help out when she finally gave birth to her extra special firstborn. Charles became the spare part to her family, who all thought ill of him. His strategy for peace and avoidance of conflict gained him no respect, and he quietly lost his footing in his marriage completely.

It is not surprising, then, that his son Freddie also grew up to disregard his father and have little respect for him. There was little in his environment that advised him otherwise, but some of the reasons for this were of Charles's own making. He survived in the relationship by doing what his wife wanted him to do: earning the money, driving her to the shops, paying for Freddie's expensive private school and taking them on holiday. He would do all of these things without question, wishing to please and keep a smile on her face, to maintain the illusion that the marriage was working. Unhappy as he was, his abiding principle was that he just could not fail at marriage. That would be too much shame and disillusionment for him to bear.

He told himself that he was willing to tolerate anything – even when she began bullying him into submission and treating him with disdain. When Charles adopted the role of the family butler, the child knew no different. His father had become a servant to mother and child, and within a very few months of the child's birth, mother and son had become the primary unit – a love affair had emerged: 'There were three of them in this marriage and the doting grandparents made five.' Charles tried to hold on to each passing day as it came, but he gradually came to reject Freddie, and the child knew it and felt it.

June was thriving – and why not? She had everything she wanted in life. They had managed to buy their own home through a generous donation from the out-laws, which Charles had not wanted to accept. But accept it he had, and this weakness moved them forward so that the Little King could be born into a home that was owned rather than rented. She did not have to work and could remain at home doting on her child twenty-four hours a day. Her glory was in motherhood and to her, she may as well have been local royalty as she took her baby in his pram down the high street of Blessingham. She knew all the shopkeepers and local people by name, and they had known her from childhood. Her perambulation to town would make her day. A trip to the shops where everyone would recognise that she was the mother of a baby boy who was perfect and beautiful was all she required to feel perfect herself. She spent her days in a reverie of maternal joy and the glory of her unique child was reflected to her. As far as she was concerned she had made it. Everything was in place in her life. All the building blocks were there. She would live as local people did, just as her parents had done in this farming community. All of this was as normal to her and as inevitable as the passing of time, and the geological and geographical processes that formed the Somerset countryside and laid it flat, making a natural pathway for water to flow.

Chapter 4

Who Is Watching You

Their struggle was recorded by the octogenarian Gwen Knight, living five doors down from the Bradshaw household on the opposite side of the road. Gwen was enjoying the prospect of her morning tea with her closest companion, Abigail Farley, one day as she held forth on her opinion. They would frequently observe the mother and son going by on their trips into town, and as the child grew older their trips to the park, the toddler group, and then the posh private infants' school.

Gwen was fully retired and able to observe and scrutinise life to the full without the necessity of holding back on her thoughts any longer. She was both wily and wise and, even though she had no children of her own, spotted very soon that this Bradshaw child was out of control, and considered that the mother 'completely ruined him'.

She chattered to Abigail as she wheeled in their tea and biscuits on the tea trolley. They sat in the front room looking out of the window, which had a panoramic view of the road from one end to the other. To the left the road led to a small housing estate; to the right it led to a small T-junction.

When they reached the T-junction, Gwen could see whether the inhabitants turned right to go into town, or turned left to the rough track that could reach the river that flowed on through the countryside. She knew the river well – the River Exe, heading from a stream in the tiny village of Simonsbath, babbled through the county of Somerset and then expanded massively into the adjoining county of Devon and out to sea via the Exe estuary at Exmouth.

Gwen joked to Abigail that being in her lounge was like being at the cinema. But watching was much more than a hobby for them both. Even after Abigail went home Gwen would resume her afternoon shift and keep her seat late into the night. Abigail, being more inclined to record information following a lifetime as a secretary, took things a step further and really did keep a diary of the small daily events that they observed and discussed. No subject was too sacred between these two well-practised custodians of Blessingham life. Although they were invisible except to the very few, they felt this cloak of invisibility only added to the importance of the role they had carved out for themselves. In this world, Gwen and Abigail felt no despair at all at the limitations of old age. Together they had uncovered and developed the gift of quiet watching and waiting which is silently bequeathed to the elderly. They may have looked like two vacant old women staring from the window and gossiping, but they were far from this.

The two veterans had uncovered together one of the secrets of life itself: that it never actually comes to a halt and that it continues for ever, like their gossip and the River Exe. As a result, these ladies felt they had found their purpose. Their watching was their art form and their goal was to consider the implications of the universal forces unfolding through the small events that they saw through Gwen's window. They were devoted to their task and to each other. Together they were strong as they chattered, bantered and considered. They concluded that their importance to life was not over. They were the sisterhood of hope. Ordinary they may have looked, but few knew what Gwen and Abigail knew by now.

'There she is with that little horror,' Gwen said. 'Do you know, I saw him pull up flowers in the park the other day and it was so obvious that he needed to be told off. Instead, she thanked him. Abigail, how wrong can a mother be in spoiling a child? I swear that one will end up in borstal. I can see exactly where he's heading.'

'Two sugars, Gwen. And a little extra – I need it today, and have you noticed that the child has a big head?' Abigail dunked her biscuit in her tea as she considered the matter and blurted out her unedited thoughts as one can only do with an old friend.

'What? Literally?' Gwen gave her three sugars, knowing that this was what she really meant when she said she needed more.

'Well, yes, literally he has quite a big head, but I mean in his personality. He's only four and it's as if he is the boss of everything. It's a most unattractive quality in a child. My children knew where they were in life. I think it makes them happier. Speaking of unattractive, I also think he looks odd.' Abigail half meant what she said and realised that her words sounded unkind, but she did find him a very unappealing little boy, and she considered this uneasy feeling.

'How do you mean?' Gwen wasn't sure whether Abigail was going to make a joke or not.

'Like he's possessed.' Abigail finally blurted out the words.

'Oh, I see,' said Gwen. 'Well, I've not had children of my own, but I've seen enough in my time and looked after enough. Pass the biscuits, dear, I really want to try those "peanut cookies", as they're called; they look much more interesting than digestives, though why we have to start calling them cookies, I don't know – "peanut biscuits" will do nicely.'

Gwen sipped her tea and crunched her biscuit, enjoying the new taste of peanut which she thought was very agreeable.

'How is it that you eat so many biscuits and still remain stick-thin while I am most careful about how many I eat and look as if I eat cake all day?' said Abigail. 'I just cannot eat another one but would love another tea from the pot … two sugars again, dear … don't skimp.'

Gwen knew that Abigail was only half-joking when she made observations about Freddie and the way he looked. All the same, she went back in her mind to see if she had seen signs of demonic possession in Freddie when she had watched him over the previous weeks. She had not thought of that before. It was a sad indictment of a child that two women should be joking about him in this way, but his behaviour was noticeably out of the ordinary. Despite not having had children of her own, somehow, she knew this little boy's behaviour was a problem for his parents.

Gwen knew about relationships and knew about people. Of the two friends she was the more dominant and sure-footed. She had worked her whole life in service as a housekeeper and she understood how to read someone from the way they looked. When you always lived and worked in other people's houses you had to learn to do this for your own security. You had to notice the climate around people and make predictions about what was going on in their minds. Gwen had been so good at this that her employer, Captain Shields, in his dying days had bequeathed her his home for all the hours of mind-reading she had offered to him. This was a gift for the dedicated care and patience she had shown him; he was grateful for her simple human kindness that turned his slow demise into a more comfortable experience and gave meaning to his days in the departure lounge of life. He returned to her the great gift she had given him. The difference in their social standing became irrelevant to him. He had been a handsome, cultured man with status and money and she had been a plain and sensible woman who apparently only understood housekeeping. But he admired her with a passion for her capability and enduring practicality that made his life so ordered following the death of his wife.

They chatted daily, and he came to understand that her housekeeping had taught her science, and that her observation of people was the study of psychology, and that her nursing and care had the skill of any professional medic. There was nothing ordinary about her at all. She became his muse and object of fascination in the life that was left in him. Her care for him was an act of devotion in which she took great pleasure, and which gave her purpose. The act of giving fulfilled her lifelong ambition to serve others to perfection. As he became more ill she cared for him as if he were her child, and her importance to him increased beyond measure. He wanted to give her something for the immense love and loyalty she had shown him. So he left her his home and, with this great gift, his heart. The house became a monument to the devotional love that had flowed between them. She was always grateful for this act of generosity that so handsomely repaid her for years of service, but which gave her also an abiding sense of the something wonderful that had quietly passed between them unspoken, daily.

So, living now in the same road as the Bradshaws, Didcot Lane, in this comfortable home in her retirement, she had time to wait and watch and mull over the comings and goings of daily life and reflect on these with Abigail. If the householders in the road but knew, they would never have bothered with CCTV or burglar alarms to record visitors to their homes. They could have asked Gwen and Abigail for every detail.

'I'm very fond of Charles, you know,' said Gwen. 'He gave me a lift the other day. It was blowing a hoolie out there and I was holding on to the lamp post and had to stop myself flying out like a flag, and he came and put his arm round me and guided me into his car. All the ladies in the street chat to him. Jolly decent young man, I think, and he cuts my grass.'

'Oh, good. I wonder if he'll do mine. Could you ask him?' Abigail took time out from her tea-drinking to enquire.

'I'm sure he will, dear, if I mention it. He's always here doing one thing or another and helping me out. My guess is, he doesn't want to be at home, but what's it coming to when he prefers to spend time with an old woman like me. I see unhappiness and despair all over his face – just like the Captain used to have when he had his episodes of pain and had to go on medication. I know the signs of a depressed man when I see one. I've a good mind … in fact, I think I will … I'm going to have a word with Angus.'

'Can you do that, dear? I mean, he's a doctor; I don't think he can talk about his patients.'

'Angus can talk to me. Don't worry, Abigail, I will be discreet. Anyway, Angus relies on our talks for certain pieces of information about what's happening in the town. He's one of those who understands us and our role here at the lookout post. Don't forget – he may call on you one day. Here, have one more of these before I eat the lot. And let's keep our eye on that little boy too. He's just a child, Abigail. We can't really blame him if he thinks he's an adult. I blame the parents.'

Abigail drained the china cup, having first spooned out the remaining soggy sugar at the bottom directly into her mouth. Then she picked up the handbag that was resting down by her feet and shrugged her shoulders in delight at the taste of the sugar. Gwen reflected with a smile that her friend was sometimes like a child with sweeties, with regard both to life and to the sugar at the end of her tea. She made no attempt to curtail her companion's bad habit with sugar – she wanted Abigail to enjoy this small indulgence. A little notebook with a floral cover and matching pencil now appeared from Abigail's bag and she made a note exactly as directed: 'Keep our eyes on Freddie – just a child. Gwen to go to doctors about Charles.'

Then she placed the notebook on the table in case there was anything else to remember. Abigail relied on Gwen for instructions such as these at times when she was not sure what to do next with their observations. She needed to have Gwen to lean on because her friend always seemed to know what to do. This dependency made her feel happy and complete, and she would always follow her instructions to the letter. She had been told to keep her eye out for Freddie and she would do exactly that.

So, Charles was noticed and loved by people who really understood him more than his wife. If he had known how much Gwen observed and understood about his life, or the part she was going to play in it, he would have gone over and chatted to her, and he could have unburdened his soul of the panic that he felt about being trapped in an unhappy marriage and whether or not he should stay or go. He had failed to observe the principle that people who play small parts in our lives sometimes have something big to offer. But many people failed to observe what Gwen and her companion had in mind.

Chapter 5

A Call to Change Everything

The day was Freddie's fourth birthday in the summer of 1980, Charles had dutifully contained and entertained twelve little girls and boys of a similar age at a birthday party. In they came, dressed in their best OshKosh dresses and dungarees, not caring less about where the cake, jelly and ice cream landed, smearing them all over their little designer-label outfits into which their mothers had squeezed them for the occasion. Not long after their arrival, their special costumes were bedecked too with mud from the garden, and as teatime progressed they were spattered with further layers of experience – various shades of chocolate sponge and egg sandwich to which they were blissfully oblivious.

Charles had spoken to June several weeks before. 'Do you really think he needs such a big party? He's only four and he does get out of control when there's a lot going on. Perhaps a small family tea would be—'

'Of course he needs a party. He must have a party. He will have a party. Why would you question this?'

In June's mind the event was a matter of social survival, the symbolic act proclaiming her victory over life. She had the child. She had the party to prove her possession. She would invite every last mother from the preschool, all twelve of them, except for the child whose mother was a single parent. No, twelve small people would be arriving to pay homage to her little man.

Charles had responded mechanically by shopping for party food and ordering a bouncy castle. June organised the cake, a perfect replica of Thomas the Tank Engine in blue with 'Freddie' written in large letters on top – which Freddie could not read and into which he had stuck his chubby index finger just an hour before the event started in order to taste the sweet blue icing. He loved sugar and could not be deterred from getting a chair up to the pantry shelf, even though his mother had told him 'No.' When she found the damage, June asked her child, 'Did you do that?' He answered, 'No, Mummy.' She stroked his head 'My little darling. How could Mummy think such a thing.' And Freddie gave a super sugar-boosted smile and went on his way.

June put the question of how a mini finger-shaped hollow had come to be on the cake, ruining it just before the party, completely out of her mind. If her small child said 'No, I didn't do it,' then he did not do it, even though this defied even the most basic logic and the evidence before them – the chair he had put up to the shelf was still there. Such was the way of this child's mind, and it is very difficult to develop a conscience if people don't help you to see right from wrong.

Somehow this small cameo represented how good June was at hiding reality from herself and her child. His defiance was an example of the human mind's ability to exist by its own rules and to hide reality from itself. If June had been able to reflect on herself, she would have seen that the cake and the party and the excitement were not in any way about Freddie – they were about her and her need to validate her existence. No finger in any cake would unravel her fantasy. If only she had been able to see then how this would affect her beloved son's future.

Towards the end of the party there had been a call, and Charles was partially relieved to escape from mother and child who were engaged in a battle as to why the event was over and his friends were leaving. Freddie just could not handle the ending, and the fact that the fun, the adulation, the excitement, the sugar, the gifts, were all finished. He was having trouble putting this together in his mind and June was trying, as usual, to compensate for his dwindling sense of reality at the end of the day.

Charles's initial thought upon hearing the phone was: *Leave it, there's too much to do here, clearing up and settling Freddie down.* On the other hand, he'd had enough and wanted a distraction. Too late – his reactions to phones were automatic: 'Blessingham two six two, three thousand, Bradshaw speaking.'

A pause, then a young man speaking politely: 'Sorry to trouble you with an unexpected phone call, Mr Bradshaw. I am the son of Katrina

Allsop – I'm Harry Allsop? My mum said it was OK to call. I don't want to surprise you if it's a bad time.'

Surprise me? What's he talking about? Charles had completely missed the name the boy had mentioned and reacted with speed to discharge himself of this sense of unwanted encroachment. 'No, sorry, I think you've got the wrong number and I don't take sales calls on Saturdays. I don't know anybody by that name. Thank you.' He was about to hang up when the teenage voice ensnared his attention.

'No, I think you do? Katrina's my mum and she knows you. She told me about you.'

Charles stopped short, jarred by the name, his memory alerted by the single word 'Katrina' and, as he juggled with the unwanted recall, he shifted from foot to foot, uncomfortable, unable to settle. Left, right, left, right, his legs would not let him relax or stand still and ouch, a stinging sensation in the front of his groin. He was beginning to feel there was no escape from the call and the waters were rising around him. What he felt was panic. He realised he needed to urinate, and that he had to continue this call out of June and Freddie's earshot, even if he did not know why. 'Sorry? Er, hang on a minute … I'm just going to pick up the phone in another room. We've had a party here today and it's still a bit noisy.'

He picked his way down the corridor towards a quieter room, stepping over balloons, sweeties, wrapping paper and Bang! he had stepped on the edge of a tightly pumped purple balloon that had burst and made him jump. He heard Freddie laugh from the other room because the bang had startled his dad.

He reached the only remaining quiet room in the house – the den. He closed the door firmly behind him, making sure that the latch had caught, and stood by the window continuing to shift from foot to foot. The stinging from his bladder would not go away. There was something going on here that he didn't like, and both his brain and his body were on high alert.

'So, which Katrina are you talking about, then, because I'm sorry I don't know a Katrina Allsop, and even if I did I would not be holding a conversation like this with someone I don't know, so really you must have the wrong number.'

He made to put the phone back on the receiver. He needed to urinate, and this annoying young idiot was trying to sell him something.

'It was Katrina Stuart. That was her maiden name, the one you knew her by. She married, and now she's Katrina Allsop.'

'What? Look, excuse me, young man, you've caught me at an inopportune moment.'

'Oh, do you want me to call back at another time?'

'No, I do not. Wait there.' He hid the hands-free receiver under a small scatter cushion on the settee and fled from the room, up the stairs two at a time, crashed through the bathroom door, locked it behind him for privacy even in this moment of terror, and leapt across the floor to bang the toilet seat up, yanking his zip down, thinking: If June finds out about this she'll kill me.

His mission completed, he then returned to the quiet room and with caution closed the door. He glared at the phone under the cushion, ready to shut down the receiver and switch the damned thing off. But he was met by the curious sound of a voice singing. He recognised the Bob Dylan song from a young voice, slightly off key:

'About having to be scrounging your next meal

How does it feel

How does it feel

To be without a home

Like a complete unknown

Like a rolling stone …'

He thought that the song was coming from a radio somewhere, but he raised the receiver and the sound became louder.

'Hello?' he said.

'Oh, just practising while I was waiting. We've got a gig tonight.'

For Charles, the situation just seemed to be becoming more and more absurd – now he had a teenage salesman practising Bob Dylan down the phone while he waited for his mum's old boyfriend to have a pee.

'So what is all this about?' said Charles.

'This is gonna sound strange, but I know Katrina was your friend when you went travelling with her around 1965, and then, you know, she had me the following year. Like, I'm your son? She said I could call. Like, it's not a big deal, I just thought we should say hello. They said I could. Well, they don't know exactly I'm calling right now but it wasn't hard to find you in the *Yellow Pages* – Bradshaw Associates?'

Three seconds of frozen silence and then the news hit.

Why does the truth always feel like a shock to us? His instantaneous response was to defend himself from this life-wrecking information that had just crashed into him and knocked him over. As if life wasn't difficult enough already.

'Excuse me, is this some kind of joke? Really, because it's not very funny, young man, whoever you might be. That's quite enough of this game now.'

'No, really, I wouldn't joke about this. I couldn't think of another way. I'm awfully sorry, I can put the phone down if you like.' The voice that had been at first adventurous and confident suddenly became timid and shaky.

The whole scene was shifting, and Charles realised that this was not some silly prank. He remembered his love affair with Katrina Stuart, as she was called then, and he could calculate and start to make sense of why this adolescent voice with a similar tone to hers might be calling him now. She had been confident and spontaneous, even impulsive, in a way that this young person appeared to be. Even the Bob Dylan song fitted with her whole carefree demeanour. Memories surfaced in his mind of the sounds of the late sixties and the beautiful, brief love affair that he had forced himself to forget. The purple silk dress she was wearing that night, the way it slipped from her shoulders, the wine sweet as dates they had drunk until they lost all inhibition, the evening heat that helped them to relax, the surrender to their bodies. He had lost her, and he had tried to forget about her. But now life clearly had found him. This boy was not messing around; he was telling the truth, and he was on the end of this phone.

'Look, just stay on the line but give me another minute.'

'OK. My dad warned me about this.'

Charles covered the phone again and sat with his eyes closed gasping for breath. Wet, more wet tears streamed down his face combined with sweat sliding from his forehead and the fluid emerging from under his arms, his collar, his feet. Bodies are made from so much water.

He began to talk himself back into control – to find the man, the hero he thought he was. 'Look, I won't talk now if you don't mind. Let's meet and discuss this. It might make more sense.' And as quickly and calmly as he could he made arrangements with the bright young man purporting to be his son.

Chapter 6

A Meeting of Minds

They met at his office, Bradshaw Associates, in Blessingham seven days later, by which time Charles had had a chance to collect his thoughts, but this achievement was not without further struggle. Within an hour of the call from Harry he had gone down with a fever, shivering and sweating, vomiting, and with a fierce headache. He spent a fretful and restless night tossing and turning as he battled to make sense of the emerging picture – the process of taking someone new and unexpected into his heart.

The armour-plated vehicle of his life had been caught by a roadside bomb. He could not make the adjustment, his body would not get comfortable as he struggled his way through, mumbling and babbling in his sleep. Even June had taken pity on him and let him sleep all the next day, assuming he had a virus. The idea would never have occurred to her that his collapse had psychological meaning. He could hide his distress from her in that dark warm space under the duvet in the guise of sickness which she understood more easily. She brought him jugs of iced water and put a bucket by his bed, closed the bedroom door and left him in peace. The next night she moved into the spare room so as not to catch the virus and to protect Freddie. His fever broke within forty-eight hours and he emerged from the mental and emotional struggle with himself as a man resigned to accepting his past, and realising he was still living in the present. By the appointed day of the meeting with Harry he had returned to the office.

'Alright? You look a bit rough, mate.' His cheerful business partner,

Ryan, teased him when he saw Charles looking pale and tired as he arrived at the office. 'Trying to get out of the monthly review meeting, were we?'

Ryan Butler was one of the predictable people in Charles's life; he was a gifted accountant, five years younger than him, stunningly good-looking and gay. The office was his stage and he lit it up every morning when he arrived there. He seemed to be untainted by life's disappointments even though he must have had many, and was consistently enthused by making their business flow energetically. The partnership could have been a wonderful marriage, filled with complimentary characteristics and matching tendencies: Charles's pessimism and caution countered Ryan's risk-taking and excitement, and Ryan's love of accountancy complimented Charles's insurance sales skills. When Charles was down, Ryan was always up. Most importantly they believed in each other and trusted each other. The office became a haven for Charles and even though he was struggling by now with depression, he always gave time and attention to the demands of their work, so as to honour the contract they had together.

'Funny guy,' Charles responded. 'I was sick as a dog. I'm OK now, thanks. Need to get my head down and catch up. Talk later.' He went into his office. Blandly painted in magnolia and sparsely furnished this was just the familiar territory that he needed that day. He took his place at the large oak desk, sank into his executive chair, and looked at what needed to be done. He stacked the files requiring his attention in order of priority, sticking a yellow Post-it note covered in scrawled handwriting on top of each one. *Ah,* he thought, *the haven that order and structure can bring to the stirred-up mind.* He lost himself in this activity for a while and was ready when his receptionist buzzed him at midday. 'There is a young man called Harry here to see you, Charlie. He says you are expecting him.'

Charles was ready. He had to admit that he thought Harry, as he entered, was a beautiful looking boy, and taking him into his heart was not only not difficult, but also instantaneous. There was an openness about the young man, and an obvious excitement about life which was totally appealing as he paced across the floor towards Charles's desk. Charles felt he was looking at a younger version of himself, as this tall, slender, gangly young man – with his mother's red hair down to his shoulders – came towards him with a natural confidence, wearing jeans, and a T-shirt that proclaimed the teenager's identity: 'My real home is Glastonbury.' Charles was powerless to resist him – as powerless as he had been with the boy's mother. He was bowled over and had to sit down for the first few minutes to contain himself and stop from staring at his son.

'Wow, my real dad. Wow. This is really something. Can I call you Charles? I'm Harry.'

'Well I think I might have known that.'

'Sorry I surprised you on the phone the other day. Mum and Dad were furious that I'd jumped ahead; they were going to call you. They're gonna talk to you. They made me come today. They said "You started it, you finish it." Like, they made me take responsibility for my actions. Cool, huh?'

The boy held out his hand. Charles wanted to crush him with a hug, but refrained and transferred these tendencies to a look on his face which he hoped would do the job. *Hugging at this stage is not right,* he thought.

'Mum didn't want me to call you. She married Gordon and I always thought Gordon was my dad, but he knew that you were my real dad. Gordon was your friend, too, I know. He's been a great dad and we've all been really upset since Mum finally told me that you're my real dad. I wished she'd told me when I was younger. It might have been easier for us all. Anyway, I said she can't really expect me not to contact you. So, here I am. I just want to say hello, really – Mum and Dad are good with that. Gordon wants to formally adopt me, so we would need your permission for that even though his name is on my birth certificate as my father, but still, it's important to meet you, I thought, right? So, yes, here I am, this is me.'

'No, of course, of course, well done you – jolly brave, I'm really glad you did that. Tell me all about yourself. Would you like a coffee?'

'Well, I play the guitar and I've got my own band. We practice in the garage. I love all the old rock stuff, you know, Pink Floyd and The Rolling Stones, and folk stuff like Bob Dylan I really love. Yeah, Dad says it's his music, but he doesn't understand. I mean, it was clearly written for my generation.'

Charles smiled, and Harry chirruped on like an excited little bird on a branch. The story was to become crystal clear when he remembered that Katrina had cut off from him as suddenly as she had appeared to turn on to him on that sultry night as they camped in Iran and they had both gone to look at the stars. He had loved and waited for her ardent attention for months, flirting with her and making himself indispensable in his support, so when she gave the signal he was as powerless as he felt now in this very moment. But she had disappeared after they left Tibet and was never in touch again. He was devastated but assumed that he had made a thoroughly minimal appearance on the stage and screen of her life. What was for him an adoration was for her some playful fun and another adventure. How different could the intentions of two minds be when engaging in an act of coupling. For her the lovemaking had been daring, for him the heroic fulfilment of his dreams.

On the way home on the train, Harry watched the Somerset countryside speed past his window. Miles and miles of flat green pasture filled with sheep and cattle, so different from his suburban existence in Surrey with his mum and dad. The meeting played over and over in his mind; he felt they had spoken man to man and he liked the sense that Charles was treating him as an adult. He didn't really understand why Charles had said that there was a possibility that his wife, June, would not accept him, but he had listened to what Charles said – that just now was a difficult time and therefore they needed to be careful about how June was told.

Before he left, Charles took Harry for lunch in town at Billings Gourmet Burgers. They munched their food with pickles and fries, Charles slightly anxious and looking over his shoulder in case he might bump into June out on a shopping trip, even though he knew she would never be in a burger bar. He was quite amazed that Harry could down two burgers, double fries and coleslaw with a milkshake as if he were eating a light snack. He had never previously been exposed to the mysteries of the teenage appetite. Charles then drove Harry to the station and tried to shake his hand to say goodbye in a businesslike fashion. Hugs might have been on their minds. However, in the final calculation they settled on the handshake goodbye, but with full hearts as they each held on to other's hands while studying the other's face, and shook for an extensive amount of time so that the actual act of the handshaking became unimportant and the expressions on their faces was the real focus of communication.

Neither of them hid from the current of electricity that passed between them, and neither of them registered any concern about the mirror image in the other's face. In fact, they were both enchanted with each other in that breathtaking moment. They had met and accepted one another and the encounter was good.

For Charles, something at last emotionally alive had happened. For Harry, finding Charles was like finding a piece of the jigsaw of his life – not a central piece, but one of the outer, straight-edged pieces to help complete his picture, one of those edges that gives the clues to finding all the others, fundamental to the core picture he was to have of himself.

Charles went home dreading the outcome of breaking the news to June who was fragile at the best of times, burdened as she was with covering up the extraordinary behaviour of her child. He knew in the back of his mind that Harry would be the straw to break the camel's back of their relationship and that she would not accept his son. However, he bravely decided that honesty was the best policy, that timing would be everything, and buoyed by the meeting with Harry he had a portion of hope. Maybe this would be a joy for her rather than a burden.

'What? What are you saying? How can you … how can you do this? How selfish of you to think that we can have this boy introduced into our lives. Never, never mention this to me or my child again and I will not discuss it with you.'

'I couldn't be sorrier, June. I know, and you're upset and I don't blame you, I was, too. I know it's tough going but he's a lovely kid—'

'Lovely kid? You already have a "lovely kid" in case you hadn't noticed. We have a beautiful boy and you hardly have time for him, so I'm damned if I'm going to let you bring in another child to start ruining what we have. I hate you for doing this. Why couldn't you have kept it a secret like any self-respecting man.'

There was no discussion, no planning, no possibility of explanation as she fled the house for her mother's, banging the back door so hard behind her that he thought the windows would break.

He should have kept it quiet, but he'd had such a sense of hope, of something new that Harry had brought to their meeting. He pulled out his rarely used handkerchief and wiped his face. No one was there to see him now, so he just took his time and let the waves crash over him. Once he'd settled he recognised a new feeling. A feeling that was new, but old, like … what? And then, in the instant, he realised that this new-and-old feeling was the heroic release of the sense of freedom that was forming in his mind.

Chapter 7

Things Can Definitely Get Worse – the Years between 1980 and 1988

Separating from June should have happened more quickly. Yet the loyalty and decency of this man meant that the marriage ran on for longer than imaginable. Charles was shocked by the arrival of Harry into realising that he had never fully given his heart to June anyway. The result was that being together in the same house now was a marriage of convenience for them both.

It was 1980 and Freddie was four when Charles and June produced one more baby: Anthony, the child conceived as part of a plan by June to keep her husband in her home for as many years as possible. To some extent she succeeded, but time eventually caught up with them. For now, though, Charles was ashamed of where he was in his life; he was afraid to leave and this kept him in place with her.

He had been momentarily baffled and taken by surprise as she opened the bedroom door on a sunny afternoon when he was preparing for golf and Freddie was with his grandparents. She flicked off her flat shoes, pulled off her black tights and panties and kicked them to one side. She pulled up the hem of her skirt to her waist, exposing herself to him, and then lay across the bed. She was staring at him with an uninhibited and relentless predatory stare. She said nothing.

He managed to completely misread the scenario and did not pick up on the implications of her behaviour. He was a man getting ready for golf and for victory. Very little got in the way of this ritual, even an offer such as the one so obviously presented. He cut a helpless image as he pulled on his golfing trousers and was reduced to hopping on one leg as he accidently stood on the opposite leg of the garment. He stumbled, and just managed to stop himself from falling over completely.

'Are you OK, darling, is something wrong?' he said.

Not many men would ask that when a woman lay supine in front of them with no knickers and their skirt pulled up to their waist, but Charles was just not used to this kind of proposal and he certainly had not been let in on the fantasy that was exploding in June's head and smashing her inhibitions so that she could make this thing happen. Instead of feeling sexually excited, he felt very nervous and wondered if she was unwell. He was completely unable to understand this ambush.

'I'm perfectly OK, Charles – shall we get on with it?'

His lack of connection with the moment was not what she had in mind and it annoyed her immensely. A wonderful surge of impatience began to overtake her whole body, making her legs shake and forcing her into an animalistic role that, in fact, if she allowed it more often, was always lurking just behind the scenes of her daily life. An exploitative excitement arose within her and the sexual charge it gave her made her ready. She was impatient and lost all reserve.

'Come on! I want it now!'

He caught up with the plan and was unable to control the surge in his own body as it responded to the discharge of her pheromones and the intoxicating rudeness of the sight before him. It took less than sixty seconds to rip off his own pants and mount his wife (who seemed, to him, to be behaving uncannily like a prostitute) so that he could meet the demand that she wanted sex now. A mixture of familiarity, the warmth of her skin, and his affection for her flooded through his system as he panted, and she groaned, and years of pent-up frustration were exposed and came to a climax with one final shove from him and one final exhalation of release from her. He collapsed to one side onto the bed and began to mumble.

'Oh, thank you, darling, if only we could do that more often I'm sure we'd be better for it.' And he pulled the coverlet over his bare posterior, which felt rather exposed and ungainly now that the ferocity of their sex had been discharged. But June did not hear. She had already left the room and gone to the bathroom, where she lay on the floor with her feet resting on the side of the bath so that her pelvis tilted upwards to enable his semen to make use of gravity and stay inside her for impregnation. Her plan had been executed. One sex act to cement her family back together. There was an almost biblical beauty to the scenario.

***

'Something is up,' Gwen observed to Abigail some months later, as she poured their afternoon tea and made her friend's particularly sweet with three sugars and offered her today's cake, which was Battenberg. She knew that Abigail loved the pink and yellow squares in the cake and the sugared marzipan icing on the outside, which she always pulled off and ate separately. Gwen did not take any sugar for herself, but she felt the sugaring of her friend's warm drink demonstrated her warmth for her.

'Something is definitely up, dear, and it will come to no good. How did she get pregnant? We know she doesn't like sex,' Abigail said.

'Oh!' Gwen was surprised. 'How do we know that?'

'She told her friend who told her own mother and I know her mother very well – Brenda, you remember her from school. Good at needlework? Always made her own dresses? Better turned out than anyone? She was slightly annoying but always friendly? Then she ran the alterations department at Astleys for years?'

Gwen nodded after each descriptive remark.

'Yes. Yes, it's coming to mind. Ah, yes, of course – vacuous Brenda. Made a great alteration to my grey Berkertex suit that kept it going for years, and always took up the Captain's trouser hems for him. Yes, of course. How is she, Abigail?'

'Marvellously well, still taking on alterations and working. We meet occasionally for a catch-up and I'm sure that's when she would have told me about June not liking it. I'll check my diary. I would have made a note. I felt that was an important point, Gwen. By the way, have you spoken to the doctor about Charles? I'm sure he would want to know how worried we are about him.'

'Yes, I chatted with him at the surgery the other day. Angus says we should just keep an eye. You see, it's his mental health we're worried about now. He just looks so unhappy.'

Abigail made an entry in her flower-covered notebook, which was lying ready on the coffee table: 'Charles B. … keep an eye … mental health.' Sitting with Gwen and enjoying her tea, she flicked through the last few months of entries in her notebook just to see if she had anything of interest to raise. She noticed another entry from some months earlier that she had forgotten to mention. 'A while ago he had a burger at Billings Gourmet Burgers with a young man who had long red hair looking a bit like a hippy.'

'Oh, were you up there for lunch?' Gwen took a pleasant mouthful of her tea.

'No, but Genevieve was up there with her grandchildren having burgers as a treat and she mentioned it to me as we bumped into each other in town later that day. She had thought how unusual it was to see Charles B. with a hippy. Then we thought nothing of it. But I did make a note. So, there you are. It's all in the notebook, Gwen.'

The ladies resumed their business and their tea. Abigail put her yellow marzipan icing to one side temporarily while they talked. They were most concerned about the meaning of this new event. The baby. The event did not seem to fit, and as yet they could not explain why.

When June announced her pregnancy, Charles was forced to banish Harry from his life forever. Harry would not be allowed into their family and he would never meet his half-brothers by Charles, at least not until they were adults. June made him promise.

He was forced to explained everything to Katrina over the phone. It was a difficult call for him, filled with memories and imaginings that were controlled and held in place by a constructive need to communicate well and urgently. The call was a very adult, businesslike conversation dealing with the facts. By now, Katrina had become the woman she had always intended to be, and Charles was surprised when he heard her voice. He had never previously taken much notice of how ruthlessly she got what she wanted in life. He quickly synchronised with her tone and her intention on the matter of Harry, and saw that she had always known how this plan would work out; here she was some sixteen years later, precisely where she had expected to be. Her voice was still deliciously quixotic and vibrant but of course, he finally noticed, she retained that ability to capture every conversation and make it her own, to be in command of the moment while at the same time holding on to a unique brand of femininity that had always been enchanting.

'If only you'd told me, Katrina.'

'I'm sure you'll understand, Charlie, that if I had wanted you to know you would have known. I was always in exactly the position I wanted to be in, and you have no cause for concern or to be sorry. Now all we need to be clear about is whether you will want to see Harry more regularly and create a relationship with him. Gordon and I are open to it if you do.'

'I'm sorry, Katrina, please explain to Harry. I can only be truthful; I think world war three will break out down here if I have anything to do with him. June is just not able to accept this, and we are going to be busy with a new baby. My marriage is not in a good place and Freddie has behavioural problems that we are going to have to sort out. Please give Harry my love, tell him that he is a son I would have been proud to call my own, and tell him that if things change I will be in touch. Tell him, Katrina, that it's not his fault, will you, and that I will be thinking of him? The poor chap will be confused. Of course, there's no problem with the permission for the adoption. Just send me the papers to my office in Blessingham. It's totally right that he should be adopted by Gordon. And I have to say thank you. You will never know what a *gift* he is to my life.'

Eight More Years

For eight more years Charles lived in Harry's heart and mind in a comfortable place even though they were not able to see one another. There was too much going on for Harry for him to fret over the father he had barely known. Over this course of time, he grew from a teenager into a young man, learning from life as he went, singing and writing his songs, falling in and out of love and searching for meaning and identity as young people do – always believing that they are the only human being searching for this meaning, which they also believe is uniquely their own. He read philosophy and politics at the University of Reading, which turned him into even more of a thinker, even more of a storyteller of life. Then, remarkably, the dreamer in Harry did a volte-face and decided he wanted to learn more about physical reality, and swopped his songbook and guitar for the uniform of the Royal Engineers. He broke one more heart before he left home for his life in the forces, and that was his mother's; Katrina finally had met her match when it came to broken hearts.

For Charles, life was less comfortable. He longed for this connection with his past and idealised the possible relationship he could have had with Harry, occasionally finding that he spent his time imagining a meeting with him and catching up on his life, but he soon closed down these happy, warm imaginings and faced the reality of his existence. With as much finesse as possible, Harry was painted out of the scenery of the Bradshaw household.

And there was now Anthony – eight years old, born of that sexual ambush by June. Charles had been resigned to the birth of another child into the house, even though it did not make him happy. He had lost sight of his own happiness long before, but he had thought that at least June would be content and that this might resolve things for them, and that maybe Freddie would calm down if June had to give her attention to another child. Maybe it could be a blessing for them, or the child would be a glue or a salve to bind them all together.

Looking back, it was hard for Charles to trace how the course of the journey he had taken through life had seemed to lead nowhere except to him sitting at his desk with his head in his hands, muttering. 'My God, this was not what I had planned. I didn't know it was possible to live with such despair.' He was just going through the motions of life, his soul waiting in the wasteland for a new existence to begin to rise, the pulse of life gently drumming on the back of his mind.

When Anthony was born, he was a chubby little sweetie full of smiles and dimples, golden-haired and peaceful. He slept and ate, chuckled and cooed when he was awake, all in a comfortable rotation. Everything about the child had harmony and rhythm – something Charles had never been able to see in Freddie. He would go home from work and hold the baby happily in his arms while June got on with Freddie, managing his misbehaviour and, according to her, making sure Freddie did not feel pushed out.

Absolutely no chance, thought Charles as he nursed Anthony. He was pleased to feed the defenceless little chap, change his nappy, bathe him, give him his bottle and cuddle him off to sleep to keep the peace.

These moments with his young son became the highlight of his day, the way that he as a father was able to belong in his family, and the delightful infant came to expect this ritual of time with his dad. The pair bonded through peaceful contentment just as much as June and Freddie bonded as the days passed and their suffocating relationship with each other was challenged by no one, though observed by many. So rather than glue them altogether, young Anthony unwittingly rather caused a further split in the family proceedings. There were now two groups of two in this family: Freddie and June, and Anthony and Charles, plus another two in the form of June's parents just a hundred yards down the road, all doing the best they could to survive.

They belonged to each other, this little band of human beings dispersed in comfy homes along their road in the town that was built into the Somerset Levels. They belonged to each other. The bonds that bound them did just that – bind them. They were not free, and at least one of them at any one time would be struggling for consciousness at the expense of the comfort of the other.

Anthony grew into a sturdy, joyous little child and he embodied all the happiness and freedom to which none of the adults in the family were entitled. Charles loved to watch him as he learned to sit up and then crawl and toddle, and then as he started to speak his first words. All too soon, his stocky little frame was squeezed into a green school blazer with his name sewn into the back and he proudly held his satchel and headed off for infant school. His brother was reasonably good-natured to him unless he perceived any chance of his mother giving him her indulgence, which by now he felt was his own domain. Love, indulgence, being the centre of attention, and a growing sense of entitlement were the hallmarks of Freddie's expectations in life, and he claimed this territory through either manipulation or aggression, whichever was the most successful at the time. June was jubilant that she had two boys, and the second boy fortunately caused her no anxiety whatsoever. He seemed to just fit so easily into the space that was available and was also quickly subservient to his older brother, appeasing him whenever he could and making all manner of offerings to keep the status quo: his sweeties, his toys, his affection. How much in his lifetime was he going to have to offer?

Charles knew he was going to have to interrupt this family machinery to make some time to raise the issue of Freddie's behaviour; it was the elephant in the room and he knew this confrontation would throw a spanner in the works.

'Get off him, you little bastard.'

With those words he had pushed his elder son to one side so that Freddie stumbled, fell, and was silent for a moment. He was calculating, resetting his system after a surprise. He cried with anguish and humiliation that his dad had been so hostile to him and went running to his mother.

'Mum! Dad pushed me. He hates me. He said a bad word.' Freddie's sense of his father's disregard in that moment was devastating to him, but he saw it as an opportunity to ensure yet again his mother's devotion for him.

Charles could not believe he had uttered such destructive words about his son. He was mortified with himself – ashamed – but what's more, he realised that what had come out of his mouth was the truth. His hatred and contempt for his child and his wife had been laid bare in that split second when his defences were down and he needed to protect his younger son.

To regain some composure, he went outside for a cigarette at the end of the garden. He had recently taken to this habit as a form of passive compensation for all that he endured. The ritual of the comforting clicks of the lighter, the small amount of heat as he lit the end of the cigarette and the ignition and puff of smoke were all as important as inhaling and the stubbing out at the end. He clicked and lit up and sucked in a deep lungful while he stared at the scarlet hibiscus bushes hoping that they would offer him forgiveness. He blew the smoke heavily away from him and pushed his hair back from his brow several times. He could not accept what had come out of his mouth towards this child, and he was contorted with anxiety.

Charles knew that he could have hurt him as he pushed him away and, equally, that Freddie could have hurt Anthony as he pushed him. A chain reaction of frustration had erupted in a split second. He could not bear the sense of his own physical power in relation to that of his twelve-year-old. The hibiscus flowers still offered no absolution and so he stubbed out his cigarette on his stubbing-out rock and walked down the path and back indoors. He was ready.

'Don't you *ever* touch him again. And don't you call my child a bastard. Ever. He's your son. That's tantamount to abuse, what happened there. I'm going to have my father speak to you about this. What the hell's the matter with you?'

Several days later, following another letter from Highlands Senior School about yet another detention due to Freddie, for fighting in the playground and drawing blood on a child's face so that the young boy had to be sutured at hospital, Charles decided he just had to have that conversation with June. Freddie had seriously hurt this child, whom had previously been his friend, and the boy's parents were furious and complaining and questioning why. The headteacher, Mr James, invited them to come in for a meeting to discuss the problem. This most affable of seniors was two years off retirement and a walking encyclopaedia on child management. Most kids subjected themselves to his every whim without hesitation and with a joy that they were making their beloved head teacher happy.

It was true that they mocked his tweed suits and flannel shirts and oddly matched ties with unreadable motifs on them, and that they would not have understood the emblems for Freemasonry or for Lord's Cricket Club. True, also, that they sang little songs about him behind his back regarding his bald head that shone under the light when he took assembly, and the tufts of remaining grey hair that struck out in a professorial manner with a clear mind of their own. 'Mr James, he shines so bright, with his bald head under the light.' But aside from these acceptable bids to shun authority, his pupils, overall, knew that he was important to them. Happiness for Mr James was seeing his vision of the twin spirits of harmony and learning playing a duet together throughout his school daily. He was their Pied Piper and the children followed as if entranced by him. He did not lead them – they danced with him.

With Freddie, Mr James was not beaten, just concerned that the boy was not as happy and carefree as the others. He knew exactly that most of the boy's problems were because he had been allowed to become overprivileged with too great a sense of his own importance. Mr James knew that he had to get his parents to understand this. There was to be no child in his school who had more authority or knowledge than himself.

Charles made one last futile and fatal attempt to raise the issue with June. 'Look, darling, I'm thinking about Freddie's behaviour: we have to get some help now. I'm concerned about how this rubs off on Anthony. All of these power struggles, all this endless angst; two camps in the house with me and Anthony getting on with life, and you and Freddie doing your own thing.'

'What do you mean "get some help"? Nothing is wrong. Why the hell do you hate him so much? No wonder he is so badly behaved with a father who hates him and ignores him. God Almighty you are a ridiculous and rotten father to him. I wish to God you would just stop. He's just going through a stage and being a normal boy.'

There was no point, Charles knew, in taking the matter further. June just would not budge. They made yet another trip to the school and reassured Mr James that they would absolutely ensure that things started to change. Charles wrote yet another letter of apology to parents of a wounded child, because as usual Freddie would not do so as requested and showed no remorse. Mr James resorted with Freddie to his least favourite position as a leader, and gave him a warning that he might have to be excluded from the school if he hurt any more children. Freddie was left to contemplate his fate. At all costs he felt he had to hide the fear that this caused him, and he did this with bravado.

So, despite Charles's efforts, nothing changed except that within himself there was a psychological movement, downward and degenerative. Charles fell into a mental decline, his mood thickening like fog around him, his smoking increasing as he wracked his brains for a solution.

He knew he was lost in depression when he found himself crying at his desk and unable to get on with his work. To add to his anxiety and despair he was getting behind on visits to his clients for their annual financial reviews. They had not started to notice yet, but he dreaded the idea that time would pass and yet another cataclysmic disaster would emerge in his life in the form of a failed business. He was cheered only by the loyalty of his business partner, Ryan, who was propping things up right now, and to whom he would soon owe a long overdue explanation about what was going on. He consoled himself on this point with the thought that there was plenty of credit in the bank between himself and Ryan in the form of a trusting and long-standing working relationship. The length of time that they had spent together, and the fact that the business bank account literally *was* in plenty of credit, formed his own insurance policy against even further disaster and slippage into financial debt.

Somehow, Charles imagined that young men like Ryan – gay and extremely beautiful – did not have the kind of emotional problems in relationships that were experienced by heterosexual people. Then he thoroughly rebuked himself for such conservative and homophobic thinking, and resumed the line of thought that Ryan was a deeply understanding person who, when Charles finally confessed all, would fully understand.

Of course, Ryan had his own challenges in life – being gay was not a walk in the park, especially in 1988 when homosexuals were almost being demonised through media hype around awareness of HIV and AIDS. He was flesh and blood and just wanted to be taken as seriously as everybody else.

What Charles had failed to note, was that Ryan was already cognisant of all of his emotional problems, and fully understood the causes. Charles failed to recognise that Ryan had eyes and could see how his partner was struggling, and also that he had rather special clients in Blessingham who oversaw everything in the community – Gwen Knight, his close neighbour, being one of them.

Gwen and Ryan were outsiders – two of a kind. She was old and on the way out of the system, and he was gay and always living on the edge of being pushed out of the system. The assistance he gave to her with her complicated annual tax return created only a thin veil over their more meaningful connection. Ryan thoroughly enjoyed the cake that Gwen always brought for him, and he reserved extra time for their meetings. She knew his favourite was chocolate-and-hazelnut brownie, and while they ate this and drank tea he found out all sorts of very informative things about life in Blessingham. She was both a source of surprising insight into the minds of the locals and, frankly, a source of business, as well as offering him a sense of comfort and belonging. There was always much for them to discuss. There was too much else for Charles to think about for him to notice that Gwen popped in once a month and that she spent a longer amount of time than the average client chatting to his business partner about extremely pressing issues much more important to life than a mere tax return. In truth, her tax return only needed one meeting a year.

The reality, then, on which Charles now focussed was that his life had become joyless and without meaning. When he daydreamed about a trip to the doctor for sleeping tablets (even though he was sleeping well) and then hatched a plan to save them up and take them (about thirty, he thought) in the office all in one go so that the kids and June would not have to find his body, he knew that his sadness had reached a clinical level. He had also tried drowning his sorrows in moderately priced white wine. He could, by now, drink a bottle a night after dinner and experience almost no effect – except for the fact that June was disgusted and banned wine from the house during the week.

Enough of his brain, however, was preserved from the chemical effects of depression that he was able to ponder more sensibly on the idea that he might one day be able to reach out to someone who could help him with all this. He had tried and tried. He just could not find an answer, and in his mind's eye he had become an anti-hero.

Chapter 9

A Nice Man Called Colin

As if startled from his dream, Charles picked up the phone from his desk, dialled and found it was his dad on the end of the line. He blinked his eyes as if just waking up, and realised he had called him without thinking. Maybe the drum beat of his morbid thoughts had taken him there, or maybe there was enough common sense in him and enough self-preservation to know that he had to do something and reach out from his despair.

'Dad, I need some help. I can't do this on my own any more.'

His father put down the phone after talking to his son. Nobody, just nobody, could have been more pleased than he that his boy had called him. Finally, his chance had come to help him.

'I think we ought to go down, dear. Just a visit. We could stay in that nice hotel on the ring road outside Blessingham, because I'm certainly not going to stay with them. That boy of theirs is out of control and, frankly, I find him very difficult.'

'Peter, he's your grandchild, don't talk like that. I know he's difficult, but someone has to love him.'

Never one to hold back on his thoughts, Peter had learned through years of working with thousands of patients as a doctor in the National Health Service that one had to be quite immediate with one's thinking in order to be effective. The only thing that had stopped him intervening on his son's behalf before now was the common sense and judgement of his wife, who had so far told him he was not to comment. Peter had guilt about his fathering of Charles. He had been an absent father, giving too much time to his work as a paediatrician. He had never been able to tell Charles how remorseful he felt for this.

Now he was retired he had acres of time to consider his failings. What Peter did not mention, was that the family secret was out and his own bad dream had come true. Charles, his adult child, mirrored the exact same depressive tendency that he, Peter, had suppressed in his middle years of adulthood. Not even his wife had known of his own personal journey through despair which he had masked through overwork and tried to forget. It seemed to Peter, that day, that the mind will not let you forget the important things in life, and that these will always come back to you in some form or another.

The momentum of this first desperate phone call of the day gathered, and Charles took the advice given by his father and made an appointment with the town's doctor, Angus Kennedy, for that same evening. He made a ten-minute appointment at the town surgery, and sat in the waiting room telling himself that this was ridiculous as there was nothing wrong with him, and that his call to his dad had only been a moment of upset. He rehearsed his lines as he waited to go in.

Angus was at his desk as Charles opened the door, his stethoscope around his neck, sitting in his commanding black leather swivel chair as usual, leaning back as if he were sunbathing, and with his hands behind his head. He was massively built – like a shot-putter – with red hair and a beard. He must have stood at six feet six tall, and many of his patients tried to estimate his actual weight. Charles wondered how his heart managed to pump the blood round his enormous frame. Bet nobody bullied him for having red hair.

Adding to Charles's confidence in Angus was the fact that he was not a shot-putter, but that he did play at the golf club and had a handicap of ten. Now, that's pretty good going for a fellow who does not have a lot of time to practice. With all the male logic that Charles could muster, he thought that if Angus could make a handicap of ten without practice, then he could probably get a handle on depression.

Angus's great bulk belied his sensitivity to human beings and his understanding of both the body and the mind, and his life's intention, formulated as a small child, to be a healer. And the healer he had become was a very modern doctor, most concerned with the general well-being of his patients. He had learned that the body was the mind, and that the mind was the body. He listened intently to all that this patient and fellow golfer had to say about feeling suicidal, bleak and contemplating the best way to die.

'OK, Charles, now let's cover all the bases here. I could give you some medication, but I think from what you are telling me I will want you to see someone in Clinical Psychology before we medicate. You do seem very low. What are you struggling with? Is that boy of yours troubling you?'

'Err … well …'

'Come on, Charles. Our kids go to the same school and I get to hear the gossip. Look, we can get this sorted, you know. Go along to Psychology and see if we can get you some family therapy and sort out all the problems while we're at it. It can't just be that depression has crept up on you for no reason. I've watched you recently – you've not even been down the golf club for a game. Something's wrong. Let's get it sorted. I'll write today and ask for an urgent appointment. But come and see me every week until you get notified of one. I'm going to keep an eye on you. Does June know?'

Angus knew there was a problem with their marriage. The trouble was obvious to everyone, and anyway, this GP was also favoured by visits from Gwen who, besides stopping by to have her blood pressure monitored, frequently availed him of all current necessary information about local people when she attended for her regular check-ups. He always gave her a double-time appointment: he felt this was good medicine for her, and good local reconnaissance for him. He knew that she had an influence with a significant group of elders in the community, and she was his link to the powerful 'Republic of Retired Peoples of Blessingham' (his own favourite term for this tireless group who seemed to have energy for everything). He had even contemplated a social study of why they seemed so alive and well and so interested in life – could it be the fertility of the minerals in the soil of the floodplain?

He loved Gwen's sense of decency – her antennae were tuned to the towns intelligence in a quiet but, he had to admit, not exactly unspoken style. In her own way, her politics on life were as radical as his. Gwen had been in the town all her life and she knew that everyone was better off if they joined up, worked in unison and thought together. She had spoken of her concern about Charles for years, watching his joyless face as he walked past her watch-point. By the time Charles actually arrived for an appointment, Angus knew everything anyway, just as Ryan knew everything anyway, too.

'I don't want June to know,' said Charles.

Angus smiled to himself and thought that she would probably be the only person in Blessingham *not* to know that Charles was depressed, but never mind … 'Fair enough. Make an appointment for next week, Charles. Remember I'm here to help you, and by the way, you can call the Samaritans if you need to talk. Damn good, they are, at this sort of stuff. Here's the number. Now, be clear with me that you *will* call them if you need to. I don't want you doing anything stupid. I mean, we can soon get this sorted out. If you feel you may succumb to those suicidal thoughts, then go to A & E: they can get you through to Psychiatry. We have to take your thinking seriously – you know, seventy-five per cent of suicides are men. Because they refuse to talk about it. And I'll monitor you for a while … Next!' He called in his next patient before Charles had even had time to close the door.

Something changed for Charles in this meeting. He had reached out to two men that day – his dad and his doctor – and they had responded easily and generously to him. There was also the additional comfort that, in some unspoken way, Ryan had his back covered at work. If he only knew how many hands there were that joined together to provide support for him in what he felt to be his isolation. He just had to start to see that there were others, too, who saw him. Depression, though, stops us from seeing. There were many words spoken of understanding: some obvious, some invisible, some professional, some very ordinary indeed. Depression may have stopped Charles from seeing that support, but in good time there would unfold before him a future that included that ordinary brand of love from many people.

It took only three weeks for an appointment to come through. People in the countryside, for some reason, seemed happier than those in the cities, and waiting lists for mental health services flowed quite easily in the more sparsely populated south-west.

His appointment day came around and he had not told June, although she did notice that he seemed more alert and less preoccupied than usual that morning, and that he ate some breakfast – eggs on toast – which he usually declined, preferring just very strong, sweet coffee to jolt his brain into thinking. He had put on his favourite pink shirt, with cufflinks and a matching tie. She did wonder why for a moment, because she did not really like him in pink and had planned to make that shirt – a present from a grateful client – disappear from his wardrobe. But she was distracted by a more pressing and demanding presence than Charles and his shirt, because Freddie was refusing to go to school that morning.

Charles checked in at reception and sat in the waiting room staring at the cover of a *Good Housekeeping* magazine that proclaimed '5 Easy Steps to More Harmony at Home.' He began to think that this was not the place to be for a man, and he wished he had turned the car around and gone home.

The waiting room was dingy, clinical and cold, and he could not find anything that comforted him. He searched for a lavatory. His stomach was not used to breakfast, and the eggs were churning. He thought he would make his exit look as if he was taking a visit to the toilet and then at the last minute just turn sharp right towards the exit and head down to the car park. There was so much to do at the office and he did not really need this meeting. He was just mentally crafting the final detail of his escape plan (a polite call back to reception at a later time to let them know that he had left) when a broad presence loomed over him, blocking the electric light from his reading material. Was this a predator blocking out his light, or another part of the invisible chain of support?

The presence was a clean-shaven young man with a pleasing face who must have been ten years his junior. Charles thought that the young man was going to sing when he opened his mouth and a soft, round, Welsh and harmonious accent emerged; he found it beautifully soothing. In contrast to the melodious voice, the youth was built like a rugby player: short, stocky and very broad, and Charles thought immediately that he seemed like a man who could handle himself both on and off the rugby pitch, and he liked the feel of that very much indeed. Perhaps he was in a man's world after all. This potential rugby player, choral singer and all round friendly guy, he noted, was also wearing a pink shirt and matching tie, similar to his own. They exchanged pleasantries, and Charles was led into a private therapy room.

'Can I call you Charles? Call me Colin. Obviously, we're both men of good taste, Charles, so that's a good start.' He flapped the end of his tie as he said this. They both smiled. 'Got a letter from your GP, and your Depression Questionnaire showed that you are struggling with some moderate depression and suicidal thoughts. It's usually about thinking. What do you think is the problem?'

Colin looked across at Charles, who was sitting and staring with his mouth open. Words just could not come out.

'Just speak openly and frankly about your life, Charles.'

Charles had to admit that there were some difficulties in his life. No point in pretending any more. His life right now was the reason he was feeling so ghastly. In fact, he knew only too well what 'the problem' really was – he just had not been able to tell anyone. So, his list of apparent problems was recited gradually. He was worried about his son's behaviour, and yes, his marriage was at an unhappy impasse. He was concerned about the effects of these things on his youngest child who, as yet, was relatively unscathed, but surely it was just a matter of time before he, too, began to suffer. But Charles had managed so far, and if he could only get over this damned state of mind maybe he could carry on … and once he had started to speak he could not stop the cascade of consciousness that began to slide forward and he realised that he had been holding all of these thoughts in, and out it came – the truth.

'Trapped in a loveless marriage … can't handle my son, can't seem to get a handle, shouted at him, pushed him, he hates me, I can't get near him, such bad feelings about him, such bad feelings about her, found out I have a child from my past and can't be in touch, just don't want to be there. I'm just so ashamed and trying to hide it. Losing my grip at work and my poor Anthony … my poor Anthony.'

By the end, he was sobbing and gasping for air between his words, completely taken by surprise at his outpourings, and even more surprised that the man in the pink shirt with the smile was offering him a tissue.

'Take it easy, Charles. Here, grab a tissue. Take your time. No problem with the tears, you let them be. It's only human to hide a sense of shame. But many people have these kinds of problems and it's just a case of getting them out in the open and getting a perspective, and reflecting on the pieces to find a solution. It's a bit like putting a jigsaw together, and when the picture is clear I suspect you'll feel better, but these things are never uncomplicated. It won't be easy and may take a bit of time, but it's better to sort these things out rather than keep brooding on them, because that is what'll cause depression in the long run, when you're trying to solve a problem inside your head that needs to be outside your head – see what I mean? Do have another tissue – plenty there. Great that you can release some of that emotion, Charles, it'll do you good. Wash some of that stress away. OK?'

Charles struggled with the idea that, frankly, in his world, crying in front of a stranger was the close equivalent to wetting his boxer shorts. He was completely mystified by the experience and felt that something was very wrong. Colin, a master of soothing, worked for the rest of their time together to put his mind at rest.

'It really is OK, Charles, to have a good cry. That's what we do here. Emotion is what the mind is all about. Our brains like it when we express emotion and, you know, no one can control these thoughts forever.'

When the taller of the two men in the pink shirts left the Somerset Centre for Mental Health and Well-being that day, he already felt relieved of his great burden. Why on earth had he not troubled to talk to someone before? He realised that he had been pushed into a corner completely and that he had let things get on top of him. He had given no consideration to his own feelings and could not share anything with his wife. He was grateful to have talked to this young man, Colin – a virtual stranger, yet a fellow traveller in pink who had been able to offer more support and solace in one hour than he, Charles, had experienced in the last fifteen years. He decided he would do more of this therapy, to help him through. There was finally some hope, some light at the end of his dismal journey. There was no tunnel any longer – life had expanded as much as his breathing. The tunnel in his brain was illuminated and had dissolved into an ocean of hope.

Later that day, he returned home with a sense of enthusiasm for the first time in years. As he walked up the path through the garden to the back door of his home, he clutched a slip of paper for an appointment with June for family therapy in two weeks' time. He recalled that the last time he had felt this peaceful was when he had sat and sobbed about the fact that he would never see Harry, his new-found son, again. More than that, he realised that he had lost not only Harry, but also his dignity, his pride, and his zest for life.

Harry had been a symbol of the love he needed in his life, and rather than seek this and struggle, he realised that he had checked out on himself. He knew now that he could not exchange these things for the sake of a marriage; you cannot barter with what you can never give away. All his efforts, all his work, had been an endeavour to protect himself against pain and humiliation. His whole career was built around insuring people against the uncontrollable forces of life, the waves of energy that will claim us all in the end. He existed to insure and protect others – and himself – from the vastness and relentlessness of reality. Today, he had found that he simply could not continue to do that, and that the only way forward was to turn around and face up to life with openness and vulnerability and to embrace the vast ocean of the inevitable that we neither know nor understand.

He stopped for a moment on the path and sat to collect his thoughts on the rickety garden bench in the golden, mid-September Somerset sunshine. The air was warm and the sun had heated the wood of the seat slightly and this made for a light and pleasant encounter with this evening that was slightly scented with late-summer flowers. He knew that this was his pivotal moment and he was amassing his energies. A little zephyr of breeze blew some early fallen leaves towards him, as if playing. He drew a deep breath and then one more and then his thoughts were set.

Although the bald truth of his life was painfully uncomfortable, somehow this truth and pain was far more bearable than trying to pretend that there was no problem. He sat looking at the marigolds on the verge of the path, noticing how they had bloomed on into late summer and early autumn, marvelling at their magnificent show of fearless orange and their deep maroon centres, and he felt that he had let some of the heroic colour back into his life. He went in.

Chapter 10

A Child's Death Fantasy

'I absolutely will not be going to the family therapy clinic with you. What has that got to do with me? You went behind my back and talked about me to the doctor. The only problem with that boy is that you are too weak and you avoid discipline, and when you do discipline him you shout at him and I hate you for doing that and so does he.'

Freddie listened from the landing where he stood in his pyjamas holding his breath, his eyes staring. He was glad that his mother was screaming at this father. Somehow her rage appealed, and chimed like a bell with the disturbance in his own mind that thudded in his brain. Only right now, the craziness was going on outside of him, not inside him – and that was nice. It did not happen too often, as Dad usually co-operated with everything Mum said and this kept the household in order as it should be. But Dad seemed to be trying to say something different, and it was creating something like static electricity in the home. He would not forget this moment of truth. Somehow, it was his moment in the household.

Anthony joined him on the landing in his winceyette cowboy-patterned pyjamas, looking sleepy and unbothered, yet taking his lead from his brother. Freddie silently told Anthony to go away, shooing with his hand to send him back to his own room and then indicating in a motion which showed that he should shut the door. Anthony nodded to acknowledge his instruction, and without questioning it went straight back into his room and closed the door. He had the comforting sense that his bigger brother was in charge. He put on his TV to watch the football and waited to see what Freddie wanted him to do next.

Freddie hoped that things were going to get noisy and he did not need his younger brother to know the way things were going. He would explain things to him later and have him understand all that he needed him to understand. This was the way of things, and always would be, between Freddie and Anthony. He strained hard to hear the voices from below.

Charles remembered his moment in the cube-shaped room with Colin the mental health nurse. If he could do that – break down and speak the truth to a stranger – he could do this argument with June.

'You're right, I *am* weak. I have no control over Freddie and you have all the management. It's wearing you out, June, and not good for you or Anthony. I'm not willing to put up with it any longer. If you won't come to the appointment then I'll go on my own, but there will be an appointment.' As he gathered momentum his dignity returned, and he was no longer afraid of speaking his mind to his wife.

The couple continued their heated discussion in the quiet room with the soft-seated settees made with feather cushions, which absorbed the sound and buffered their raised and intense voices. Upstairs, Freddie realised with some disappointment that there was not going to be a lethal fight that night and that his parents had reduced the tension through dialogue. In his fantasy he had hoped that his mother would scream viciously and kill his father – perhaps stab him with a knife from the kitchen, that one with the big handle and massive blade that she used to cut meat with, or perhaps she would take out a gun that she had hidden somewhere and shoot him in the head like he had seen happen on TV. He was very excited by this idea. He could then come down and be a ruler in his home and ambulance men would take his father's body away solemnly in a bag. He would not say goodbye. Because he was a good boy, he would help his mum mop up the blood which would be up the walls and in a puddle on the floor where his dad had lain gasping his last breath, and he would make sure that Anthony did not see. He would tell the police that his father had attacked his mother and that she'd had to protect herself by killing him. He would cuddle to her soft bosom and sense the special warm scent of her body and feel comforted. Now, though, all he had was just a conversation between the two of them that he could not hear properly. He wanted to rush and get in between them and break the conversation up. They were getting too close – their voices sounded contented with each other. This alarmed him because he was not used to anyone being close to his mother except for him.

He retreated from his lookout post on the landing and tiptoed to his bedroom, quietly sat at his desk and pretended to get on with his maths homework just in case Mum appeared. His disappointment would not go away. He knew instinctively that something was about to change in their home, but it would not be through the murder of his father.

Once his aggression and the cortisol swishing through his brain – engendered by the thrilling death fantasy – subsided, he felt empty inside and so very lonely. And when he felt lonely he just felt angry and the whole cycle of discontent in his mind started up again. He felt like a clown with a sinister painted face and huge red lips curving up to his cheeks in a permanent smile. Yet he was constantly unhappy inside the mask of that painted clown face.

He took out his ruler and ruled his page. Just for a moment, he hoped that things would change and that someone could rule a line in his life that would change everything. He would like a good, straight, and heavy black line that could be carved out under the chaos of his thinking so that he could start again on a new life. Underneath the mask, the clown who was in control felt like a performing puppet with a relentless puppetmaster jerking his strings. He wondered what it would be like if he was not the puppet any more? He wondered who he would be … but only for a moment. He never thought this thought again, and he never understood who the real puppetmaster of his life was, who it was that made him behave in the ways that he did. But he did wonder about death, and whether it could be the solution to his problem and be the line that was finally drawn in his life to help him feel safe. He was not thinking of his own death.

Anthony came into his room. He was allowed out of his own room now. Anthony. Ah, yes. He could always rely on Anthony to help him feel better. He told Anthony to go down and get them both milk and biscuits, which the child did immediately and without question even though he was quite tired and not hungry or needing milk himself.

Like a little butler, Anthony balanced on tiptoe quietly down the stairs and walked by the lounge room in his pyjamas and dressing gown with no slippers on his feet and could just hear his mum and dad still talking in there. He hurried past. His bare feet slapped on the cold, tiled, kitchen floor and he quietly shivered as he opened the refrigerator door for the milk, and winced as the light blazed out at him. He poured a large glass of full-cream milk for Freddie and a tiny bit for himself, just to show that he was willing to drink milk with his brother, but really he did not need any inside him and it was just for show. He put some chocolate digestives on a plate and placed them on his favourite 'City of London' tray, which had beefeaters and red buses stamped all over it.

Then, carefully, in order not to spill milk, he gently padded up the stairs on the balls of his feet to meet with his brother and give him his evening snack and watch his face adoringly as he ate it. He could see that Freddie was quite satisfied with his evening and he, therefore, was satisfied too. This was the way of things for Anthony.

Chapter 11

One Try at Family Therapy

June only attended one family therapy appointment with Charles. The problem was that she had everything to lose and nothing to gain as their relationship took a turn in the direction of more honesty. She was going to be invited to move from a position where she used her weak husband for everything she wanted in life, to a position where she might have to make changes and think more about her relationship with him. She might even have to admit that she did not love him or even care about him, and that her goal had only ever been to have a magnificent child, such as she saw Freddie to be. The boy was her dream come true and she was blind to anybody else's needs, happily putting her own to one side too, allowing the ongoing existence of this child to complete her.

'So, what do you think is the problem here, June? You go first – let's see if we can understand this.' Their allocated family therapist, Dr Isabella Fratina, was a grey-haired, sure-footed woman dressed in colourful garb – she wore the kind of frock you might find in a niche boutique, giving the impression of kind, measured thoughtfulness combined with professional determination, power and a certain regard for creativity. She had a straight back and she seemed continuously pleased with herself, if you were to judge by the imprint of pleasure that the years had inscribed on her face.

This seemed very odd to June. Why would this woman be proud and pleased with herself, and about what? Why should she, June, be speaking to a Spanish woman with hair that was too long and coquettish for her age? What did Spanish people know about life in Somerset where families were private and dealt with their own business? June had put on a rather businesslike little suit that morning, bought from Marks & Spencer a few years earlier: navy and well-fitted, paired with court shoes.

'Er, sorry, what makes you assume we have a problem? You don't know anything about me. We don't have a "problem". I've only come because my husband asked me to. People just don't understand Freddie. He is so unique. We probably will have to change schools. They've got it in for him in that school. That headteacher, Mr James, seems to persecute him if you ask me.'

'Well, there's a challenge for us to think about, June. Do you think that's true, Charles, that you need to put in more discipline?'

'Yes, I do think it's true. But there is a problem in that he won't let me discipline him. He won't listen to a word I say and by now he hates me. He will only listen to his mother, who controls every aspect of his life.'

'So, do you talk to each other about that? Do you get to think about how to manage the power in your relationship? I find this is often the source of conflict and unhappiness – how parents are thinking about power and authority and how that affects children, who need to know who is in control.'

'Why would we need to talk about it? What do you mean' "manage the power"? We have to look after Freddie – what are you talking about?'

June was genuinely baffled, and as a result worked herself up into a frenzy of defensiveness. There was something going on here which she could not grasp, and she felt panicky. She felt that Dr Fratina was talking over her head, and talking to Charles over her head at that. It was as if there was a secret language that seemed quite clever and which only they understood, and suddenly she felt out of her depth and anyway, why wouldn't Charles support her? Instinct helped her to find the answer to her plight. She clutched her handbag and looked at her shoes. They were patent, and she could see the outline of her head in them. She was contemplating her exit and getting ready to leave this very strange little space into which they were packed and in which they could not help but look at each other's faces. Right now, she preferred to see her own face in her shoes. She did not wish to look at Dr Fratina's Spanish face, and she would kill Charles when she got home for not helping her today.

'We don't talk about anything, actually.' Charles spoke in a quasi-nostalgic tone while wondering if June would slam the door after her when she left, which he was sure she would do. He could see she was going to go. He did feel, somewhat, that Dr Fratina did not quite know how to talk to his wife – she clearly did not understand the principle of eggshells at times like this.

The doctor persevered. 'I can see you're unhappy about this, June. I hope we can help you to feel more comfortable in talking about these things. But I wonder what it's like for Freddie that you two don't talk and matters are left unresolved. What's it like for Anthony? What's it like for both of *you* if there's no communication in your home. Are you all sad in your house, or do you all just feel bad?'

Dr Fratina stopped, and during the pause she seemed delighted with her creative framing of their problem, but essentially she was throwing down the gauntlet to them, albeit in a velveteen and very smooth cover. She had drawn a line in the sand for discussion, but she was not the only person in the room who would be drawing lines.

June clutched her handbag and eyed her coat – which she had hung carefully on the back of the door – taking note of whether she could get it down in one movement as she went out. She was visibly shaking with rage now at this suggestion that they needed to think more, and she was making up her mind. Would she be in or would she be out of this discussion? Would she fight it or would she run, and would her usually faithful lieutenant be covering her back in this fight for ideas and values? She was not sure of him at this moment.

'You can tell me what you want me to know, but we know that Freddie is struggling with his behaviour. That can't make him very happy,' said Dr Fratina.

And this gave June the chance to present the picture as she thought it should be, a chance for an assault on the story that was emerging in this room about her son – that it was about them. She ventured now to the front line of the battlefield to fight for her dignity. She laid down the marker.

'Look. This is how it is. He is actually very happy indeed. He is loved and has everything he wants in life. We give him everything he needs immediately – what else is there to think about? You might be able to give us some tips on how to make his life better and how to cope with the unreasonable demands that people seem to make on him. But we don't want people interfering in our home and our affairs. If you saw how happy

Freddie is, you would not be saying these things. Now, why don't we take the conversation from there?'

Charles wished desperately that Colin was there to see them that day, but Colin did not work with families.

It was Dr Fratina's move, but June continued.

Charles was counting down to the outcome.

'I have no intention of talking to a stranger about how I feel. I completely love looking after my son. I have merely come here today to try and make my husband happy. This is what my life is about. *He* talked me into this.' She jerked her head in the direction of Charles. 'I knew this was a mistake.'

Despite her words, despite her attempts to wrestle and pin down her opponent, she was being counted out. She tried to appear elegant as she grappled with her coat, which was a little high up for her as she took it from the peg. She was losing the battle here today.

'So … it must be difficult for you both to go around and around in circles without getting anywhere. It must be quite frightening. Freddie must feel very alone – more sad than bad, and nobody can reach him.'

Dr Fratina edged towards her point.

They were all in position. Charles knew from June's collection of her coat and the look on her face that the meeting was pretty well over, but he was concerned by just how upset she looked when she heard the possibility that a psychologist was framing her son as unhappy, when in fact every minute of her working day was spent in pursuit of joy for him. Charles's instinct was to protect her from this truth now, and he really wished he had not put her through this. She was just not ready. He knew well enough that she would not cope and had not realised that Dr Fratina would be quite so intent on pursuing the sharp face of reality. He should have explained to her the need to go easy on June before they started. June had moved from being defiant and ready for battle, to desperate and ready for retreat.

Dr Fratina continued, after looking briefly at her shapely coral-painted and manicured nails on the back of her outstretched hand. Taking a good intake of breath and exhaling slowly, she launched her final weaponry. She was perfectly relaxed in her delivery.

'Well. We made some start and thanks so much for sharing your thoughts. I wonder if you want to bring Freddie along next time. We did have some feedback from school to say that they are worried about him and that they think he is challenging and, as they say here in their report … "possibly even dangerous to other children". They did have to clear the classroom one day as he threatened to knock a bookcase over the teacher. They would've classified that as an assault and called the police had it gone any further, and your son could have ended up with a criminal record. He's at an age where he can be held criminally responsible. I think that safely illustrates the extent of the problem we're facing here. June, you don't think that's a problem, but Charles is worried by it. So why don't you two talk some more and we can meet again next week. It will be nice to see Freddie.'

June was standing with her hand on the door handle as the volley of information scattergunned over her. 'Er … I don't know, I … it wasn't like that with the bookcase. It was an accident.' She was fumbling with her words, and with the door handle. 'No, really, I'm not sure; I think the teacher got in the way,' she mumbled. She had just been told that her son was heading towards criminal behaviour in which others were becoming interested. It was not just about his hyperactivity as she had thought. It was now about something bigger, about the state with all its terrifying authority knocking on her door in the middle of the night and taking her dream of her perfect boy away.

Chapter 12

The Decision That Made Itself – Summer 1988

Charles's father had visited Blessingham as he had promised and stayed in that hotel and spoken to his son without visiting June and the grandchildren. It was an unprecedented step, but Peter had been sufficiently worried about his boy (a grown man, he knew, but he was still worried, and he was still his boy) that he felt that new measures had to be in put place. He only made an overnight stay as he did not want to bump into his daughter-in-law, and he went into Charles's office to see him instead of to his home. He arrived at the reception of Bradshaw Associates with a serious face. It was the sort of face he had always reserved for events in his life of a very grave nature. This was the face that would emerge when he was about to perform a risky procedure on a sick child, when his clinical team would snap to attention and work in complete unison with him, taking his every direction.

Ruby, Charles and Ryan's office junior and receptionist, snapped to attention too as she noticed his demeanour, and responded with swift efficiency to the face before her at reception. She announced his arrival and saw him into the office. She could see this was no time for small talk and this was a day, she decided, when she would make coffee for Charles and his visitor without being asked.

Peter and Charles sat across the desk from each other in solemn parlance; they were discussing the death of a relationship.

Ryan, who would normally have interrupted to say hello to Peter and banter and joke with him in his usual sociable manner, did not even stop by. Charles's office colleagues sensed that a summit meeting of significance was taking place, and whispered to each other in the reception of the office about what it might mean. Ruby, despite her anxiety, stopped short of letting Ryan listen at the door, and so the conversation remained private.

'I just can't do it any more, Dad, and I'm making them all unhappy. Freddie may be better if I am out of the way. Dr Fratina at family therapy has said that maybe it's the dynamics between myself and June that are disturbing him. He needs some behaviour management, and he is more likely to respond to June than to me. The kid just won't let anyone say no to him, and that's a big problem. And we're the ones causing it.'

Peter winced as his son told him about the physical aggression he had shown to Freddie. It was as if he were being paid back for the same reactions he had shown as a father. Charles unburdened his heart to his old man, who listened more carefully than he had ever listened to his son in his entire life. All the time he told himself that this was his chance to give back for all the listening time he had missed in Charles's childhood, and for all his impatience, and the shaking and slapping he had administered in the name of it being good for the child. In all that impatience, he had lost his son. Now he could see that life had gone full circle and Charles was losing his own son, but for a different set of reasons. Peter genuinely felt it was best for Charles to move away, especially when he heard that Freddie was getting hit rather too often by his desperate dad. He knew what desperate dads were like – and the effects of hitting.

By the end of his visit, Peter had offered to provide a deposit for a home rental, and had advised Charles that his new base needed to be at a reasonable distance from June's.

The office door opened, the meeting fell out and Charles was curious to find that Ryan and Ruby were extremely busy in reception together, getting on with something of apparently great importance that looked like nothing more than a tidying up of the phone directories. They did not usually have anything to do with directories in their daily work.

Peter went and shook Ryan's hand warmly. The pressure was off now, and Ryan chatted amiably about how well the company was doing. Charles's father left at 3.00 pm to drive the five hours' eastwards to Kent. It was a long drive for an octogenarian.

With his father's permission and blessing in place Charles's life had changed and moved on forever. He sat in his office, ordering his work so that it would be ready for him the next day. It was a banal activity but it distracted him from the seriousness of the decision that had been made, which caused his heart to pound and his head to swim as he tried to hold on to the everyday reality of the office. It was a solemn day that he would never forget.

The old man wept silent tears on the drive home through pouring rain under a lowering sky as he listened to Mozart's *Requiem* on his CD player. He had finally gained redemption in his relationship with his own child. His heart was bursting with emotion as he was caught in the crescendo of Mozart's tragic choral piece that brought to life the bittersweet sense that he had of his son's broken dream. He could give his boy back the hope and the chances he felt he had taken away in childhood, but he could not mend his marriage for him. He recognised and accepted during that drive the universal truth that no man, however clever, can stop his children from engaging in the intensity of life's truth. He was glad it was a five-hour drive. He would feel better by the time he got home to Peggy.

Back in the office, Ryan and Ruby had no further need to tidy telephone directories. They did not know what had happened at the meeting that day, but they knew that they would eventually.

Chapter 13

Breaking News – Autumn 1988

Finding accommodation to live in is not a difficult thing to do in life. Telling your wife that you are leaving her because you are desperately unhappy – that's a hard thing to do. Charles had his new rental accommodation signed up within three weeks of his decision and his father, good to his word, had supported him financially and had loaned him the money for a deposit on the property.

Charles took nothing but his clothes with him: no furniture, pictures, mementos, not a single pot or pan, no linen or towels. He had nothing but what he was wearing as he walked out of the door with two suitcases and a leather holdall. This was all he possessed after twelve years of effort in his marriage.

June, by prior agreement, had taken the boys to her mother's home for the afternoon that day and they had known nothing. Charles and June had at least been able to make a reasonable plan for his leaving day without arguing or falling into blame and recrimination. He had kissed Anthony on the forehead as he left to visit his grandmother, knowing that his relationship with the child would not be the same again. He held his son's head in his hands for a few seconds as if letting go was dangerous to the child. But he had to let go in the end. Freddie shrugged off his hug – he knew there was something different about the day and was suspicious of his father's motives with the hug.

June ignored him as she closed the back door behind her firmly, as if to crush and break to death the chord between her husband, and herself and his boys. She was perfectly conscious of what she was doing as she clicked the latch shut and knew that the day was painful for him. She savoured the moment as she squeezed the back-door handle down and slowly let the lock click into place. A deep sense of wanting to punish him shuddered through her arms. He could leave but, by God, he would pay for it, she thought, as she stepped steadily down the garden path with one boy at each hand. And from that day forward she remained true to that silent oath.

Charles waited, sitting in the house until they were completely gone, listening only to the sound of his heart beating and pulsing in his chest. Then the silence of the family home enwrapped him, as if trying to hold him there. His body became heavy as he sat and stared at the back door that marked the boundary between the present with his family, and the future of his life alone. Soon, his turn would come to go out through that door. When the time was right he would leave to begin his new life, but he was wracked with guilt about putting himself first in this home where his own psychological needs barely existed. His heart said stay and his brain said go and the conversation between these two vital organs echoed around his mind. He slipped to his knees from the kitchen chair and allowed his whole body to sink to the floor.

He was on that floor for half an hour, subject to the attention of his righteous inner torturer, until he broke and his rational thoughts interceded and he decided to take control.

'OK, I get it, you can't leave that to which you truly belong, and it feels like if I go something bad is going to happen, but I do need to get out of here before June gets back and finds me on the floor like this.'

These spoken words jolted him to his senses. The fight with himself ended and he kissed the ground that faced him: the cream and gleaming clean linoleum floor. He was kissing his family goodbye from this home base, but he knew now through the mercy of some evolutionary force that they would always exist for him, as he was their creator.

Later, he had time to reflect as he looked out of the window of his new abode – Town End Cottage. This was a well-worn, two-bedroomed, Victorian red-brick building in open countryside on the edge of their home town. For now, the dwelling seemed the perfect place to bring his broken heart; it had pretty gable ends to the roof, and the window frames and doors, probably original, had been painted over and over again through the years to protect the wood from rotting, as the Somerset rainfalls soaked all. The abode may have been originally a woodcutter's cottage or perhaps the home of a senior farmhand who had earned the right to a shelter with more status. For now, it offered the perfect haven for Charles.

***

To walk up the River Exe from his house to June's in Blessingham took about forty minutes if you were prepared to cope with a rough track, nettles, briars and fox traps. Not many people wished to do this, especially when the river flooded. To drive round the ring road and through town in a car also took about forty minutes if traffic were taken into consideration. You could choose which route – through the evolutionary pathway visited only by those committed to nature, or around the tarmac of the suburban route.

This day, he chose the tarmac route, although with his heart being linked as it was to evolution and having a mind of its own, he would have loved to take the natural pathway. The location of the cottage meant that there was a tactful distance between the warring couple, and that Charles did not have to travel far for work or to visit the boys. These were very early days, and he felt both grief-stricken, and more alive than he had since he was in love with Katrina and was belting around without a care with her across Iran in a Land Rover. He now had so many polarities to face in his life – he feared the future and embraced it, felt a sense of loss at the break up and yet was excited and energised by the whole journey. So, here he was now, on his own living with all those mixed emotions in a small, slightly damp cottage. And there was no way that June was going to make it easy for him or accept the situation, because she had everything to lose.

When Freddie finally got to hear the news that Dad had gone he responded minimally. He had calmed right down and even, like his mother, seemed very pleased to see his father when he visited. Freddie, too, had realised through his father's absence that, despite all the disdain he had seen demonstrated by his mum towards his dad over the years, he might have some value as a human being. He wanted more than anything to impress him, but saw that there was less opportunity to curry favour with his father than there was with his mother. But for Anthony, the second son, born out of a desperate ambush by his mother and entirely innocent of his origins, a bond was much easier to sustain.

Charles could not get anything wrong in the eyes of little Anthony who, like his father, had grown into the habit of keeping most of his thinking to himself within the confines of his family. These were thoughts that the child felt to be dangerous and which he had to hide at all costs from Freddie, although he did not hide them from himself. The main thought hidden was that his dad was marvellous. He never said anything about that. And another, that often came to mind, was that he thought that his dad needed more love. He never said anything about that either. There were seriously suppressed thoughts in his house with Mum and Freddie. He also believed that Freddie was a marvellous big brother, but he never told his dad this. Nor did he, in fact, ever contradict Freddie in any way because that led to bad results. In his mind, it was as if Freddie were the authoritative father and Charles were the big brother. And thus little Anthony was a very quiet boy with many thoughts in his mind that were often upsetting to him. Yet his little face – at least the one he presented to the world – became a picture of compliance around his family, and everybody marvelled at how he seemed resistant to nothing, whereas Freddie protested about everything.

When Charles had prepared all the paperwork for the one year rental on the cottage and knew the date on which he would be leaving June, he broke the news. She was in the lounge; he went in and closed the door behind him.

'I'm so sorry, June. I've made a terrible decision. I'm leaving. There will be plenty of money for you and I will pay the mortgage. You will have everything you need. But I just can't do this any more. I owe you an explanation. I've had to give up on our relationship. You won't stop and think about us, and so I can only tell you in this way. I'm so unhappy that I have wanted to die. I'm leaving so that I don't try to commit suicide. I wouldn't do that to you or my boys. I care about you, but you don't love me and I don't think I love you. I'm just a small bit player on your stage, June. I'll call you and make arrangements to see the boys.'

'You … you can't,' she stuttered, although she did not actually feel upset. She just felt angry that he had got the better of her on this occasion and that she had been taken by surprise and had not noticed what he had been planning. For her, the worst event had already gone, and that had been the meeting with, and the information from, Dr Fratina at the family therapy session, and she was never going to let anything upset her like that again. This event was easy in comparison to that morning when she had met with that woman who had said those dreadful things about her parenting and her son.

Charles was sitting down now and facing her, his hands placed on his knees in case he accidentally grabbed her hand to entreat her one more time to make a change.

She stared towards the window. She really did not wish to hear him further. He was dismissed from that moment onwards. He had given up on them. She had heard enough. She countered her despair by planning her next move. She would go down to her mother's within a few moments, where she knew would be well received.

He read her mind. 'I'll ring your parents and get them to come over for a while. I don't want you to be alone,' he said. This was the most powerful – heroic, even – that he had been for a long time.

June sniffed the air and surveyed the landscape of the room, contemplating what she should do next. What shocked her most, was that the power within their relationship had shifted and taken a different turn. The tug-of-war rope had been dropped by her opponent and there was now no longer a game to play. The rope was slack and she was on the floor. She knew her parents would help her. They had always told her that Charles was useless. This was the moment they were proved right. She fetched her coat and left Charles with the children, and was away down the road to tell them what he had done.

The day he had picked himself up from the floor and walked out of his family home he knew it was unlikely that he would ever return. Anything, he thought, anything had to be better than the living lie that his life with June had been to that point. He had waved to Gwen and Abigail at their window as he went down the road and turned right into town. They both waved back, genuinely pleased to see him. Charles made a mental note to speak to Gwen when he next saw her in the high street. He must let her know what was going on. *Although,* he thought, *she probably already knows I'm leaving.*

'I think he's leaving, dear,' Abigail told her friend as she watched and waved. 'I saw suitcases in the back of the car. He was crying, Gwen, definitely. I saw the tears even though he was trying to be cheerful with us.' Abigail had picked up immediately on the significance of this sighting.

'I know, Abigail. I know. How much worse can this get for him?' Gwen was deeply upset: Charles was no longer living in their road. He was such a pillar of strength for them in many practical ways when they needed him, always willing to lend a hand. She was genuinely sad and felt a sense of loss, but she knew that this was so much more than a personal loss; people like her never dwelt on personal losses for too long.

The ladies looked at each other knowingly. This was a loss for Blessingham – a change in one person always meant, they knew, a change in all the people. They were partially excited that they would monitor and bear witness to what that change would mean, but they were also respectfully cognisant for now of both the personal and the political significance of the moment, and knew that they should continue their surveillance task and not get in the way of history as it flowed past their window.

Gwen made more tea to comfort them. She dried her eyes and blew her nose in the kitchen. She did not wish to upset Abigail, who squeezed the crumbs remaining on her plate together, so as to create an extra delicious mouthful of cake. She knew her friend would not want her to see the crying.

'Well, let's keep our eye on this situation,' Gwen said resolutely, arriving with the teapot. 'I think something is changing. Can you make a note? And I will make a point of chatting to him when I'm next in town. He won't be going completely.'

She had already reconciled herself to the situation. Old people with much experience are able to resign themselves to loss more quickly. If only everybody knew that, they would not patronise elders quite so much, and more, they would revere and respect them for their knowledge of the world.

'Already done,' Abigail said. 'I've made a note. I'm sure he will be pleased to see you. This Madeira cake is just delicious, Gwen; another wonderful bake.'

Chapter 14

More Room in a Broken Heart

Charles had driven across town, stopping at the supermarket on the outskirts of the ring road. It was dusk. The frosty air and the unforgiving darkness settling on hedges, trees and tarmac matched his mood.

Everything hurt from crying; the great waves and sobs that were the inevitable result of a broken connection had thoroughly unsettled his whole skeletal system. His cheeks remained raw as they met the chilly air, having been sluiced with salty tears.

How could he leave them? The words still echoed faintly in the back of his mind now. The minutes ticked by and he thanked God for the growing darkness which made it unlikely that anybody would see him. He wiped his face again and blew air out from puffed cheeks.

'Come on now,' he said out loud. He could only go onwards or he would go straight back to them and to the warmth of his home – whatever he had to put up with in life from June.

His practical mind had kicked in when he realised that he not only had no food, but also no plates or anything with which to eat food. He felt like a refugee at that moment and wondered how refugees got along without a credit card to buy all they needed. His way was always to think of others less fortunate than himself, and this distracted him from his grief. He could, though, have been a refugee at that moment. A refugee escaping from an oppressive regime in which he had not been free to think.

Piling the shopping trolley high with immediate necessities was the perfect distraction. He had to think clearly now in order to survive. In the trolley were assorted implements: a saucepan, a frying pan, some eggs, some sheets, a duvet etc. He still desperately hoped no one would see him. How would he explain this pile of household goods and his red, tear-stained face? He finished the task as quickly as he could with his head down, manoeuvring the trolley erratically as it became heavier and heavier, trying to convince himself that this was a normal shopping outing. He deliberately did not engage in banter at the checkout counter, despite the cheerful countenance of the young woman trying to help him pack. He pushed the trolley back to his car, straining with the weight and wheels that still would not co-operate, the last humiliation of the day, and then drove to Town End Cottage and let himself in through the front door of his new life.

Charles stood and looked around. It was cold and basic but a space in which he could exist and in which everything now was possible. As his eyes took in the shapes and shadows of his shelter, he allowed a trickle of hope into his heart.

Plodding methodically through the things he needed to do to put the house into shape for that first evening was a helpful distraction. His mind, which had been in turmoil, started to obey the commands of his body and the task became a meditation and a refuge, a defence against the misery that he feared would never end. He was dusting some cobwebs from the corner of the bedroom, and with his heightened state of sensitivity couldn't bear to kill the medium-sized spider that had made its home there. He pushed the arachnid gently with his forefinger onto the duster and made towards the window, tipping it out with some regret onto the window ledge into the cold night air, as if he were repeating the pattern he had just experienced of pushing himself out of his warm home into the night with his bags.

Itsy-bitsy spider climbed up the water spout,
Down came the rain and washed the spider out …
I know nothin' stays the same,
But if you're willin' to play the game,
It's comin' around again.
Don't mind if I fall apart,
There's more room in a broken heart …
Charles murmured the refrain to his spider friend:
'Don't mind if I fall apart,

There's more room in a broken heart …'

He was captivated by the harmony of the tune and the comfort of the simple nursery words as they went round and round his head in a loop and offered a sedative to his sorrow. The song became his mantra as he worked, and he even dared to sing it out loud as he moved around the house locating everything that he would need to anchor himself down in his camp. The song in his head continued as he remembered the words:

Baby sneezes,

Mommy pleases,

Daddy breezes in …

He started to notice things that made him feel pleased rather than things that upset him. Carly Simon filled the stage of his mind.

Baby Sneezes …

He liked the outlook across the patchwork fields of the flat, moonlit countryside.

Mummy pleases …

He ran his hand over the marble of the fireplace in the lounge – original Victoriana marble, framed with cherrywood, ornately carved and imposing; he thought he could light a good fire in the iron fire basket to warm the place up.

Daddy breezes in …

His gaze turned to the sofa and chairs covered in violet tulle, slightly shabby and well-worn but comfy and with curtains to match; these had clearly originally been a very expensive and well-made set of furnishings.

I know nothing stays the same …

He felt the stone kitchen floor under his feet and ran his hand over the silky, old-fashioned, Formica-topped kitchen table.

But if you're willing to play the game …

He spent the evening unwrapping packs of new sheets and towels, making up the bed with a hot-water bottle to reduce the dampness, and putting his clothes in the wardrobe which smelled of lavender mothballs, a waft of nostalgia that stimulated his nostrils.

I know nothing stays the same,

But if you're willing to play the game …

He hoovered the floor and wiped the windowsills free from dust. He was left with piles of cellophane and cardboard on the floor, which he cleared up to take to the recycling centre.

It's comin' around again.

As he completed the tasks of adjusting to a new environment he felt physically tired but mentally better, and reminded himself that he had a life that he must lead and that he must be ready for work tomorrow.

So don't mind if I fall apart,

There's more room—

The business. The business had come to mind. He really wanted to start to give the business his full attention. At least now he could use all of the psychic energy that he had been investing with June and the boys to revitalise his work.

It was 9.00 pm and the autumn night-time had taken over.

In the cupboard under the sink he found firelighters, and just outside the back door in the shed was a neat pile of logs beautifully dry from the summer and covered in lichen. He returned to the lounge with an armful, inevitably inhaling another intoxicating smell: the spicy pungent odour of the wood, an old spruce. He crumpled some newspaper in the fire basket and set fire to the corner of one small piece of cardboard. The flames soon caught, and he fed the centre of the fire with increasingly bigger pieces of the boxes, totally focussed on the goal of making himself warm and comfortable, and utterly lost in this primal craft.

Eventually, there was enough heat and roaring in the flames for him to add some twigs and the smallest log, on top of which he placed a few more firelighters just for good measure. The fire roared up the chimney beautifully as he opened the vent below the grate so as to feed the flames with oxygen. With his task complete he stood back to admire what he had created. Then, adding to his sense of comfort he went to the kitchen and pulled out a half bottle of brandy he had bought that evening at the supermarket and poured some into a slightly chipped floral bone china teacup and remembered that he was hungry and that there was a sausage roll to eat. No need for a plate now, he was a man in his cave. With this sense of arrival, he locked the back door, pulled the curtains to in the lounge and sat on the settee, staring and staring at the crackling fire.

He stared at the fire and his mind held still for a while. The intense labour, delivery and immediate separation were complete. Like most births, it had been messy and painful while he was delivered. He knew he had many more miles to travel on his journey and he did not have any map of the future. Charles just had this moment of respite as he sat in front of his fire in this cold, damp little cottage by the river on the edge of Blessingham. Tomorrow …

***

Following this brush with the grimness of separation, his life developed, and back at the office he had to block the telephone calls that June made to him up to half a dozen times a day. He knew she had her parents to lean on and this assuaged his fear that he was leaving his family alone and vulnerable – on the savannah in his mind – ready to be picked off by predators. This was the picture that kept presenting itself.

He was making a new set of rules for himself. This helped. He would support his kids, he would help June out financially and ensure that they were kept well, but there was no way – no way – that he was going back to that kind of life or that kind of relationship, however much he stood shivering as he entered the shabby little cottage on his own in the evenings. Whatever the fight and however much he missed them, however ashamed he felt that he had hung on for too long, that struggle was over now.

One survival strategy he developed, which was quickly noticed by Ryan and Ruby in the office, was to work late and have a takeaway from the town before going home. This way, he could get through some files, eat his food, and then go into the cottage with a contented stomach, put the oven on for a few hours to warm up the place, and after a few mugs of hot sweet tea and a biscuit in front of the evening news the water tank would be heated and he could undress, take a hot shower and then head for the bed heated by the electric blanket. He realised he was heading from one heated electrical implement to another within the cottage but he did not mind – it was keeping him warm and mentally afloat. There was an upside to his new regime; he was working his way through acres of files at the office. He had never felt so on top of his client's work and their financial needs. Ryan was impressed by the way his partner had caught up with his backlog, even if his shirts did appear to look as though they needed an iron. They had been ironed as Charles stood by the stove in the kitchen, although not up to Ryan's impeccable standards. Eventually, Ruby took pity on him, and Charles brought his shirts in for her to do. Ryan just could not stand an unkempt man around the office and had encouraged Ruby to make the offer.

So, what would he do on his first weekend in his cottage on his own now that he was a single man with a toothbrush with no holder and unable to finish off his shirts to a decent standard? No, he would not fall apart. He was in the car before he thought more about his losses, his bag packed. He was not falling down that hole again, not plummeting into that chasm in the ground of his being where he was slapped around by his heart. He would do what any self-respecting aspiring hero would do when challenged to a weekend on his own in his little cottage without his family, and visit Mum and Dad.

Chapter 15

Coming Around Again

The five-hour drive through the rush hour traffic of the overcrowded M25 motorway and down the M2, dodging the lorries that were heading to Dover and the Channel Tunnel to cross to Europe, either by boat, or underground on the train, gave Charles plenty of time to reflect on his knee-jerk reaction to get out of the house. As he drove in the inside lane he was sandwiched between a petrol tanker behind, and a Marks & Spencer delivery lorry in front; he read the sign on the back of the lorry – 'Am I well driven? Call 020 268 7380' – and really did contemplate calling to say how pleasant his journey had been. When you are lonely you tend to seek opportunities such as this. With these thoughts and wrapped in the gentle droning of the car engine, his attention strayed and he quickly became worried that he was lost.

Signs for Canterbury, Folkestone, Margate and the Channel Tunnel showed he had not missed his turning, and he felt excitement in his legs and a smile crossed his face without even being invited. Somehow his body knew this territory, and some part of him could smell the salt-laden sea and could hear gulls wheeling overhead already. There was a restorative call about Kent: home, the sea, and Mum and Dad. These were aspects of his treasured past that were enduring and reliable and he needed them right now. His past was calling him with its arms open.

He threw himself at his mother and father and they huddled together under the cobwebbed porch light, their arms weaved around each other without any embarrassment. Peggy's tears were to be expected, but Peter's were not, and his father quickly drew out his maroon paisley silk handkerchief and wiped his eyes and then his forehead as if to portray the idea that he was wiping away perspiration rather than tears. Charles looked away while he did this. When they entered the glow of the interior, Charles noticed immediately how easily warm and cosy felt the familiar domain of his childhood. The grandfather clock in the hallway, which had been there from his birth, continuously marking the passage of time, softly struck 8.00 pm as his father shut the door on the cold night and switched off the illumination of the porch.

The simple roast chicken dinner, with cauliflower cheese and mashed potato followed by bread-and-butter pudding for dessert, filled his stomach and soul and soothed his mind. After his week of singleton takeaway suppers this was a magnificent feast. His mother knew it would warm him. Peter sat in his fifty-year-old wing chair which Peggy had recently reupholstered in Mitford Check – pink and yellow, with covers on the arms so that he would not spill tea or rub newspaper print onto the expensive new linen and spoil her labours.

The after-dinner talk was small and Charles was quick to set up the chessboard. This was been risky because Peter was competitive and did not like losing, but Charles needed to take his mind off things and did not want an argument with his dad about his life right now, which he knew would happen if he was not distracted and would upset his mother.

Words did not have to be exchanged as the board was set up. The younger specimen could beat the old man into submission in half a dozen moves. He had his father's king cornered within twenty minutes of the game starting, challenging him comprehensively with a bishop and a knight on the corner of the board. Peter was baffled as to how he had done this and felt intense annoyance such that Peggy had to remind them that this was only a game. Charles laid down his father's king on its side ceremoniously, as if it were dead. Peter showed due deference, bowing his head, and after a few moments challenged his son to another game by setting up the pieces. The argument was over.

Peggy, however, said no, and that it was 'Time for bed with cocoa.' It was Charles's turn to admit defeat. He could take his father down with the chessboard but he was not arguing with his mum over bedtime and cocoa, grown man and aspiring hero though he was. Anyway, he quite liked that he was not in control as he retired to his room in a cocoa-induced stupor;

his mother, having observed that her son had lost weight, had treated him and topped up his cocoa with full-cream Jersey milk. With his stomach full, lined with fat from the drink, he slumped onto the mattress where his body fitted into the predetermined curves that matched his memory.

As he fell asleep he contemplated the dramatic change that was taking place in his family. He realised, as he reflected on the conversations between them, that his dad had never known the wound of separation in his own marriage to his mum. Somehow her hard work had turned into a form of devotional love and they had forged a complete life of acceptance of one another that served them well in their old age. They had never had to navigate the dreadful sinkhole that opens in the lives of modern families due to unresolvable differences. They were doing their best to understand, and he realised he had to nurse them through the unknown territory as much as he was nursing himself. He ruminated on these last thoughts before sleep in the familiar surroundings of his childhood, and wished that familiarity could return to his adult life, but he no longer knew what kind of prayer to offer up to achieve this.

Life looked and felt better following a long, apparently dreamless, sleep in the bed of his childhood. One of his mother's cooked breakfasts would inspire the hero in any man, and he engaged with the food with a new-found vigour: bacon, eggs, fried bread and tomatoes. They were quiet around the breakfast table as they concentrated on the serious matter of nourishment for the day, only interrupted when Peter got up to make a second pot of coffee for them all. They were in no hurry for breakfast to end. Charles would have sat with them and eaten all day, a long, lazy experience with no sharp ending in sight. They replaced any further conversation with the newspapers, walks by the sea and football on the TV. The weekend passed without event or meaningful conversation – except for tones of consolation from his parents, which was all he needed from them.

And so, they were done. He spent one more night and ate a final large and hearty breakfast before he drove back to Blessingham, and to his musty little Town End Cottage that had an empty fridge and had to be heated by putting on the cooker as soon as he got in the door, and a bed that was warmed only by activating an electric blanket an hour before retiring. So different to the feather and down in which he had been enwrapped that weekend. This was all he had now, but he had connected with his past and that rich storehouse of memories that formed his story and his identity.

The past can sustain us at difficult times, and having been greeted so comfortably by so many aspects of his youth that weekend Charles felt that he may now have a clear road ahead of him. He was not entirely confident but at least he could imagine something of his future. He still longed to be a hero of some kind, but he was reminded of his father's favourite biblical phrase that 'a living dog is better than a dead lion', and he laughed out loud.

Chapter 16

Unknown from Ardent

In a brighter and more hopeful state of mind Charles rumbled into the office of Bradshaw Associates on the following Monday morning with a badly ironed shirt, which, he knew, Ryan would notice, but since he felt rinsed through with the possibility of life for now the shirt did not matter too much. And as is usual when you meet the world with hope, the world meets you back. That morning he came across something very unusual in the front area of the office – an attractive woman in her late thirties wearing a navy dress, the white collar of which was partially covered by a side ponytail of thick blonde hair.

Unbeknown to him, this woman was wearing her favourite dress, made by the designer label 'Curves Aloud' – renowned for subtly enhancing women's natural curves – together with the most expensive pair of matching navy shoes that she could find in her wardrobe. She thought that the ensemble would make her feel good for her first day in temporary work, and her presentation was carefully crafted to give the impression of confidence.

How well this woman knew the psychology of dressing. While there was no outer display of nervousness whatsoever, she had not enjoyed the circumstances that had finally forced her to work through an agency as a temp. Some would have thought that she had not flinched when she was made redundant from her prestigious role with the global accountancy firm, Ardent. But she had flinched. The company had downsized that year and let their most expensive managers go in favour of promoting less experienced people who were prepared to work harder for lower pay. She had been with Ardent for ten years, and was one of the managers they let go. She had left her office trying to maintain her composure while carrying the personal effects from her desk in a box that had previously been full of packs of A4 paper; these items included a calculator, her pens, five lipsticks, two large books on taxation law and two bottles of perfume that she had forgotten were at the back of her drawer. She had signed up with an agency that same day – carrying her box with her – ensuring that there was no gap in her work record or income whatsoever and that she was back at work in a new job the following week. Now she was here, in a little local firm, busy with farming accounts.

Charles only glimpsed an assured and composed picture as he walked past her (as if she was not there – he was feeling rather awkward, as if he should have recognised her). He knew nothing of the story behind the woman in the navy dress with the white collar. He felt there was some expectation that he should have known her, particularly as she was on the business side of the reception desk rather than on the visitor side. He went straight into his office, dropped his briefcase, picked up the phone to ring Ryan and struggled out of his coat while still holding the mouthpiece. At the same time, he stretched across his desk and pushed the door closed to give him privacy now that he had shaken off his outer garment into a heap on the floor. These are the sort of gymnastics that are needed when one feels that one might not quite have got the point of a sudden visitor to the home who looks as if they are confident that they have every right to be there. He needed to gather the right information in private to prevent any further embarrassment. He spoke down the phone in a whisper, even though he had total privacy and Ryan was only in the office next door.

'Good morning, Brains.' He always thought of Ryan as the brains of the partnership. 'Is that a woman in reception?'

'Uh, yes – last time I looked. What's wrong with your memory, Charles? We said we'd have a temp in for a month while Greg was on extended leave, yes? Remember now, do we? Her name is Alicia – she's a qualified accountant, in between jobs now and so doing locum work. Fortunately for us she's a very skilled tax consultant who used to work for Ardent. We've got her at new-customer rates with the accountancy staffing agency, thanks to my nifty thinking and smooth talking. So, make the most of having her here, especially as she says she doesn't mind what she does to help while Greg gets a break. Therefore, we won't fall to pieces while he's away, although it must be a bit of a comedown for her to end up in a little office in Blessingham when she's been a big hitter in the city. Lucky for us, though. OK? Remember now? How's things, anyway? We haven't caught up for a while. Let's talk soon. How's life in that cottage and, by the way, why are we whispering? And don't forget to give that shirt to Ruby for an iron – it looks as if you've been trying to manhandle the ironing board again.'

Charles wondered where his head had been in the last few weeks, because he absolutely had not remembered at all that Greg, their trainee accountant, was away on a youthful jaunt across Europe on a railcard and they were having a temp in, particularly to support Ryan's work while he was completing year-end accounts for their clients. He looked at the pile of files on his desk, looked in his diary, looked at his watch and asked Ruby to get him a coffee while he got on with work. Ruby told him to get his own coffee and that she was not his mother. He was pleased with her response, and satisfied that nothing had changed in his office except for the new temp. Ruby and Ryan were as caring and familiar as they had always been. For the first time in many weeks he felt he could think clearly and give due attention to his clients. But first, he backtracked to reception and extended his hand to the temp with a warm smile on his face, to redress his initial rude omission.

'So sorry, and good morning to you, Alicia – it's Charles, Senior Partner. I didn't realise who you were – we're lucky to have you with us. Hope you don't mind, but I need to get on. Up to here in work.' He pointed to his forehead. 'Just ask if you need help. Ruby knows how things work around here. Don't hesitate.'

Alicia responded with a soft smile, and extended a well-manicured hand. 'Thank you. No problem, I think I can cope.'

Charles went back to his desk, thinking, Alicia, Alicia … that name rings a bell. I'm sure I've known an Alicia.

Ruby brought him a sandwich at lunchtime even though he had not asked for it, but she still refused to make him coffee. Somehow things seemed to be as they should be in the office that day and Ruby, his teenage protégé, was not disappointing him.

Chapter 17

A Ruby So Rare

They had taken on Ruby the year before at age sixteen when she had just left school. They only needed some help around the office with the everyday hiccups, and to ensure smooth running and efficiency. Reception had become chaotic with clients, especially the farmers who needed herding and organising and who were just as likely to walk into either of their offices unannounced. Charles and Ryan believed that an office junior would fit the bill, and they advised the local jobcentre that they wanted someone with good people skills, good mathematical ability, a willingness to do anything that needed doing and a great manner with difficult clients.

When they were alerted by the curious sound of a brawl in reception on the day of interviews for prospective candidates, they rushed to the scene to find a vision of supervisory practice in action. A tall, handsome and very broad red-haired young woman was holding two youths by their shirt collars and staring down at them while they struggled to be free, not from each other but from the humiliation of being held by a girl who was not much older than they, but who was advantaged by her height and size.

'What do you want me to do with these two?' The young woman speaking in a soft Somerset accent caused Ryan to immediately think of her as styled along the lines of Boadicea.

Ruby, the red-headed referee of the fight, had stood out from the crowd that day, as she had been quite prepared to knock together the heads of both the young men concerned after one of them had provoked a fight by criticising the other's cheap suit. She had been next in line for the interview, but instead Charles and Ryan had sat and had a cup of tea and a biscuit with her in a debrief, because they had completely lost their focus and confidence as interviewers and were anxious after such disruption. Charles also noticed that she was not at all scared, as he had secretly been, and he thought that this would make her an asset to the team. Ryan's nerves then overcame him and he could not hold back, his eyes brimming with tears; he felt thoroughly humiliated by the experience, and was shaking from head to foot from the shock of witnessing such unleashed youthful aggression.

The young girl offered him tissues and spoke in comforting tones and did not seem to despise him for this at all. 'There, there, just stupid boys … you don't want that sort in your office. I was at nursery with them. They're no different from then.'

She was the obvious choice for them and they asked her to start the following week. But Ruby became very much more than just a junior. She became 'their' Ruby and they became 'her' boys, as she referred to them. Although they had not quite planned this reversal in power between a sixteen-year-old and the senior partners of the office, it suited them both temperamentally to be cosseted in this way. She was the thermostat of the emotional system of their office, and not even Gwen could have predicted the role she would play in future events as she took control of her chaotic boys.

Chapter 18

Eating Alone

Charles put down his work and thought that he had better wrap up before he got his figures wrong or started to file things in odd places. He had phoned June and said he would go to see the boys and decide about a suitable time to see them for the following weekend. She was not there but her mother, Brenda, took the call. The obvious hostility in Brenda's voice was like driving through a hailstorm in a convertible with the roof down. Brenda had always hated him but now she had a good excuse and every ounce of disappointment in her own life was focussed and projected onto him. Instead of thinking about that demanding husband of hers, her own interrupted dreams, and how she hadn't got the sort of life she really wanted, she could see Charles as the devil who had spoiled her daughter's life. Really, Brenda's own aim in life was to be 'a lady', and if not the lady of the manor then at least the lady of the house. Ladies, she felt, had entitlement, had power and gave orders rather than made requests. They wore smart clothes that meant they did not do housework and they got driven to places in the back of the car rather than map-reading in the front for their forgetful husbands.

In keeping with her vision, she now adopted the voice of Her Majesty while Charles attempted to consult with her on his requests and her wishes.

'It's not convenient for you to just "pop round".'

Charles explained that it would only be a short visit to make a plan about the future.

'Well, only half an hour, we have appointments this evening.'

Who is we? he thought. *Is that her and Prince Philip?* A realist, and republican at the best of times but especially when faced with Brenda's delusional association with the House of Windsor, he purposefully piled his work up for the following day and pulled the blinds down.

As he passed through reception, he saw the woman in the navy dress with a white collar and blonde hair in a ponytail talking on the phone, remembered who she was and noted that he had neither taken any notice of her all day, nor uttered a word to her. He waved as he went past and caught her eye. She waved back, still talking on the phone. He thought: Alicia, though he barely noticed himself having this thought as the door swung closed behind him.

She packed her own working files, locked them securely in the filing cabinet and went in to see Ryan. 'Do you mind if I go?'

'Not at all – you get off. Thanks for everything today, Alicia. Amazing you just got on with it, don't ask me how. It seems like you're capable of anything we throw at you – where did you learn to do that? Nice to have you here.'

She smiled to herself as she walked out of the office wrapped in her camel coat, tied at the waist to protect her from the freezing October air. As she threw her black patent Chanel handbag over her shoulder and carried her briefcase in her opposite hand, she manoeuvred downstairs to the front door, breathing a relaxing exhalation, pleased to turn her back on them all, pleased that her first day was over and had gone so well. Why so pleasing? Ryan had noticed that she appeared to be able 'to do anything.' She had learned this from an early age when she did the ironing for her mother, laid the grate for the fire and kept the younger children under control. All that responsibility in childhood was not wasted. She thought she could do anything and today, yet again, she had proven herself right. In addition to all this she had quickly put herself in the right position with 'Mistress Ruby', as she referred to her already in her mind, not disrespectfully, but perhaps in full recognition of her role as a 'herder' for the office. She had shown the young lady the respect that she clearly commanded, and got on with her work. And she had noticed that Charles, while he seemed to be very much on the outside of the duo of Ruby and Ryan, clearly had a commanding role to play and she thought he had been charming and friendly, if a little forgetful – did he really forget she was due in the office today? Tomorrow she might find out why Ruby would not bring him coffee, whereas she had been supplied with plenty all day.

It's been a good day. I like it here. Nice group of people. She could assert this to herself with comfort, and her intentions for herself were intact after her day in this new environment, a day that could have knocked all her needs for security out of place as she exposed herself and her ability to complete strangers for their appraisal.

She slid into the driver's seat of her BMW, clicked her seat belt into position, turned on the evening news, pushed the gears into reverse, looked carefully in her rear-view and wing mirrors and reversed smoothly out of the parking place, driving home through the evening traffic across town to her warm cosy flat, her little haven from the world where she would prepare her evening meal for one and take a hot bath with essential oils before retiring. She was tired from the strain of working in a new environment but felt contented and somehow stirred and joyful, although she could not quite pinpoint what exactly had opened up for her that day.

Charles, meanwhile, was steering his way through the evening traffic on the ring road to June's house, and was certainly not thinking about the temporary accountant in the office, nor was he feeling stirred and joyful. He was relieved as he saw that, knowing he was coming, Brenda had apparently gone back to her own house. He felt a growing sense of dread as he walked through the garden and knocked on the back door – the door that was not his any more. The door that he used to take for granted as much as he took dawn and nightfall for granted. Not any more.

Knocking on the door caused him pain, as much as it had caused him pain when he walked out of it the previous week to go and live in the cottage. But he knew now that this process was about pain and that he had to live with this happening, live through the experience, and there was no avoiding it. So he knocked and waited while he felt the frosty ground nipping at his feet through his shoes and the chill air brushing his temples.

Anthony opened the door to him, and in a rush of warm air his youngest child threw himself at his father while at the same time telling him he was doing his maths homework and needed help. 'Go and get it. I'll help you,' Charles said, panicking, his mind beginning to race about how he could help his vulnerable little chick left in the nest and exposed to all comers. This was the very thing he dreaded – letting his child down, not protecting him, abandoning him with his maths homework so that his vulnerability was exposed in class. His mind raced to resolve the problem now, so that the child would be safe when returning to school. He held the pencil that Anthony passed to him hard in his fingers and focussed his mind immediately on the long multiplication problem and how he would explain the sum to his son. His shoulders were hunched, and his brow was knitted in much the same way as it used to be when he tackled maths homework at school himself.

Freddie would not come for a hug, but Charles managed to show his intent to care for his other child, and ruffled his hair, gave him a cheery hello and searched for his eyes. His boy ignored him, his shoulders stiff with the effort of doing so, his stubborn chin jutting forward as he focussed on his computer game with his face set and eyes cast down in a sulky pose.

June ignored Charles too, and got on with getting tea for the boys. She was in the kitchen with her apron on and listening to the radio while concentrating on making sausage, chips and beans for her sons. The words from the radio were a muddle in her mind as it raced along on the task of how to convince Charles that she was not interested in him any longer, when in fact her heart wanted him there. All this she considered in her mind with her head bent down to the cooking as if she were bowing to the shrine of a beloved God and making an offering. She shut the kitchen door and hoped that Charles felt thoroughly shut out, as she made sure it did not close quietly. Only the muttering of the radio and the spitting of the frying pan could be heard by him now on the other side of the door.

Freddie observed his mother's decision to shut Charles out, and observed his father for her as they were now in the same room, noticing that his dad seemed rather cheerful and energetic. Freddie was not used to this, and he was startled and alert to see this different sort of man. This was not the man that he knew so well from the moment of his birth when he had been placed in his arms; he was used to his dad doing as he was told, and helping Mum out, and looking rather sad. Freddie had also noticed that his mum had been unhappy recently, and he was old enough to realise that what had happened had serious consequences for his own life. His mum had spoken to him about Dad leaving the home, just for a while, to think about his work. He did not believe this. Dad had left because of him. He knew it. He was sure of it. It was because he was bad.

At first, he had been pleased – so pleased – and he enjoyed Brenda and Dick coming to the house more and indulging him in play and constant activity and treats, and Mum could spoil him as much as he wanted. He liked this. But there was now an interesting change. Dad seemed bright and detached and unaffected by him. This was shocking to him, and he was not used to being shocked by his father. He did not want his dad to see that he was either startled or upset.

So instead of things getting better they were worse, he thought, as he stared at his computer screen as if he were ignoring everyone when in fact he was thinking, thinking about what to do to change this confusing and discomfiting feeling as soon as possible. He noticed that Anthony right now was doting on his dad and leaning on him comfortably and lazily so that he almost got a cuddle as he leaned in, his little body relaxed and soothed by the closeness of their connection. They were pressed close to each other and Dad was helping him and showing him in a kind way with a soothing voice. That annoyed Freddie, jarred him somehow inside in another frightening way that made him feel alone, separated and outside of them both; he had to change it, and so he called his brother over.

'Anthony, come over here with me. I'll help you with the homework. I know how to do that maths.'

And Anthony hesitated, but left his dad, looking at him for approval and hoping he would understand as he went over at his older brother's command, feeling sheepish that he had been caught out; he had automatically put his father first in front of his brother as soon as he saw him at the door as he stood in the cold. But he had needed his dad. He realised now that this had been the wrong thing to do and that it went against the rules in the house. Now he had to show his brother that he was putting his dad in second position, to put things right.

'Can we come to your house?' Freddie asked, standing up.

'Of course. I came to sort that out. I'll get you on Sunday.'

'No, get me on Saturday. I'm busy on Sunday with my friends. Get me on Saturday at ten o'clock.' Freddie stared at his father and did not take his gaze off him while rocking his foot on the ground, backwards and forwards as if he were a little rutting stag. He was not ashamed at making this demand. The full weight of his stare was on his father.

'No, son, I'm sorry – I can't get you on Saturday. I'll get you on Sunday and we can have a nice day down by the river, maybe go fishing. You'll have to change the arrangement with your friends.'

'No. Saturday.' Freddie put his hands on his hips and puffed out his twelve-year-old chest and his cheeks went red. He was outraged.

Charles let the idea that his stance was not working fall aside. He recalled the 'broken record' technique that Colin, the mental health nurse, had shown him when trying to help him be more assertive. Repeat the information in a calm and kindly manner. There was no negotiating going on and he was not to show fear in the encounter, as this is what allowed children to take control of parents.

'No, son – Sunday. I'll confirm this with Mum and look forward to seeing you then. Sunday, it is, fellas.' He rubbed his hands together industriously.

With that, Charles gave Anthony a hug and spoke with him gently, saying he could not wait to see him 'on Sunday' and that they would go over the maths again then. He made ready to leave, pulling on his overcoat. He knew he had to face the cold air, but before that he had to face June. He would have loved the warmth of a cup of tea but June did not offer and he did not feel he had rights in this home any more to ask for a simple warming beverage.

He spoke to her on his way out, saying that he would call her the next day to make time for them to talk, and that maybe this was not a good time now. He tried to make eye contact with her as he spoke but she would not look at him and continued her frying at the stove, turning the sausages so that they browned on all aspects of their circumference. This was always hard to do with a sausage at the best of times.

June's mother had briefed her on this kind of scenario. Charles, they had confirmed between themselves, no longer deserved any positive attention whatsoever.

He should not have come, he thought. He should have made arrangements with June over the phone.

He waved to them all from the window by the back door and that feeling came over him again, that terrible feeling of loss and abandonment, especially compounded when he heard June noisily bolt the back door after him. The chill air jerked him out of his cramping despair and back into the practicalities of what had to be done. At the car, the lock was not yet frozen over and he thanked God for that and switched on the fan heater as he started the engine. The initial rush of cold made his legs and feet freeze before he could adjust the direction of the blast up to the windscreen.

As he drove up the road to the ring road, the car warmed and the screen and his mind were clearing. He felt that his response to Freddie had been the right one as instructed by Colin, and again he made vows to himself that he would help Freddie by being straightforward, but kind and clear with him in future. He hoped this would bring them closer together in the long run.

As his journey continued, he talked himself through his remorseful state, and his logical mind clicked into gear as he moved through the gears in the car. 'No going back.' He spoke to himself in strict but comforting terms. 'You have your own home now, get back to Town End Cottage and get some dinner on for yourself, get that oven on and light the fire, this is what you have to do next.'

And back at his old home, June and Freddie were sitting at the family table eating tea with Anthony. They ate in silence except for the clinking of cutlery on china. They were sharing the same realisation that things were never going back to the way they had been before.

Anthony could not eat his tea, and had to go to bed with a stomach ache. This was the only way he could introduce his mother to the idea that he was desperately upset.

While June took Anthony to his room, Freddie ate what was left on his brother's plate.

Chapter 19

To Everything There Is a Season – Spring 1989

The initial months of darkness passed at the pace of the turning earth. Following the winter gloom at Town End Cottage, the spring of the following year heralded new shoots of life in the surrounding garden of the ancient homestead in which he had taken asylum from his personal war. Charles struggled with his solitary existence but learned to shuffle through life after his separation from his home and children. One foot forward, another follows, one foot forward, another follows: keep going. In the garden there was evidence of growth that gave him hope. He was changing. He could sense the vibrancy that was gradually emerging in him daily. He had entered the cottage a broken man. He was recovering now.

'If Winter comes, can Spring be far behind?' he muttered to himself involuntarily one day as he looked at the frosty grass from the kitchen window, remembering the lines he had learned at school from Shelley's 'Ode to the West Wind'. He had not known what the words meant as a child. He knew now that Shelley had been writing about hope.

The snowdrops came first, pushing their heads from the forbidding soil still frozen in January but defied by this petulant and solitary single-minded winter flower that thought the snow was its sunshine. And, as if the whole garden were conjoined and the plants chattering and talking to each other having felt the confidence of the little white winter flowers leading the pack, everything else seemed to tag along behind. The snowdrops nudged the delicate lilac and gold crocuses, which arrived by Easter, and they tapped along the wire to the daffodils and tulips, which trumpeted their presence in swathes of clashing gold and purple, signalling to the grape hyacinth and meek little pink woodland cyclamen that it was time for them, too. This intelligence was picked up by the yellow forsythia bush that looked too old to continue, gnarled as it was by years of fighting the elements, but which came into bloom anyway for another year. Not wanting to miss out, the camellias burst from dormant bud to lively flower in their clay pots. By late spring the garden was humming and buzzing like a power station, feeding from its own vibrant energy and further fuelled by warming damp sunlight towards which the world now turned its face.

Charles noticed all these things with a brighter mind and a more open heart than he had possessed just nine months before. By late spring he could bear to sit some days in the humming, buzzing little bower of wild ivy in the corner of the garden, and his misery was diminished while something as intoxicating as the lilac perfume provoked his emotional system and took its evocative seat in his mind.

The summer came and the garden demanded that he dance with all of this growth and, beyond his own will, he was spurred into activity. He had to mow the lawn, which was thick with daisies and buttercups, before its growth spoiled the chocolate-box-picture effect of the whole scene. While the heads of most of the daisies and buttercups were shorn, he left a corner of the grass to grow wild and long to display these common little yellow and white grass flowers, the proletariat of the garden. He felt for them in that way.

He clipped the ivy that was tumbling and surging over the Victorian stone wall that marked the boundary of the garden. He also took to feeding the birds from the old bird table, encrusted with lichen and rotting with age, with crumbs from his morning toast. He had noticed at least four different types of common garden bird that he could name, having learned them in childhood from his mother: the thrush, the sparrow, the blackbird, and the unmistakable robin which, he noticed, despite its sweet reputation had been ruthlessly sucking, pulling and stretching without shame, long fat worms from the damp ground. Ryan and Ruby would tease him later in the day because he popped out to the hardware store to buy birdseed. One weekend even found him putting fresh emulsion on the lounge walls of the cottage to brighten it up inside as much as it was brightened outside.

He had chosen the colour to match the lilac bush that had so encouraged him and impressed itself on his mind.

In short, Town End Cottage had transformed from a transitional camp into a home and haven, and the treasure that he had found was from the openness of his broken being. His self-fulfilling prophecy had come true – the prophecy he had sung about as he had first entered the cottage in his state of despair – *There's more room in a broken heart …*

The problem for humans is that we have a choice about change, whereas a garden, and animals, insects, birds, trees and flowers, thought Charles as he lingered one morning by the bird table, do not have a choice. For humans, making a choice about altering the course of your life is exhilarating and empowering as well as frightening. It involves a leap of faith combined with alterations in attitude and adjustments in behaviour. The braver and bolder we are, the more we are empowered to make the changes we want. Charles now felt firmly rooted and planted rather than being a vulnerable seedling in his new life, and he wanted to strike out and construct a future for himself to show his colours – to be the hero of his boyhood dreams.

In line with this development many other aspects of his life fell into place. Business was good in insurance and they had branched out into the field of investment portfolios. He now worked hand in hand with Ryan as he built up the accountancy side of the firm, whereas they had previously been two separate entities under the same roof. Their consultancy continued to serve the local community of farmers, traders and business people in their financial dealings, and they had some more wealthy clients now too: Dobermans, the milk processing plant in Somerset, and Webbers, the south-west parcel delivery group. Many times, Charles had had to clear mud off his office floor (Ruby refused) after his farmers dropped by with a query on farm insurance, or to leave their careless bookkeeping on scraps of paper for Ryan to make sense of, and he always kept his wellingtons in the boot of his car for visits to their farmyards. Ruby had become adept at helping Ryan organise the farm accounts. She understood every scrap of sodden paper, every envelope with figures on the back, and every tea-stained receipt that was thrown at her.

Somerset farmers are a surprising contradiction of muck and money, and Charles was observant enough to acknowledge that these men and women of the most ancient of professions were the complete backbone of his business, and indeed his life, now and in the future. This kept him busy and absorbed in the detail of his industrious office, and this absorption brought him satisfaction and peace of mind that was quite aside from his private life.

The local GP, Angus, pondered the state of these dynamics as he cleared up after his evening surgery. He was content that his patient Charles had pulled himself through his valley of darkness, but he wanted to get June into the women's group he had set up in the surgery, run by one of his experienced counsellors. He aimed for her to be empowered rather than reliant on serotonin inhibitors. That way, he thought, she might also manage Freddie better and stop living as if she had a child in an alternative universe where children ruled over adults rather than vice versa. This was well noted by him independently, and besides, Gwen had been into the surgery for her monthly blood pressure check that day and had updated him with essential reconnaissance that reinforced his confidence in his assessment.

Gwen had guessed he may welcome this help when June had found her pruning her roses one warm afternoon and had stopped to complain to her about what an unsympathetic doctor she had. Gwen had not agreed, but had noted all that was said.

Gwen had also given him the startling nugget of news that she thought that Charles was dating. She had discussed this development with Abigail, and Abigail confirmed her suspicions: she had seen him walking from his office with a woman whom she described as being well dressed and having long shoulder-length hair and a nice face. (Gwen checked carefully that Abigail had not mistaken the woman for Ruby, which would have been a reasonable mistake, given her eyesight.)

'No, not a reasonable mistake,' said Abigail. 'This woman was at least twenty years older than Ruby and half her dress size, and had yellow rather than red hair. You know, she reminded me of the young Grace Kelly when she married the Prince. No, a woman not a girl, dear. He's dating!' Gwen, of course, had to pass on the information down the line to Command Control at the surgery.

Angus had seen pictures of Grace Kelly when she married Prince Rainier, and so he immediately got the idea of elegance and glamour and he was pretty sure that he knew the woman who was being referred to. That could be tricky, he thought. He did not repeat his thought to Gwen: she knew already it would be tricky.

***

'So, you've been dating Alicia for six months now, Charles,' said Colin, the mental health nurse, in one of their closing sessions.

'Oh, God, yes. Frankly, it's like living in paradise compared to the last thirteen years. I feel so damned guilty for having her in my life. Why should I be so lucky to have a companion like her? I struggle with that so much, and it's about time June got to know about it, you know, but I don't want to upset her or hurt her. If telling her that I was leaving was a challenge, then telling her about Alicia will be bringing hell and damnation on my soul for eternity and beyond.'

'But you're not with June – we were talking about that before – you wanted to bring closure to your relationship with her. You've been apart for eight months now, and you were thinking that you wanted a divorce but you were struggling with that. It seemed that you were thinking of her. It's great, you know, that you are so thoughtful of others and so decent that you will ensure that they have all they need, but you must keep being aware of what *you* really want and need, Charles. Remember – don't forget yourself again. You're entitled to a new relationship, it's not like you had an illicit affair and had been cheating on June, but you're making it sound that way. People do move forward in relationships in this day and age.'

Charles warmed to his subject, just as Colin had intended; he leaned forward with his arms on his knees and discussed more of his worries. 'But Mum and Dad had such a stable relationship. Mum was, I know, always tolerating difficult things. I felt I should do the same. I know it's over, and I'll make sure June has all she needs. I have this sense of duty to her. They can keep the house.'

'Let's break that down one piece at a time. All that "should" and "must" … you'll be heading yourself towards a good dose of stress. Let's build on your assertiveness and what you've learned so far about what *you* need. So, what's the hardest thought you have about the whole thing?'

'My poor kids. I've really let them down, you know. I let go of my soul in that marriage for the sake of a quiet life. Freddie is completely aghast that there is another me inside, and he can't come to terms with it. He thinks I should revert to who I was a year ago and I just can't do that. I can understand his confusion. I didn't assert myself with June, or with him, and I asked for nothing for myself. And now my kids, frankly, are suffering. Freddie thinks that everything should go his way, and Anthony is so compliant, trying to keep the peace; he frighteningly reminds me of me. I've got to help them move on a bit, you know. That, I do owe them.'

Colin relaxed with his ankle over the knee of his opposite leg, and sat back in his chair. From all that he knew, there was a clear reality about some of his client's concerns regarding his wife's possible reactions to his new love.

Chapter 20

Going Mad and Staying Mad

June went mad and stayed mad when she heard about the 'new friend', from none other than her mother, the aspiring Lady Brenda, who had spotted Charles with Alicia in the smart Michelin-starred restaurant that sat snugly in a village on the outskirts of Blessingham. Brenda had been at the bar with her lady friends from the bridge club when Charles swept through, holding the hand of a woman who she thought looked remarkably like the young Grace Kelly. Brenda had been transfixed, and as soon as she was dropped off by her friend at home she called her daughter.

'No, darling … very common. Really unattractive and rather plump and plain, and clearly no breeding. Yes … very, very common.' Common was the most insulting word in Brenda's lexicon, the exact opposite of good breeding, which meant everything to her. 'Looks like some sort of clerk or secretary from the office. Clearly no competition for you whatsoever but I felt you ought to know.'

There had been other possible sources of information for June. Ruby's mother supplied her organic home-made cheeses to the restaurant in which the new couple had been spotted, and the proprietor kept her informed about the glamorous woman who had turned up on Charles's arm and, in turn, Ruby had been told the information at the family dinner table. Ruby told her mother not to say a word to anyone. This order was noted and adhered to, because her family knew how to keep secrets. In the event, Ruby had already known, because Alicia herself had confided in her, and Ruby and Ryan had discussed the matter from every angle over many cups of coffee and different brands of biscuit. In this case – unusually for Ruby in relation to Charles – she gave the matter a good approval rating. Ruby would not speak to anyone, but the news was out in Blessingham.

June had threatened, taunted and cajoled Charles on the issue of this new mystery woman with whom he was sharing dinner at the smartest restaurant in Somerset. She had thrown things and invoked the wrath of her parents and, by far the worst and extreme of all, she told Freddie the news of his dad's affair with a common and plain looking office clerk, and Freddie, already shocked and traumatised by the changes in his life, was pushed a little further to the edge of his remaining sense of reasoning and self-control.

To show their support, June's parents arrived unannounced to speak with Charles at the office. Dick and Brenda clearly came dressed for the occasion: Dick was in cords and a navy sports jacket, with an open-necked shirt, and a cravat in saffron and red paisley, looking sturdy and solid as if he were ready to slip off the jacket in preparation for a fist fight; and Brenda was neatly attired to needlepoint perfection in a demure green dress with a puritan-style lace collar, suitable to her age and her state of mind, and carried what Charles knew to be her best handbag, which for some reason he found menacing as he noted it was carefully placed on the floor by her chair.

There they sat, across from him at his desk, glaring at him in silence, holding him in their sights. They had, they thought, a right to be there, as if Charles remained their property.

He thought they looked like a parody of a lord and lady of the manor – something he knew they both aspired to be – out for a spot of shopping in the town and a quick meeting with their accountant. He knew that when Brenda was trying her utmost to impress, her voice could sound very similar to the Queen's. The two of them were a vision of self-appointed importance and quasi-aristocracy. Unusually, despite their standing and sense of entitlement, Charles did not offer them refreshments as he might normally have done. This ought to have been a signal to them that their relationship with him had changed. This was something that they had not yet fully understood, but would soon. He stared at them in return across his desk. He recalled from somewhere in his mind that this was called eyeballing, and it was what heroes did when they were preparing to win.

'How can I help you?' he asked in his best client voice.

'Help me? Help me?' stuttered Dick. 'It's not *me* you need to help; it's *you* that needs the help, my boy, and your wife and children. From the day I walked my daughter up that aisle to meet with you at the other end, to be married in the presence of God Almighty, I knew it was the wrong thing and that you'd let her down. Fifteen thousand pounds that wedding cost me, including the cathedral choir from Taunton and the vintage Rolls-Royce. I provided a quality luncheon for eighty people that day who bore witness to your vows, and so you can't wriggle out of this that easily. I can get them all here, if necessary.'

'Er, no, that won't be necessary, thank you, Dick.'

'The cake alone cost nearly five hundred pounds, and that was fifteen years ago.' Brenda delivered this additional evidence in a magisterial tone.

'Quiet, Brenda, leave this to me.'

Brenda took a breath, ready to take her part. Like a child in a school play she had her piece ready and she was going to deliver it despite the growling warning she had just received from Dick to be quiet. She delivered her speech.

'You married in church, Charles, and had your children christened in that same church. Our daughter has been a faithful wife to you and now we hear that you are seeing someone else; you have finally broken all the rules. You'll have to answer for it all in the end, you know. I knew from that trip to Marrakesh in the Land Rover that you told us about that you were a rule breaker all along, and we heard all about your illegitimate baby.'

'It was Tashkent actually, Brenda, in Uzbekistan, rather than Marrakesh, which is in Morocco. And I don't think that Harry has anything to do with my split from June.'

He gave himself a moment. His response was remarkably well controlled considering the torrent of writhing emotion behind his stiff presentation. The middle prefrontal cortex of the brain had won the day over the limbic system, and he had not bellowed at them as it dictated. He put his hands on the arms of his chair, levered himself up to standing position and took determined strides towards the door, which he opened decisively.

'I appreciate this must be very difficult for you both. But June and I have been separated for a year now and going through a divorce process, and I am entitled to my private life. I won't keep you, and I have a client in the waiting room. I'm sure we'll be in touch. Ruby,' he called, 'can you see

Dick and Brenda out, darling?' He knew that this was one occasion when Ruby would help him, and he also knew she had been listening at the door.

'I won't keep you any longer, Dick,' he said again. 'Thank you for calling by and for letting me know your thoughts. It's also great that you do so much with the children. Thank you for that too.' Polite but firm, his feet rooted to the floor, the door remained open, he would not show fear, he would not cower. They were leaving the room and he was the hero he wanted to be. This was the Charles Bradshaw equivalent of throwing whisky in Dick's face and telling him to get out of town fast while pointing his shotgun at him, with his cowboy hat perched effortlessly over one eye. Pointing the way out was his equivalent of throwing Dick head first by the seat of his pants into the dusty road.

Brenda gathered her bag and stood up, taking Dick by the arm and leading him from the room, holding his hand. Dick swung his other arm in a loose fashion, looking at the ground as she led him out. Charles mused that he looked rather like a monkey being led away by a zookeeper after a chimpanzee's tea party.

And there was Ruby, a vision of delight, in the corridor waiting to guide them away. She towered over them both with a dazzling smile on her face as if she had not heard a thing. With the confidence and sure-footedness that she doubtless displayed when moving two of her best cows from their milking stall back to the pasture, she stood now between Charles and his visitors with her arms slightly apart as if to shoo them in the right direction. A well-choreographed exit was performed, respectful of the elders, soothing and calming, giving them back their dignity as they herded in the right direction. The door was closed behind them.

Now Charles could allow himself to react from the neck downwards, and he slumped into his chair and stared at the wall with his legs and arms shaking. He shook his head and then let it land on his folded arms atop his desk for a few moments. He was recovering from the heights of emotional stress. The speed of his recovery back to normality increased when Ruby came in to check that all was well and to bring him coffee. Her gesture did not go unnoticed.

He did not particularly like himself for the displacement of his pent-up frustration and negativity onto his in-laws. He was, though, especially pleased that Alicia was not working in the office any more to witness this unseemly spectacle. She had left some months previously, as their junior team member had returned from his leave. They had kept her on for a few extra months, using her expertise. It enabled them to lay down a new tax system for the office, and Ryan had thought that it would be well worth the cost of continuing to employ her to help the company move forward.

The sobering thought of her finding him in this undignified enactment of the negative residue of his past pulled Charles back together very quickly. He retold himself the story and found more respect and compassion for Dick and Brenda, who clearly were upset at the break-up and doing their best to do something to change that. The fair-minded man that he was soon came to the fore as he munched his biscuit and slurped his coffee, and he began to realise that it must be a painful loss for them to see their daughter alone.

His heart began to speak now that the anger was subsiding and ebbing from his system. He had loved them once as he had loved his own parents. He had not always thought of Dick as an old fool, and they had always been warm and loving to him as if he were their own son. He was sorry for his rage and their humiliating rejection from the room that morning at his instigation. They were elderly, and he felt some remorse that they were silenced and clearly hurt as they clumsily defended themselves from their grief. He envisioned Dick's hunched shoulders as Brenda had led him by the hand out of the room. Now he felt their grief as he tried to put the event in its place.

His closing thought was that he should have asserted his authority over them years ago, just as he should have asserted his authority over Freddie, and then it would not have come to this.

Chapter 21

Interaction With a Woman

In the quiet moments that followed Dick and Brenda's departure, Charles could contemplate the freedom that was now offered to him in his life and his thoughts turned to his new love for whom, frankly, he would eject anybody from his office. He absolutely knew, that day, that he wanted Alicia with him. In the previous few months he had been learning the joy of a love that was combined with authenticity and vulnerability, rather than the defended pretence that he had to admit he had allowed to become the fabric of his marriage. Somehow, Alicia managed not to overpower him in the way that June had done. She had what he thought may be termed as 'soft power'.

His first observation of her resilience and determination, though, could not exactly be called soft power. It had been in a difficult scenario during her second month at the office, before their relationship ignited, when Freddie had come in on his way home from school to ask his dad for extra pocket money. This was an ad hoc occurrence and this time Charles had been tied up with a client, a particularly difficult farmer who was unhappy with the premiums on his insurance for his lambs, so much so that Charles had had to admit defeat on understanding the problem and call in Ruby to help translate the situation.

As Alicia was passing through reception, Freddie had noted that she was a member of the team and the only one free for the attention that he required at that moment. He approached her without hesitation, assuming she was a secretary. He wanted new headphones for his portable CD player, having lost a pair at school that day. Freddie, now in his first year of teenage life, depended heavily on drum and bass music tingling its way through his headphones to keep his mind focussed. The rustle, boomps and tings of the music occupied his mind and took him away from everyday existence, giving him relief from his depression and the worry that something in his life was horribly wrong, and that he might at any moment fall off the edge of a cliff that existed in his mind into a chasm where no one would catch him. The restlessness of the music matched the constant activity, undulations and jerks of his own brain; he felt as if he had found a much-needed friend in these sounds that echoed his neurological patterning. So, the headphones were as important to him as any other part of his body, and therefore he thought his dad should provide them. He had heard his Grandma Brenda and Grandpa Dick refer to this new rule that Charles should provide for expensive things, and so he had decided to test this out as he walked home from school that day. He barged into his dad's offices, which were so familiar to him, or at least he felt *should* be familiar to him, or had been part of the familiarity of his life so far – he had been visiting them since he was able to walk. He decided to wait in reception to ambush the first person to come his way. This happened to be Alicia.

'Hi. Dad's busy and I need some cash. If you let me have it, then you can get it from him later as I'm in a hurry. I need new headphones – they're a hundred and ninety pounds.'

He put out his palm to receive the cash, looking a surprising sight: a young teenager behaving like a belligerent adult, his school tie half undone and a stain on the front of his blazer, staring at Alicia intrusively as if she were an object, or perhaps even a cash machine.

She was stopped sharply in her tracks. Whose child was this? It felt bit like she was being mugged, and she hugged the pile of files she was holding to comfort and protect herself from this disconcerting canvasser.

Unfortunately for Freddie he had chosen the wrong person, but he was a creature of habit and was only reproducing behaviours he had learned long before.

There were some people in the office who were used to his ways and who would have given him the money, probably from petty cash in the absence of his father, just to have him go away. Ruby, obviously, was not one of them, and had he run into her in reception he would have said nothing. He might even have glanced away. In fact, he was quite afraid of Ruby. Ryan, though, would have given him money, and the apprentice accountant and the bookkeeper would have handed it over, too.

Alicia's response was brusque. She clearly did not know who Freddie was, although the familiarity of the features was beginning to dawn on her, but certainly not the rudeness of the tone. She was both fascinated and repulsed by this youth accosting her for money. He could have been anybody having walked in off the street begging, as far as she knew. Had that been the case, she might have responded more favourably. She had observed less objectionable and more respectable and worthy street beggars in her time. Instead, she had an arrogant young man who was almost her height staring her in the face with his palm outstretched as if she owed him something.

'Excuse me, I don't think we've met, have we? I don't give money to strangers, especially when they don't even have good manners.'

'I'm not a stranger. I'm Freddie Bradshaw, and my father's in there. Either you give it to me or I go in there and disturb him. Whatever you like.'

Alicia wasn't having that. 'Yes, whatever you like young man. You go ahead and disturb him and then face the consequences. It's not my problem. Excuse me, please.' And she pushed him back with the pile of files that she carried in front of her in a sort of inoffensive bumpsadaisy fashion so that he had to step aside.

Freddie was aghast. Who was this woman answering him back? What was that tone in her voice? He was not used to women speaking to him in this way. Unfortunately, he was learning the ill-informed and archaic misogyny of his grandfather, unbecoming to most men but certainly not fitting for a child of thirteen.

'How dare you,' he said, repeating an oft-used phrase from his life at home.

'You go right on ahead. I'll speak to your father later. Walk straight in and ruin his relationship with his customer, why don't you. Then we'll see where your pocket money is coming from, and next time you come in here you show a bit more respect to me, young man. I don't care whose son you are, and my guess is that your father would not want you to be speaking to his colleagues in this way.' And with that, she went to the room she was sharing with Ruby and dumped the heavy pile of files on her desk.

She was hot and flustered and unsettled at being accosted in this way by Freddie, but even more unsettled by her own reaction, particularly as it was Charles's son, whom, by now, she was wanting to impress; she started to think she had overreacted to the situation. What was it that was happening to her in that moment to make her react so aggressively? To her, it was alien and illogical to be so cross with a child of thirteen who you didn't know.

Ruby noticed that a red flush had appeared on her colleague's chest, and went to get her a glass of water, which she knew would settle this down. Redheads are used to managing reactions in the skin, and Ruby knew the value of water to any mammal.

Alicia gulped the drink with a grateful glance and pretended to look at her files, but she was not really taking any notice of them. She felt like the scene had been an assault on her values.

'Was that really Charles's son? God, he hasn't got his father's concern for manners. What an unpleasant child. Does he usually behave in that way?'

Ruby tittered with her hand up to her mouth when she heard what had happened. She had long ago ceased to be shocked by Freddie's rudeness. She completed the picture for Alicia on the story of Freddie, whom she and Ryan had secretly nicknamed as 'Damien' for the purposes of their private conversations. Damien is the child protagonist in the film *The Omen*, about a child possessed by the Devil; the name did not need explaining to Alicia. 'That must be a problem for him,' she said. But she remained mystified and disconcerted by her own reaction to the boy, even after Ruby's explanations. After a few moments of file-flicking she excused herself to the ladies' toilets, and in the secrecy of a locked cubicle she leaned on the door with her face in her hands. This was a quiet few moments in which she could contemplate the depth of her discomfort. This small rest in which her hands took the heaviness of her head gave her a chance to consider all the information she needed to, and to settle herself down so that she could regain her composure. She had not been able to think quickly enough to manage Freddie in that moment. She could not place the scenario anywhere comfortable in her mind. This was difficult for her; she, who managed everything in life smoothly, had had her competent defences overwhelmed by the spectre of a boy's unreasonableness and defiance.

She had fought all her life, since she was strong enough to stand

and influence her environment, to manage her mother's erratic, hostile and particularly demanding temperament. Meeting Freddie in reception had been like a bad dream about meeting her mother, overwhelming her defences, taking her by surprise and knocking her momentarily off balance. This moment of recognition, that she had met the shadow of her worst dream in the face of this young boy, was enough to console her for now and quieten her fear that something threatening had come back into her life. Something that she was entirely geared to resist at all costs.

For now, she understood and had resettled her agitated senses. Next time she would be ready for Freddie, just as she was always ready for anyone who activated this show. The matter resolved, her private view of herself complete, she let herself out of the cubicle, washed her hands and refreshed her eyeliner, contemplating her image to ensure that all was in place. Her vigilance was back intact and she could breathe again.

Freddie didn't go into his dad's office. He went straight home, but he did not forget the interaction with this woman, to whom he referred as an office worker when he described her to his mother because he could not conceive of a woman being in a senior position. He told his mother how rudely he had been treated, without bothering to mention his own part in the event.

This single encounter, unbeknown to any of them, was the first in a chain of events in Freddie's mind, and indeed in the mind of his mother, that he would link together as he created a vendetta against this woman who, at that moment, was completely blameless in his life, except that she would not be spoken to in a disrespectful and demanding manner. The only common ground that this thirteen-year-old teenager and this thirty-seven-year-old professional woman had was that they were connected to Charles Bradshaw, and neither of them would be beaten.

Chapter 22

A Time to Love

To everything there is a season, and a time to every purpose under the heaven:
A time to be born, and a time to die; a time to plant, a time to reap that which
is planted;
A time to kill, and a time to heal; a time to break down, and a time to build up;
A time to weep, and a time to laugh; a time to mourn, and a time to dance;
A time to cast away stones, and a time to gather stones together;
A time to embrace, and a time to refrain from embracing;
A time to get, and a time to lose; a time to keep, and a time to cast away;
A time to rend, and a time to sew; a time to keep silence, and a time to speak;
A time to love, and a time to hate; a time of war, and a time of peace.

Had Freddie known that his behaviour towards Alicia that day at his father's office would create an excuse for the couple to grow closer, he would have not gone there at any price and would have lived without the expensive headphones. He had no idea that the way he had presented himself in the reception wore so heavily on Alicia's mind that the end of her working day found her walking into her employer's office to talk with him about his son.

That conversation was the beginning of her lifelong love affair with Charles Bradshaw, a love affair that began with a conversation with him about his relationship with his son, and then his relationship with life, followed by an even longer conversation over their first dinner. This was the same dinner at which they had been spotted by Brenda and, of course, the restaurant proprietor.

Charles was both profusely apologetic and furious about what had happened when she had bumped into Freddie. Their conversation continued over several hours: Charles's broken marriage; his consequent therapy with Colin and Dr Fratina and how he was trying to help Freddie to turn his attitude around; his single life at Town End Cottage; his mum and dad; his love child Harry … and, since she was still listening, his trip in his youth to Iran and Tibet.

Alicia, having now spent some months in the same building with him, did not care how they started their first in-depth conversation, just as long as she had an inroad into a communication that symbolised just how close she wanted to be to him, and how much more she wanted to know about him, and how, by now, every instinct in her wanted to protect him from the crisis with his son, because she knew already that she was more capable than he was of doing this.

Charles, in return, secretly, did not care if she came into his office and demanded that he take her to dinner, nor would he have minded what she wanted to talk about, as long as she wanted to talk to him and him alone. He was besotted with her, based on, he had to admit, very superficial reasons: the way she tied her hair back; the clothes that complemented her curves; every word that came out of her mouth; every file she managed to skilfully and competently organise for their company, somehow transforming chaotic figures into reason; the feminine connection that she had made with Ruby; and every bit of respect that she showed to Ryan.

Contrary to her fears, Alicia's immediate management of Freddie only increased Charles's admiration for her, although she later thought that she could have softened her response, and made a resolution to make a fresh start with the boy.

And so, Alicia became an ally in his quest to help Freddie pull himself together, but they became so much more than this to each other in life. A very few months more and they were inseparable, and their relationship then had little to do with Freddie and everything to do with them, and their need and longing for the other.

Freddie would never understand, from that time forward, why he was not the centre of their relationship and was no longer the focus of his dad's attention. They thought that they had many years to help Freddie come to terms with this.

Alicia's view of Charles Bradshaw was not unrealistic. She could see that he had a vulnerable side that was totally exploitable, and that Freddie was taking full advantage of this. The great fortune of their meeting was that she was not a person who had any need or intention to exploit anyone. She could stand alone in life if she wished. She saw Charles as an equal and treated him respectfully, even on difficult days when she did not agree with him or when he was at his least heroic. She admired him and enjoyed him just because of his decency and his desire to help others, and they fitted together like a hand in a glove about the things that mattered to them, like being grateful for every moment, speaking honestly and treating others respectfully.

He felt happier than he had felt since his romance with Katrina. This far distant memory produced pasture in his mind and body from which new memories could emerge and grow. He started to live his life again.

Any visionary, any witch creating her spell of love, any mathematician developing an algorithm that can slice into the universal laws of number … any of these might stand together and collectively shake their heads and say 'No' when it came to imagining the outcome of this relationship. But all of them would have wasted their time, for they had forgotten the power of love to transcend all reason, the call to belong in the heart of another, and the psychosis and forgetfulness that occurs in the addictive chemistry of the brain that ignites the human attachment system, saying, 'I want nothing but you.' All too late for the warnings of our Greek chorus, and for a woman whose very fabric was created to bind and heal the psychopathic tendencies of her deranged mother. Too late to turn back for a woman and man who were drunk on love. To Alicia, therefore, Freddie simply looked like a child in need of help. And Charles was the flawed hero, who needed her help, too. Thus, Freddie, with all his difficulties, became part of the attraction.

Chapter 23

A Time to Hate – Autumn 1990, Town End Cottage

Alicia had determined to make a constructive start with the son of her lover, and she knew that Charles desperately needed to see some signs of progress in him. Early autumn of that year found them planning for her to be at Town End Cottage with Charles when the boys came to visit.

She arrived at lunchtime on the Saturday that they were coming around for supper and a film. She spent most weekends with Charles these days, abandoning her own flat and preferring to be with him. Town End had transformed for Charles from a damp purgatory into a cheerful little hub of quaint Victoriana. Neither of them minded waiting for the immersion heater to heat their bath water, and there was no need for an electric blanket when they snuggled so closely together in bed to keep warm. Alicia was always cooking something so the oven was always on heating the kitchen, and Charles needed no excuse whatsoever to make a log fire in the evenings at weekends as they sat thigh to thigh, hand in hand on the comfy sofa and gazed into the flames. The Town End rental property had almost become *their* cottage now, and this development did not go unnoticed by Freddie when he arrived with his brother later that day.

Charles had been out shopping with the list Alicia had made for him so that she could prepare the food, and the plan was for her to cook for them all. She had laid out in clear handwriting the ingredients for her signature dish – lamb rogan josh.

Alicia, despite efforts in her previous marriage, had not had her own children but she had a good idea about what boys of fourteen and ten might like to eat, and had imagined their pleased response when they tasted the warming flavours of the curry. This, she thought, was her chance to practice her nurturing skills on two boys who might be her friends, maybe even her surrogate sons.

This was the transformation Charles had hoped for, and now dreamed about, in his developing life with his boys and with Alicia. He knew by now that they would be moving forward together and that she wanted this too but, for now, the simple act of him buying the food and her cooking made him want to sing out loud as he had done in the choir at school. Instead, he settled for the absent-minded gentle singing of a folk song from the sixties that bubbled into his mind:

'To everything, turn, turn, turn,
There is a season – turn, turn, turn,
And a time to every purpose under heaven.
A time to gain – A time to lose,
A time for love, a time for hate,
A time for peace, I swear it's not too late.
A time to build – A time to break down,
A time to dance – A time to mourn.'

Alicia, on the other hand, instead of singing on her way over that morning, had been so cheerful that she stopped off at Blessingham's only department store and treated herself to a new lipstick. This is no absent-minded and mundane act for a woman. For some, it is the way that they celebrate when they are happy. They are painting their colours for the whole world to see, the equivalent of showing their best plumage and fluffing out their feathers: their mating signal to their chosen one. The exotic names on lipsticks are often drawn from nature – nobody ever stops to think that lipstick is directly linked to the process of evolution, not even the cosmetic companies who produce this possibility for womankind to show their primitive calling, unaware that it is essential that we honour our original selves born from nature. That is why women will spend a lot of money on lipstick and hide it away in secure little boxes and packages for the appropriate moment of display. So, in the local department store in Blessingham that morning Alicia could be found at the Chanel counter slashing splashes of colour onto the back of her hand in a meditation of greatest importance, during which the rest of the world momentarily faded into the background. She transcended every critical voice in her head – tarty, prostitute, barmaid – all the criticisms her mother might have levelled at her if she dared to reveal the full display of her sexuality and attractiveness. Today she would have none of these voices. She was a woman with lipstick and a bank balance to afford it.

The salesgirl understood this, giving her customer plenty of time to play with the testers, knowing that it was impossible to interrupt at this crucial moment, though she carefully watched her prey for the right time to pounce.

Crushed Candy, Soft Rouge, Petal Pink, Peony and Poppy crowded her senses until the most obvious colour for her came to light, and she settled for Flamingo Pink, the one that pleased her the most as she studied her reflection in the mirror. Her colours could be seen.

The salesgirl moved in to complete the transaction. She was swift and efficient and it was painless: boxed, tied with ribbon, and wrapped in a small carrier bag and popped into Alicia's large shopper, the ritual completed with the provision of scented tissue to remove her practice splashes of colour from her hand.

***

'Oh, lovely, lovely!' Charles said, not really relating to the experience, but it sounded nice and looked beautiful, and he got it all over his face as she kissed him and had to go and wash it off. He was delighted.

'Did you get the film for tonight?' she said.

'What? Oh, damn,' he said. 'What an idiot. Completely forgot. So busy checking out all those spices you sent me for. I'll have to go back. We can't do without that.'

'Here,' she said, taking a fifty pound note from her purse. She couldn't find any other notes so that would have to do. She was always so generous. 'Let me get it.'

'No way.' Charles squeezed her hand. 'That's so sweet. No, I'll get it. Look, I'll go back now, and then pick the boys up from their mother's on my return. How about I take them to the playing field for an hour and we kick a ball around and they can run off some energy – give you a bit of quiet. Are you OK to get on?'

She thought that would be nice after a busy morning attending to her plumage. She put the fifty pound note carefully back into her purse, noticing that she had no other change and hoping that she would not get caught out over the weekend with a need for coins. She put on one last splash of the new Flamingo Pink before settling down to the serious task of crushing her spices for cooking the curry.

She moved through the shabby little kitchen of Town End Cottage with her usual precision and ease as she prepared to produce something that she imagined would appeal to the hearts of the sons of the man she loved. She wanted to find something to love in both boys, and could not imagine that this might not be possible. At this stage, as she comfortably wrapped her apron around her waist and pulled the strings tight, she was unable to foresee that the boys might experience her gain in life as a threat to their safety and security.

She put up her hair in a clip and washed her hands in preparation for the performance that was to come in the kitchen. For now, she could anticipate none of these difficulties, and she wiped the little Formica-topped table clean and laid out the individual ingredients. The windows steamed up so that the afternoon light turned her preparation area to gold, and as the kitchen became warm the scent of the musky spices pervaded the room.

She measured and washed the rice and counted out strands of precious and delicate saffron that would turn the ordinary whiteness of the mundane grain to a pleasing and exotic colour, as if creating alchemy that would intoxicate the young Freddie and bring him into her golden world of the golden kitchen in the golden sunlight.

As if to complete the divinity of this picture, she clicked on the radio as a background to support her sorcery. A familiar tune mixed with the cinnamon and cloves as they were crunched and pounded in the wooden mortar and then she watched the spices melt into hot oil that would draw out their essence and perfume, a blend that she would later taste to see if it was worthy of her intention. The familiar tune was one she used to hear on the radio as a child; it was one to which her mother would always sing along, bringing her out to a new mood, and some momentary refreshment and refrain from her apparent continuous hostility towards, and frustration with, life and people. Perhaps the tune was an omen that Freddie would think of her in a new way. She remembered the words as she toasted slivered almonds to a light brown in a heated frying pan:

To everything, turn, turn, turn,
There is a season – turn, turn, turn,
And a time to every purpose under heaven.
A time to gain – A time to lose,
A time to rend, a time to sew,
A time for love, a time for hate,
A time for peace, I swear it's not too late.

She saw Charles's car in the drive before the boys saw her. She watched the scene anxiously. This was her moment. Freddie got out of the car and slammed the door shut way ahead of his father and Anthony. She was still sure that Freddie's mood would change as soon as he was relaxed and felt at home around her and they had had some fun: just as her mother's mood changed when she worked hard at pleasing her. She murmured her tune as she watched him pound the path to the door: 'To everything, turn, turn, turn …'

Freddie pushed his way through the back door and her hopeful face disgusted him. He had not wanted to see her there at all, let alone in a receptive state with a kitchen stinking of foreign food. He brushed past her and she quickly had to step to one side as he went through to the lounge and walked around the rooms of the cottage without even saying hello. As if the arm of a record player had been jolted and scratched across a record, the tune changed. She was left with an abrupt end to her plan to connect with Freddie, and an introduction to his intentions for the afternoon.

Instead of brooding, her thoughts turned to what was possible. Anthony, she knew, was a naturally more affable child and he was easier to calculate. Yet his face had an imprint too, and she felt that he was hiding behind the compliant bright smile that he presented to the world. While Freddie pushed his way into everything in life regardless of the feelings of others, Anthony held back and was watchful and did not let his emotions show easily.

The newly bound couple had talked for many hours together about the two boys. Their discussions were part of her heartfelt commitment to

Charles to help him with his children. Up until now, Charles had been seeing them on his own, and the weekly event – usually a Saturday, from lunchtime after their morning choir practice at school – always troubled him. Afterwards, the couple would have supper together, which she would cook in his absence. Following their meal, Charles would talk with her as they sat and stared at the fire in the little lounge of their homestead.

He was tortured by this weekly experience. He just could not connect with Freddie and draw his son close to him; their afternoons together usually ended in a power struggle with the boy still trying to dominate his father, whether arguing about arrangements or being aggressive when they kicked a football around.

What was plain to Charles was the painful fact that Freddie did not and would not accept his father's separation from his mother, and even now, a year later, Freddie was more entrenched on this issue than ever.

Alicia had at first thought that Charles was worrying too much, but her mind was open to what was happening. She had great common sense and her upbringing had taught her how to manage difficult people. She was relaxed about the whole thing and determined that she could manage anything thrown at her; in one of their many conversations she stretched her legs across his lap and squeezed his hand. 'I'll be alright, darling; and *it* will be alright. He can't help what he feels any more than we can help how we feel.'

But even Alicia had to admit to disappointment with Freddie rampaging through the cottage at this moment; he was seemingly looking for something.

Freddie *was* looking for something but he did not know what. He just had to search because he thought his mother would want him to search. He was like an animal marking his new territory as he desperately sniffed and scented each room. He did not speak to Alicia to say hello as he passed by, though Anthony stopped for a chat.

Charles watched and knew that he had to take control. He followed Freddie, who had reached their bedroom, and was outraged when he found him by their bed. 'What are you doing in here?'

They stood on opposite sides of the double bed with the light shining through the window. He stared at his son and his son stared at him. Which one of them was going to dare to state the obvious?

'Private, Dad? Since when has your room been private. Your bedroom wasn't "private" in Mum's house. We went in there when we wanted to get things or find you. We slept in there if we were ill. So why not here?'

There they stood, with the afternoon sun turning the walls into luminescent gold and reflecting off the pale yellow of the antique-rose-patterned bedcover, with the crows laughing cruelly outside in the bare November trees – man and boy staring at each other across the room, across the bed. It was obvious to Charles why Freddie should not be in there, but not in the form of anything that could be said to a child. This obvious information, for adults only, sleeps deeply in the hearts of children, ready for revival in later years when they themselves awake sleepily from the moratorium of the taboo of sexuality; that form of adult bonding lies only a dream away from a child's consciousness.

This oldest taboo of all lay between father and son at that moment, throbbing in their hearts, coursing through their veins, their brains and their bodies, and that same river was about to fork, and their emotional paths diverge once more. This moment of pathos was also a moment of torment for Freddie, who had the sense that something beyond his control now separated him from his father, something more deeply alluring and beguiling than the love between father and son. He could almost, but not quite, grasp what this awakening pain was. He had been searching for the cause of his pain and the source of the river of discomfort inside him.

The bed shared by the new couple stood between them now, but the obstacle might have been a whole world, a wedge, a flooding river that they could not cross to reach each other. A river that would drown them, a river in which someone would be drowned. Freddie, at nearly fourteen years of age knew, at a semi-conscious level, why he could not go into this bedroom: the bed. He could not accept the bed with the pretty rose-and-lace cover. There was nothing that could be said between him and his father, nothing that could repair the chasm that had opened to separate their two worlds.

Charles guided Freddie by the arm down to the kitchen to find Anthony helping Alicia. He was grateful for the sanity of this domestic scene. She had tied Anthony into a striped apron so that he looked as if he matched her. He was so relieved that at least half of the equation was working like a dream. He propelled Freddie into the kitchen and instructed him to say hello.

Alicia took his hand and held on firmly, shaking, and clasping it with her other hand so that he could not easily escape, and found her most consoling voice. 'I'm so pleased to meet you, Freddie, we had a bumpy start last time we met didn't we, but never mind. Do you like curry, really? Your dad said you did so I got to work, and here's Anthony showing us his moves in the kitchen.'

Freddie, realising he was surrounded by a compelling amount of good mood from everyone, managed a non-committal growl of hello. But then said that he wanted Anthony out of the apron.

Anthony might have undone the ties immediately, but his dad said no, leave him, and again he propelled his oldest child gently by the elbow, into the lilac lounge where Alicia had lit the fire, drawn the curtains and switched on the lamps, successfully conveying a sense of comfort and warmth. Watching TV was the obvious solution to occupy Freddie's mind, and Charles clicked through the channels to find some football. 'There.'

'Put the film on, Dad.'

'No, later, Freddie. We'll watch it after supper, together. Something nice to do together.'

'I'm not watching together if you mean with her.'

'What do you mean?' Charles closed the lounge door. 'What do you mean, exactly?'

'I'm not watching with her. Simple as.' His nonchalance was an attempt to successfully hide his fear that any connection with this woman would betray his mother.

'Freddie, don't be so rude, please. Alicia is a friend. I hope you are going to show some respect this afternoon or we won't be having much fun. She's gone to a lot of trouble to make us food. Come on, now.'

Alicia could hear all this from the kitchen despite the closed door, and she was already deciding how she would cope.

'I don't respect her and I don't respect you. Mum says you have a girlfriend and you shouldn't have. It's hurtful to Mum. You should be at home with us. I won't be speaking to *her* today. And I want Anthony in here with me, not in there with her. I only came today to see you. I thought she'd be out.'

And so their early tea of lamb rogan josh with saffron rice, and Peshwari nan bread stuffed with sweet pineapple, sultanas and grated coconut, was a quiet and tense affair with Freddie trying only to make conversation with his dad and Anthony, and Anthony looking panic-stricken and not knowing what to do, while Alicia asked Freddie questions to which he would not respond.

'Hey, how was your football this afternoon? What position do you like to play, Freddie?'

For an impressive amount of time Alicia was undeterred and unaffected by the brick wall of defiance from him, but she eventually had no option but to ignore Freddie. She was left with no choice but to speak only to Charles and Anthony about the most banal things, making a heroic attempt to hide her increasing well of sadness that every hope and dream she had had about this most orchestrated meal was going to be burned like something accidentally left on the stove for too long.

The elegant meal was lost in the stress and anxiety of the little quartet sitting in the kitchen of Town End Cottage. Freddie, with a mental hold over the situation, had them all in a pincer, his intention being that they would not get to know one another. He would not tolerate his father being with this new woman, and none of the muscular tension, headache and distress that this controlling behaviour caused him mattered – he simply had to ward her off, keep the door closed on her and push against it with all his psychological might.

Charles thought that the afternoon could not have gone worse and he was furious, already making vows about how to prevent this outrage in the future.

Alicia felt the awkwardness and, despite employing all her defences, felt the discomfort of the situation seep into her skin. Eventually, as she digested the rich warming curry, she gradually metabolised the pressure and relaxed a little more as she overcame her disappointment and accepted reality. At least the magic of her own cooking was not wasted on her. She began to think of the meal as medicine and an antidote to her initial sense of failure. The mission had failed, it was true, but she was becoming more interested in the situation and less upset. What she was most worried about was the dreadful way in which Anthony constantly tried to appease his older brother, trying to compensate for his extreme rudeness. God, what a childhood for him, she thought, as the last piece of nan bread was split between Anthony and his dad and she pulled out some home-made mango ice cream with chocolate fudge sauce, which kept them all busy. Anthony made appreciative sounds and loved the sweet sharp taste, willing to take the risk of being glared at by Freddie.

'OK,' said Freddie. I'm ready for the film. Let's get on.'

'I don't think so, young man.' Charles's voice was re-energised. 'There's the small matter of table-clearing and some washing-up to do first. And I haven't heard a thank you yet.'

'Yeah, whatever. I'm not washing-up and I'm not clearing the table.'

'OK, that's a shame, so also you will not be watching the film. But just as you wish, I'll give you a few moments to decide.'

He was drawing on all the information about 'consequences to behaviour' that he had gleaned from family therapy and in his meetings with Colin. *Stay firm and fair. There will be consequences to unacceptable behaviour.* The theory was the easy bit and the role play was a pushover. The actuality of facing his child across the table and changing the behaviour-pattern of a lifetime, was quite another matter.

Some half an hour later Anthony was tied back into his striped apron, and he and Alicia –in her own apron – had cleared the table and were washing-up together. They pottered around and, on his own, Anthony was trying hard to show Alicia just how helpful he could be, wiping plates and placing them carefully for storage. The door between the kitchen and the lounge was closed firmly and Charles was in there again, talking with Freddie about the consequences of his behaviour that day. The moment of primitive realisation that had passed between them in the bedroom was entombed in their consciousness. Now was the time for reasoning. At first Charles tried giving him hope, understanding and reassurance about the seemingly impossible situation that existed in his mind. He put his hand on Freddie's arm and searched for his eyes, which were not given. The room was warm and scented with lavender; the logs crackled and burned their own story.

'I know it's difficult … all very new … but Alicia is a kind person. If you just offer a smile you don't have to speak much, but there is no need to be rude, Freddie, I'm not prepared to accept that any more. I know you're hurt and disappointed. I do understand that.'

Charles was performing to the textbook. But Freddie did not come up with the responses that the textbook might have indicated. He stared ahead with his arms folded. He did find the fire a nice dreamlike distraction and decided that he would enjoy this, but that he would challenge his dad. His dad did not know how he was feeling. This was a good thing about being a person – you could hide your thoughts. *He* did not know exactly what his thoughts were, as they were rather muddled, but he was not moving his position. The bed with the rose-cover was wrong and he would defend his mother from the bed. That, he did know. From his knitted brow to his scrunched-up toes this was what was going on right now.

This annoyed Charles, and he tried one or two threats such as: 'We'll just have to leave you out of things, unfortunately.' But he knew abandonment of the child to get results was not in the textbook. To give himself thinking time and to prevent an escalation of his own rage, he left Freddie in the lounge and went to Alicia and Anthony in the kitchen.

Alicia was eliciting a conversation from Anthony about his time in the cricket team and the books he was reading, including the *Wisden Cricketers' Almanack* and an autobiography by the legendary cricket umpire called Dickie Bird; this chat was rewarding to the youngest boy, who was finding a chirruping and cheerful little voice of his own. It could be true that Alicia was not the slightest bit interested in cricket, but nonetheless her questions indicated to him that she was fascinated to know more, and he could certainly let her know more about the almanack, which he knew by heart. Then Charles entered in the room.

'Look, darling I'm going to take him home. He's not in the mood. I'm so sorry.'

Anthony's face cracked, and tears welled and brimmed, flooding his eyes and gushing down his cheeks. Alicia felt for him. The whole experience had been ruined by his brother's determination to spoil things. Anthony had tried so hard to be friendly and affable, even conceding to the apron, which he knew would attract his brother's scorn. She was cross.

'Let me have a word with him.' Without seeking a response from Charles, and still in her own apron, she went into the lounge and closed the door.

Charles, meanwhile, sat with the inconsolable Anthony – inconsolable not particularly because his brother had been rude, but because he was a bright kid and he had worked out exactly what the afternoon's events would mean. He did not know about the bed; he was ten, and did not know about the meaning of beds except that you could snuggle in your mum's bed if you were ill or had a bad dream. That was all he knew about beds. What he knew, was that Freddie was never going to accept Alicia, and he knew what happened when Freddie made up his mind.

In his young ten-year-old heart Anthony had held some hope that today would work out. He knew that today was supposed to be about something hopeful. He wanted his dad to be happy. He missed his dad, but he knew that his dad was better now. He liked Alicia. She was pretty, she was kind and she talked to him. She clearly was interested in cricket. He had shared the almanack with her. He felt brighter and lighter with her around. She was funny and made jokes and she could cook better food than his dad. Most of all, he knew that his dad was safe with her, and that made him happy. If Dad was safe, he could be safe. He wanted to be part of that, and he had been looking forward to this Saturday for weeks. His instinctive disappointment was because he knew ahead of time that the day was ruined, and that meant that something would be ruined now forever. He did not know what that meant about his relationship with his dad and Alicia. He just knew from the bottom of his child's heart that what had happened was not good.

As Alicia breezed into the lounge she found Freddie rummaging by the side of the settee. He quickly sat up straight as she entered, and stared at the fire. She wondered briefly what he had been doing, but ignored her sixth sense that something unusual had been going on. Instead of hostility, which could easily have been the outcome, she displayed her 'Let's give this another chance' face to Freddie.

Her communication was intensely immediate. Her hair was not tidy and her lipstick had worn off. Her presentation had no polish. She was down to the bare bones of life. Something had to be saved and she was good at saving things.

'Now, I know this is tough for you, sweetie, but I am your friend not your enemy. We can have such fun on Saturdays together. Think of all the things we can do. Dad is still friends with Mum. He tells me she is such a nice woman; I'm sure of it. Come on, let's turn this one around. Let's go to Dad and tell him we're going to try to get on, and then let's put that film on. Yes? You know, Freddie, there is a saying that I want to share with you: "Your enemy is your friend who you do not know well yet." I love that. What do you think?'

'Well you'll know nothing about me, then. You'll never be part of my life and you'll never be part of my mum's life and you'll never be part of my brother's life. Also, you'll never be part of my dad's life – ever. You've caused my mum and dad to split up, and for that, in my view, you're as good as dead. As far as we, the family, are concerned you don't exist and you never will exist. If you don't disappear out of my dad's life, I will kill you. I hope you understand that.'

Alicia was shocked into stunned silence, staring at his face while her brain raced to think what she should do or say. She was being threatened by a fourteen-year-old boy. Was that really happening? In slower motion she went to the fire and turned the glowing logs with the poker so that the heated but untouched side of the wood could catch in the embers.

She felt Freddie staring at her back while she did this. She knew that he hoped she would react and that this could be one of those times when everybody shouted, and then he could shout and it might put an end to everything. He wanted that, and she knew he must not have that opportunity for a violent outburst. She stepped away from the fire and put up the guard, hanging the poker carefully in its metal container, just to be on the safe side. She always wanted to be on the safe side of things. In all her lifetime of difficult personalities she had never encountered an actual death threat, and she was going to have the last word.

'That's OK, Freddie. It's time for you to go now.'

She walked pace by pace from the fire to the door, closing it decisively behind her, leaving Freddie where he was on the settee, now staring at the scorched logs. She shut the door as firmly and purposefully as his mother would have done. The interaction was closed. Her file on this chance for hope was complete for today.

'You're right – best to take him home.'

Charles responded with deliberate movements. He picked up his car keys, took his coat off the peg, grabbed the coats for the boys, stacked some plates to one side that did not really need moving, and instructed his sons to get their things as it was time to go, using a clear, certain tone of voice that neither condemned the disaster of the day nor encouraged it. He was moving in to mop up, as both he and Alicia worked as a couple now in step to bring closure to the scene of their defeat.

There was a silence while Charles organised and guided their movements to repack the boys into the car, holding the lounge door open as Freddie walked through. Events seemed to glide as if everyone were skating and the kitchen had become an ice rink of smooth movement, a chain reaction, a conveyor belt towards the exit. Freddie walked out cuddling his day bag in front of him, patting the side with an artful look on his face. Anthony's tears were shuddering to a halt, as he struggled towards the door.

Alicia gave Anthony a hug and she noticed that they were still in their matching aprons. She marked the end of their time together by twirling him round and undoing the strings, then twirling him round again, pulling the apron over his head, ruffling his sandy hair back into place with a smile that found his eyes as they looked up into hers. 'Don't you worry; you were such a great kid to be with today. Don't worry at all. Hey, see you soon, Anthony.'

Charles passed him his soft, woollen, blue, tartan scarf, which Alicia took and draped around his neck, tying it at the front, pulling it up over his large ears so that he was muffled and soothed and warm, shutting out the world so that he could not hear anything any more, just for a while. Anthony offered a weak smile that covered the pain of something broken in his mind which kept making his eyes prick with tears, and then walked to the back door where Freddie waited for him, watching and noting the soothing dance. Anthony hung his head as he walked out of the door.

'Be back soon,' said Charles. He looked over his shoulder at Alicia with a picture of resignation on his face, the sort of look that men have when they leave a football match and their team have lost that day.

She knew they would talk about the day later and, on his return, would discuss the results of the match and its ramifications for them. She folded the two aprons slowly, matching them up symmetrically, creasing them over, dropping the ties into the folds, folding again, smoothing them, nursing her wounded dream and Anthony's broken heart, patting the neat package, and putting it in the drawer. Now the time for tears to prick her eyes had come, and she stood still in the empty kitchen, lamenting the implications of the day. Eventually she wiped her face with her hand, defiantly refusing to find a tissue. The dream was temporarily postponed, but not over.

She retreated to the lounge to enjoy the fire. She would have her moment of peace. She picked up her handbag from the side of the settee as she tidied round the room, automatically but absently looking inside it to check that her private world, the interior of her handbag, was still in order. The black leather sack felt strangely depleted, somehow, as she sat down and lifted it onto her lap and rummaged through the contents. She searched, feeling sure she had left the new lipstick package in there. Dig as she might through the contents of the soft dark interior, Alicia just could not find what she already knew was missing. She searched around the room in other places, craning her neck into corners, pushing curtains to one side just in case. No, she remembered putting the package in her bag – the important new lipstick with the specially chosen colour of Flamingo Pink that reflected the new identity emerging for her and her life with Charles.

She would not have been careless with anything as important as that. She took everything out of the bag, as if hoping still to find it in some corner. But the package was no longer there. She dropped the sprawled contents back into the bag, scooping them all up from the coffee table at the same time. Like a sleepwalker, Alicia checked beside and behind and even under the settee, then she returned to the bag, looking again, noticing now her purse, and she checked this too. The briefest glance delivered the even worse news that something else was missing. She was sure she had put a fifty pound note in there earlier that day; fifty pound notes are so big, and she would have seen the edges peeping out if the money was still there. She knew she had put it there, the note she had tried to give to Charles for the film that he would not take from her. Perhaps she had put the items upstairs. Sometimes she put money on the dressing table upstairs, but nothing was there. She checked the surfaces, she even checked in the drawers – nothing. No, she was sure – she had put the lipstick package on top in her bag, and the note in her purse.

Charles drove his boys to their home in silence and thought the best tactic was to let things rest now. He clicked on the radio and let the talk and chatter comfort him and fill the air.

Freddie read this silence as him having won the day. He was quite satisfied. Everything was ruined. The day had started with his dad and football, and ended at Town End where a sense of possibility and celebration and colour had descended into shattered fragments. But something new had started for him already; something he could feed off, something that quite resolved the startling truth that he had discovered about the double bed that had stood between him and his dad earlier that day when he had gone into the bedroom. A new thought had come to him suddenly as he was sitting in the lounge in front of the fire, and that thought was keeping him full and happy now as he sat next to Anthony in the back seat, cuddling and patting his rucksack.

Aside from the chatter on the radio not a word was spoken, the only other sound being some sporadic sniffs from Anthony who was hoping his baffling torrent of tears would stop before they reached home. He did not want to upset his mum. His dad passed a handkerchief into the back of the car for him and checked in the rear-view mirror to see if he was OK. He put on the blower and turned up the heater to warm his youngest son. Anthony blew his nose and then distracted himself by watching the passing fields and looking at his image in the passenger window, which became illuminated like a mirror as the street light shone against it from the other side. He felt very alone indeed, even though his dad sat only eighteen inches in front of him and his brother was only the same distance to the left of him. He would be pleased to see his mum, and perhaps then he would not feel so lonely and the pain in his stomach would go.

Freddie could not wait to see his mum either, but for very different reasons.

Having delivered his cargo of two boys to their home, Charles opened and then closed the back door of Town End Cottage, shutting out the cold dark air and locking the door behind him. As he did so, the sound of his return woke Alicia from her sleepy hollow on the lilac settee. While she smiled and reclosed her eyes to see if she could stay unconscious for a little longer – although she could not quite remember why she needed to do this – he put on the kettle and made them some tea, bringing the spotty pink china teapot and bone china matching cups and saucers in on a tray with some milk and biscuits, and placing it on the coffee table to give the tea time to brew. The fire needed replenishing and he found another log, larger this time than the two that had incinerated in the last half hour of her slumber. There was just enough hot ember and skeleton from the previous logs to scorch and bring the fire roaring to life in a few moments.

He took her hand and sat staring at the grate with her, as if a whirlwind had been through the house and torn everything down and this was the quiet after the storm. They found comfort in these quiet moments of togetherness, soothing each other through their entwined hands, seeing each other through the feel of their skin. This silent closeness was all that they had left after their day of shattering realisation and hostile reality. They could regroup from this. The warmth in the room multiplied as the burning of the new log accelerated.

Alicia sipped her tea. 'It's very strange, Charlie, but my new lipstick and a fifty pound note have just disappeared out of my bag. I've searched everywhere and can't find them. I just can't think where they can have gone. Did you move them somewhere, darling?'

Her question hung in the air for a few seconds. 'Oh, God, no!' Charles chinked his cup into his saucer, placing it dramatically onto the coffee table. He dropped his forehead into his cupped hands and expired heavily. There was no hiding from this and he knew exactly where they had gone. When she saw his face, her own fears were confirmed.

Chapter 24

A Time to Get, a Time to Lose

'Pink lipstick!' Angus contemplated the picture, leaning back in his enormous leather swivel chair in his familiar posture with arms folded behind his head and a leg across his opposite knee, giving the impression of doing a yoga exercise while at the same time reclining in a chair and undertaking a consultation.

'Yes, really – Flamingo Pink.'

Gwen was perched beside his desk with her sleeve rolled up awaiting her usual blood pressure check, a procedure which was always combined with information sharing. The cake she had made for him sat in a tin on his desk by the side of a stethoscope and his blood pressure kit. Her feet barely touched the floor as she sat, but her stature had no relevance to the role that she played in the life of Blessingham, or to the significance of this meeting. She was of the view that this exchange of knowledge was the lifeblood of her town. That is what was really being tested here today – not her blood pressure.

Her briefing today concerned Freddie, his behaviour with his mother, and the general comings and goings of the family in her road. Her information was only for the ears her GP and town ally, Angus Kennedy. 'In addition to which … a very unusual thing.'

'What?'

'It relates to Mr Taylor down at the paper shop. He has a Lifeboat Fund box on the counter – the transparent box for Exmouth Lifeboat, in the shape of an actual boat, where people can put their loose change for charity? Kids are always pestering parents to put coins in there.'

Angus did not know, but he nodded his head as he was sure of Gwen and her methods.

'Well, the boy put a fifty pound note in there as a donation. Now, why on earth would a young man of his age do that? Most teenagers would buy alcohol or share cigarettes with their friends, but sadly, he hasn't got any friends with whom to share contraband. His mother says she is short of money, so she can't have given it to him. And I know Charles wouldn't. So why, and how?'

'Maybe the young man has turned over a new leaf, then, and has found that giving is better than taking; or maybe he was trying to offload a fifty pound note that was not his. Either way, that poor child seems to be upsetting someone most of the time and, Gwen, you'll get me struck off for gossiping. And I know you like a tipple, but we must not encourage the youngsters.'

Angus felt that he should at least make a stab at looking as if he was being a doctor undertaking an examination. 'Now, come on, let's look at that blood pressure, young lady, and I'll be taking a blood test today. You look a little bit pale to me. You are sleeping OK?' He then returned to the thesis of the day: 'I think that it's most unlikely, though, that she would wear pink lipstick – it's really not her style.'

'No, really. I'm sure she has a boyfriend. Things have moved on. I honestly saw June wearing bright pink lipstick in town yesterday.'

Gwen extended her inner arm, and Angus gently rolled the blood pressure cuff around it and began pumping the gauge.

'Ah, well,' Angus tried again. 'Life moves on and that's a blessing. Perhaps people down your way will be happier if Freddie is less disruptive because his mother is happier. And speaking of happier, this cake is definitely going to do the job for me, Gwen. Coffee and walnut – it must be my lucky day. I know you said to share it, but I'm not going to.'

He let go of the rubber handpiece that pumped the blood pressure apparatus, and observed the mercury in the pressure gauge as it dropped down. 'You'll do, my girl. See you in a month. Keep me posted on developments. By the way, how did you know the lipstick was Flamingo Pink? How can you be so exact?'

'It's our new friend, Hulio. Abigail checked for me in the store. She was looking for the Helena Rubinstein counter, and noticed the same colour in a display and stopped to ask the nice young man in there what it was, and he told her all about it. One of his girls was on the counter that day. Abigail thought he was a most handsome and charming young man, and when she said she loved his outfit he was thrilled and gave her a lot of attention. She was quite taken with his looks and his attire, which she described to me exactly: tight leather trousers with a chain hanging down the side, a very tight flowery shirt with no tie, hair down to his shoulders and wearing mascara. She thought he was probably an out of work model, as he was one of the most handsome young men she'd ever met. Hulio took her through the entire Chanel range of lipsticks before helping her eventually to find Helena Rubinstein counter, and he wasn't even disappointed that she didn't buy Chanel and only wanted to know about the pink one. She's going to see Hulio again next week, as she promised him we have another friend who wants to go through the range, and she wants his recipe for panettone, which apparently he rather favours. Hulio is Spanish, you know. We're beginning to think that he is very much part of our group and can help us with our grooming. He gives free consultations, which should keep us busy. But besides all that, Angus, I just don't see why June would suddenly appear out shopping in this lipstick. It's very unusual behaviour from her, very out of character. It's a strange turn in the works and it's too strange for me to ignore.'

'OK, well I know you'll let me know. But one more thing, Gwen, dear, speaking of Abigail; I want the comrades in here for their flu jabs this year. Not like last year when you all gave me the runaround. Have a word, will you – winter flu kills more older people than any other illness, and it's a lot of paperwork for me if you all go down at the same time.'

'It's for sure that something will take us out, Angus. Flu might be a nice way to go. But I'm sorry about the paperwork, so I'll tell them to be here. See you soon.' Gwen knew there was no chance of any of her fellow Time Lords going for the jab, but she did not like to disappoint him. She would go for hers with Abigail soon. That would keep him happy.

With every other aspect of his professional life scrubbed as clean as a surgeon's hands, perhaps this small amount of indiscretion on the part of the doctor would be something of a mystery to any onlooker. Better understood, though, this gathering of local information could be conceptualised as an act of sanity in a job where humanness is viewed generally as a failing, and where every aspect of one's vulnerability must be bottled up to an impossible degree. In Gwen Knight, Angus had chosen exactly the right correspondent for indiscreet and curious gossip. Gwen corresponded with the part of himself that wanted to be involved in the story of life, rather than forced into the role of a sterilised expert. Why were people always surprised when doctors, like the legendary Anton Chekhov, showed themselves to be human and have needs?

Once Gwen had left the surgery, Angus took a moment to reflect on the conversation and allow the content to link with other pieces of information in his mind. He was very concerned, and not just about the unusual event of pink lipstick being seen on his patient June Bradshaw. He had seen young Freddie up on the golf course on Saturday morning a few weeks ago when the lad had thought that no one was watching. Believing that what you do when no one is watching is really the measure of anybody's conscience, Angus had been surprised at what he saw: the teenager whacking the ground continuously with a golf club in a very aggressive and purposeful manner. Very curious behaviour in terms of golfing etiquette, and the amount of aggression that the boy had shown made it look almost as if he were possessed.

What was most worrying, was what he had found when Freddie had left the area and he had gone over to see what the boy been whacking; he had noticed crows gathering there in an excited huddle. When he reached the spot, the birds flapped and hopped a few yards away, not in a great hurry to leave their treasure. There, on the ground, were the remains of at least four large dead toads, smashed to pieces on the manicured grass of the golf course, blood, sinew and mucus spread everywhere. *Christ,* thought Angus, *that's a bit of a bloody mess.* A sickened reaction from a doctor who was used to blood, and who had been top of the class when dissecting toads at high school, and who had owned and completely taken down to the bone his own personal cadaver at medical school. This was not a medical dissection: this was a massacre. *Little sadist. What the hell is wrong with that kid?* He had made a note to himself to talk with the educational psychologist attached to the surgery, about the meaning of adolescents who sadistically bash toads to smithereens when they think nobody is looking.

Meanwhile, the story of the pink lipstick continued its journey through the town, and Charles was in his office on the phone to June.

'No, June. Seriously, I'm sorry, but there seems to be some confusion. I didn't send a pink Chanel lipstick as a gift via Freddie, and I haven't split up with Alicia. I'm afraid that Freddie has stolen it from her handbag and made up a story. He is also highly likely to have taken fifty pounds from her bag as well, so you can tell him from me that he won't be getting any pocket money for a month, and that I will reimburse Alicia on his behalf. June, this is really worrying, we've got to do something about that boy – he has a bad attitude, bad manners, and now he's a thief and a liar, and something of a fantasist. I'm very worried about him and I think he needs help. I know we're separated, but this is one area where we have to get our heads together and be of one mind.'

June studied the upper side of her finger nails, half wondering if Chanel made a nail varnish to match the lipstick that Charles had sent her via Freddie. She did not believe his explanation. 'I think it's you who needs help, Charles. Freddie would not make up a story like that without some basis for it. There is no smoke without fire, and my boy is no thief. I think you gave him the lipstick and now you're backtracking. Freddie has not got fifty pounds, I can assure you of that. He has plenty of pocket money from his grandparents. On the other hand, you don't give him a penny, and maybe he's trying to tell you something. It's not nice to accuse my son of these things.'

Her brittle voice did not hide well her disappointment and the hope she had felt when the 'gift' arrived via Freddie. She had been sure Charles was sending her a message that he wanted her again, just as she had hoped, and just as Freddie had hoped as he put his plan into action. She wore the lipstick all the time, reapplying it to go to the shops, and wearing it around the house. But maybe now she would put the thing to one side. She was not exactly sure if it suited her anyway. Charles had talked to her again about professional input for Freddie, and she did not really know what he meant, and anyway, the growing disappointment about the source of the lipstick was playing on her mind, and she felt a crushing sense of humiliation and disappointment that needed to be dealt with as a greater priority.

'Either she's losing it, or I am,' Charles mumbled as he put down the phone. He did not feel as if he was losing it. He felt as if he was finding it. The terrible day with Freddie just that weekend had cemented and bonded him with Alicia in a way that poor Freddie had not imagined. His plan had backfired, but one cannot be surprised when the plans of fourteen-year-old boys fail.

Charles had thought he would lose Alicia forever following the assault on her personal possessions, but there was no confrontation that night in front of the fire after the lipstick had gone missing, and Alicia realised that Freddie had stolen it from her along with her money.

Instead, she held Charles's hand and considered his face. 'Look, its clearly too much for him, Charlie. The boy just cannot cope with me being in your life. I love you enough to step aside if it's going to cause these problems for you and, to be frank, I also find him rather disturbing. He threatened to kill me; I could have him arrested for that. And he has a terrible way of exploiting people, like you and Anthony. I just don't choose to have that kind of person in my life, what with having had to keep my mother sweet and restrained for the whole of my childhood. Do I really need to marry a beautiful man with a child who behaves like my mother in her most psychopathic moments? I don't. I absolutely don't, even though it's going to make me as miserable as sin itself to lose you. It could be for the best that we face this now.'

'Best for who? Not for me it's not, and not for you, and not for him either. No. It's not for the best. No. I'm not having it. No, no, no.' Charles stood up and paced the room. 'No, I'll find a way. I'm not losing you. I've already lost one love in my life due to my complete gullibility, and I've lost the connection with my son Harry due to Freddie and June not coping. I'm sorry, but this bullying has to stop somewhere. Go, if you wish. But I tell you, I will find a way to sort this child out. If necessary I'll keep him away from you, Alicia. He need never come here again. I'll see him on my own and he can disturb me. I'll take every measure to see that you're not affected, but I need you and I want you in my life. Please, don't go. I've been thinking about boarding school for him. It might sort him out if his mother's not there to protect him.'

Their life together was hanging in the balance in that moment, but her decision was not hard to make. She wanted to sit on the settee with Charlie and hold his hand for the rest of their lives. She made one more attempt to test the strength of the decision she was about to make: 'But he's going to interpret you acting in that way as putting me before your first family, darling, and that'll be worse than anything for him.'

'No, it's me putting myself first, Alicia. Me, and what *I* want in life. Nobody is taking that away from me now. It starts here. I implore you to let me put this right and don't leave me. He has to learn.'

She would think later, when she was on her own, would weigh all this in the balance again. She would ask herself why she would lock into a relationship with a man who had a kid who was clearly not right. But she knew now, that despite the self-remonstration that would occur later, she would not change her mind. She did not need Charles as he needed her, but she did want him, and would be led by her heart in this moment. And they would find a way. The fire was fading and the room became cooler; time to go to bed. Time to give up on the day and go to sleep on promises.

***

Just as he had clunked the phone down on his conversation with June, and just when he hoped that this would all soon be over, and before he could take a breath … Ruby put him through a call from Angus Kennedy, who had decided to inform Charles of his concerns, and to advise him on seeking some psychological assessment for Freddie. He relayed the story of the toads. Charles coupled this in his mind with the complaints from school and the bullying from the past, there was only a short moment of hesitation before he decided what he would do next. As he put down the receiver he felt like a cornered man, with no choice but to act.

And so, the circle dance of life was completing itself through the gossip grapevine in Blessingham:

> Watched by the old woman, Gwen, who studied life continuously,
> who noticed the lipstick on the mother,
> which had belonged to the father's lover.
> She, Gwen, talked to her friend Abigail,
> who talked to the counter assistant in the store,
> who would talk to his friends too as he sold the lipsticks,
> and to whom the doctor, Angus, also spoke,
> asking him to encourage the women to take their medicine to keep them living.
> The doctor who saw the youth playing alone, killing toads,
> was put through to the dad by the receptionist, Ruby,

who knew everything anyway from the farm where the chatter
also went on.

The doctor spoke to the dad:

Who would make a decision about what was happening?

Then Freddie, the boy who was bullying, who was still, for now,
lost,

in his own world completely,

unaware that voices were joining together to make sense of him,

to intervene, and bring him some peace if he would only let it
happen.

Would he let it happen?

Would his mother let this peace happen?

Would her life become complete following the terrible rupture and
the loss of her fragile dream,

which her son tried to fix by stealing the lipstick?

The gossiping, the poetry of life, and the weaving of information to a
pattern continued in the town:

As always from the day the sun dawned on time,
As gossip always would do in service of the divine,
Not mere idleness but something fruitful.
It takes a village gossiping to raise a child.

Chapter 25

A Time to Cast Away Stones

Daniel Sanderson threw his fishing rods into the boot of his beloved BMW, along with his wellingtons, his warm, quilted waxed jacket and a tin of bait. The bait was laid down more carefully so that the writhing maggots did not spill out again and creep into the passenger seat as they had done on one occasion.

His wife had been disgusted with him and would not go in the car for weeks after that. The vehicle became a car for fishing: 'the fishing car'. A peaceful compromise had developed, whereby they used her two-seater for any occasion when they went out together to anywhere that required decent clothing, and the fishing car if they went out for a walk with the dog. The dog loved the back seat of the fishing car. For weeks after the event relating to the maggots he found interesting things there at which to nibble. Daniel's wife could not be angry with her husband forever, but that did not mean she had to accept a repeat of the behaviour. She did not have to share anything with maggots, but she did have to share everything with him, and this was the way the marriage worked. She knew her rights, and he and his maggots knew their place. All was well.

Into the front of his fishing car, then, he threw his briefcase and overcoat. He would have liked for the fishing tackle to be in the front of the car and the briefcase in the boot, as a symbol of how much he hated his job, but he accepted that this was the way of things and how his life had to be for now. He muttered to himself as he prepared for his day. One more coffee should eject him out of the house and catapult him into the office for what he perceived to be another day of people who did not have a clue how to manage their offspring. He was sick of children who could not behave and parents who could not get their kids to behave, and he could not wait to go fishing at the end of the day. But, unfortunately for him, he was an experienced psychologist specialising in education and child behaviour, and he was needed. He had a good eye for a sociopath, understanding as he did the difficulty of living within the petty constraints and rules of modern society, but he knew by now that there were some kids who were just going to go to prison and there was little that anyone could do to prevent that. He kept this kind of view to himself.

He did not really like the science of psychology, and in fact knew very little about the subject. He did not feel that the subject ever quite captured the essence of human nature and, where knowledge of it might help explain human behaviour, all those experiments did not solve the mystery of life itself, which he thought was far more interesting. Waiting for a fish in the water … now that solved many mysteries. Psychology had been a soft option when he ticked the box on the university entry form. As a student, he thought this subject that hid knowledge was one up from sociology, and two up from studying the arts.

Psychology had been all about behaviour and experimenting with rats and a bell pad. And at that time of his life, he had been so stoned for half of his lectures that he frequently formulated his own ideas and did not listen much to his professors. On one occasion – as a measure of his independent thinking on life and as part of his own personal experiment with a particularly strong form of marijuana – he was found setting his rat, Juliet, free out of the lab window, with a tiny green ribbon tied round her neck in a bow. He wanted to see how long it took to get a reaction and how far the rat might travel. The ribbon was there so that he would know that Juliet was his own personal rat, and because all rats look fairly much alike. He was nearly thrown out of university for this but managed to blag his way back in, although they would not have let him back in if they had known the full extent of his personal experiments with LSD and other hallucinogenic drugs in the name of psychology.

Later, he drifted into educational psychology at a time forty years before anyone had really formalised the profession. He hated the organisation of it all. Lines drawn between disciplines were, in his view, merely an attempt to create power structures to make members of the profession feel small and inadequate and not think for themselves, and he hated feeling small and inadequate. He despaired as he thought of the jumped-up little psychologists coming through the system these days, who thought they knew it all and had mastered the science of understanding people through psychometrics, and who babbled about neuroscience. He thought they were all so shallow. He smiled and was comforted as they were buffeted and bruised by the turbulence of the job when reality and that mystery called life came to greet them. Then, he could be the comfortable, affable man that he knew he could be, and help them all out with a sense of generous largesse that only comes to those who have truly experimented with a radical and free identity in their own youth. Thus, for this alone, the younger psychologists in his group loved and revered him, and put up with his rudeness about the profession.

In his more senior years, he loved to give the impression to his juniors that he was a more reliable source of information than they would find in a rat with a bell pad, or in a textbook. This reliability was reflected in his bulky stature, which he seemed to have to drag around with him, and the tweed suits and soft flannel shirts that his wife made him wear. He was not a nimble man in any way except when he was fishing, and then he could flick his rod and make a fly-and-line dance like a ballerina across the surface of the water. If only some of the troubled kids that he encountered would take up fishing, he frequently thought, then the world would be a better place.

He knew what the problems were and what the outcome would be when he looked at the details on the referral form, and he was bored already by the case of Freddie Bradshaw. He had been around all the cycles of behaviour that were possible in children of this age: mutilation of frogs, arson, stealing, bullying and death threats were all part of a familiar constellation of behaviours. Nonetheless, he had a job to do, and he would need to do his work as quickly as he could if he was to get a few hours in down by the canal with the rod and line before dinner tonight.

He began by formalising the gossip that he knew always erupted around difficult children, and started with a trip to the school, taking information from Freddie's form tutor. He planned his day – a trip to the school would give him time out of the office for lunch, and that would be at the Fisherman's Cottage café so that he could check out the chatter.

Then he could speak to Freddie's parents in the afternoon, and tell his boss that he was nipping home to do some paperwork and look at the child's medical notes, when in fact he would be down at the canal on his primary mission for the day. In effect, he would be playing hooky, in another mirror of his professional work, but this finer point eluded him as he made his plans. But first things first; teachers were usually a direct source of good information for someone like Daniel and he had no intention of wasting any time that day. He cast his line.

When he met with Ms Byron at the school it was clear that his appointment had interrupted her own busy schedule. He thought he could understand her annoyance at cutting into her lunch break.

She gave him a direct stare as she savoured the ham-and-mustard on wholemeal that she had to eat during the meeting, and followed this with a delicious drawing in of strong sweet coffee that made her feel better. She would have preferred to give her total attention to the sandwich, but she successfully split her focus both ways.

His mouth watered as he tried to wade through the detail and cut to the quick of what he wanted to know, which he knew he already knew anyway, but for the sake of formality and looking as if he was earning his salary he continued with the meeting and was tortured by the sandwich.

He was dealing with yet another professional half his age, but never mind. He sighed quietly inside: this was all part of what he had to do.

Ms Byron wasted none of her precious minutes in conveying her experience as Freddie's form tutor. During the consumption of the first half of her sandwich, as she appeared to be listening to Daniel while tearing at the meat and mustard, she spoke of Freddie in staccato-type utterances and minimalist sentences which, when roughly translated, stood for 'I'd prefer not to deal with this horrible child.' At the same time, she was trying to be as polite and as professional as possible, talking in a sort of code about Freddie. The conclusion was that it was felt there was no hope around this boy. She had studied all the child behaviour codes in her teacher training modules, and she just could not find a technique that tied the boy down or made a difference.

Daniel folded his arms across his barrel of a chest and leaned comfortably forward. 'So … he's a narcissistic little sadist heading for a career in politics?' He had tried to make her laugh. But she didn't find it funny, he realised, as he looked at Ms Byron's face.

'His only career is likely to be at Her Majesty's pleasure, after he has either seriously hurt someone or engaged in a corrupt activity by exploiting vulnerable people.'

Thoroughly rebuked by the young woman who could have been his daughter, and following the scrawling of a few notes, Daniel sauntered off to the student counselling suite where he would meet the boy who was the other most important thing on his mind that day.

Freddie had been called unexpectedly from class to the counselling suite and was bewildered and cautious and did not like the disruption. He had been listening to his drum and bass music. His teacher from the maths class had allowed him to keep on the headphones that day, as she recognised that this helped him to settle and concentrate and meant that he did not disrupt the rest of the class. He liked very much being in the jingle jangle of his own world. So, with the headphones on, Freddie swung open the door with a swoosh, without knocking, and sat down without being asked, all the time staring at Daniel Sanderson with the ting ting swish boom of the music swimming through his head. Freddie cut a dishevelled figure with his tie knot slipped halfway down his chest and pulled to the side, and the top button of his white shirt undone, which was strictly against the school dress code. He just about managed to keep his blazer on his shoulders.

'What?'

Daniel indicated, through the gestures of pointing to his ears and moving his mouth, that Freddie would have to remove the headphones for them to converse. The psychologist noticed the Bang & Olufsen equipment and wondered who had bought such expensive goods for a child to take to school. This was his opener: 'Smart pair of earphones you have there, bet they cost you a lot of pocket money. Nice to meet you, Freddie.'

'Nah, Dad bought them. Since he left Mum I can get him to buy expensive stuff.' He ripped them off clumsily.

From that comment alone, the case was closed as far as Daniel was concerned, but he was comfortable in his seat with the boy in front of him and continued. There was always more to be said. He had nothing to lose by exploring the boy's expression further – there was always more depth beneath the topsoil of narrative. He knew well that there were always the worms beneath the surface of the world that caused everything to grow. He drummed his fingers softly on the table, and spoke.

'I'm here to help out with your behaviour. I think your mum and dad are a bit worried about you and so they got me in. I'm Daniel. Tell me what you think it is they're worried about. I'm really interested to find out from you.'

'I don't know.' Freddie shrugged his shoulders, looking disinterested.

'I bet you do know. I bet you just don't get time to think about it. OK, what goes well for you at school?'

'What goes well for me? Nothing. I don't like school.' A shake of his head.

'Well, lots of kids don't like school but they get through well enough, Freddie. What would you like to do instead?'

'If I knew, I don't think I'd tell a random stranger what I think I want to do. Is there anything else you have to know?'

He picked up the earphones as if to put them on and block out the consciousness that Daniel was putting before him. 'I don't think my mum would want me to speak to you. She didn't mention it. I expect it was my dad who called you.'

Daniel knew the conversation was finished.

He swerved smoothly into the gravel forecourt of his lunchtime haven and parked up the fishing car, checking the bait to see if they were still alive and contained in their box in the boot before going into the Fisherman's Cottage café. He was relieved that his new bait box was holding out against the constant wriggling of hundreds of maggots who wanted to be free. He studied them with affection. *'Use him as though you loved him; that is, harm him as little as you may possibly, that he may live the longer.'*

These words, by Izaak Walton from the *The Compleat Angler*, came to mind, and he reassured himself that it was fine to care for his maggots more than his job and the unhappy child who he had just seen. Izaak Walton: now there was a man who, through the centuries, had understood the mind of the fisherman and who was with him in spirit. Right now, Daniel was entering a doorway beyond which maggots and flies could be revered like treasured artefacts. He spoke to his fellow anglers over a ham and mustard sandwich and a mug of sweet tea, and much completeness passed between them. The sandwich had remained in his mind since his conversation with Ms Byron that morning. He passed a pleasant hour catching up on news of the local pike and the latest havoc the brute of a fish had wreaked in the canal, and what colour fly would be good to catch it with.

***

June was on form that afternoon. She'd had a new haircut from Justin, the latest hairdresser to arrive in Blessingham, and who had been fully trained at Vidal Sassoon in London. Her mother had treated her, as mothers do for a beloved child when they are flailing around trying to find a direction in life after a bruising end to their dream. Justin had captured the angles of her face perfectly with his snipping, and the short bob swung dynamically when she turned her head. It boosted her confidence, and she had stopped by for her very own new lipstick from Hulio, the new man at the Chanel counter, whom every woman in town – whether teenage or old age – was now visiting. Her neighbour, Gwen, had directed her there quite passionately, pronouncing that it was better than a trip to the doctors; June wondered why the old woman would know this, especially as it turned out to be true.

June had recovered from the Flamingo Pink debacle and still did not believe that Freddie had taken the lipstick from that woman. How would he think to do such a thing? She found that the best policy was not to raise the issue of this with him any more and not to think about it. This was always June's position on difficult things, and it could be said to work at times: don't think, and all will be well.

But she was filled with indignation today, poised and ready for the curtain to be raised on her meeting with Daniel Sanderson. She had been put in the disdainful position of having to meet with this educational psychologist by her husband and by the school and by her doctor and, as soon as she had finished, she fully intended to make a complaint to the authorities for picking on her son. For now, though, she decided to adopt a new approach, and when Daniel Sanderson was let into the house from stage left it was to a June in a proud and dignified state of mourning who was having a very sad time at the end of her marriage. The dark-red dress was the next stage on from black and thoroughly masked the contempt she had for the meeting, although her portrayal of grief was not a lie.

She was sad at the end of her marriage. But she did not truly recognise that there was an end to the relationship, because she just could not yet envisage her husband not being in her life. He had been there for twelve years, and she was just beginning to realise that there was more meaning to their union than Charles being a willing servant and a weak father. She was starting to recall his kindness to her on frequent occasions, his endless patience, and she thought that she would never find another man who would be quite as malleable, and she missed his presence, his closeness and his warmth. So, she did not feign her upset, but its presence did not distract Daniel Sanderson from the fact that her son had something of a problem and that he thought this was related to her parenting of him.

She was polite and cordial and made her professional visitor a cup of tea and offered this with a home-made shortbread biscuit. They sat at the dining room table and the hot tea was placed before him in a lilac cup with a gold rim, and the biscuit tin left open so that he could take more if he wished. He noted the comfy home environment, the warmth of the room and softness of the decor, and thought that June was rather dainty and refined; he wondered how this all connected with the incredibly rude child he had just met at the school. Then he realised that it fitted rather well. If you were so dainty and so above it all you just might not notice the difficult things that were going on. Daniel meandered through the conversation with the mother, and the problem was conveniently and convincingly placed at the door of the father, who was described as weak and disinterested in her son.

'His father has never shown enough interest – I do wonder if there is something wrong with him?'

'So, you're worried that there might be something wrong with your child?'

'No, I mean his father – Charles. He's so vague and misses the point of childhood. He doesn't notice him half the time. Perhaps he has a psychiatric condition that is troubling Freddie. Did you think of that when you came here questioning me? Charles has had depression. I hope you're aware of that for your records.'

'You know, Mrs Bradshaw, every bully I have met has a parent willing to shield him or her.'

'My son is not a bully and I do not shield him.' She spluttered as she quickly placed the lid back on the biscuit tin which had, until that point, remained open to him on the table.

Time for Daniel to do some real work. He put the one last mouthful of his remaining biscuit back in his saucer. 'There is plenty of evidence to suggest that he *is* a bully though, June – can I call you June? – and that he is willing to exploit more vulnerable children. I don't think that the school has time to make up these stories. So, June, I'm starting to think that we need some behavioural management strategies, and maybe some additional parenting skills …?'

As he headed towards his car, Daniel heard the back door close firmly behind him. He should have seen this coming by the look of alarm on her face, and he wished that he had got that last bit of biscuit in the mouth before he was ejected. He should have stopped, perhaps, and found another way to present his ideas to her, but it was all too late. He was tired of being tactful today.

He drove down the road a little way and parked up while he phoned the office and spoke to his boss from his car phone – one of the first that had been installed in this 1990 BMW model. It was a little luxury that he had allowed himself, with his wife's permission once he had persuaded her. It had already been useful for calling her if he was going to be late home from fishing and this alone had helped to convince her that it was much-needed. Now he was calling his boss – his other wife, as he sometimes joked to himself.

'Yeah, hi, Lydia, just thought I'd forewarn you: I think Mrs Bradshaw is going to put in a complaint about me. What did I do? I suggested more parenting skills. OK, just thought I'd let you know. See if you can head it off at the pass. The local education authority will have an even bigger problem if this kiddie gets kicked out of school, and the state will have a problem if he ends up in the slammer with an antisocial personality disorder. I think we're seeing at least a conduct disorder here. The child is being intentionally harmful at times, and without any parental management we're going to have a costly problem on our hands, and I don't just mean the money. Yeah. OK then, see you tomorrow. I'm going home after I've seen Mr Bradshaw, to do a bit of, er, paperwork. Let's hope he's got more sense, for Christ's sake. Yes, alright, Lydia, I know you're a Christian; sorry for the profane language, but ask yourself – what would Jesus think?'

Daniel had a much longer conversation with Charles when he met him in the office of Bradshaw Associates. He was fascinated and flattered by the tall, broadly built young woman in knee-high red suede boots, a short, tight leopard-skin skirt, and purple nail polish who met him in reception and who took an enormous interest in his work.

Well, he thought that's what she was doing – making a fuss of him – but in fact Ruby was making sure she had all the facts to hand about what was happening here regarding Freddie and the visit from the educational psychologist, so that she could talk to Ryan later and give him the details. They needed to know what was going on so they could support Charles, she told herself, but really – they just needed to know what was going on.

As part of her role as convenor, as she had appointed herself for the day, Ruby mustered tea and more biscuits, this time chocolate digestives, plenty, on the tray laid before him.

Charles raised an eyebrow and knew that he should not get used to this. Seats were found, the phone was switched off, and Ruby pulled the door closed saying she would leave them in peace and deal with Charles's calls. She shut the door convincingly behind her.

For the first few moments of the meeting, Charles was stumbling with the idea organising itself at the back of his mind that Ruby would take his calls without question. But the matter before him was of much greater importance, and he soon settled and explained the whole story of Freddie's life so far as he saw it, while Daniel took notes.

These, he later he read back to Charles, because by that time he thought he was in enough trouble back at the office for one day, and wanted to show that he could stick to protocol, and the best way to demonstrate this was to scrawl notes.

'So, tell me if I've got this right so far: a difficult birth, hard to settle. Mum took over the parenting, so hard for Dad to get a look in, it never changed. Dad took a back seat and admits not being strong enough with the boy, and boy seemed to have more of a relationship with the Mum than with Dad. Dad got depression, has had treatment, family therapy, left the family home, admits smacking too hard on more than one occasion, shouted at him too loud too many times. Depression lifted once left and been away now for nearly two years, new relationship, happier. Freddie always difficult, always got his own way with Mum, hard to keep in routine. Maternal grandparents spoil the child with everything he wants. He won't accept Dad's new partner. Threatened to kill her.'

'Yes, that's about it. Sounds dismal, doesn't it. I'd like us all to sound a bit smarter, to be honest.'

'Well, he doesn't have any respect for adults, you see, Charles, and that's the root of our problem. He has totally withdrawn from the world as a defence. He's bright enough but can't be bothered with learning. Why *would* he be bothered? He feels he's entitled to everything, and that's a bit of a growing personality problem for the future. His mother protects him from himself and he's getting away with some quite malignant behaviour, frankly, and so I'm not surprised he felt free to make a death threat. He feels he can knock everybody over like skittles.'

Hearing that, Charles hung his head and there returned that awful and familiar feeling that he was to blame for everything. The 'I'm to blame' symphony orchestra started to tune up in his head, the conductor tapping his baton on the music stand. Charles tried to verbalise the symphony to Daniel. 'It's like having the sword of Damocles hanging over my head, to be honest. I can't see what I can do with the boy. I can't control him, and his mother is increasingly determined that he will have his own way. I wonder if she uses him now to get at me … you know … as if she can't have my attention so Freddie will get it … in all the wrong ways. I can't let him ruin my relationship with my new partner and, unfortunately, he sees that as a rejection, and that I choose her over him, and, frankly, I do in a way. Not to mention my youngest son, who has become completely withdrawn and won't speak a word to me about anything. I just don't know which way to turn.'

A comfortable silence sat in the room between the two men. This lack of the need to verbalise comes from people having built an alliance, a mental resonance between themselves. Daniel looked at his watch. There was only another half hour to go. He could fish in the dark if necessary. He ventured to the window with his cup and saucer in his hand and watched the Blessingham High Street traffic crawl past, slowed up due to the wet weather, headlights lighting up the late afternoon, everything shiny with rain, grey with lack of sunlight yet lit by traffic lights – a palette of grey, and soft neon lemon, smudged and softened by rain. The tension of the day faded to the back of his mind and he let the late afternoon sounds enwrap him. The steady buzz of traffic through the High Street, a seagull that had flown inland to avoid the rain, separated from his pack, reeling and cawing on the thermals.

'There's always boarding school.'

The comment hung in the air, floated in the atmosphere, rang in their ears. Both men looked at each other, wondering who had said it.

In an unguarded moment, Daniel had come up with an unorthodox solution that he knew his boss would not like: 'You can't separate children from their parents as a solution,' is what she would say in horror. Yet he continued.

'He'd be out of the way, safe, and someone else could teach him how to behave. Hopefully he'd meet boys who have twice the capacity that he has to be a bully – that should iron things out. You can't do it, and June certainly won't be able to; the grandparents can't, and your partner can't be exposed to his hatred for too long. I just know we're not going to budge this child very easily without some interruption to current proceedings. We have to think out of the box.'

Charles felt they were speaking in a forbidden language – what if June was listening? He could not help himself but to check around the room, and for some reason glanced under his desk as if someone might be under there or, perhaps, he would find that they were being recorded. He tidied a few things on the top of the desk, and put the top on his pen and laid it very straight, ready for action.

'Do you think his mother would accept that?' said Daniel.

'If the idea was sold to her on the basis that it would bring some additional kudos and status to his life … yes, I think she might. Underneath it all she's tired and it all wears her out. Yes, I think she might, and her parents would love the plan, especially if I were having to spend money on the whole project.'

'Can you afford it, Charles? It's a lot of money.'

'My dad would help. There's the trust fund from his father, always there if we need it.'

'Well done you. What a good idea,' Daniel proffered, knowing full well that it was his idea in the first place. 'I guess you could visit him at weekends and he could go home to June in the holidays. It's an unorthodox solution you've come up with there, but I like it. Well, I think I must be off – I'll get these notes written up and mention your ideas in the conclusions. I think this could help everyone out of a spot of bother, and not the least, Freddie himself, who must be struggling with this. Call me if you need any help with finding schools. We need one with an excellent behaviour management regime.'

Daniel left quite delighted with the outcome of his day, escorted by Ruby. He was impressed by how readily available she was to help him as soon as he opened the door. She walked with him to the exit, full of smiles and chatter, telling him about a cider festival on the moor that weekend. When she got back to the office, Charles shouted through door.

'Ruby … get my dad on the phone, will you?'

She responded immediately.

'Do it yourself … I'm talking to Ryan.'

And Daniel, at the very end of his day, completely satisfied with the roundness of his solution, headed through the pouring rain to the canal to catch a very big fish that was bullying all the other fish.

Chapter 26

A Time to Rejoice

A single event can have many meanings, depending on the interpreter and their relationship to the event. Some life events hold more power to provoke feeling than others. Births, deaths and weddings are in that category. These events are evolutionary in nature, the depth of meaning just beyond our grasp yet not beyond our experience. Weddings, for example, have the ability to provoke mixed emotions. The union of a couple can be a threat to some and a joy to others, depending on the status of the relationship that they have with the subjects of the celebration. A relationship based on high levels of dependency may mean a loss of status, a loss of power or control. If the relationship is one with more freedom of mind, then the response may be more joyful and the union seen to be of benefit to the community in general.

In the case of Charles and Alicia's wedding, this mixed bag of emotions was to be expressed throughout their hometown. They married some months after Freddie had been shoehorned into The Academy Boarding School in Somerset and left to settle. Charles had waited for the eruption and protest from his son over the event, but the reaction never came. Freddie went very quietly indeed through the gates of the school with his suitcase in hand. He showed no emotion and, just for now, his father was not questioning the peace in his life. He simply seized the day and asked Alicia to marry him, never thinking about what the effect might be on Freddie's mind, never seeing that his son's interpretation of this event was that of a further wound that would strengthen his resolve to rid himself of this unwanted intrusion into his life: this woman now given validity through a marriage – this evil stepmother. The boys would not be at the wedding and would not know about the matrimony until some months later. Charles was through with worrying about their reactions. He just wanted to enjoy his day, and for once just to take care of his own happiness. He would deal with any fallout later.

They had thought it would be a very quiet affair in Taunton registry office. Nobody needed to know apart from the two witnesses who were to be present. Since Ruby and Ryan were in attendance in this role it would mean closing the office for the day and, once Ruby had a hold of the news, the event became the most talked about story in town – everybody was gossiping about the marriage. The news, once spilled, fluttered further than any box of confetti on the April breeze. The interpretations and the personal meanings of the event began. The wires were buzzing in Blessingham.

Abigail and Gwen were excited and hopeful that this marked a new start for them all, including June. They had thought that sending Freddie to boarding school was a master stroke that would benefit his mother and brother and, indeed, the children in his former school, as well as Freddie himself. They discussed the hopeful ramifications over tea at one of their afternoon sojourns and clinked their teacups together, toasting the outcome.

Conversely, June was struck with horror that things had got this far without her noticing. The story was running away from her control and she had a lot of catching up to do. The information caused a frantic and upsetting time for her, and she kept the news from the boys so that the story would not affect them. She spent many weeks checking to make sure the announcement was true. This had become a hand-wringing tragedy of great magnitude, and she could hardly bear to face each day with the thought that she had nothing more of Charles to which she could cling.

Her parents, Dick and Brenda, had to nurse her through each day for weeks, finding the task of consoling her impossible. They were horrified at this final betrayal of their daughter and of their grandchildren. This event meant something so final to June's life, that it was like a death; in their minds they raged and roared about Charles's inadequacies, and in their hearts they grieved for the loss of the years that they'd had when he was married into their family, and wondered if they should not have taken him for granted quite so much.

The corresponding set of grandparents on Charles's side, Peggy and Peter, received the news warmly yet with some despair. The change of partner being now so definite was frightening confirmation to them that Charles's marriage had ended. They had never experienced this in their own lives, even though they read the papers and had friends with children who had divorced. They held on to the knowledge that their much-loved son generally acted in the best interests of all concerned, but they had been in touch with June, and thought that she was embittered to the point of madness. They did not understand this modern-day rite of passage of the second marriage – it was a new world, but they would gradually get to grips with the change, they knew that. Their open minds and affection for their child meant that they would adapt.

Angus Kennedy thought the wedding would bring some closure for the family and a new beginning for them all. He was pleased to see at least one of his patients happier with his life, yet gave a sympathetic ear to June and really did wonder about giving her the antidepressants that she so firmly demanded.

Hulio at the Chanel counter seized the moment as a wonderful opportunity for sales, and offered Alicia a free makeover in preparation for the day. He wanted to do pictures for the local paper but she would not let him. Alicia's happiness brought him sales; June's despair meant she would not be in for lipstick in a while.

Alicia excused herself from Blessingham, purchased a day-return ticket to London – taking breakfast in the buffet car for a treat – and went shopping in Knightsbridge, where she spent the middle of the day in Harvey Nichols taking advice on the best possible outfit for a woman of her age – nearing forty – at a country town registry office wedding. She returned with a simple well-cut shell-pink Chanel dress for her special day, and a cream straw hat that had lilac flowers falling all over the brim, together with a matching lilac tie for Charles. She spent a fortune on this one outfit but felt fully justified with the outlay. On her return, she insisted that Charles have a new suit for the occasion, though this took some serious persuasion. He liked the comfort of his old 'best' suit. Eventually, he attended the gentlemen's outfitters in Blessingham, and purchased an off-the-peg Hugo Boss piece that, once worn in, would become his new best suit. He was not too keen on the idea of the lilac tie, but he was not of a mind to argue, and the thing grew on him. At least Ryan had approved.

On a Wednesday lunchtime in May the small wedding party

walked across the cobbled courtyard to Taunton registry office for their appointment. People were going about their daily affairs, noticing briefly the smartly dressed, joyful quartet heading towards the town hall. They were used to seeing small wedding parties in the area and took little notice, although Ruby's rainbow colours caught the eye, as did Alicia's charming lilac-strewn hat. The day was thick with the scent of spring, everywhere peppered with pink and white blossom, and warmed by sunshine yet with a slightly chilling breeze that toned their senses. They had not bothered with traditional flowers – the only flowers were in Alicia's hat and on the apple and almond trees surrounding the courtyard. The bell at the church of St Paul's chimed twelve strokes, each being a call to sobriety, a call to the hour of midday, and their chatter slowed and then ceased and became solemn as they entered the porch of the Edwardian registry office building. With bells, whether funeral or wedding, the effect of the sound is much the same – to draw in the attention and focus the mind in the moment.

With most small events that have a big meaning the emotion expands as the event unfolds. What Alicia had thought would be a formality, with her signature on a piece of velum, exploded and became a beautiful and unexpected wave of emotion on which they were both carried, staring into each other's eyes and holding on to each other as if life could end at any moment, indeed perhaps at that very moment.

And perhaps that is why we get married. We are all so afraid and fearful that life may end at any moment that we wish to bind ourselves to another and give some meaning to our wretched solitariness. We seek permanency when we know full well that it is not ours to have. So, we make our declarations and contracts with each other and the words that we use will probably never again have such meaning. Those words take on a life of their own and become part of a lexicon that binds us forever. If only we knew that we were always adding to the narratives that bind us every day of our lives, we would perhaps be more careful about what comes out of our mouths, although at weddings and funerals and christenings we seem to be more cognisant of what we are actually saying.

As the civil ceremony progressed, the solemnity of the occasion unfolded before Charles and Alicia, and they were on the threshold of a new beginning.

'I do solemnly declare that I know not of any lawful impediment why

I, Alicia Isobella Millward, may not be joined in matrimony to Charles Rupert Bradshaw.'

Ruby suppressed a giggle, not knowing that Charles was also a Rupert. She was nudged in the ribs by Ryan, who frowned at her, and she soon came to her senses. She was just excited to be part of the day and soon she was reduced to tears, and Ryan had then to give her his handkerchief and a consoling look.

'I call upon these persons here present to witness that I, Charles Rupert Bradshaw, do take thee, Alicia Isobella Millward, to be my lawful wedded wife.'

Ryan took a step forward and everyone wondered what he was doing until he began to recite Shakespeare's 'Sonnet 116':

'Let me not to the marriage of true minds
Admit impediments. Love is not love
Which alters when it alteration finds,
Or bends with the remover to remove:
O no! It is an ever-fixed mark
That looks on tempests and is never shaken;
It is the star to every wandering bark,
Whose worth's unknown, although his height be taken.
Love's not Time's fool, though rosy lips and cheeks
Within his bending sickle's compass come;
Love alters not with his brief hours and weeks,
But bears it out even to the edge of doom.
If this be error and upon me proved,
I never writ, nor no man ever loved.'

Alicia went quiet, her knees had finally started to shake. Like a Catherine wheel of energetic colour and laughter the four rolled back across the courtyard as they fell in for their lunch table at The Wisteria – a Michelin-starred hotel in Taunton – and a luxurious menu of lobster, and strawberry-and-vanilla cream cake, and a champagne cocktail for starters.

The staff were ready for the newlyweds, standing to attention and clutching the opened bottles to their chests. At the request of Charles, Ryan had arranged for Gwen and Abigail to be taxied from Blessingham to share lunch with them. The chauffeur-driven ladies were excited to be there to join in the event – the full details of which they would later disclose to strategic members of their group within the town. Abigail would speak to Hulio, and Gwen would speak to the town's doctor. For the event, they had found their prettiest hats from the back of the wardrobe, which were not taken off for the entire afternoon. They felt giddy and light-headed as they sipped the golden bubbling liquid that slipped so easily down their throats in such a comforting and instantly cheering way. They were not used to any drink except for tea, and the occasional glass of sherry. Despite casting care aside, Abigail was ready with a pencil and pad and nobody could stop her from slipping into the kitchen to accost the chef and demand the secret of his strawberry-vanilla sponge cake.

Ryan was official photographer for the day and could be relied upon to produce the best shots of them all, although there was some problem with explaining to Gwen how to use the camera as she tried to follow his instructions for taking a picture of him as a part of the wedding party.

'It didn't click, dear.'

The party of six from Blessingham rode on the wave of completeness for several hours that afternoon, fuelled by sweet sticky cake and glasses of champagne, the older ladies having theirs sweetened with cassis because somehow they did not like such a dry taste.

There are billions of such moments of harmony all over the world every day – not necessarily special occasions – most of which go unreported. Small moments of affection, gladness or giving transacted between ordinary mortals during ordinary matters. So much of the goodwill and harmony of everyday living is dismissed and goes unnoticed. We bury simple happiness when in fact it is the treasure of life that gives some meaning to breathing.

This particular small happiness, though, would not go unreported, as journalists were present: Gwen and Abigail were the recorders of the occasion, and its relevance to the town would be thoroughly put to work on their return to their everyday lives. The small wedding in a small market town under the bell of St Paul's was a marking of time for the couple and for the witnesses who were present. The day would lodge in their minds, as these occasions do, as a marker, a life event, an afternoon when time was able to stand still and be remembered and recorded. There was, for the moment, no need to worry about those who would be less content about the occasion.

Chapter 27

Time Passing

They returned to the ordinariness, the bone and muscle of their existence pulled down by gravity and the weight of life's demands. The honeymoon was too quickly over. Not many moments had been spent considering the hard face of the reality of their lived experience – which was a good thing on a honeymoon – but the pressure of lived experience always comes to find you. They had not discussed Freddie or what would happen in the future, or how June was going to react, or any concerns about Anthony. They only knew that they had needed this time together.

So from their week in the plush opulence of the George V Hotel in central Paris they returned to little Town End Cottage in all its Victorian simplicity and without any trimmings. Their home, still a little damp in places, nestling alongside the river, deep in the heart of the flat Somerset countryside with spring bursting into early summer all around it, was made more comfortable now with some fresh paint and soft furnishing fabrics, which suggested something more than an ordinary working man's lifestyle for which the building was originally intended. The earliest inhabitant of this humble cottage would never have guessed that the simple shelter would one day be described as the height of fashionable design. But here, their playtime ended, and the next stage of their lives began with Charles ready to face the office and the urgency of insurance, while Alicia hung her pink wedding suit in the back of her wardrobe covered in light plastic and got out her navy two-piece and flat shoes for the 6.45 am train from Taunton to Paddington, ready for her new temporary accounting contract in the City. The timeless luxuriant breakfasts in bed of the honeymoon were exchanged for hasty slices of toast with coffee, and a kiss goodbye before separating for arduous days of work. They soon adapted to the routine. The story of their lives as they continued required much of their attention now.

The tale of Anthony emerged as a surprising low point for them both to grapple with as time pressed forward. As Freddie went off to boarding school with a disconcerting amount of non-resistance, Charles had thought that Anthony would come out of his shell and feel that he could have his own mind about his dad's relationship or, indeed, anything else in his life. He was coming into his early teen years and perhaps, too, he could have a quieter time at home with his mum and enjoy himself more, fill his own boots with his own feet, and fulfil his own destiny. But the reality of Anthony's mind, rather than being communicated to them directly, slowly began to dawn on them, and it showed a very different picture. Alicia, now his stepmother, would be first to understand what the boy was thinking. She woke up one Saturday morning and said she'd had a dream about Anthony:

'I dreamed he walked into Freddie and they became the same person, and there was no Anthony any more – just a Freddie. It was a very short dream – no more than that. Anthony walked into Freddie and became him – morphed.'

Charles had learned about Alicia's dreams and knew to take careful account of her psychic experiences as she portrayed them, even if they did not make immediate sense to him. He knew her well enough now to understand that her world encompassed an imagination which included lively dream states that held meaning about both of their lives. She dreamed about everything: her work, the garden, her friends. Her story of life would play back to her at night as the front of her brain switched off and she became paralysed by sleep; all her unfulfilled wishes and urges would interplay and collude with the gods in a form that would be re-presented to her in a mysterious code for her to understand or decipher when she was awake. Such is the nature of dreaming. The couple often spent time interpreting her sleep experiences. She liked and accepted her dreams, even if she did not fully understand these mysterious representations of her existence in the world.

They sat at the kitchen table with their Saturday morning tea after a hard first week of work, trying to make sense of the latest imagery. No – it was inconceivable that Freddie and Anthony could become the same person, as suggested by the dream state. They were so different. Anthony was a thinker. Anthony would never do what Freddie was doing in terms of actively showing hatred towards his dad and stepmother.

Even the Saturday morning tea could not stimulate their imaginations on the dream's meaning, which led Alicia to feel like a helpless prisoner because she could do nothing about something she did not understand. She thought that Anthony liked her, but the dream said he was willing to be the exact same person as his brother. To her mind, this did not bode well. But what if Alicia was mistaken, and that instead of Anthony morphing into Freddie, she was wishing that Freddie could morph into Anthony? Perhaps her wish was for a childlike Anthony who could possibly offer her the love that she craved. Thus, cleaving to the smallest possibility that Anthony's early acceptance of her could give her some hope of peace and harmony, the dream had fed back to her the story that it was possible that Freddie might turn into Anthony.

We forget that dream time is not the same as the time of our social world. We easily misunderstand that, in the world of the gods, time does not even exist at all. The story of Alicia's dream, therefore, from the time of dreaming to the time of realisation, took another four years to complete, starting with the sequence of events that sent Freddie to boarding school and finishing with an outcome that the couple could not even yet imagine.

The decision to send Freddie away was a turning point for Anthony, much more of a turning point than hearing about his father's marriage, which did not mean a lot to him.

Anthony was young and was not his own man, and he was completely influenced by the mind of his older brother, who intended now to disturb his young protégé's relationship with their father. Freddie had concluded that if he could not have a relationship with his dad, nor would his younger brother. A few whisperings and comments here and there at the right time changed the whole landscape of connections within his first family, with their mum, and this second family, with Alicia, which he hated and thoroughly rejected.

'She wants Dad to herself now and wants us both out of the way.'

'Dad can't love either of us if he put her first, and they didn't even invite us to the wedding.'

Whisperings such as these were most effective. Anthony could not talk to his mother about the thoughts that circulated his mind like a merry-go-round that would not stop. 'Don't upset Mum with all of this,' Freddie had told him. The story of Dad, therefore, had to remain the same in the Bradshaw first family. The view was consolidated. Dad did not want them any more. Freddie carefully and repeatedly reminded his brother that Dad and Alicia had caused the pain that they both felt, and that their mum felt this same pain. He carefully added layer upon layer of cement as he built the story, ensuring that Anthony was as fixed as he was in his views as the concrete set.

Anthony had tried to split himself into two families. He had tried very hard, but he had failed, and from now on he would be nice to Dad and Alicia when he saw them. He would smile and comply and then go back to his real home. He had started to become part of Freddie's mind.

Charles and Alicia at first started to notice this decision when he visited them. He began to speak to them with a flattened tone, as if he were a robot in their house. Alicia observed that his smile changed to something disingenuous, that he chose to show no gratitude for the things they tried to do for him and that he kept checking the time to go home. Eventually, it became clear to them both that the heart of Anthony was no longer with them.

Anthony had been able to make his decision because he knew his dad would not be angry – he would be sad, but not angry. It was safe to reject Dad, but not safe to reject Freddie, who would be even more angry if he did this and would very likely threaten him and even punch him into submission. Freddie had told him the story. And his position did not change over the weeks and months of visits to Dad and Alicia that were part of the family arrangements with June.

Yet the dreamer's dream still needed time to perfect itself. The dream itself was not yet satisfied that the curtain could fall at the end of the performance. The stage was set but only one part of the story had been performed. Never be fooled into thinking that a dream is a one act play … this is very unlikely. It took many more years of disappointment and failure for Alicia and Charles before the real meaning of the dream could be realised.

Anthony now visited for a Saturday twice a month, with Freddie not visiting at all, even though he was at home from boarding school at weekends. They accepted Anthony's deadpan features and the brick-wall defence that was set in place, which Alicia thought was so like Freddie's own brick wall.

***

The weeks and months that followed Anthony's solution became years, and even milestone celebrations of birthdays and family Christmases did not change the position he had decided to take. Alicia thought it was just a matter of more effort. She always tried hardest at Christmas, and at Town End each year she set to with increasingly elaborate decorations, making a traditional Victorian family Christmas in their little cottage of the same period which, in her imagination, automatically gave anyone a sense of warmth and belonging.

Charles was left with dismay, and Alicia gradually realised that her Christmas baubles were not going to speak to Anthony, just as her Easter Sunday lunches and elaborate hand-decorated Easter eggs did not speak to him, their holidays together in Portugal in the sun did not speak to him, and nor did the family barbeques or even the fourteenth birthday party she hosted for six of his friends, which his mother would not have at her own home. Nothing spoke to him, and he did not speak.

Alicia found herself looking up the condition 'selective mutism', wondering if he had some disorder that affected him, but she discovered that this state of mind in a child is psychological and behavioural in nature, and she was therefore left to think the impossible thought that she knew was true anyway: that Anthony *chose* not to speak, and had rejected them. And besides, he could perfectly well use his voice in his mother's home when he wished. The thought that was unthinkable was that Anthony had crossed the bridge to the other side, and he may have burned the bridge behind him. Nothing she did or was going to do would change that. No amount of effort was going to make a difference.

Dreams are not erased over time. They do not simply go away. A dream dreamed is a reference manual for the future. Time marches on and people change in line with dreams. Dreams do not change in line with people. And anyway, there was more of this dream to come for the story to be complete. The couple finished their drink of tea and went for a walk along the river. Walking together is another good way to think, and in those days they took to walking often along the wide River Exe, so close to their home.

Chapter 28

Four More Years

Charles did not have the strength to fight the power of June, Freddie and now Anthony, who had joined together to lock him out. He found this isolation from his children an unbearable reality which he could only cope with by turning his attention elsewhere, distracting himself to something more hopeful that he could share with his wife. He could not reconcile having found a new love with having lost the children who were the loves of his life and his biological link to the world.

The two opposing thoughts clashed like cymbals in his mind in an irreconcilable cacophony. So he concentrated Alicia and hid the pain of this loss from her, saving it for quiet moments, just as she hid her worry and concern from him. Night-time saw them in the same bed but withdrawn into separate worlds now, with their two separate stories, uttering their separate solutions. She, still muttering wasted prayers of hope that the boys, by some miraculous transformation, would come round, and he, simply praying without thinking for a child who loved them, yet at the same time not really stopping to think where that child would come from.

Then there was the dream that came on another Saturday morning a week before Christmas one year: sitting in her winter dressing gown at the kitchen table with their morning tea, Alicia told Charles that she had dreamed a happy and joyful dream about dancing hand in hand in the garden with a red-headed child. She cried as she told him about how they already had the child with red hair who would love them … but that he was not her own. They had forgotten, but the dream had remembered for them – there was a child who embodied all the qualities they would have wanted, dreamed of and prayed for, rather than the rejection that was received from the boys. Charles was now free to renew his relationship with Harry, his son by the red-headed Katrina Allsop. That child had been there all the time.

***

Four more years had seen more activity and growth at Bradshaw Associates, mainly through Charles's enduring and reassuring presence and due to the hard work and productivity of Ryan; so much so, that another new legal arrangement was formed, a kind of marriage between these two men, and the company became Bradshaw Levison Associates as Charles joined with Ryan in a union of trust and productivity that was very much like matrimony. Charles remained in his dream role of hero and protector of the company and, despite all the teasing that continued from Ruby, he was a cornerstone to the company's longevity. Charles saw himself as the carthorse of the company, plodding along at his own pace, while Ryan was the creative entrepreneur with vision, who brought wealth and fresh seams of income to the organisation. This was a lifelong relationship which became, along with his marriage to Alicia, the buttress to Charles's life despite the many twists and turns that were going to happen.

It was becoming a family affair down at the office; it was not only a hub of commerce but also a hub for the community, which was unusual for a company in the area. Farmers would pop by for coffee or tea as instigated by Ryan and Ruby, who thought that the networking would be good for business, and they invested in a new hot drinks machine for this very purpose. As they had extended their range of activities to include will-writing, they had many senior citizens drawn in for the convenience of a local hub where tea and biscuits were always available. And of course, this included Gwen and Abigail, neither of whom felt that their visits had to include business. They were simply friends of the company by now.

The ladies were still the centre of senior communication for the town and, if anything, they knew more now about what was going on, rather than less. Their friend Dr Angus visited them weekly now, under the pretence of checking blood pressure and other vital signs, but they always knew he was really checking for what cake had been made and what was going on in the town.

Angus recognised that since Abigail's arrival on the scene Gwen's house had increased in its importance as a control centre of communication for the town elders. He could justify the forty-five minutes a week spent with them on the basis that he got to know what was going on with virtually every patient on his list over the age of seventy. Not for the first time, he considered writing a paper for *The Lancet* on his community research, but knew that his professional body were not yet ready to hear about his unconventional community data collection methods, and certainly would not be ready to make sense of his connection to Gwen and Abigail. He was content with his own measures, although he had put on weight but could not cut down on the cakes, which he felt were good for his soul rather than his waistline and was still weighing in the balance which was of more importance. The ladies had swayed him towards their point of view that sugar was reviving, bringing this notion with them from the previous generation who had depended on sugar and accepted its benefits, rather than seeing it as an enemy of the health system.

Over these years, then, there were losses and gains to be had for everyone. Charles bought Town End Cottage and had Ryan's partner landscape the garden, revealing some of the historical beauty of the old stone walls. They found a well that had been dug centuries before but which had become hidden by a conspiracy between ivy and time, and it gave them free water for the garden and for washing the cars. They found a late eighteenth-century plough, also covered with ivy, that became an ornamental feature, and they found shrubs as old as the house itself. Charles started to take pleasure from the world of gardening, which was something nobody could have predicted.

And then there was June and her life back at Didcot Lane with her boys. June had made peace with herself and her daily life was a series of small contentments: taking care of her boys, keeping home, caring for her own ageing parents and volunteering for Meals on Wheels to provide hot lunches for the ageing community. She made peace with herself, but she never made her peace with Charles, using any opportunity to criticise or defend from the happiness that she heard about in his life as reported by Anthony, who twisted his reports on his dad to the negative to please his brother. She did not progress into a relationship, although she considered a few dalliances with some suitors, who saw her as an attractive option until they found that she came with attachments in the form of Freddie and Anthony. Her boys in themselves were not the problem as much as the communications that the boys made to the interested parties. Of the men who were interested in June, few survived the initial surveillance and sense of doom from Freddie, and only one progressed to a second date. One look at the face of this teenage boy would help them to realise that they would never own or even share the territory that surrounded June, and that this world belonged solely to her son. Men are good at reading this signal at least, territory having been their rite of passage for many thousands of years. After two years of this familiar pattern of territorial posturing from Freddie, June settled for no more dating, convincing herself that she would put future relationships on hold until her boys were grown up. This kept the household in a comfortable position. She became handmaiden to her growing sons and her contentment in this role was beyond normal imagination.

***

Back at Town End Cottage, after four years of marriage, the conversations between Charles and Alicia took a sudden turn.

'I just don't think I can do this any more,' Alicia said.

'Do what any more, darling?' He put some more bread in the toaster. He knew exactly how she liked her toast especially, on a Saturday morning. The radio chattered in the background about weekend matters.

She sat with her head down, looking at the table like a twelve-year-old who is bad at maths waiting to take a maths exam.

He was worried she was ill. This would explain everything, and he was relieved at his powers of perception. He felt her forehead, lifting her face to his as if she were a child. She was pale with dark circles under her eyes and had clearly not slept well. He could recall now that she had been tossing and turning all night. He wondered if she had a temperature, because that would explain everything very comfortably.

'I didn't want to have a period today!' She sobbed, flopping her head onto his shoulder.

He wrapped her in his arms. 'I know, darling … believe me, I do know … I really do know.' He thought he almost knew now.

'Your children hate me, your ex-wife hates me, and we don't have our own baby … and I've been wondering if it's possible that I am such an awful person that I'm not destined to be loved by children. I just work. Children are not for the likes of me. I don't belong in that world. Do you think we're being punished? You don't talk about Harry. Are we being punished for Harry? You never say a word about him, it's as if I'm banished from that world – pushed away. You don't want me near your children and they hate me!'

'No, you're right. I don't talk about Harry. It's just that he is so well and truly banished from my mind. I don't know why, darling … it's just, I thought—'

'I thought you were ashamed of me and you didn't want me to meet him.'

'No, no, not at all. I just literally put him out of my mind—'

'It's like work is our baby.' She was coping beautifully with reality now. It was out there.

'Well, yes, work is the baby. I thought that was good for us … the company working so well and the office feeling like a family. I guess with Ruby and Ryan feeling like part of the family … I guess I just took it for granted that you were happy, and made a massive assumption that that's what you'd prefer.'

'Well, you got that wrong.'

'I got it wrong. I am so sorry … I got it wrong.'

He looked helpless in his pyjamas and she smiled softly, because sometimes he could be so remarkably inept and hopeless that he made her smile, and if she did not smile she might be annoyed. So better to smile.

'Look, darling,' she said. 'I'm forty-three and you're forty-seven. It might be a little late for a baby for us, but it feels like a failure. I feel like I failed. I don't want to, but every month … I feel like I failed.'

'OK, so which problem are we solving here. Are we talking about the boys hating me or you, or us having a baby, or Harry coming back into our lives? Because I've got them muddled. Which one do you want me to solve first?'

Her eyes went wide.

He decided he would take control.

'Right, now here's where we are, and here's what we're going to do. You're going to the doctor to check out the baby thing, and I will come with you and we will talk about it to Angus and establish the position with fertility; you want a baby and we'll have a baby, and I couldn't be happier even though it wouldn't have been my idea.'

'I'll go on my own. It's obviously my fault. You already have three children.'

'Alright, my darling, you go on your own.' He passed her the tea and put in a teaspoon of honey to sweeten the taste. 'Enough now. We've done it. Faced it down. It's on the agenda. I know it hurts you, and it doesn't hurt me because I'm a stupid bloke and I haven't been sensitive to it. I get it. I don't want you in pain. That's all I know. If you want a baby then I want a baby, and that's where we're going. I just didn't know that's what you were thinking … I only just caught up. Now, what was number three on your agenda of things, because they all seem to be the same thing this morning? One was the boys hating you, two is the baby, and three is?'

'And three is … we're going to have to think about Harry sometime.'

'Right, Harry. Shall we do that some other time? Do you think we've had enough for now? Come on, drink your tea.'

'We've put it off long enough. Now is the time. It won't solve any of our problems, but it's there for us to deal with. He's even getting into my dreams. Maybe I'm dreaming that for you.'

'Well look, darling, it might turn out badly. We've had quite enough difficult stuff. Harry might hate me, and out of my three sons he's the one who has a just cause … and I don't need that, Alicia … I just don't need that. I've got quite enough to deal with, with the other two.'

She slowly sipped her tea, watching him over the top of the cup. Something was shaking at her for this meeting between them and Harry … something in her bones, in her dreams; she knew where she was going with this even if she did not know why. It was almost the end of 'honesty in the kitchen' time – this would close the deal, and she also knew Harry would be good for him. Sometimes when you love people you know what's good for them better than they do themselves, and sometimes they fight you on it.

She was no longer upset, and she found a smile that showed she was soothed and a squeeze of his hand that told him she was calm and sure. She sidled onto his lap, and it was his turn to have his grumpy face taken into her hands. She considered his eyes, and he sat helplessly with his arms down by his sides while she kissed his forehead and then squeezed his cheeks so that he looked like a hamster.

The nerves in his face twitched so that he had to smile and then he had to laugh, slightly grudgingly, because having your cheeks squeezed does make you do that. It was ridiculous to be sitting in his pyjamas with his wife on his lap in her nightie while he was having his cheeks squeezed as if he were a hamster, but that is what it came to on this morning when they sorted out the matter of the baby, being hated by his boys, and why they had not been in touch with Harry.

Chapter 29

A Time to Every Purpose Under Heaven

A foggy Sunday morning in January – with the church bell in the village just chiming once to indicate half past eleven – found Charles and Alicia on an ivy-covered porch ready to knock on the door to Harry's home. They were hiding behind chocolates, flowers and wine – offerings to the God of Hope that this meeting would go well. The journey had taken longer than expected and they had found it difficult to find somewhere to park. And now they were momentarily confounded as to whether they should ring the clearly signed doorbell, or knock with the ample lion-head knocker. They had discussed so carefully what they would take and how long they would stay and what overall message they wished to convey, and concluded that you can never express enough respect and gratitude when someone else has raised your child for you, when you have ignored them for the whole of that child's life and he is now a grown man and then they, the ones who did all the hard work, generously invite you for lunch.

Standing on the doorstep was supposed to look spontaneous and cheerful in nature, but was in truth as choreographed as any stage production to manage the fear that it would all collapse into disarrangement. With assistance from wardrobe and props and many dress rehearsals taking place in their minds, their underlying nerves were heavily disguised in preparation for the opening curtain. From Alicia's carefully chosen navy coat that was deliberately without any trimming or ostentation, to Charles's suit with a tie, also navy, chosen by Alicia. (She often chose his ties these days.) They took one last enquiring search into each other's faces before they decided to use the knocker rather than the bell.

'Ready?'

'Ready.'

The tall young man who opened the door to them from the inside that day was a mirror image of the older man on the outside opposite him, the same height and the same look of curiosity about life. The very real difference was in the red hair which, Alicia would establish within the following few seconds, belonged to the genes of the younger man's mother, Katrina. Despite Harry's easy cordiality, the same amount of stage production had gone into the opening of that door from his side as on his father's. All this preparation in the name of keeping friendly in the face of an exceptionally unusual situation, although one might question how much effort it was for the younger of the two to choose jeans, a T-shirt and flip-flops in which to answer the door.

While Charles had battled with possible rejection on one side of that door, his son had battled with some ambivalence, rehearsing both the 'Why bother now?' and the 'Hey, it's good to see you, anyway,' stances, weighing up the two options and then deciding on jeans and flip-flops for the door opening ceremony that was now taking place, the chosen garments and footwear representing relaxed acceptance rather than tense ambivalence.

It was not so much the awkward handshake that was worth a photograph for the family album, but more the few split seconds before it that were of significance and which could not possibly have been rehearsed or captured on film, but were somehow logged in the minds of all of them. The silence and slightly open mouths would show that they were all completely taken by surprise to see each other, despite the clearly orchestrated arrangement that had been imagined in detail from both sides.

The surprise for Harry was that his dad had grown older since the last time he saw him. Charles's hair was grey nearly all over, and Harry had not imagined, as younger people do not, that the passing of time would have had an impact on this middle-aged adult who was his father.

Charles was surprised that Harry still looked like he did when he was younger, except that he had lost all trace of gauche teenage awkwardness. He forgot to imagine what fourteen years of growth looked like, during which time Harry had grown from a sixteen-year-old slouch into a thirty-year-old man in his own right, and did not look remotely like the teenager

Charles had remembered. Their faces were on the same level, and he could hardly have ruffled Harry's hair as an act of affection as he might have done with his own sons if they had both still been receptive. The stare in his eyes gave away his surprised but unvoiced thought: *How the hell do I relate to you now that you're six feet four?* His plans had not anticipated this concept of bodies growing taller.

Alicia was surprised that this meeting had finally happened at all, and that there was a mirror image of her husband right before her on the doorstep the same height, and same build, only with red hair. Mostly she was disconcerted by the jump in her belly and the sense of enchantment that she felt so immediately upon meeting this boy who was now an adult. To save her embarrassment, she felt she had to cover up the idea that she had dreamed she was dancing with him, for now, anyway, except that she was so excited she really did feel like telling him straightaway, or grabbing his hands. She resolved from that moment onwards that this relationship would not be spoiled in any way, and that this was her chance for redemption with stepchildren.

Harry's mother appeared to be confident as she approached her own front door, but she too had to manage the emotion of surprise. *Did I really have sex with this man and have his baby?* She smiled through her stare at the conservative yet admittedly charming-looking grey-haired man standing on her front doorstep. In her own split second she resolved this initial shock, and could sense through the reaction of her body that this was, indeed, the man. She was remembering when she had not expected to remember at all. She had thought this day was all for Harry and had forgotten, as mothers can easily do, that she was a key player.

Her husband, Gordon, stood beside her to meet the genetic father of the adult son who had been his baby since birth, when he had cut the umbilical cord in the delivery suite for his wife and promised the tiny infant that he would care for him forever, no matter what. Harry had always been his baby. He was shocked by how vehemently his brain needed to impress this upon him right now. As he greeted Charles and Alicia warmly, his hair prickled slightly on his head.

Meanwhile, their twenty-year-old daughter, Sophie, twisted her red hair around her index finger and watched their greetings unfold. She was surprised that they were all surprised. They were, she thought, all remarkably awkward in the way that they tried to cover up this emotion. What was the point? If her truth were known, and it would be known eventually, she was a little envious that her brother Harry could now tap into the generous resources of two fathers.

There they all stood in freeze-frame on the threshold of a new beginning that foggy morning, hardly suppressing their turbulent emotions in the strangeness of the moment, before someone pressed the start button and they began moving and smiling as if it were a stop:go party game. Etiquette saved the day and comforted them; they sprang back into action and the procession decanted from the tiny stage of the ivy-framed doorstep where emotions had been so intense, into the ample auditorium of the comfortable home where reactions could be diluted. It is not so much the emotions we have about things that are awkward, as the way in which we try to cover them up that makes for remarkably interesting human behaviour.

Charles kept a smile on his face to cover all bases, and excused himself to the gentleman's room to take a small respite from the strain of being extremely engaged in this visit to the family of his long-lost son. He concluded, as he rose to use the furniture in the bathroom rather than just sit on it and stare at the wall, that the joy of the day made him feel guilty. He ran the bathroom tap and washed his hands in the warm water, the subtle smell of geranium-scented soap pervaded his senses, and this calmed him. He reminded himself that this was what Alicia wanted, and he had seen her face today and she was happy; this thought dominated the others, and re-energised him as he left the bathroom for round two of engagement with the family, hoping that he had flushed all thoughts of June from his system and would now not be too preoccupied. He remembered what sorts of things could happen when he was preoccupied and, as a result, he double-checked to make sure he had straightened his tie and done up his fly properly. And then the bathroom was free, which was timely, because Alicia would soon be wanting to use it.

When he returned to his seat at the lunch table Alicia was talking to Sophie about her plans. He could hear from the tone of her voice that she was feeling confident now, and enjoying her conversation with the young woman who was holding on to her every word. Had she been given to bouts of triumphalism then today would have been her day, but it would not have been like her. She had caused this to happen, and it was right.

In her own retreat to the bathroom for the regrouping of her thoughts, Alicia took the opportunity to talk to herself in the mirror:

'Now, learn from this. You can't possibly be accepted by everybody. It's not as if their rejection threatens your life, but today, yes, you got it all back. Yes, yes, yes.' She smiled, comforted, and applied some lipstick, noting Katrina's choice of expensive hand soap and the light green designer tiles around the sink that matched exactly the green of the lily pads on the Monet print, which she thought she might like to replicate around the sink of her own bathroom at home. Then she steadied herself, and gained her familiar sense of control by focussing with great seriousness on her eyeliner.

Nobody really knew that person, not even the one staring back from the mirror. She was barely conscious herself of the girl who'd had to give up on her own real needs to keep her mother happy, and keep the peace and care for everyone emotionally in her home. The girl who learned to cajole, comfort and create in every moment so that she could survive with her own thoughts intact but hidden from view. The woman who was so wounded by what had gone on with Charles's children, who wanted to bully her into submission so that they might break the relationship to relieve their own fears of abandonment. Today, she was having none of this, and she was neither cowed, bent nor broken. A few moments, and she would regain her composure and her refreshed look would be completed with a spray of J'adore and a quick brush of her hair. Her self-reassurance accomplished, she flushed the toilet so that it at least sounded as if she had been in there for the right reason, and closed the bathroom door behind her.

They all had their private thoughts that day and took opportunities to escape to quiet places to examine them. Thoughts relating to the past relationship between Katrina and Charles, for example, were not given weight and not part of the group discourse over lunch as it progressed from the carefully chosen soup, to the simplicity of the risotto and salad, and then to the confection of the strawberry meringue. This, all prepared by Gordon, who was entitled as much as the others to his own set of thoughts as he retired to his kitchen for preparations of both food and mind. This domain was his private world. His meal had said welcome, and his internal struggle, he assured himself, would be addressed another time. Gordon the doctor, the healer, the family man, was a creature of good measure. For now, his main consolation for a challenging day was that this was all for his beloved child Harry, and it would be good. He was naturally an emollient character and a healer, but he had questions that he would be asking of Charles.

Right now, Harry was enjoying conversation with Alicia, and he perceived her already to be part of his future. She was so easy to talk to and it was somehow easier to face her, a stranger, rather than Charles who was powerfully familiar, bringing out unimagined emotions for him, so much so that he had to keep a distance for a little while yet; he protected himself by talking to Alicia.

Forming a room of their own at the lunch table, the two women were chatting after the meal: one, whom Charles had loved earlier in his life with a passion, and the other, whom he loved now more deeply than he felt he could ever love anyone. He could see something similar between them. He would ask Alicia later, and she would explain: 'I guess we just know what people need. It's what happens when you stop putting yourself first and try to imagine what everybody else requires to be happy. Katrina needs her son to be connected to you for his sake – not her sake. I need you to be connected to your son – for your sake and our sake. Keeping each other happy, darling. This is what we try to do for each other.'

It was soon teatime, and the January sun dipped low in the sky. Some rooks cawed in the empty winter trees that surrounded the garden, and the grass out there was beginning to look as if it would soon be covered in frost. Harry turned on some lamps to add some light to their conversation before he slid onto the velvet-covered chesterfield opposite Charles, his posture earnest, as if he were going for an interview. Charles's own seat opposite him was an exact replica of the settee on which Harry was sitting. The two men appraised each other from their parallel positions across this empty gap of fourteen years with only a coffee table between them, each wanting to fill the space with something, not knowing quite what, but each at least wanting to put something good in there.

Charles was looking at someone who was mature for a thirty-year-old; he wondered how that had happened. Harry had changed from the gawky hapless kid he had last seen, into this intense character who, despite the jeans and T-shirt – now covered with a beige sweater – carried himself with gravitas.

Harry smiled, pleased but awkward, softening to the conversation. His body leaned forward and he put his elbows on his knees as he sensed the humility of the man who sat before him. 'Mum and Dad are fine about me being in touch. Yes, let's keep in touch, Charles. I'll come and visit. What about your boys? They must be teenagers by now. They're half-brothers to me – that'll be even more weird. Maybe I could meet them?'

'I'd like that, but I think it would be futile unless there's some miracle and they have a dramatic turnaround in their thinking. I'm not very pleased with them. They won't accept Alicia, and they've completely rejected me because I've remarried. It's all about June needing it to be that way, just like she needed me not to be in touch with you. I don't think I'd put you through their rejection of you right now. I'm sorry if that's disappointing. You can try if you want, but I just can't see how it would work out.'

'Hey, I thought you guys might want something sweet.' Katrina could see something was happening. 'I'll just put this tray down – pour yourselves some tea, Harry.'

The tea was a good distraction. Harry poured for them and passed Charles some yellow sponge with a cake fork. He kept his eyes on the spout as it met the edge of the second cup while he spoke, and Charles stirred his own cup but watched his son's face. He thought how he had never gained mastery of the kind seen is his son right now, this naturally inherited confidence and belief in life and his inherent right to exist. But as they talked that day, in the quietness of the family lounge with the curtains shutting out the blunt winter darkness, everything made such total sense: the reason why he had been so attracted to the mother of this child; the reason why his child had become the hero he had always wanted to be; and the reason why Alicia had to scream and beg him to get him to visit today. So, he left that day with a sense that at least one aspect of his life had a sense of completion and that there was the possibility of a relationship with one of his sons in the future.

Chapter 30

A Time to Pray

Prayers never stop being made in the human heart, although we don't know exactly the science of them being either heard or answered. They are often made at night-time before the brain closes for sleep, before it drifts into the state where people are at their most helpless and vulnerable, but prayers can be made at any time of the day. Atheists might refer to prayers as a list of human needs; neuroscientists might think of them as a function of the brain, the cognitive mind integrating comfortably with the needs of the limbic system; evolutionary psychologists might call prayers a product of the current stage in the development of our group thinking. And ordinary mortals who have a need for a god, whichever shape that god takes, simply call the thoughts that they chatter at night before they go to sleep 'prayers', and they are comforted by them.

Alicia, for example, had her prayer to see Harry answered in the end because her husband co-operated with her. Harry became something that was wholesome and complete in their lives. Alicia had her remedy there, but she did not have her repair with the boys, and she did not have her baby, and so her prayers continued but changed track. Being a practical woman, she knew she had to help prayers along and help herself, and to do this she would visit the doctor over the issue of getting pregnant, as promised to her husband, but she thought she could not go to the doctor about the two teenage boys who hated her. She did not see the two issues in her mind – the baby and the boys – as interlinked. She was sure her doctor would know nothing about these difficulties with Charles's family anyway. Why would he?

***

He had scrubbed his hands, and Angus Kennedy now sat at his desk tapping his pen onto his notepad, which advertised sertraline – a drug for depression. He was thinking. He did not like sertraline and never prescribed it to his patients. He only kept the notepad with the advertisement as it had been given to him for free and he did not want to waste the paper. He was another example of someone who made prayers. His prayers were that his patients would find ways to manage their depression without having to resort to the power of drug companies who made money out of their ordinary human unhappiness. His prayer for himself was that his paper on 'The Power of Healing in the Community' would be published in the medical journal *The Lancet*. He felt that doctors should know their patients better to treat them better. And as a case in point he knew plenty about what was going on for Alicia Bradshaw, the patient with him now, who was getting dressed behind the screen following an internal examination.

Gwen helped him put many people's stories together, and was someone who contributed to his prayers for better community medicine coming true. He played the same role for her, supporting her prayers that the community should care for and support one another. These are the kind of prayers that older people have when they are set free from their youthful ego. They surrender and realise the pointlessness of being so individualistic and selfish. Their joy is to be found in a better community, and so Gwen's prayers were easily linked with those of Dr Angus, and they would commune together on their common goal.

The only visibly unusual thing about Gwen's relationship with Angus, if anyone was interested, was that her medical notes showed she had a twenty-minute appointment each week, whereas all other patients had ten. But nobody would be interested in this or think it unusual. She was an old woman in need of time. It was up to him how much time he gave to his patients. Her notes would not reveal that she also had a razor-sharp brain, and was a community archangel, the purpose and meaning of her work never really to be known except in her prayers, where she prayed for something good to happen in her life every day, and that she brought good to the lives of others. She was quite beyond the selfish narcissistic prayers of youth, and Angus played a part in her prayers being met. He was on her team … or was she on his? So, a longer appointment was needed. If anyone wanted to record the science of how prayers are met, they might start by looking at the liaison between this patient and this doctor. But to return to his current patient:

'You're fine, there's nothing wrong with you, Alicia. Many women these days have babies after forty. I don't suggest we start any fertility treatment. Nobody ever tells women the cost of going down that kind of road: it's quite toxic to the system and the chances of success remain at less than thirty per cent. You never hear those figures. Besides, it's not available on the NHS and will cost you thousands. My suggestion is that you learn to relax more, cut down on so much work, eat well, take folic acid and have sex at the right time each month. You have a stressful job, and I know you and Charles have been through a lot in the last few years. It's easy to lose sight of goals like this and think they will happen automatically. Get a fertility thermometer and start to register those fertile times on a graph. I can't give you one on prescription, but they're available in the chemist. When you have sex at the right time each month don't forget to put a pillow under your hips and keep your bottom at an angle so that everything stays inside for as long as possible. We don't want any of the little blighters getting away. All you've got to do is give Charles the signal at the right time.'

These conversations were so embarrassing, but Angus had such ease with them that Alicia was quickly not bothered. So, as she stepped carefully back into her knickers and pulled up her tights, thinking that there was nothing more that could humiliate her in life, she listened to his commentary without a second thought from behind the curtain. She was cheered and hopeful at the information he gave her, and immediately became tearful from relief; warm salty liquid filled her eyes and gushed down her cheeks. She took out her tissue. Blast, why did this have to happen now and why did he have to see this!

But he did see her.

'Is there anything else worrying you about this, Alicia?'

'No, it's just been hard to pull anything like a family together. I don't know if you know, but the boys have been awful and that's made me feel like a total reject. I've tried every way to pull it together, and I just can't.'

He did know. 'Really? I can imagine that must be difficult.' He was not imagining at all. He had heard perfectly well from Gwen just that week that the boys were being obnoxious towards Alicia, and he was glad of a chance to pull this conversation out of the bag. Another coup between himself and Gwen that no one would ever know about. He was sure that stress and worry over the boys would reduce Alicia's chances of pregnancy.

'I don't know why they still trouble me, really. We know there's nothing we can do about them. I guess I see it as something of a personal failure.'

'My view is that if you can't change the situation then you must change your response to the situation,' said Angus. 'Meanwhile, you need to manage your anxiety, and I suggest you take up some form of 'stress management'. I think you have a choice. You can have some counselling through the NHS but the waiting lists are long. I think you'll get a lot out of simply focussing on a new goal, combined with stress management, a little bit less hard work and lots of sex at the right time of the month.'

Charles was not surprised that Angus had put Alicia's mind at rest, and resolved to thank him when he next saw him up at the golf club. He played with the idea that he might even let him win a few games for that. Alicia had bought the fertility thermometer on her way to the office to catch up with Charles, and came and sat on his desk facing him that afternoon, with her legs dangling between his and him holding her hand while she told him everything. How he was going to respond to her new world was important. He was not going to let her down now, knowing it was hard for her to have exposed in this way her most tender self – measuring her sexuality against performance targets in terms of an achievement and outcome, measuring his own, for that matter, but he was not so worried about that.

'This could end up like an Olympic sport if we're not careful, my darling, all this limbering up and getting on the job. I don't want to set up yet another stressful unsuccessful scenario.'

'No, quite. So I found a yoga class.'

'Ah. Brilliant.' But he had not thought of yoga. 'Now, do you want me to come with you, because I think I could come up with a good lotus position even if it is a class for girls.'

'No, really it's OK, thanks, darling.'

He was encouraged. 'No, because I *can* do that.'

'No, you can't. This is for me, but I've been researching that gentle exercise like yoga and walking can decrease stress. We could do something relaxing together like walking. How about we unwind with a stroll in the evenings? There are some beautiful footpaths around here along the river and across the fields, and we've never taken the time to explore them. This could be a new pastime together, and it would help us to connect with nature a bit more, and with greenery and fresh air. You may walk with me if you wish.'

'I may walk with you. Thank you.'

He was still reeling with relief from being rejected from the yoga class, but felt he had got off lightly, and registered in his mind what was needed on his part to contribute to her well-being. His way to help signposted, he got out his Ordnance Survey maps as soon as he was home. He was onto this.

Men can feel so helpless when being told that nature must just take its course. They are quite determined, always, that they can help things along.

Genuinely excited by the baby issue now, he was not going to let her down. He had time to think about it. This was all he had needed. He thought that even though he was older he could enjoy fatherhood again. When you love someone as much as he loved her you want them to be happy, and you'll surrender to anything in the end. He concluded his life was very different and that they could build something new based on fresh dreams. Nothing was going to spoil this for her and he found himself clenching his fist and tightening his jaw as he vowed this to himself. He took her shopping and bought her some stretch outfits for her yoga class, and reminded her to leave the office early. These are the small and thoughtful ways that men can help.

Chapter 31

The Greatness of Life

Alicia sat quietly and began to see that it was, as Angus had said, her own mind that was revolving round and round with the problem of Freddie, becoming more of a problem than Freddie himself. She accepted that it was natural that she was worried and would try to anticipate what he would do next. That is what minds are for – to second-guess danger. And was he such a danger now? She had to ask herself, although she did not really have the answer to this. She had to assume not. As she disciplined herself to sit quietly at a certain time each evening, focussing on her breathing, she noticed how she could control and slow down the ideas that simply repeated themselves time and time again until her head was aching and she became a victim to her own wild and fearful thoughts. She could see it now: the thoughts you have about the problem may be worse than the actual problem itself. She found she even felt compassion for Freddie, who was simply stuck in his own toxic unhappiness and unable to move forward. She thought what a miserable life he must be having and how much he must miss his father, and she experienced a flutter of enjoyment at this thought, but accepted that revenge, too, was as natural as love. She began to surrender and find some peace at last. The restless dreams stopped, and she slept more deeply. But some instinct made her careful enough. While she could think about Freddie compassionately, she did not feel that she could fall into the trap of being too sympathetic. Freddie had done nothing to show that he was a safe and reasonable person capable of reconciliation, but he had shown a ruthlessness that was inconceivable to most people. Some lurking force in her suggested that she should continue to be cautious of him.

Mindfulness is not all about sweetness and light, she thought, and this doubt about Freddie just would not go away. Our brains frequently tell us when it is right to be cautious. She accepted the distance between the two families just as it was, without pushing or pulling any more towards how she thought it should be. She could not control Freddie, nor could she predict him, any more than she could really control the thoughts in her mind – she simply had to accept the whole situation as it was given to her. And here lay her answer to peace of mind. She had also found flotation, which put her in touch with the mighty centrifugal forces of the world of which she would become a part while lying in the liquid; there, devoid of worry, she vowed to herself: 'I am going to have a baby … nothing, but nothing, in this world will ever stop me … ever.'

Flotation took place in a huge tank at the health spa, an enclosed space full of salty water in which participants, who were willing to overcome their scepticism, floated for an hour in the limpid azure pool, surrounded by violet rays and soothed to sleep by Mozart on the piano.

Charles wondered if things could get any weirder when she described this, but he noticed immediately that it was of great benefit to the woman in his life, who was making an art form out of stress management for them both. He had learned to respect her new ideas, especially as they seemed to work. He was told to prepare for his turn in the tank and, like most men who are ordered to attend the spa by their wives, he could not wait.

At first, she thought it was just too odd to step down three steps into a deep pool of warm salty water in a tank about half the size of a single garage. The initial problem for her to overcome was that she could not swim, let alone consider floating on her back; she had never been able to swim, and had little inclination to learn. She recalled an embarrassing time when she had tried to swim with Charles when he went to the pool with Freddie and Anthony. This, another failed attempt they had made at a family outing. She'd had to stay down the shallow end and hold on to the edge as usual, but she had enjoyed splashing in the warm water and feeling the enjoyment of everyone around her. She had been excited by holding a bright orange float, kicking her legs behind and going a width across with Charles walking beside her, his hand under her stomach in case she sank, the boys watching from the side, their arms folded, their chins tucked in. She really did look like a child splashing in the water that day, but she felt quite happy – kicking her legs with a piece of polystyrene held in front was a big achievement for her. She had been surprised as Charles pulled her out by the hand that Freddie had stared her in the face and scoffed, and then had made a joke in Anthony's ear so that he too laughed about it. She was quite sure that this small failing of hers not to swim was held in his mind against her. But she did not give the incident as much weight, in truth, as she might have done. She could not imagine that anyone would be able to hold such a thing in mind to use against her. Not being able to swim was very low on her list of worries, and it rarely affected her life. At school, her teachers just shrugged and left her on the side. She was so good at maths that they used all the time she could have spent trying to learn to swim by putting her in for maths competitions; they were not bothered that she did not like the water or swimming, never thinking that it may be an essential survival skill that could save her life one day. Instead, she turned herself into a helper if she ever had to go to the lessons, taking off her shoes and socks, fetching floats and balls into the pool for the other kids, and minding their towels and watches.

Right now, in her determination to move forward, and with the promise of the tank being the most effective route to relaxation in the new millennium, she stepped down into the water in full trust of Flo, the assistant of the day. She began to panic on the last step, pulling back from Flo's hand. 'How can I float if I can't swim?'

Flo, the petite blonde and impossibly glamorous assistant, enjoyed helping people with these first few moments of worry, going down with them in her one-piece swimsuit with gold buckles precariously clasping the material together at the hip and centre of the breast, as she introduced them to the experience.

Despite the flimsiness of her attire, Flo was a reassuring presence and was able to persuade Alicia to float on her back with the aid of her hands placed between her shoulder blades and under her bottom. Chatting merrily, she gradually took her hands away without Alicia realising, as one might do with a child, and then took great pleasure in saying 'I've not been holding you for exactly a minute now,' and watching Alicia's unbelieving face, anticipating the usual response, which was for her charge to stand up immediately, and Alicia did. Then Flo urged her to do it all over again.

After one introductory session, Alicia began to realise that she could get in the pool and float on her back as if she were lying on a blown-up lilo.

Flo left her there when she could see that she was confident on her own, and switched off all the lights except for one small violet ray that lit up the inner sanctum in an eerie soft glow that was both entrancing and comforting. She made sure that Alicia realised she could open the door from the inside, as she knew that many people would panic about a sense of being locked in. She took extra time with Alicia, who had a double dose of fear to deal with on her first session with her disadvantage of not trusting water.

Alicia tried the door once and then, reassured that Flo would come and wake her in an hour, and that if she had any problems there was a buzzer on the side and she could call, as most things she did in her life, she decided she was going to give it her best shot.

Flo was pleased with her work, but if she had known the precise extent of the part she had played in Alicia's life, and the long-lasting effect of the flotation learning, she may have been even more pleased.

Over time, Alicia's fear subsided and she relaxed, and could make sense of her fearful response that was now ebbing away. She fully understood that her experience of Freddie as a stepson had revived her deepest memories of having a hostile mother, someone she would like to have loved wholeheartedly, but at the same time someone around whom love was combined with a tenseness and danger, making her feel inherently that all was not well and that she had to work hard to put things right. As the weeks went by she realised she had fallen back into trying to put this thing right with Freddie, when in fact she absolutely could not, and realised now that this was not her job. Gradually, the threat that he brought with him receded in her mind; he became a person in the distance – not someone who was in the constant foreground of her life. She liked this. Just occasionally he came to the front of her mind and now, when she noticed this, she would go to her tank or take up her yoga or walk along the river and breathe life deeply back into her mind, and the thoughts of him would fade and she would repeat her new-found mantra: 'Goodbye, Freddie, sorry it didn't work out but it wasn't my fault.'

Things came good for Alicia, and she simply enjoyed the sweetness of her busy and now buoyant life with Charles. She was drawing on her reservoirs of strength rather than on the emotion of fear, and it was as if learning to float had saved her life.

Chapter 32

A Time of Reckoning

By the time Freddie Bradshaw was eighteen and had been at the Academy Boarding School for four years, they were quite happy to be rid of him. The headmaster commented to his deputy that if the school had not fallen on hard times financially and they had not needed the income, they would have expelled the lad in his first year. But they persevered with him, mainly because his paternal grandfather was so prompt at paying the fees and donating a sum each term to the grant fund for less well-off students. Little did they know, that from the grandfather's point of view, he was only prompt with payment and a contribution to their charity because he wanted his son and the rest of the family to be at peace, removed from the difficulties posed by his grandson. He made a generous regular donation so that they would not fail to keep him in the school.

Unfortunately for Freddie he was unpopular with most of the staff, and any of the friends he did have he tended to exploit at some stage or other, leaving them bewildered and shocked. He would always choose to dominate the vulnerable and lonely kids, steering clear of the better resourced ones, who just ignored him. Freddie did not see why he should do much schoolwork and was unable to think of the consequences of leaving education without any qualifications.

In fact, understanding consequences in life continued to be a big issue for him. He appeared to think there would never be any comeback for any of his actions, which included: encouraging the second formers, aged twelve, to smoke and drink; turning two of the fourth formers into 'fags' – a custom that had been banned in the school for a decade; and once stressing one of the school cleaners by ordering her to clean out his wardrobe as well as the rest of his room, insulting her so much that she left the school immediately and could not be persuaded to return. The cleaner could not understand how anybody could show such disregard for her. That episode caused quite an argument and the lack of respect nearly got him expelled, but a donation to the grant fund was due to be made, and Freddie was allowed to stay.

There was just one member of staff who seemed to understand and connect with him, and as a result Mr Andrews became the link between Freddie and his social world, including all the other staff in the school.

Once, Freddie had put a fake turd outside the headmaster's office, causing much distress, especially to another cleaning lady who had to clear the item up and found Freddie laughing at her as she did this. This woman, proud of her trade and not to be taken for a fool, realised it was a fake dog poo when she tipped it upside down in her dustpan and saw 'Made in China' written on the bottom. She took the offending object to the headmaster, who was most surprised to see the curious shape in her hand. She placed the item on his desk. Freddie was called immediately. He never owned up, but the incident had his hallmark all over it.

Freddie's reprieve was probably down to the goodness of Mr Andrews. In fact, his continued attendance at the school was because Mr Andrews promised to take care of the matter, and saw to it that Freddie spent a week cleaning up the school playing field, which included the removal of cowpats left by the local cows that had recently roamed onto the property from the field next door. Armed with a shovel, Freddie found out exactly what it was like to clear up excrement. Andrews personally had to supervise the punishment, which was completed so that everyone was satisfied that proper reparation had been made. The headmaster particularly enjoyed watching across the playing field from his office window.

Freddie was too overcome on that occasion to plan revenge, which he was rather prone to do, but in any case he would not have created a payback for Mr Andrews, with whom he had formed a loyal bond. He considered Mr Andrews to be like a father to him. A decent father, one he could trust. It was more likely that any future need to be mean would be directed at another cleaning lady, or someone else he considered inferior. Unfortunately, despite his young age, he had already developed misogynistic as well as sadistic tendencies.

Charles knew that Mr Andrews had taken Freddie on in mind and spirit, and never let this kindness go unacknowledged. The school knew this too, and for his efforts Mr Andrews was promoted to Head of Behaviour Management within the school with a raise in salary that helped him to support his wife and family, and which meant that the school could add another string to their bow, telling parents at the back of their brochure that they could take on and manage children with difficult behaviour. This eventually brought a new income stream to the school. Somehow, just as Mr Andrews prayed for and intended, everything he took up seemed to multiply into good, and he was highly thought of for his behavioural management plans for the difficult kids that the school encountered. It is possible that the role even spawned a new career for him. Charles spoke with him one day.

'What can I do, Mr Andrews? I just can't break through the barriers.'

'I know it's a challenge. He knows that people hate him for being a cruel little dictator. He feels inadequate and thinks that being grandiose will cover this up. Or he tries to deal with it by being the class clown, and that goes down moderately well some of the time, but the fact is, Charles, he has just been given the wrong idea about life. He is obsessively close to his mother, is afraid to let go of her, and feels it was wrong of you to leave her and so, consequently, he hates Alicia. Even I find the things he says about her frightening. I gave him a detention last week for what he said about your wife.'

Charles drew breath. 'What? What did he say?'

'He said she had no right to exist,' said Mr Andrews.

Charles drove home wondering how the hell you helped a boy understand acts of misogyny against women, when he himself loved his own mother so much. How much more perverse were things going to get and how much more would they have to take?

***

At six o'clock in the evening at Freddie's home, a champagne cork popped from its bottle and gold liquid came spurting and frothing from the head and dribbling down the sides. The two drinkers exchanged luxurious, proud and contented smiles.

He mopped the excess champagne up with a serviette and poured two glasses to just below the rim, passing one across. She sipped the first sip without taking her eyes off him, a pink lipstick mark creating a delicate tattoo on the glass.

'Happy birthday, my darling.' She gently lifted her glass and touched his glass with hers before putting it down carefully on the table, and cutting into the sponge cake with his name iced on top in blue, which was filled with cream and strawberries that oozed out from the sides; she passed him a piece on a plate with a napkin and fork. 'Here's to my birthday boy … enjoy!'

'Thanks, Mum. I can't believe I made it to eighteen.'

Freddie was celebrating his entry into adulthood with his mother. She was trying to cheer him up. He had been disappointed about leaving school and was finding it hard to get a job. Freddie had assumed that the world of work would all be his automatically, that he had a natural right to the status that his father had.

He had been offered summer jobs by the employment centre. One such job was cleaning chalets for the season at Golden Sands Caravan Park, one of the popular holiday camps in Somerset.

'What? No, thanks,' he said to the girl at the counter. 'I don't clean. That's women's work. What else have you got?'

She was a little surprised, but was willing to overlook this comment. 'Well, it's all seasonal work, but there will be the apples to pick in September – that usually gives a lot of employment opportunities, and it's well paid. And with the summer evenings there's plenty of overtime.'

'Don't foreign people do that?'

'I beg your pardon?'

'Don't Polish people come and do that?'

'No, they don't. I'm sorry but I will have to ask you not to speak like that when you're in here, Mr Bradshaw. It's offensive and it contravenes our Equality and Diversity policy.'

'Yeah, well what about my rights to an opinion then, love? Whatever. I'll find my own job. You clearly haven't got a clue.'

The young lady behind the counter marked his card to say that he had spoken out of turn, and consulted with her manager about the incident, which had surprised her and caused her some discomfort.

And Freddie went home to his mum to proclaim his condemnation of the jobcentre and of Polish people who came to pick apples. She agreed with him without a second thought, but secretly planned to call Charles to talk to him about giving her son a job. She might as well use him for things that were useful to her and her goals for Freddie. She was sure all would be well in his future as soon as he got started and people realised how special he was.

'Call your dad. He could start you in the company.'

'Come on, Mum, I haven't spoken to him for years.'

'It doesn't matter – call him. He's your father. He has an obligation to help you. You speak to him first. I'll call him later. Do it now, darling, while we're thinking about it and then you can go off and enjoy yourself.'

It was four years since Charles had talked to him, let alone seen him. Time had worked on Freddie and he had grown physically into a man, and in some respects his mind had developed. He had even greater expectations of life, he recognised himself to have the power of a man, his voice was deeper, his muscles were stronger, and his refusal to have anything at all to do with Charles while he was attached to Alicia was more rooted than it had ever been. He had been working on the matter in his mind continuously and he had formed his conclusions. Charles knew that he would not have changed, and was sharply reminded of the existence of his son as Ruby at reception told him who was on the end of the line. He knew that he would have seen Freddie before now if his son had changed his mind about him and Alicia in any way.

'Put him through.' Charles felt a nervous fluttering in his stomach. For some reason he was already forming the word 'No' in his mind, not even knowing the reason why. He overrode this strong compulsion for now.

'Hello, young man. It's been a long while since we've spoken. I hope everything is OK?' His tone was thoroughly defended.

'Everything's fine. I only rang because it's the summer holidays, I left school and need a job. Mum thought you should give me something.'

The immediate image of Freddie creating havoc once more in his peaceful and well-ordered emotional world was too much to bear. His foot went down on the ground and he stood up in response to the request, trying to control what came out of his mouth next. Every piece of armour in his defence system came to the fore in the few split seconds between the request and the response.

Freddie tapped his fingers and looked at his watch. What was there to think about?

'I'm sorry, son. I can't employ you. I don't think that would work. Besides, Alicia works here again now and I don't want you upsetting her. So, no. I can't help you.'

Freddie's jaw dropped, and a crimson glow crept up his neck to his jaw. He dropped the phone into its holder, wrestled in a fog to get his favourite beige hoodie from the coat hook by the door and went out, mumbling to his mum that he was going for a walk.

June had heard the call and knew from the short length that it had not gone well. She picked up the phone as soon as Freddie was down the path and out of sight.

Charles knew exactly who would be on the phone next, and he was not responding. He pretended to himself that he was getting on with his work without a second thought. But he was annoyed and flustered and had to put everything down in the end and submit to the panic that was flowing through his mind. He was used to an emotional distance from Freddie and he was not going to change that now. He knew that having him on the premises would mean instant conflict. He certainly would not tell Alicia of the near miss, and that she might have had to work shoulder to shoulder with the stepson who hated her. He had grown adept at making sure his wife was not upset by these incidents.

He did not want her upset now. She was eight weeks pregnant and he could not have her worried. Thinking about this took his mind off his annoyance. They were absolutely delighted, just dying to tell everyone, but were waiting for the twelve-week scan before they did so. Angus had told them it was standard to wait until the end of the first trimester, which was a vulnerable period for miscarriage. Alicia was feeling sick now, but enjoyed the waves of nausea and every rush to the bathroom that meant her prayers had been answered and her dream had come true. Charles was not having her upset and, to his own surprise, he had banished his son from his kingdom to protect his wife. This was the final curtain on their relationship, and his paternal love for Freddie, he had to admit, had come to an end that day.

Chapter 33

A Time to Watch Your Enemy

Freddie was muttering to himself as he walked past Gwen's house to the end of Didcot Lane, his head bent low, his shoulders hunched as if he were fighting with the world. He was so engrossed in a sorrowful dialogue with himself that he was unaware of her presence, watching him from her vantage point over the lane – her picture window. She saw him go to the end of the road, keeping his head down, and his hood up and then she noted that he turned left at the junction at the bottom with no hesitation, darting off down the rough, narrow, footpath there that led to, and then ran alongside, the river.

'That's funny,' she said aloud.

'What's funny, dear?' asked her cosy compatriot, who was watching Wimbledon on the television. They loved Wimbledon and soon they would have strawberries and cream while they watched with a glass of afternoon sherry. They did not usually have afternoon sherry, but Wimbledon was an exception because the tradition was a celebration of the summer and the enjoyment of cheering on their sporting heroes while savouring the flavours of the season, which included strawberries, cream and sherry. At Wimbledon, everybody else was drinking champagne, but these ladies preferred the sweet sticky comfort of their cream amontillado, which was minus the sharp bubbles. This year, Wimbledon 1994, they were focussed with intense enjoyment on the strength of a young man called Peter, although everyone else called him Pete – Pete Sampras.

'Why is he turning left?' said Gwen.

'Well, he was just lunging for the ball, dear. He had to throw himself at it.'

'No, left at the end of the road. There's nowhere to go except down the bridleway that leads to the river and the open countryside. It's very overgrown, not many people will venture that way – it's not a nice walk, loads of nettles and wasps nests. So why is he going down that way?'

'It's three miles,' Abigail responded.

'Three miles to where?'

Abigail was reluctant to take her attention from the game. 'Three miles to where Charles Bradshaw lives at Town End Cottage … if you follow the footpath and are brave enough to get through those nettles and thick brambles without being scratched or stung and still find the path, and if it's not flooded, of course. I don't think we'll ever be walking down that way Aww, no! That one went over the line.'

Gwen continued her conversation. 'That's the third time I've seen him go that way this week. Once he turned right and went into town with his brother, but three times he's gone left down that impossible path that leads to the river and eventually past his dad's house, and always at the same time of day, in the early evening.'

'I expect he's stalking them, Gwen. Now, come and watch – they're slamming this ball around with all their strength.'

Gwen scribbled a pencilled note in her diary, and when she finally sat with her friend she did not relax, a frown remaining across her vexed forehead. A question had crossed her mind that would not go away.

Abigail did notice her look and that she was not rested, but she would talk to her later when they were sipping their sherry. That would be a good time. They always talked about questions together, and they always came up with answers – she was sure of this. So sure, that she could carry on with the tennis for now.

If the truth were known, Gwen was annoyed because she wanted to follow Freddie Bradshaw to see what he was up to, but she knew that if she followed him she would not be able to keep up. All the same, she was tempted, but her old body would not co-operate with her youthful curiosity, or with her capacity to imagine tragic consequences from simple beginnings. Turning left at the end of the road rather than right had roused her suspicions. Her imagination might have been youthful in its agility, but was old in the tooth in its sense of reality.

She put the matter out of her mind for the time being, and decided to watch tennis with her friend. Her curiosity and imagination were getting the better of her. She could think about it later. She must not spoil this special time. They never knew how many more Wimbledons they had in front of them and she wanted to be with her friend, and so she turned from their window – their lens onto life – and back to her dear friend who was glued to the other screen in their lives: the television. Gwen smiled at the irony that, while they watched the youthful strength and civilised aggression of the players dressed in white on one screen, she had been watching from the other screen with some concern, the entry of a youthful and aggressive young male, dressed in a beige hoodie, to the wild abandonment of the disused footpath. She wondered what this would come to. Her note was in the diary. She smiled and allowed herself to be distracted by Abigail's choice of Wimbledon earrings for the day, which on this occasion were little gold tennis racquets that swung as she turned her head.

Chapter 34

All Cried Out

Freddie enjoyed the three mile walk down the bridleway. The exercise helped him to clear his mind of the upset he was feeling after the phone call. His shoulders unhunched as he got into his stride. With the number of times he had walked that way recently he had worn himself a clear path with the swathes of nettles brushed to one side, and he had taken secateurs with him just the week before and cut off the determined brambles, which were thick and immense like octopus tentacles and reminded him of a science fiction novel he had been made to read at school where weird plant creatures would come and strangle unsuspecting humans. The day that he badly snagged his arm on them he had vowed to get his own back, and had returned with the cutters and snipped them off. He had to keep his shirt sleeves down for ten days before the scratches would heal. His mum did not notice as he snuck out the secateurs from the garden shed in his jeans pocket.

After this work was done it was a pleasant, less hazardous, walk and the late afternoon August sun was warm on his face. For a while he forgot his worries, his upset about not getting a job and the rising panic that he was somehow inadequate and helpless. But nonetheless, despite his attempts to push away and forget this idea, the deep shame of what had happened today with his dad emerged in the private thorny pathway of his thoughts and brought tears scorching to his eyes and brimming over the lower rims, gushing down his face.

They had told him at school about his attitude, saying that nobody would ever employ him, and now he had to admit that they might have been right. But the call to his dad severely upset him and angered him so deeply that he felt he could barely hang on to reality and that he might go mad with the unfairness of it all. He went over the conversation in his mind. His dad had said no, he would not give him a job, but the tone of his voice was what Freddie remembered rather than the words. As he walked along, his anger subsided and was replaced with sadness at hearing the familiar voice of the father he loved saying no to him. He had heard no plenty of times before, but the no this afternoon had had such a ring of finality, as if a door were slammed shut between them that would never again be opened. His lip began to quiver. He could see no justification for the slammed door and he felt he had done nothing to deserve it. He was filled with a self-pity that melted his own heart towards himself, and now he was sobbing as he brushed passed the nettles that stung him, on the way to his destination.

This new sense of himself as a victim of injustice built up and reached a crescendo so that he nearly choked with crying and had to mop his face with the sleeve of his beige hoodie, sweeping away the tears and wiping his nose until the wrenching in his gut echoed into his mind and he was able to form the thought that he had actually been abandoned, the thought finally reaching his lips so that he said the word aloud: 'Abandoned.'

His dad had dumped him, and at this final realisation he could walk no longer. He creased over and crouched down, and if anyone could have seen him they would know that he was crying the inconsolable tears of a child who had been pushed away. His sense of the situation was perfectly correct. His father had abandoned him that day, once and for all.

Nobody was there to hear, and so his emotions simply took a hold and he bawled out loud for some minutes before he could bring himself to stand up and walk further. The birds in nearby trees that lined the pathway panicked and fluttered temporarily away until the noise was over. He walked on, and after a mile of grief had been expressed and the emotion had subsided into something different, he was able to walk calmly and with purpose as he remembered his goal for the day. He began to look out for the special hidden spot he had made for himself in the grass. By the time he got there he was feeling more peaceful, all cried out and the little place at which he had arrived was his haven.

He had been waiting all week and watching in the early evenings from this straw lookout as his dad and Alicia went for their walks together. He could lie on his stomach in the long dry grass about a foot from the edge of the river, and peer through the blades and see them go by on the opposite bank. Then he would wait half an hour or so as they walked out of sight and along to the bridge further upriver and turned around, and he would see them come into view again as they walked back the other way, holding hands, laughing, chattering, and kissing on occasion. They were carefree and at ease with each other, and were as regular as clockwork in their pattern of walking.

He smiled to himself as they ambled past today. If only they knew he was there, he thought. They were about thirty feet away across a wide part of the river. If he went downstream about half a mile he would find the bridge where they turned around to go back and he could, if he wanted, cross over and watch them from their side of the river, but he decided not to do that. That might be a bit close, and he had practised in his mind explaining such a meeting away if they were to bump into him or spot him, but it would not be easy, especially as he wasn't known for a love of the countryside or walking. He was quite sure that they went down to the bridge, and maybe hung over the wooden crossing for a minute or two, watching swans go under or fish bathing in the deep green pools lit by evening sunlight, and then turned around and walk past him but on the other side, going home probably, he thought, for their dinner, to sit together in front of the fire and enjoy belonging to one another.

That evening as he watched them he noticed that Alicia was wearing her loosely fitted cotton summer frock and that Charles was in his shirt sleeves. They were walking slower than usual and she looked a little tired, perhaps a little fatter around the waist, and he could see dark circles under her eyes, but this did not mean much to him. He did not know what he was watching at the time, that there were three of them on that walk, that they were a new family developing and enjoying life together.

If he had known the truth about the new baby, his mission would have had even more purpose. For now, he simply continued with his observations. He looked at his watch and noted the time. They were regular in their habits and they could be timed down to the half hour. By six o'clock, you were guaranteed to see them. They did not always come together. Sometimes she came on her own, but his dad never came on his own. Clearly, she was more committed to walking than he was, and Freddie calculated that his dad would come at weekends but not so often during the week.

Once they had gone and were completely out of sight, he walked the half mile further down to the bridge himself, up the few steps and onto the planks of the platform. He leaned against the wooden hand rail noting that it came up to about the height of his pelvis. Freddie took a good look down from the central point of the bridge, putting his hands on the rail and stretching them out, leaning on them and pushing hard at the structure to test the strength. The water was deep and emerald dark in the centre so that you could hardly see the bottom.

The depth might have been six feet in calm weather, but not as deep as this water could be if there was heavy rainfall. He knew that when there was a good downpour his hiding place in the straw grass on the side would not be available to him, as the river would flood her banks and spread out. He knew also that, when this happened, the waterway at its deepest almost doubled its depth, rising up to the wooden platform, even sometimes seeping over the bridge itself. The channel would then be transformed from a beauty spot fit for walking, into a place of danger, and there was a sign at both sides of the bridge that warned: 'Beware – deep water. This bridge can be slippery.' The sign showed a figure in black falling backwards, with a red exclamation mark at the side indicating quite well what could happen. Freddie knew that over the years there had been accidents at the river, perhaps up to one drowning a year, with a body floating downstream to the sea and eventually found thrown up on a beach miles away at Exmouth. Everyone knew to look there if someone, especially walkers, went missing along this river in Somerset after heavy rain.

His thoughts wandered as he walked home, and he made links with other pieces of fascinating information that became a map in his mind, his earlier upset of the day forgotten. Over the past few weeks at home he had been watching nature programmes on the television, and his mother was thrilled that he was taking an interest in natural science. Something specific had caught his attention. If June had asked him about the most interesting piece of information he had found, rather than making overblown assumptions about his desire to be a natural scientist, he would have told her – because she would never have guessed what this meant to him – about crocodiles and how they hunt their prey.

Crocodiles have developed the art of killing their victims in a fashion that causes them the least possible effort. For example, a crocodile can kill a hippo almost four times its weight. They simply clamp their jaw onto a leg, hold the creature effortlessly under the water, and fix them there until the struggling and thrashing stops because the hippo's lungs are filled with water and they are dead from drowning, whereupon the croc can engage in the reward of ripping the still warm, but newly drowned creature to pieces. For crocodiles there was no need for weapons or drawing blood. They just used water.

This documentary had inspired Freddie to think of hunters and the hunted. Today as he headed home, instead of being the wronged victim he felt that he was a hunter, wading through the long rustling grasses, with nature and the wild calling to his senses helping him to feel he belonged in the evolutionary world of passions and instincts. Despite the terrible emotions of the day, he had returned to feeling powerful and at one with the world. The sun was dipping lower and was bright orange mixed with red on the horizon between the earth and sky. It was cooler now and he shivered a little, but he felt powerful as the call of the wild was pulling him closer to her heart. He pushed forward on the path back home, down his personal private pathway now cut to his own specification, his mind filled with thoughts of the couple laughing as they had walked alongside the deep river, and he remembered the terrible blow to his pride he had suffered earlier that day and he knew what he had to do to solve his problem; he told himself that he would have the last laugh and that his mum would be proud of him.

Chapter 35

The Invitation

'Alicia.'

She, running along by the river, did not hear him. A tidal wave rolling in close behind her, water towering and curling over her head, her heart pounding, the wave rumbling relentlessly closer and closer and faster than she could run and then consuming her, crashing down, carrying her off in a torrent as it swept on and on to the sea.

'Alicia.'

She fought the unstoppable force as it crushed her under its power, gasping for breath, terrified of drowning, trying to hold on to something – the salty warmth tossing her and dragging her under, tossing her and dragging her under, and then throwing her out to deeper water. Struggling for breath, she began to shout: 'I can't swim, I can't swim!'

'Wake up, darling, it's OK.' Charles was fully awake now, concerned, shaking her arm gently. 'Goodness me, my love. I know you can't swim but it was just a dream. It's OK, I'm here.'

She opened her eyes. The nightmare had all been so real, that now the bedroom felt like the unknown compared to the dream that had felt like a part of her world. She was sobbing, still struggling to catch her breath, saturated in sweat but not, to her confusion, the water from her drowning in the sea dream. Big salty tears ran down her face. She was distraught.

He pulled her in close to his side as she shook and cried like a baby in his arms. 'It's only a dream, darling. Here, snuggle up. Come on, you're safe now. Look, I think your system is a bit topsy-turvy with the baby. You'll settle down in a few weeks and the nightmares'll go away.' He pressed her warm sleepy body against his, her damp cheeks spilling tears down his chest.

Alicia nestled into the crook of his arm and he cradled her, falling easily back to sleep, comforted by her closeness, her smell, the warmth of her smooth skin and the reassurance that she was safe.

But she did not sleep easily. He was confident that all was well, but she continued to shudder and cry quietly to herself, trying not to reawaken him, her tears falling down his stomach now; she wiped them away with the sheet, knowing that something was not right. Her dream had told her, as dreams do tell you. She did not tell Charles the whole truth about the dream, about Freddie, who had emerged from the wave before it swept her away, grabbing at her in the water and pushing her under. She did not tell him that bit – she really tried these days not to distress him with the dreams that were starting to emerge again in her mind. She had worked so hard, she had come so far, she was over all that. Yet somehow, she could not pretend to herself, and something was on her mind, trying to communicate with her, spilling again into her dreams, such as this one. She could not explain it.

Eventually, she dozed with the thought that Charles was probably right that pregnancy was a shock to the system of a forty-three-year-old woman, and this thought comforted her. She put her hand on her swelling pelvis just above her pubic bone and smiled before she nodded off, telling herself that thoughts were just thoughts and were always worse at night-time, and that all would be well in the morning and why should she be worrying about anything at this magical time.

When they awoke, the sun was shining through the gap in the curtains at Town End Cottage, and the dream had submerged itself beneath the waves of her consciousness as she got on with the routine of their day. Hungry this morning, she ate bacon and egg with toast that Charles had cooked for her while she was in the shower, but within ten minutes she threw it up, running to the bathroom and kneeling at the pedestal, grabbing her hair out of the way just before the projectile vomit splashed down the pan. Charles waited in the kitchen, squeezing the car keys in his hand, concerned for her as he heard her retching down the toilet, but he consoled himself that there was not much he could do. It was normal and natural that this should be happening now, he told himself. He put some plain biscuits in a plastic bag for her to nibble in the car, and took out a small bottle of fizzy water from the stack they had prepared in the cupboard for her to sip. These precautions usually prevented her from vomiting in the car, at least until they got to the office.

'Only another month, darling, and this should all be over. Angus said we could expect it to last three months.' Ten weeks, only another two to go.

***

Freddie had planned a cloak of invisibility. He had always found it hard to think through the consequences of his actions until their completion – even as a child he'd had this limitation. So, he thought his preparations were rather clever, and he was a little pumped up with his sense of mastery over his situation. This was partially because of the constant unmerited praise he had received from his doting mother and, in turn, his grandmother. He believed that his acts of deceit were invisible to others because they were invisible to the most powerful women in his life.

Thinking of powerful women, he had been stalking Alicia every evening on her six o'clock walk for weeks. Down to the T-junction at the end of their lane, turn left, then along the partially hidden footpath: only about fifty minutes to find his hide and settle. He knew to be there for at least fifteen minutes before the hour. He knew that rain or shine she would be out for that walk. He also had learned much about the ways of the river as he nestled in his secret straw nest. The water's pathway could be as benign as a stream or as destructive as a tidal wave – all depending on the summer rain that came down from the hills. It could be your friend with a light trickling flow when the weather was good, or your deadliest enemy in heavy rain. The river was a mirror of life itself, both giving and taking away: filling quickly within minutes after moderate rainfall, and levelling out again just as quickly as if nothing had ever changed; heightening by two feet just because of a summer deluge, and reducing to a trickle the next day, with no one ever knowing what had happened.

Over the weeks, this waterway had become *his* river in his mind – his territory. He liked the idea that he owned the river, that Alicia had no right to walk there and that he had to stop her. Just as he felt that his father was *his* father, and that she had no right to have him for herself. The idea that the river belonged to him gave him power, and rubber-stamped his authority, validating his plan.

Meanwhile, he was seen a lot at the gym. He went every day, knowing it kept him out of his mother's way when she thought he was job-hunting and busy, and there was a nice man down there who took some interest in his workout, helping him to build his biceps, and to lift weights high over his head, and to perform handclap press-ups. The man had no idea that there was some purpose to this bodybuilding, and no idea why Freddie had set a goal to lift up to nine stone in weight high above his head. 'That's the weight of the average woman,' he joked with Freddie one day. 'You'll soon be able to pick the ladies up.' Freddie laughed with him, and was comforted by the sexist narrative of entitlement that fitted with his view of the world. With his watching and observing and his muscle practising all taken care of, all Freddie had to do now was wait for the weather to turn and to see if his brother was going to help him.

***

Most brothers would assume their older brother was joking if they said 'Let's kill the stepmother,' but Anthony responded with urgency to what had been said. He knew his brother's mind, and knew that he was not joking.

'Don't be so crazy,' the fourteen-year-old warned him.

'It's not crazy, it's normal. It's normal. People have always done it. They do it all the time all over the world. In Africa or India it would be easy to kill someone and hide their body, or leave it for an animal to eat if you didn't like them. When you can't get someone to do what you want, you to get them out of your life. Killing them quickly is the best way. Nobody's going to notice. It's only in this country where the rules are so restrictive.' Freddie took a few gulps of enjoyment from his lager.

Anthony's eyes grew wide. This was seriously abnormal thinking, even by his brother's standards. Nonetheless, he scoffed with him, but hid his face away. 'Yeah, yeah, I know what you mean.' He never wanted his brother to think that he was not onside. They did not even bother lowering their voices over this conversation. They felt emboldened to be themselves when in their mother's home, and were sitting in Freddie's bedroom as he undertook his daily sit-up and press-up routine.

Anthony did not like sit-ups or press-ups. He noticed how Freddie could do loads of them and still hold a conversation as his biceps bulged under his T-shirt, and how he could clap in between. He tried to appeal to his brother.

'You don't solve a problem through murdering someone though, Freddie. She's pregnant – you know that, don't you?'

'My point exactly – we're not having that, are we? What if she has a boy? Someone to take our place, hmm? Anyway, no one will know – it'll look like an accident. It probably will be an accident. It's the perfect crime. I've got it all planned. The only person who'll see me is her and she'll be dead. And it won't exactly be all my fault; it's not my fault that she can't swim if she falls in a deep river. That's another thing that happens all the time – people accidentally drowning. I read about it. And they fish plenty of people out of that river. Look, you don't have to watch, you don't even have to come. Just keep me covered when I tell you. Give me an alibi for when it happens. Say I was with you. That's all.'

Anthony sat on his brother's bed with his face in his hands, rubbing his eyes and exhaling hard because he absolutely knew that his brother was going to try this and that there was nothing he could do to stop him. He stared at the blue carpet. The blue carpet gave relief to the turmoil in his brain, the blue carpet offered him a haven of tranquillity; if only he could disappear into the blue, blue carpet. But he could not. This was real and was going to happen and he felt sick and started to cry. He could never stop Freddie from doing anything he wanted – he never had been able to – and he knew that this time would be no different. But he also knew that this time there would be dire consequences that would play themselves out before his eyes, in which he wanted no part but in which already he was implicated. There was no escape from the plan that Freddie had shared with him unless, perhaps, he could disappear and become one with the carpet. It was hopeless. He knew that the consequences of drowning Alicia would make the rest of their lives unbearable, whereas Freddie thought that her existence was the unbearable matter. Anthony searched his mind for a solution, but there *was* no solution to Freddie. The only solution he had was his usual one, which was to keep quiet and pretend this was not happening. He mumbled to his brother that he was meeting someone and left the room.

'Don't worry, it'll be OK.' Freddie sat with his arms folded. 'I'll take care of things.'

'I'm going to forget we had this conversation, Freddie,' Anthony mumbled, as he left the room.

'That's exactly what I want. You just forget we had this conversation.'

Anthony slipped past his mother. 'What are you two boys up to?'

'Just chatting, Mum. Freddie's doing his home workout. I'm popping to practice at the golf course before dinner, OK?'

'It's so nice that you boys get along so well.'

Chapter 36

A Time to Kill

Towards the end of August the deluge came. The evenings were drawing in slightly but not so much as to render darkness by six o'clock in the evening, which was the time fixed in Freddie's mind. From the rain and the cloud of the day there was a brooding blue blackness to the sky, as if it were bruised. The water had been bucketing down like a tropical storm all afternoon. This was good for the gardens of Somerset, which were dry and parched; the rain fed the underlying water table and reservoirs, refilled the streams and rivers, and enriched the pastureland, turning the colour back to deep green. The windscreen wipers squeaked across their screen as they drove home from work, the traffic slow; Charles decided that it was not the time to walk that evening. The ground was wet and slippery underfoot, even on tarmac, and they were both tired.

'Anyway, that river will be well up. You're not walking down there.'

'No, I need my walk. It helps me relax. Come on.'

'No, darling, let's give it a miss. It's slippery and soaking, stay home.'

Her face screwed up slightly at his imperious tone, but she knew he was tired and only being protective of her. Now three and a half months pregnant and brighter by the day, she was feeling energetic again and excited by the rain. He knew it was pointless to argue. They pulled into the gravel drive of Town End Cottage, made shiny by the rain, and ran in for cover with their briefcases over their heads.

They drank their tea in the kitchen while listening to the local news bulletin, which warned of localised flooding and advised people to stay indoors. This was commonplace in Somerset. Alicia was not really listening, but instead looking out of the rain-spotted window, noticing that the downpour had reduced to a gentle patter against the glass.

'Well, put your wellingtons on if you've got to go, it'll be muddy. And keep well away from the edge, will you. That river will be wild after a day like today. I'm not sure … I think I should come with you.'

'No, it's OK. You're tired. I'm fine, and I could do with some thinking space.' She plodded upstairs and changed out of her office suit, which was getting too tight. She would have to get some new clothes. She would go walking, just a short walk; maybe twenty minutes would freshen her up, and the rain was subsiding now. That evening, she chose her other coat – the lovely bright-red Italian one made of cashmere, with a silk lining – to wear for walking and to throw over the light cotton dress and cardigan that felt so comfy after the restrictive suit, which she had thrown at the bottom of her wardrobe. Things were changing: her waist was changing, her life was changing, she did not fit her old life, she did not fit her old suit. She did not want it any more.

'Bye, darling,' she shouted as she went out of the door to Town End Cottage.

'Oh, I thought you'd gone already … are you sure you won't change your mind?'

'No, the air's so fresh – I need to be out there. It's OK. I'll be careful, I promise.'

'Hmm. Well, tread carefully it's—' The door slammed on his words. '—muddy and slippery out there.' He worried about her with water – she had never learned to swim. But he watched her buoyant step as she went down the path looking so full of life, yet very alone, and he wondered if he should change his mind and throw on a coat and catch her up. He settled for the settee watching the BBC six o'clock news with his feet up, keeping his eye on the clock – twenty minutes, she had said. He would give it half an hour.

Alicia felt that Charles was missing out on the vitality of the evening. She nearly went back for him. She did not like to be far from him these days. The electricity in the air after the rain caught her imagination. Somehow the thunder seemed to have freed up the oxygen in the atmosphere and everything smelled so clean. She felt she was experiencing something beautiful in the walk after the rain. And so, in the careless mixture of a luxurious brightly coloured coat with clumpy wellingtons, she strode down the riverside that evening breathing in sharp and intoxicating air.

The deepened river was gliding past, flowing with immense muddy torrents of water that was rushing its way down the valley from the hills and into the riverbed, filling the channel right to the edge and spilling over. The water, as was expected in these parts, had filtered down off the moors and hills following continuous and steady rain all day, and had been added to by a torrential downpour later in the afternoon. Alicia smiled at the ferocity of the water in the river she knew so well, and was somehow thrilled that it was so out of control and wild. She felt like a carefree child, and was thinking that she could not feel better, and how grateful she was for everything. Every step was energetic, and every splash with her wellington, every drip from each leaf, gave her life.

'And this looks like little Red Riding Hood.' From his lair on the opposite side of the river, Freddie spied a bright red coat on his horizon. 'And she's all alone this evening.' He could not see clearly, but was sure that the figure was Alicia. He, too, was sniffing the air, noticing that the atmosphere was fully charged and ready. And there she was, looking like a picture-book character without a care in the world. And she was alone. He crouched on his haunches in the grass and scanned each step of her approach as the gap between them reduced, his eyes darting for any important information that would inform his decision.

Silence was the key: his breathing restrained, his eyes focussed, his body still, so still, yet alert and ready, his camouflage ensuring he was invisible. Yes, it had to be now. The time would never be so perfect again, the conditions so stacked in his favour. He was ready, and she must not see him. He had been waiting there for some time that evening. He had arrived early and was annoyed by how wet he had become from hiding further back in the longer grass than usual because the water was creeping up close to his usual position. An umbrella would have made him visible and, anyway, he needed his hands to be free. His clothes were soaked, leaving him so shivery and uncomfortable that he almost thought of giving up and going home and waiting for another day, but he was held back by the idea that he would not get another chance as ideal as this. The rainfall today had been perfect, and he had been waiting for weeks for this particular confluence of natural phenomena – bad weather, saturated hills, and an overabundance of water – to occur when she was walking on her own. The environment it created was unmistakably dangerous to anyone, let alone a pregnant woman who could not swim. The weather, the river and his brother were to be his perfect alibi for a crime that would be nothing to do with him, and in which his involvement could not be proven.

The ground was slushy underfoot; she approached the towpath and took smaller steps to keep steady, and pulled her coat around her and tied the belt protectively over the growing bump of her stomach. She thought that she might not go all the way down to the bridge, as there was such a chill in the air after the absence of any sun all day. But, ambling and lost in her thoughts, refreshed by the clear air, she changed her mind and kept walking, mulling over things that needed to be done: what she would cook for dinner, imagining the wallpaper for the nursery, where to buy a cot and all that they had to do to prepare a room and the rest of the cottage for the new little person in their lives.

And then, she was at the bridge, and the water was just inches from the lowest wooden plank of the platform that joined the opposite sides of the river. She would not be going on there, she thought, and with a protective instinct kicking in she put her hand over her stomach as a chill ran down her back. She was too close to the churning muddy brew below. She turned and walked back the way she had come, a little quicker now as she felt suddenly chilled. Walking downstream with the current of the river, she noted how dull the light had become and how the birds had stopped singing for a moment and how a duck began quacking urgently from behind her as if it had been disturbed. Quack, quack, quack, quack – the sound echoed down the valley. Suddenly, it came upon her that she wanted to get home and she wanted Charlie. She began to hurry.

Just as Freddie had planned it, she did not see him spring forward from his haunches, and the thundering water masked the noise of his steps as he thudded up the path on the opposite side of the river behind her. Her hood was up so she had no peripheral vision. He reached the crossing and hid from view as best he could until she turned to make her way back, and then darted across the bridge from his side of the river and ran stealthily up behind her, trying to prevent the splashes that he made with each foot as they slapped in the mud, disturbing the duck that quacked and flapped away as if not wanting to see what was going to happen.

Before she could turn around at the sense of something looming, he lurched with his final surefooted step and grabbed her in a muscular stranglehold around her neck, choking her so that she gasped for breath, her hands automatically grasping at the thick forearm that was locked onto her. Before she had understood what was happening, he had kicked the back of her knees, buckling her legs so that she collapsed backwards. He had her weight, and dragged her on her back in a cruel hold around her neck, edging himself backwards to the bridge, pulling her along in front of him, the back of the red coat dragging in mud and water. She hadn't even had time to yell out, but when she caught a breath she screamed, and it was for Charlie, half a mile away sitting in the warm cottage with his feet up, watching the clock, awaiting her return.

She screamed his name and did not stop until Freddie could not stand it no longer and slapped his hand over her mouth. Startled, confused, and unable to conceive of the worst, she had thought at first that maybe a tree had fallen on her – but from the hand on her mouth she now knew someone was dragging her backwards.

Someone was attacking her from behind: a man. She could feel the pressure of a broad chest against her back and there were grunts that were deep-rooted in a male voice and she could smell sweat. She clawed at, and tried to bite, the large hand that stifled her yells. This was useless, and so with her one free arm she reached backwards and pulled his hair, and then her nails found a face and she ripped at the skin with all her might, instinctively reacting, prepared to do anything to save the life of herself and the baby growing inside her. Her fingers drew blood, causing him pain so that he let out a short, clumsy, unchoreographed cry of 'Ow!', and that gave the game away.

She immediately knew who this was. The pain of the stinging across his face meant that he loosened his grip, and she temporarily gained some ground under her feet and tried to stand up, but her stomach was bulky, and she was clumsy and slow to find her feet. He was onto her again, and grabbed her hair and shoved her ruthlessly towards the bridge, in front of him now, with her head down staring at the ground.

She was quite willing to accept the sharp pain in her scalp to stay exactly where she was, and she grabbed her own hair further up, close to her scalp, to pull it back. Her wellingtons made her stumble again and one fell off; her coat was already off, trampled and covered with mud. She struggled to pull back from him, reduced to fighting in her saturated cotton frock and cardigan, with bare legs and wearing only one of the wellingtons. Nevertheless, she was seizing every opportunity to stop herself moving onto that bridge.

Seeing the first buttress of the wooden structure before her, she laced her arm around the railing in a hook, catching hold of her opposite hand so that she formed a powerful loop with her upper limbs, creating a momentary anchor and turning her face away from Freddie as he tackled her locked arms. She did not wish to see his face. As the struggle continued, the water thundered relentlessly under the arch. Compared to the noise of the water, the fight was a silent movie.

He had not planned for a fight back, not thinking or accounting for the idea she was that strong or might possess the survival instincts of a pregnant woman. He could not prise her arm off the railing, or pull her hands apart, but he could not stop now because she knew who he was and what he was doing; the swift, clean execution he had hoped for became dirty, and he kicked desperately at her forearm with full force in his bulky boot, eventually catching the edge of her elbow so that the delicate nerves there exploded in pain, and she had no choice but to drop her hold.

She was a wounded animal now, and he had the upper hand as she was in deep distress at the pain searing from her elbow to her shoulder blade. She bent over, nursing the limb, but she was going to continue to fight.

He did not know this woman; she had seemed such a frail little thing, like someone you could dispose of as you would a bag of rubbish. But when he had felt the force of her body against his, he realised that she was powerful and very much alive, and he wondered if he could really extinguish her life as easily as he had imagined. He knew he had no choice, and so the fight continued, just as the water continued to rush beneath them, roaring as if cheering on the winner – whoever that was going to be.

To adjust to the immense pain in her arm, Alicia pulled herself to her feet, leaning on the handrail of the bridge for support. She looked up at him through the bedraggled rat-tails of wet hair that lay across her face, and kicked out with her remaining wellington-booted foot, her other bare foot and the handrail holding her firm. The boot caught him in the groin as he loomed in front of her, intending to grab her by the upper arms and duck down and throw her over his shoulder. He doubled over and groaned, and, seeing that her kick had hit home and hurt him, she kicked again and again.

But Freddie had muscle and height over her diminutive frame, and frantic kicking-out was no match for his bulk and the level of adrenaline that was now coursing through him. He was in danger of his whole plan failing and of being found out, and this doubled his resolve. He surged forward, ignoring the blows, knocking her boot off her foot and out of the way with his hand, catching her up and hoisting her onto his shoulder in a fireman's carry. His plan of attack was back on track.

As the water rushed by relentlessly beneath them, she had one last card to play. 'Freddie! Don't do this. Leave me. I'm pregnant. Stop now.' Even then, she was who she was. She would kill him first, before he killed her and her baby. She still was not going to let this happen.

But this was to be his moment, his plan and his river. He swung her legs over the handrail first. He had the upper hand. This had been his sole aim for weeks, months and years: everything else was failing in his life except for this. His life was going to change because of this, and he would not change his mind now. He could see she was searching desperately to find something she could grab hold of, and he couldn't let that happen. With all these thoughts in his mind he formed his conclusion, and not only let her go, but also pushed her hard, very hard, down into the water below so that she had no chance of holding on to anything.

Chapter 37

Pray for Us Sinners

As soon as she disappeared off the handrail Freddie turned his head away, because he did not want to see the result of his efforts. He did not wish to suffer from what he was going to see; he had decided there would be no consequences to doing this and so that was how it had to be straightaway, as soon as it was done. He searched for her other boot and the red coat, which were to follow her downstream. They were just a few feet away, strewn and trampled in the mud from the struggle. He threw them in after her and they fell with no sound. He looked behind him, checking whether there was any other possible evidence. Had he dropped anything? He thought not, and the water would cover his tracks; the rain falling again now was already covering the marks of the struggle in the mud. That was perfect: just as he had planned. He was out of there. He was off, out of the way.

He could hear her screaming as the water bore her away, but he would not look back – that was not the plan. A screech owl hooted deep in the woodland, and he decided not to differentiate between the screech owl and her screams – he could not be held accountable if he could not tell the difference. The screech owl confirmed his innocence for him, whereas her screams may have confirmed his guilt. His plan was that it would not take long before she was silenced. As he had seen on the TV, when crocodiles kill their prey the victims simply drown themselves in the end, trapped and flailing in the water.

He did not have much time as he was due back at his mother's. He hit the bushes with his hand as he passed them, the damp wet rustling was the focus of his attention, rather than her muffled screams as she gagged on the water. When the hell would that screaming stop? He glanced at his watch, seven minutes already. That fight had taken seven minutes. His watch was his alibi now. His watch and the time and the bushes and the screech owl and the red coat floating down the river … collectively, these hailed his complete exoneration from any act of murder. It was not him. She had fallen in.

He thought that Charles would be out looking for her by now, as he ran down the puddled path with the long, wet grass brushing at his jeans, soaking him and washing away any culpability, his heartbeat banging in his ears. He feared being seen, of being found out for something he had not done. What he had just done – the murder of this woman – had not been as easy as he had thought it would be. The struggle between them attempted to play over in his mind: her many attempts to fight back, the incredible life force that he had felt … the force that he had just snuffed out … He entertained a split second of realisation that there might be something terribly wrong about it all.

But no. He had just not planned for a fight back, and in the end he'd had to push her. She might well have fallen on her own, but he had to push her because she fought. The stupid woman had tried to spoil his plan. No wonder he'd had to push her.

Like so many other times in his life when he had acted on impulse, Freddie had just felt fleeting regret at the consequences. But somehow, in his intense yearning to be rid of this woman, he had not anticipated that extinguishing her life would continue to carry consequences for him. He had planned to walk away lightly. But now, amid his panic to get away, he had to entertain a sense of remorse about the terrible thing that had happened.

And he fought it.

Something terrible had happened, but it was nothing to do with him. He was already distancing himself from the act of murder by referring to it as something terrible, a tragic accident on a wild night. He would be able to talk in this way in the future, but for now he consoled himself with the comforting thoughts that the rain continued to fall so hard that his boot prints in the mud would be covered within minutes, and that soon he would be far enough away so that he could not hear her screams, which had now gone anyway because she had fallen in the water. Thank God it was over … that terrible, terrible accident was over, and he couldn't hear the screams any more.

***

I suppose he's running because of the rain, Abigail thought, as she watched Freddie hurry past her window towards his mother's house, his arms propelling him along, his hood up against the chill. *He's soaked through, and in an awful rush.*

She looked at the clock: 6.45 pm. Even in the light of dusk she could recognise Freddie Bradshaw, the silhouette was unmistakable; she had seen it so many times, and in that same sweatshirt with the hood. She was a little sleepy as she sipped her evening sherry, which was sweet and delicious. Gwen was out at a meeting, and she had not wanted to go as she felt a little queasy. Her friend had said it was because she had eaten too much bread-and-butter pudding and that she should rest.

They had been going to a course together and learning to use something called the internet for sending letters called emails, in which they had become interested. Gwen thought it would help them connect with people. Abigail trusted Gwen's view of the world implicitly, and although she did not quite know what she meant by 'connect', she knew that all would be well in the end. The class was for the over sixties. They were both over eighty, but she liked mixing with young people. Abigail could not really make head nor tail of the course content just yet, although Gwen seemed to be on top of things and had made an order, and there was already a large screen with a keyboard installed in the dining room on the table.

'We used to have typewriters. I'm quite happy with my Remington with the nice bell at the end of every line,' Abigail had said upon seeing the new equipment.

She wondered if she should write down a note in her diary, as Gwen would have done, noting the time that the soaking wet and tired-looking Freddie had gone past the window. And she had also noticed that he had come from the left-hand side of the T-junction and so had been down that pathway again, the one that Gwen had been so worried about. It was a most unusual sight, and she would be able to tell her friend about it in the morning. She wondered if she should jot down her note in pencil before she nodded off to sleep. She had been so tired today, so very tired.

***

Back at the bridge, the sequence of events instigated by Freddie continued to play itself out. The first few seconds after she hit the freezing water were filled with terror for Alicia, who had hoped that she and her baby would die quickly as she smacked through the surface, the shock alerting her body to the fact that she was now subject to another level of assault, this time from nature herself. The shock threw the pain of her fight with Freddie Bradshaw into immediate relief. The fight would not be the worst part of her journey that evening. But there was a pattern to the way she was drowning, and she could see that her demise would not be quick. She went under the surface, taking in great gulps of icy, muddy liquid, struggling for air and fighting to grasp onto something to help her stay afloat. Had she been in a swimming pool she would have drowned very quickly, sinking straight to the bottom, but the uneven surface of the water with its continuously swirling waves and eddies kept throwing her up to the surface. She was rhythmically bobbing up and gasping for air, and then choking and swallowing water as she was taken under again; then tossed up again for a few seconds by the thrust of the current against large pebbles, a gasp of air, and then down again.

At first terrified, then struggling, then exhausted from the fight, she found herself slipping away and surrendering to the forces of the consuming waters that had a will of their own. She resigned herself to the idea that she was done for, except that there was still breath in her body even though she was slowly drowning, and her lungs were gradually filling. Fortunately for her, as her life was held in the balance and the milliseconds went by, some of the little failings in his plan that Freddie could not have accounted for were beginning to reveal themselves.

The first of these unexpected events was the speed with which her body was hurtled downstream in the water. She covered a mile in a minute. This meant she was quickly hurtled into a different terrain, one that had been unobserved by Freddie, whose imagination could not stretch as far as a mile downstream for his victim. He had not factored in that fact that water, when rushing in a torrent, moves as fast as a car.

The second unexpected event was the fact that she entered the water wearing neither her wellington boots, nor her expensive red cashmere coat with the silk lining and hood. Both the boots and the coat would have become quickly waterlogged had she still been wearing them, increasing her weight in equal proportion to the level at which she would be dragged down into the water, all according to Archimedes' principle. As it was, her attire had been reduced to a simple cotton shift dress and a light cardigan. This was something of an advantage when it came to buoyancy.

These were not, though, the most helpful small events that changed the course of the whole evening and undid Freddie's plan, because of course, none of these things matter if you cannot swim.

There was a series of additional things which occurred that evening, that even she could not have anticipated, and they were greatly to her advantage. The first, was that she knew the course of the river by heart as it flowed downstream. This lower part of the river was her river, whereas the part of the river upstream from the bridge, where she had been thrown off like a bag of rubbish, could be considered as Freddie's river. He did not know her part of the river and had not thought to explore her world. She knew every little trick and turn of that waterway, having taken in the information unconsciously during her many hours of walking. The river downstream was her friend, not her enemy.

So, as she grew used to the rhythm of being thrown upwards for air by the current and then taken down again to struggle and choke, she began to realise that she was on her back, and that, in between the ups and downs of the struggle with the great firmament, she was actually … floating … and floating was familiar. She could not swim, but she had faith that she could float for a few seconds, giving her time to gulp in some air. She knew, too, that the course of the river was about to change as she neared a familiar crop of rocks that spread across the width of the entire riverbed; these usually formed a pleasant distraction as water bumped and frothed against them. They were often completely uncovered when the water level was low, enabling children to walk across and climb up on them in the sunshine, but even when the water was at its highest levels, their smooth domes still held their heads up from the surface. These rocks, she knew, would stop her.

Towards them she hurtled in the choking and reviving cycle, on her back, in and out of the water, panicking, struggling, flailing and still reaching out with her arms like a child asking for someone to pick her up and rescue her. She was as helpless to the underwater forces as any infant, gasping now for even a millilitre of air. But she knew that the rocks were coming up fast. If she smashed her head on a boulder at the speed she was moving, she could be killed instantly – on the other hand, the rocks would stop her from travelling, and perhaps stop her from going under again if she could hold onto something or stop for a moment to catch her breath.

The question was, which part of her body would be smashed against the hard-domed surface first, and she did not mind what the answer to this question was, but she knew that her head would be the most vulnerable part. Thoughts of protecting the baby had slipped into second place, and she did not think of anything other than saving herself at that point; there was no room in her mind for anything other than breathing.

In the next split second she met the rocks, and in a reaction that she could not have planned she automatically raised her arm above her head so that it would hit first. A searing pain travelled through her body as she crashed against the first boulder, her femur, her thigh hitting first. Her body swung unpredictably to the side, so that she smashed into a second boulder with the side of her thigh rather than with her precious skull. She lay widthways across the river, wedged between the boulders, the water crashing around her. But the rocks gave her leverage to raise her head. This was a resting point, and she caught some breath at least. The water was naturally shallow here as it flooded outwards into the fields, reducing somewhat the force of the flow from the rapids upstream where their channel was narrower. The water was silken and lazier than it had been, offering her a rest and, with effort, she could keep her nose just above the flow and gasp in lungfuls of air. She was now more afraid that her leg was smashed to pieces than she was of drowning.

If the truth were known, she had half-drowned, her lungs so full of water that she was only semi-conscious. But lungs are remarkable in their desire to inflate, and still inflate they did, with the small amount of oxygen coming in now through her nasal passage. Her leg was, as she feared, smashed to pieces – her femur had cracked – and her collarbone had also snapped like a twig with the force of the impact against boulder, but she had at least stopped for a second.

To add to her good fortune of encountering natural occurrences in the right place at the right time, a willow tree that she had often considered with admiration; its majestic ability to straddle both land and water appeared to want to offer something to her in return for her frequent compliments, and from its branches, constantly soaked and strengthened, weeping fronds dipped into the water and brushed against her. She grasped them with her remaining good hand and held on with all her might, entwining the fronds around her forearm, the flexible tubers of the outermost branches of the tree with their little shoots, each with a sprouting leaf, catching and entwining through her fingers, letting her hold firm while her body spun round and round, pushed by the current so that her arm was bound completely in the branches as if they formed a rope. She hung there, freezing, semi-conscious, her dress up to her chest, her limp, broken leg dangling on the rock. And in her semi-conscious state she knew that she did not have very long to live, and so she did the only thing left to her that day – she muttered in her mind a prayer that she remembered from her convent school days. It was the prayer she said every day in assembly, and the one that she spoke when Father Martin had given her penance after confession. Again and again she muttered it, and was brought comfort:

'Hail Mary,
Full of grace,
The Lord is with thee.
Blessed art thou among women,
And blessed is the fruit of thy womb, Jesus.
Holy Mary, Mother of God,
Pray for us sinners,
Now, and at the hour of our death.
Amen.'

Her muttering continued, and for a time she was carried on the wings of prayer to a place where she was no longer cold, no longer in pain and no longer hanging from a willow tree that was entangled around her forearm, with her circulation gradually being cut off. She had prayed herself into oblivion.

Chapter 38

Finding Juniper

Jenkins was out with his master, but he was not herding sheep. He was looking for cows. They had seen the herd down by the river earlier that evening, and had one missing. At the farm they couldn't find her anywhere. For some reason, the beasts had taken to paddling in the river recently, all going in one after the other. Most unusual to see cows paddling, people thought. Concerned ramblers who knew the pasture and who had wondered why a herd of cows would be frolicking in the water, had called the farmer from the phone box up on the main road. But no, they were fine, the farmer explained – they'd just got into the habit of taking to the river when they were hot. They had found a comfortable pathway down to a shallower, broader part of the waterway by the rocks, and seemed to like dipping their hooves. That afternoon there had been twelve of them down there, happily sploshing along, mooing and exploring the stony ground in the shallows, egging each other on to go further in, one going up to her knees. The steady rain hadn't bothered them all day, but then there had been that torrential downpour at four o'clock, coming over in a thunderstorm, and as soon as that started they were out, slipping as quickly as they could up the previously sodden but rough slope that had quickly become slick with mud.

As dusk started to fall at around six, the river was at its fullest and the cows would not go near the edge of it again. Their fun was over for the day. The farmer decided to get them in for the night, and they even seem pleased to see Jenkins the dog, whom they usually surveyed with disdain. Unlike sheep, they could give him a nasty kick if they wished, but they knew when they had to be herded, and today was such a day. They would accept the authority of the fretful canine because they knew their farmer did not want to leave them out on a night like this. Later, as they were going into the barn, that he realised that one was missing. Juniper, his youngest heifer. He had wondered why the herd kept bellowing: they knew that she was still in the water.

Jenkins walked with the farmer who was wearing a rubber mackintosh, and waders that reached his waist and were held in place by braces, which he had worn in case he had to go in after this stupid cow. The dog was looping back every hundred yards or so to be by his side, sniff and wag his tail, and then go forward again, nimbly leaping the puddles that his master navigated with his heavy boots. Half a mile downriver, soaked through to the skin, the dog changed his behaviours and began to sniff the ground near the water, his snout low as he manoeuvred through the mud as if he were hoovering up with his nose. His master watched him. This meant something coming from the dog he knew so well.

When the dog's ears pricked up from the low vibration of a plaintive voice barely audible under the sound of the rushing river, the farmer knew that the dog had found something interesting, and felt a surge of relief – he was sure that it was his cow. Jenkins increased his activity and started to go mad, barking and wagging his tail and worrying at the water's edge, going back and forth between the man in the mackintosh and the riverbank, jumping up and wagging his tail. 'Come on, boy, away,' said the farmer. 'What's got into you?'

The dog for sure had spotted something, and he was not letting go of his instinct that a creature was in the water. He started to whine and entered into the river in a more defiant way up to his chin, which would force his master, eventually, he knew, to go in after him. They worked together, these two: where the dog was, the man would follow, and vice versa. The man's deeper instinct told him that his dog and friend never behaved like this for nothing, and so eventually he walked towards the water, gathering speed as he moved, his eyes straining in the fading light as he started to realise that something must be very wrong. He got out his torch from his back pocket and shone the beam towards the black river, straining his eyes to see, and then he, too, heard the sound that his dog had heard. But this was not his cow – it was a human moaning. 'Not another body in this damned river.'

He was up to his waist now, panicking, as this kind of sound from the water could only mean one thing. In the yellow torchlight, he saw the outline of a woman just keeping herself above the water by holding willow branches which were wound so tight around her forearm that it was nearly as blue as her face; the other arm hung helplessly by her side, and she dangled at an angle from the arm straight above her head, her bedraggled hair hanging at the same angle as the opposite arm, and her dress barely covering her body. He was startled by this pathetic sight and the immediate accompanying thought that she had hung herself. He began to feel as if he were in a disaster movie and, although the shock of the sight of this hanging body sent his world into slow motion, his farmer's instinct to preserve and protect even the last strands of life in any mammal made him rush forward to try and grab her, his first job being to hold the weight of the body on his shoulder while he was unwound her arm from the willow. He did not want her slipping back under into the swirling eddies that now lapped around them. 'How did you get yourself tangled up there, little maid?' he asked, using the traditional Somerset term for a female that was so instinctive to him. No response.

The drive to save this defenceless pitiful creature was overwhelming, and he felt compelled to get her onto the bank, although he was sure from what he had seen and felt from the weight on his shoulder that she was already dead. She hung limp and heavy, and farmers believe that limpness in a creature does not bode well. She was slumped over his shoulder in a manner that would have befitted any one of his newborn calves. The water was agile and reacted quickly in these parts, and he was hopeful at least that they were no longer fighting a torrent. As he moved forward, gracefully pushing through the water, he thought there could be no more surprises for him that night, but he was wrong, and he was completely startled as the corner of his eye caught another face in the undergrowth and dark shadow of the bank.

At first, he thought with some dread that it was another human being, but from the large head and snout and the pitiful sound as she recognised and called to him, he realised that it was his missing cow, Juniper, caught fiercely in the brambles at the edge, the brambles both keeping her a prisoner, but at the same time holding up her head. She was only ten feet downstream, and he had already passed her without realising while wading upstream to follow the sound of the as yet unknown woman. It seemed that the growth by the river had entrapped and saved two creatures that day. 'Uh, Christ, Juniper.' He looked at his beautiful creature. And it really upset him. An anonymous human he might cope with, but the sight of his beloved young heifer half drowned was beyond him.

His troubles and the problems he had to solve in the following few minutes as he stood in the river had just doubled, and would tax him to limits he did not yet know that he had. Somehow, he knew he could get whoever this was on his shoulder out and onto the bank, but there was no way he could shift a fully grown, if yet young, cow. He was bothered in a way that he had, up until that point, not been bothered. Being a farmer, he was a practical man and knew he could only do what he could do at any one moment in time, and he was used to emergencies from animals getting themselves into fixes. His aim was always to save life, but it was also to keep the life in his charge fit and comfortable. For now, he could only honour the oath to keep these two wretched mammals alive. He could not make them comfortable, not being out here with all this rain.

Jenkins now had a fix on Juniper, and was barking at her from the water's edge. The young heifer may have been comforted by this. She knew that Jenkins had authority in a difficult situation. She also knew that her farmer would get her now that he had found her.

Although he was a strong man, used to carrying weight, he was glad to let go of the burden of a waterlogged woman, and he unceremoniously dumped her on the riverbank, flopping her onto the soggy grass before he hauled himself out. He felt the weight of her body hit the ground and cringed, as he was concerned it would hurt her further if she was not dead already, and if the baby were not dead along with her for, if he were any judge of animal husbandry, he could already see quite clearly from her semi-naked body and tell from the memory of her stomach pressing on his shoulder, that not only was she a woman, but she was also very definitely pregnant. Still, he could only do what he could do, and the best he could achieve for now was to check that she was breathing, get the water out of her lungs, and then leave her on her side so that he could run to a phone box and make an emergency call for the air ambulance. He did not have time to consider her face, which was covered with wet hair that also fell like fingers of seaweed across her neck and shoulders. He pulled her up and hooked her over his arm, and slapped her on the lungs from behind, just as he frequently did with his newborn calves that needed reviving. She vomited up pints of filthy water, and he knew that was a good sign.

'Come on, girl. The more of that we get out of you, the better you're going to do. Out with it.'

She vomited, retching and making a pleading sound for him to stop, but he could not stop yet. He knew this. Expelling the water seemed to bring some life back to her, and maybe more oxygen into her lungs.

Once he was satisfied that as much water as possible had released from her system, he tried to lay her down more carefully, attempting to find the balance between urgent action and sensitivity to her obvious condition. As he turned her over, he recognised her face but could not quite place her. Where he had seen that face before seemed to be of little importance at that moment. Laying her in the recovery position on her left side – as it said to do in all the first aid manuals – and taking off his soaking coat, he carefully covered up the woman, and thought that the coat would at least protect her from the wind. As he covered her over, he realised who she was: it was Alicia Bradshaw from upriver.

'Always walking around here. Fancy coming out on a night like this.' He ran to the nearest phone box, his legs plodding, plodding along at an even pace – slow, but faster than he had ever run, every muscle in his body seeming heavy and weighing him down.

He had instructed Jenkins to 'Stay with her, boy,' and the dog had wagged his tail. As soon as his master was out of sight, the dog busied himself in a ritual circling of the body, sniffing the ground around her and worrying around the area as if to check for any danger. Then he approached Alicia and began to lick her face, in as passionate a way as a dog could ever lick – perhaps to warm and revive her.

Meanwhile, Juniper waited benignly in the brambles, knowing that having set eyes on her master she would be recovered eventually. She was very cold by then, but they were all cold and wet. Jenkins kept barking at her, and for the first time in her bovine existence Juniper was glad to know that he was there, and knew that if she got out of this river she would never kick him again.

Ten minutes later, Jed Cooper, Ruby Cooper's dad – for that was who he was, the farmer rescuing Alicia that night – was running up the main road to the red phone box. He dialled 999 and did not even give the operator time to speak:

'You're gonna need the air ambulance up here – Loxley Meadow, where the river widens and runs into the fields. I'll go back there and shine a torch – there's plenty of room to land, they were up there this spring with another one of those ramblers, broke his leg. Better hurry, mind, I think she's half drowned if she's not dead already. Bring one of those tinfoil covers, its bloody freezing out here. In fact, bring two – I've got a cow in the water.'

'I'm sorry, sir, can you please repeat? What else is in the water?'

But he was gone, plodding heavily back to Loxley Meadow, fully expecting to find the woman who was covered in his mackintosh dead from cold by now. This pragmatic and kindly man was upset and concerned. He had more reason to be concerned than others, for he liked Alicia Bradshaw and her husband Charles a lot, and of course his daughter Ruby had worked for them for six years. They were almost part of the family as far as he was concerned. But there was little room for sentimentality in his life. He was a practical man. Just the man to meet after someone had tried to murder you.

'What next, what next … let's see if she's still breathing. Christ Almighty, she's turned blue. Holy Christ, help me.' The dog, anxious to hear his master's now distressed voice, started barking, and pawing the ground.

'What was it you had to do? Pinch the nose, breathe into her mouth, pump the heart one, two, three, then down again and breathe … dear God, help me, please.'

He had her vomit around his mouth and he had to spit the bitter substance away but, in the panic, he probably swallowed it. He didn't really care. He was fretful now: 'I should never have left her … I did the wrong thing … Breathe, pump, pump, pump … Breathe pump, pump, pump. He did not even hear the air ambulance helicopter as it chopped the air, and the sound of chopping chopping chopping blades grew louder until it touched down in Loxley Meadow behind him. He had gone into a trance of breathing and pumping her chest.

The crew dragged him off Alicia. They could not get him to hear them. 'It's OK, mate, we're here now. Take it easy.'

He was sobbing and still counting: 'One two three, one two three …'

One of the crew handled Jed while the others dealt with Alicia and tried to orientate themselves to what was happening. The paramedic could see her eyelids fluttering.

'Alright, love, speak to me … what's your name? … Come on … that's it.'

She threw her head to the side and vomited from the side of her mouth, throwing up pints more of river water and vomit from the pit of her stomach.

'Can you tell me where it hurts you most, love? Looks as if she's pregnant.' He told his colleague. 'Better watch what we give her, there's a broken femur, looks like that clavicle is broken too, but she rolled over to vomit so I think her back is OK. I think we can get her on the stretcher.'

Alicia fainted again. The paramedic took her vital signs and found a pulse, covering her in a foil blanket and giving her oxygen to replenish her system. She was breathing, and it looked as if the resuscitation had worked. He was more worried about the farmer, who seemed to be sobbing and hallucinating, calling out that there was a cow in the river. And then the dog started to show signs of distress that his master was upset, barking, licking the farmer's hand anxiously, and then baring his teeth at the paramedic who was trying to contain him. So much for them to handle that evening: emotion, a half-drowned pregnant woman in a state of hypothermia, an older gentleman dressed as a farmer in an altered state and a dog who wanted to warn them off. All the time the helicopter was whirring and chopping the air so that they had to keep their heads low to avoid the thrust, the pilot ready to take off again as soon as they could. 'Let's get her properly wrapped up and checked over, and then leave her with me – you take care of him,' the paramedic said to his colleague.

They tried to establish exactly what other parts of Alicia's body were damaged before they lifted her onto the stretcher. Confident that it was not a back injury, they could rush now to the air ambulance to get her into the dry and out of the pouring rain that was continuing to slash onto her face, making her blink her eyes. After the dose of oxygen appeared to have brought her back to consciousness, they were able to ask her again about the pain in her body, concerned about levels of morphine due to the pregnancy.

Content that Alicia's condition was stable, they were more worried now about Jed, and talked with the police who had just arrived; the headlights of their Land Rover had appeared on the horizon and were now shining onto the scene, adding to the convergence of concerned emergency services. The officers took feedback from the lead paramedic as to what they had understood so far.

'O.K. We've got a woman who appears to have fallen in the river upstream, seems to have been pulled out by this local farmer who was reviving her when we arrived. She's responded to oxygen, she's approximately three and a half months pregnant, badly smashed femur and collarbone. We need to get her in, and we're leaving now. We'll leave it to you boys to work out what's happened. She's managed to tell us her name; she's Alicia Bradshaw and she lives upstream in Town End Cottage … you're gonna have to work on that.'

The officer took notes, and said: 'That's Jed Cooper – I'd know that dog anywhere. Here boy, here boy. He'd be the right man to get someone out of the water.'

'Well, we need to get him home. He seems to think there's a cow in the water upstream.'

'Well if Jed says so, then there probably is.'

The paramedics were not having much luck persuading Jed out of his rubber waders, which were holding water that was keeping him cold. He was shivering and crying and not making any sense at all. He seemed to be delirious, referring to a cow in the water, and fighting them to get back into the river rather than out of it. The police officers watched for half a moment before a decision was made to get him in the car and get him home with his dog, where later he would tell his wife, Joan, about the cow, and she would send their farmhands with the Land Rover to pull Juniper out and put her husband's troubled mind at rest.

The helicopter hovered momentarily above the ground, tipped its nose in a salute to the earth, and swooped off into the starless night.

Chapter 39

If Only …

The sodden kitchen door thudded shut at Town End Cottage, as Charles closed it behind him in his soaking raincoat and then ran and stumbled to answer the phone. The shrill ring only added to the confusion that was emerging for him, and he blundered forward to the lounge in his wellingtons to pick up the receiver, treading mud and rainwater into the carpet. He glanced at the clock: 7.10 pm. Maybe this was her? Maybe she'd gone for shelter somewhere and was calling him to fetch her. When she had not returned after forty-five minutes he had been down to the bridge, but could not see her and now his mind was racing everywhere. Where the hell was she?

He had heard the helicopter further downstream as he hurried back to the cottage, but it did not enter his consciousness that the chopping sound reverberating down the valley path had any relevance to his situation, and even when he saw its lights lifting into the sky as he was hurrying back from a mile upstream, he did not think of it as part of a scenario that was unfolding that might include him. He would not have wished to imagine himself or his life to have anything to do with the ominous sound of the blades and the noisy engine that were working hard to keep the helicopter airborne on such a threatening night.

The idea had not occurred to him that his wife might nearly have died in the short time that she had been absent, or that she was on board that helicopter, unconscious and wrapped in tinfoil to stop her from dying of hypothermia. He thought that he must have missed her, although he did not know how, and had hurried back to the cottage where he was sure she would be sitting in the warm and waiting for him. Maybe she would be taking a hot bath. For the first thirty-five minutes after she had cheerfully gone on her way in her boots that were slightly too big and her favourite red coat, he had dropped off to sleep. He had waved through the window, still wondering if he should go too. The light had been gently fading, but she had blown a kiss to him and had appeared so vibrant and full of energy that he stopped worrying and sat back to let go of the day and all its myriad of challenges.

He had a few moments of rest from all this, but had woken with a start and stared at the clock and, uncomfortable for some unknown reason, he had called out to her upstairs, sure that she would be back and changing out of her wet things, but she was not there. Without thinking, he had made himself a cup of tea and called Ryan, as he remembered he had promised to confirm a joint appointment for tomorrow, and then looked at his watch. She had been out for too long: over forty-five minutes for what she had said would be half an hour. Something was not right and, adding to his torment, it had grown dark in the short time that he had been asleep.

He threw on his outdoor coat and wellingtons and ran upstream to the bridge and back. The whole landscape was empty, nothing to be seen or heard bar the torrent of water rushing downstream. Now, on his return to the homestead, the phone was ringing and he grabbed it aggressively because he feared that something sickeningly unusual was happening, and he did not know what it was, and he did not like these sounds; first, the helicopter chopping and disturbing the night sky, and now the phone with its shrill tone cutting through the blanket of calm in the cottage. Each sound meant something, but he wanted them to mean nothing. He shivered, taut and uncomfortable with cold as rain trickled down his face. He rebuked the receiver. 'What is it?'

'Mr Bradshaw?'

'What is it?' His knuckles were tight as his hand gripped the receiver.

'It's the desk sergeant at Taunton Constabulary, sir.' The desk sergeant received no reply, and so he continued. 'We've got your wife at Taunton General. She's been pulled out of the river. Jed Cooper found her and identified her as Alicia Bradshaw. She was picked up by the air ambulance. We need you to get down to the hospital. We have an officer waiting.'

'Identified her, what the hell do you mean?'

'She's alright, sir, but if you could get down to the hospital as soon as possible and ask for Intensive Care. Do you have anyone with you in the house?'

'No.'

'Ordinarily we'd send an officer round, but I'm afraid we're rushed off our feet this evening with the amount of flooding incidents due to the heavy rain. Can you make your own way there? The motorway is clear, so you should be alright.'

'Yes.'

He did not even place the phone on the hook, but hurled it onto the settee. He had not been to Taunton General Hospital for ten years. Ten years, another lifetime ago when Freddie had fractured his leg after falling out of a tree. He had told Freddie not to climb so high in that tree, just like he had told Alicia not to walk down by that river tonight, and both times he was the one having to rush to hospital.

Christ, does this bloody hospital car park have to be so full? No, I can't find change for a parking ticket, and I don't care anyway.

He slammed the car door and was running to accident and emergency.

How could she have fallen in the river? I told her not to go near the edge. How could she have been so stupid? His internal tone was shifting from angry to questioning, as his mind tried to work out what had happened.

At reception, he was directed to Intensive Care down what seemed to be an interminably long and very empty corridor, with a shiny floor in which he could have seen his face had he stopped to look, each footstep echoing as he travelled for what felt like a mile, passing various doors off to the left and right. It was like being in a bad dream with no ending, and then he found the sign for Intensive Care and pressed the buzzer for entry, not knowing who would answer. The door opened automatically, and then he knew the truth – this was a dream that *had* no ending, and he was in it. He was met at the central desk: 'Alicia Bradshaw, please,' he told them, as if he had just come to collect her, which he tried to convince himself that he had. The ward sister came out from behind the desk and guided him to a small side room. He expected to see Alicia in the room, but there were only two seats – armchairs. She sat with him.

What was this? Why did she need to sit with him in armchairs? He'd seen this in films. They take you to one side to tell you the bad news. Was this to tell him … 'What's going on?' He was about to protest about being there, when the nursing sister began her delivery:

'We've got her body temperature back to normal, but she's going to be quite poorly for a few days and we need to monitor her.' The ward sister spoke to him as if he knew what had happened. He did not know what had happened. He did not want to know. 'She's going to be quite poorly for a few days.' What was that supposed to mean? *Please don't tell me that.* The nurse, born to care for others in practical ways rather than psychological ways, took no heed of the shadow emerging over him, and continued her confession of all the facts.

'We need to watch that she doesn't get an infection from that water – we must keep an eye on that. Pneumonia is the biggest risk, but if we get over those two barriers she should be in the clear. Her upper right leg, her right arm, and her collarbone are broken – her leg in about three places – and she has some cuts, of course, but these are not our concern now. We've got her on an antibiotic drip and she's still taking in some oxygen.'

He did not want to hear these words. 'What about our baby?' He did not want to know, but he may as well hear it all now. His tone flattened.

'Well, we don't know for the minute. The maternity unit will bring a mobile scanner down tomorrow morning. They won't do it tonight. We want her to rest. There's nothing that can be done for twenty-four hours. For now, she's comfortable at least, and we want to get her through the night with as little interruption as possible. We estimated she's about three and a half months, is that right?'

Charles nodded. He had heard the last few sentences, knowing that they mattered, but he continued to watch her face. Her face was not without hope, and so he would be not without hope. He was not sure what to care about now. But the interminable delivery continued.

'We've adjusted the medication according to the pregnancy, but she has to have the antibiotics, I'm afraid. They'll plaster her leg tomorrow as well.' The voice trailed off, and it was possible that the informative aria was coming to its closing stanza. All his anger now transmuted into one big question: Why? What the hell had happened? She only went for a walk. But there was more. She was going to say more. He certainly did not want to hear this.

'The police will be in to talk to you, but it was a good job that farmer was there. She would have been dead in another ten minutes.'

The police? A farmer? A smashed leg? Infection? And only two hours ago she was just going out for an evening walk. None of the dots would join up on his picture of the evening.

As he entered the single-bedded ward in Intensive Care, and the door sucked closed with its rubber seal, Charles stepped over the threshold of yet another world, and this world, a world within a world, told him the complete story of what had happened to Alicia that evening. The smells and sounds told him before he could even see her – disinfectant combined with a machine that spelled out every second of her heartbeat in a beep … beep … beep … beep. He immediately knew that it was very important to hear this beep, and that there must be no interruption. His hearing would be on alert from this moment onwards. Then his vision took in a small body under the bedclothes, looking childlike and crumpled, and he thought that they must be mistaken and this could not possibly be her, and was momentarily relieved as he was sure that they would soon apologise for a ridiculous mistake. But as he moved closer he saw her familiar face, and he was distraught as he reached out tentatively and touched the fingers of her hand. There was not much of her body not connected to a machine, wires leading everywhere to the heart monitor. There it was – that was the centre of everything now, with its continuous beeping that triggered a flash and a disturbing streak of green lightning across a small screen with every beat. This, combined with a plastic tube up each nostril for oxygen, a catheter bag hanging from the bed, and a cannula stuck into the vein in the top of her hand. This was her now, not the woman he said goodbye to two hours ago.

'She won't be getting up to go to the toilet in that state, so we thought it best to catheterise her.' The ward sister, with another volley of words, still nattering on as if he knew what she was talking about.

He knew he should be more like a man about this, but all veneer was gone at the sight of her, and he could not stop the tears that welled from his eyes and streamed down his face when he saw the harm that she had come to in what seemed like the blink of an eye. One minute the world was perfect, she slipped out of the front door in her red coat, and the next minute she looked like this in a hospital bed. He knew immediately this had not been an accident, not with this amount of harm. He heard the nurse continue to offer further explanations …'

'Her heart stopped beating at one point in the helicopter, and she had to be resuscitated. It was only for a few seconds, but she had to be revived for the second time; Jed Cooper had also given her resuscitation before the helicopter arrived.'

As the ward sister continued her monologue in the distance of his mind, his eyes took in the picture of his wife.

Her skin was grey in tone, her pupils large from the drugs, her hair was stuck round her head, and she could not return his grasp, but she responded by fixing her eyes on his face as he kissed her forehead. 'Oh. My darling, what on earth has happened to you? I am so sorry. I should have come with you.' He was far from an angry man now.

Where was the scolding she was going to receive? She watched his face and she knew that he would be tortured by the sight of her. It was urgent that he should understand what had happened, in case she died. She thought that she might quite easily be carried away, and that the task of killing might yet be completed. She knew that she was cheating death at this moment, and maybe she would love for it all to have been finished, because in this living dream she could see there was a big fight ahead and she was not sure that she was quite ready for it … not yet, anyway.

Through the mists of conscious and unconscious she had already urgently conveyed to the doctors that somebody had thrown her into the river and that it had been no accident, and their suspicions had been aroused enough for them to have spoken to the police. With more thought for her husband than for herself, she had already concluded that if this was bad news for her as she lay here on what might be her deathbed, the news would be much worse for him. Her bones might mend if she recovered, and her mind would repair, but the conflict that he was about to have to deal with when he discovered what his son had tried to do to her tonight would, she realised, torment him for the rest of his days. But he had to know.

He stroked her hand as lightly as he could, and forced himself to stop staring at her and get back in control, so that she could feel his intention to repair all of this. He would put this right. He read her mind without her speaking. 'We're not sure about the baby yet. You have to rest. They can take a look tomorrow, but can't scan you in this state.'

'The baby's OK,' she said.

He did not want to upset her, but it was hardly likely to be the case. He went on stroking her hand in response. 'What happened, darling, can you tell me?'

He had to know. She focussed her eyes on him. If she died in the next moment, he still had to know. She had to tell the truth, because the truth was all she had at this moment: 'Thrown in … Freddie … pushed me in the water.'

Beep, beep, beep, beep, beep, beep.

If the heart monitor had stopped then it would have been because his own heart had stopped. But the machine did not stop. It carried on, and it told him in that moment that her heart was beating. This was all he had to hold on to. The beep, beep, beep and the sight of the green signal across the screen of the monitor.

Beep, beep, beep. His son, she said, had tried to kill her.

Beep, beep, beep, beep. But she was lying here before him now and she was breathing, and the heart monitor was speaking to him.

Beep, beep, beep. And it was OK, because Freddie had failed, and she was not dead.

Beep, beep. She was still alive.

Beep, beep, beep.

She began to cry, but it hurt her to breathe, let alone expel emotion. They did not know yet that two of her ribs were also broken, but she did. They hurt more than anything, especially when she took a deep breath.

He could see it was hurting her. 'Don't cry, don't cry. Try not to think about it now. Just rest. I'll be dealing with it. Whatever has happened, I will be dealing with it. I heard you. It was Freddie. It's all mine. You rest now.'

Initially, he had not let this information pervade his consciousness. OK, an assault … he could manage that … but Freddie? Surely to God, no, don't let that be true. He had to ask one question.

'Freddie, darling … how do you know?' Her face confirmed the answer. She knew.

He did not have time to think this through further before the ward door swung open, and then swung and sucked closed as a figure swept into the room in a white coat, someone who clearly, from the confidence of their stance, felt that they had the right to be there at that time with no announcement or without any question whatsoever. It was the yellow paisley bow tie that emblematised the importance of the Intensive Care consultant, David Whitelaw, who strode with authority over to Alicia's bed, not even introducing himself. From that moment onward, David Whitelaw was destined to play a role in their lives, and he played for Alicia and Charles the reassuring role of consultant – he was the person in the room who held the most qualifications, the most experience, and the one who had overseen the most live patients as well as dead patients. He was the man to watch, without question. He was not concerned with politeness or emotion, which were the domains of his nursing and auxiliary staff, along with the patients. He was concerned with the science that kept people alive. And the condition of the person in this bed was a moderate challenge to his skill, even though her husband thought it must have been the worst case he had ever seen. It was not.

Charles sat up immediately; this was no time for indulging in his personal pain. He had never been so pleased to see someone who seemed to know what they were doing. Whitelaw ignored him and looked at Alicia's vital signs, which were of far more interest to him, reading her chart from the end of her bed, then moving up to her, looking in her eyes and listening to her chest.

'Not out of the woods yet, young lady. Forty-eight hours and we should know. We'll soon have you well, and we'll keep you out of pain till the morning.'

Alicia heard these words and tried to ask him about her baby, mouthing the word 'Baby' in a questioning tone, but sleep came to reach for her and she did not resist the invitation to sink gratefully into the arms of a delicious cocktail of soporific morphine. She fell into the last comfortable sleep she would have for some weeks while Charlie reclaimed his sensibilities by talking to Dr Whitelaw, although he did not pronounce many words before he became the listener rather than the speaker. Most conversations with Whitelaw ended with him having the final say.

'I've spoken to the police, Mr Bradshaw. She says it was an assault. She's been saying it from the minute she came in … says it was someone she knew, called Freddie. The police will be here any minute and I think they'll want to talk to you. I don't think they're going to get much sense out of her for now – she's well into the arms of Orpheus, which is probably for the best. That leg is badly smashed. We haven't been able to plaster her up yet, need to wait until orthopaedics have looked in the morning. For now, it's all about pain reduction, and we must hope she doesn't get an infection or pneumonia. I can't guarantee the outcome, but she's a healthy woman – every reason to be hopeful. We'll try and scan her tomorrow to see what's happened to the pregnancy. I'm sorry, I might as well be straight with you – we may need to be grateful that *she* survived, let alone her baby.'

As awful as they were to hear, Charles was reassured by these words. 'No, I understand … Thank you for helping her.'

'We can give her morphine for the pain, it won't cause birth defects if the baby does survive. We can't leave her with that amount of damage and no painkiller. It'll help her sleep, and while she is resting hopefully her body will recover itself. There are only certain antibiotics we can give due to the pregnancy, but we'll keep monitoring to see what's happening, and do all we can to pull them both through. I'm afraid we're not seeing the worst of it right now. It may take twenty-four hours to show, but I think it's likely she will become very ill because of being in that water and taking so much of it into her lungs.'

Charles realised that this was the end of the conversation. He was grateful for a lull in proceedings. He sat by Alicia's bedside wondering which fact he needed to attend to first, trying to unravel the competing thoughts pressing on him: the baby may still survive, she is going to get more ill, and his son had tried to kill her. He did not know which was worse. He was utterly disbelieving of the idea that Freddie had finally crossed the Rubicon and attempted to murder his wife, but his overwhelming fear was that he might lose Alicia, and he was acutely aware that she would be devastated if she survived and lost the baby. Right now, whether or not she remained pregnant was not something he could think about. Perhaps men, who don't carry babies inside them, can have this degree of distance from a growing foetus. He simply sat and stared at the curve in the bed as her stomach rose and fell with the rhythm of her sleep, and this movement, in turn, corresponded with the beep, beep, beep, from the heart monitor, which in the silence was both a blessing and a curse.

Chapter 40

Life Held in the Balance

Charles thought for a moment that she still looked pregnant, and without realising it he was rubbing his own lower abdomen, his hand smoothing round and round as if he were reassuring himself that there might be a baby inside one of them, either him or her, he did not mind. He did not know how long he sat beside her bed with his head bowed, holding her bruised hand and stroking her knuckles with his thumb. This was the defining moment for him, the one that set in place the rest of his life. Something was emerging from now, something important he had learned from boyhood about these moments. 'Dear God, please let her live, please let her live. I will do anything, absolutely anything. Please let her live and let her baby live … I don't deserve life, but she does. I implore you from the bottom of my heart: please let her live. I can take all the rest on the chin, I will cope with anything else, but please, let her live.'

When we pray from desperation like this, we must be careful about what it is that we are praying for. Charles said that he could deal with anything else if his wife and the baby lived. At that moment, he was prepared to throw everything else away in order for her to survive. He did not realise that the gods – whichever god you might choose – may sometimes take us at our word and hold us to the bargain. He repeated his mantra for how long, he did not know, because he fell asleep, sitting on a chair beside her bed with his forehead down on the mattress, her hand still in his, and when he awoke it was with a start.

His utter rejection of his oldest son was cemented in place. Somehow in that sleep his brain had organised itself to this decision, and there was a deep sense of finality and relief that Freddie had finally done his worst, and that he could now let him go. He had to let go of Freddie. Somehow, this terrible truth had set him free. But his train of thought was disturbed when the door to the ward swung open again and the familiar sound of the suction, to seal out unwanted bacteria in such an acute environment, was heard once more. This time the door was sucked open by a nurse who did not stay, but who put her head round to announce in a thoughtful whisper: 'The police are here.' And with no further introduction, a non-uniformed detective walked into Alicia's small ward room, and a new chapter began in the story.

The detective perceived immediately that he was not going to get a conversation out of the wired up and sleeping figure in the bed, and so he invited Charles for a conversation in the corridor, by pointing to the door and indicating that he should come out. Charles opened the conversation, as he stood taking the full force of the officer's expectant gaze, but this detective required that people talk to him only to answer questions. He, like his medical counterpart David Whitelaw, was also at the top of his game in his profession. He rarely made social small talk.

But Charles had not noticed this, and he spoke in a friendly voice in a half-whisper: 'I think she's going to be OK.'

'I know. I've already spoken to the consultant. I'm Superintendent Bloomfield from Avon and Somerset Constabulary.' He flashed his police identity card for such a short time that Charles could not possibly have looked at it, and then stuffed it back into the pocket of his well-cut herringbone sports jacket. Charles did not know the intentions of the man he was dealing with here, but surely, he thought, there could be no more surprises today.

'I think we might be investigating attempted murder here, Mr Bradshaw.' He made no attempt to buffer the conversation, or to protect Charles.

'The accident and emergency staff have reported that your wife said she was assaulted and thrown into the water by a man called Freddie. Do you know who Freddie is? Is there any reason why someone would try to kill her?'

Charles did not hesitate.

'Freddie is my son. He's eighteen. There is every reason why he should be considered to have attempted to murder her. Firstly, because Alicia never tells lies, and if she said that is what happened, then it will have happened. And secondly, he has hated her from the minute he set eyes on her at the age of twelve. Freddie is my son from my previous marriage to his mother, June. He left school this year and has been unemployed ever since, despite us spending family money on a good education for him. He will be at his mother's home, I assume.' He gave June's address.

'And where were you this evening, sir?'

'I was at home on my own. Alicia went for a walk – she always tries to walk in the evening, likes to keep herself fit. She goes along the river. She's been along there all summer. I usually go with her but sometimes she likes to go on her own.'

'Can you corroborate that, sir? What were you doing at home?'

'I watched the news … and I made a brief call to my business partner, Ryan, about half an hour after Alicia left, so you can trace that call; here's his number. But just before that, I'd been asleep.' Charles handed over the number for Ryan, but the penny was beginning to drop that he was being considered as a suspect.

'I'll be round to see her tomorrow and see if she can talk to me. Don't go home tonight, sir, as the forensic team will be on your premises.'

'My premises?'

'We must look at everything. Everyone's a suspect now.' Chester Bloomfield watched the suspect's face to see the impact of his comment. This had been a carefully timed shock tactic to test the husband's reaction. Detectives were always suspicious in this way, based on the statistic that one in three homicides where the victim is a woman will have been committed by a spouse, boyfriend or partner.

Charles was incredulous as he realised that he was now considered a suspect in the attempted murder of his own wife, this fact adding another dimension to the injuries of the day. He watched Chester Bloomfield saunter down the corridor as if he had all the time in the world, and as if he considered what was going on was commonplace.

Everyone around him seemed to know how to handle this disaster, but Charles was dazed – dazed by trying to hold the picture together. He did not know yet, but this police officer that he was watching amble along, having just declared him a suspected murderer, this Chester Bloomfield, was to become their ally over the weeks and months to come. Now though, the suggestion of the merest suspicion that he would harm his own wife was a bitter blow to him.

Chapter 41

Can't You See I'm Innocent

Freddie was at his mother's home watching television. Remarkably, he had almost put the whole event from the night before out of his mind, despite the scratch across his face and the bruising on his thighs and testicles, which had made him flinch as he urinated that morning. He felt that these battle-scars were easily explained, especially since he had leaned on Anthony so hard to backup his alibi. As soon as he had returned home, he had gone about obscuring his actions in a methodical manner. He washed his clothes in the washing machine and put them in the tumble dryer; meanwhile, he took a hot steaming shower and scrubbed himself with soap and a flannel from head-to-toe, and shampooed and then dried his hair. Then he was hungry, so he had a bowl of Frosties, and some toast covered in a lot of butter and his favourite raspberry jam; after he had eaten, he washed up the bowl and plate, and even put them away.

His mother was in bed reading when he came in at 6.40 pm. She had been struggling with a headache all day, and had gladly retired early. She had called out, 'Is that you?' He had replied that all was well and that he would bring her a cup of tea shortly, and that he had stumbled and fallen accidentally and was about to wash his jeans and hooded top. She had told him that she would do it, but he replied, 'Mum, you enjoy your book, I'll do it.' She did think it was a bit unusual for Freddie to do his own washing, but this thought soon passed through and out of her mind, as these small curiosities about her son's behaviour were in the habit of doing.

Within two hours his clothes were airing, and his boots were in the porch looking as innocent as everyone else's boots, with the mud they

234

had held from the riverbank having been rinsed carefully down the sink. For all his frequent lack of consideration to other people, Freddie was a fastidious creature when it came to clearing up. His nervousness had made him extremely careful that evening, and he was efficient at his tasks. He even pressed a crease into his jeans at the ironing board. This crease proved his innocence. Nobody who had just committed a murder would have a crease in their trousers like that.

He checked and double-checked that everything was scrubbed, and then congratulated himself on planning a bloodless crime that was in fact an 'accident', and thought that he would not have liked the mess of blood from something like a stabbing, and wondered what would have happened if there had been more than just mud from the riverbank to deal with. As it was, he smiled to himself with the thought that, as he was leaving the scene, the rain had pelted down, soaking him to the skin; it had been uncomfortable, but the idea that his tracks would be covered and turned to invisible slush was satisfying. The rain falling so hard and making the river path so slippery added credibility to the story that Alicia had fallen into the water. He had put on his cosy pyjamas and this gave him a comfortable reassurance that he was home, that it was all over, and that he was to start a new chapter in his life from the very next morning.

He had fallen into a deep sleep, in which he could no longer control his thoughts – the thoughts that maintained his truth. He could no longer protect himself from the other interpretation of his behaviour, which was that he had done something very, very wrong. He felt this in the various revolutions of his mind, as his brain turned over and examined the day's toil – disturbed yet pleased, disturbed yet pleased. He slept with these dissonant thoughts, which kept clashing and would not quite fit together. He was looking forward to the time when he no longer heard her screaming in his ears, because this was still repeating on him, rather like an undigested meal. He had found that very disturbing, as if the event in some part of his mind was not yet fully metabolised, and threatened his perfectly rational explanation the events of his evening. He must maintain this rationale now, at all costs.

Meanwhile, Anthony, unlike his brother, lay awake in the dark in his room next door, and had been there ever since Freddie had come in to talk to him at around 7.30 pm that evening, just after his shower, and while his clothes were in the tumble dryer, and just before he pressed the crease into his jeans, the crease that upheld his story, the crease that he planned with care before he went to brief his brother.

The younger brother was frozen in his bed, awaiting his brother's entry. He knew that Freddie would come in, and knew that his life would never be the same after that day, any more than Freddie's would be, but for very different reasons.

But, once he had been instructed, Anthony knew exactly what he had to do and say. He lay in bed staring into the night, focussing on the stars and moon pattern on his bedroom curtains, and wishing he could be floating in the cosmos that evening. But all he could muster from within was the dreadful sense of a teenager who has no choice about the way he must respond to a terrible situation, when every bone in his body actually wanted to say 'No!' to Freddie. It was too late for Anthony now, though, and he did not quite know that, in the end, he would be as much a victim of this crime as were Alicia and his father, and while Freddie could forget, he could not, and he stared at the face on the moon on the curtains for comfort.

People use many mechanisms to narcotise the pain of mental conflict: drugs, alcohol, even sport. Anthony turned his face to pictures of his childhood for comfort. He was looking to the moon to be his mother in this dilemma: it was all he had. And when he was not staring at the moon on the curtains, he rehearsed the lies he had to say when the police came the next day. He imagined the words that he would use, again and again and again so that he would not forget them, and so that he might believe that these lies were true and that he could help his brother maintain his alternative universe where all his actions had explanations.

***

In the morning, Freddie awoke at breakfast time when his mother called him down. But he found he had no appetite. He had been due an appointment at the employment exchange, but he rang in sick, telling his mother that he thought he had a cold coming. This, like all his narrative, was very close to the truth. He did feel sick. He passed by the breakfast table in his dressing gown on his way to tell his mother, eyeing up Anthony, who sat spooning Shreddies into his mouth, his eyes staring and fixed on the air in front of him. Mum was always sympathetic and understood illness, and told Freddie to rest and go back to bed.

When Chester Bloomfield arrived at his front door at 10.00 am, having first been with Alicia at the hospital, Freddie was sitting in a relaxed position stretched out on his bed. He was still in his pyjamas, his dressing gown folded in neat pleats around his waist, and he was watching television. He had the air of a gentleman of the manor at home in his residence, with his housekeeper providing him with snacks and hot drinks to help him fight his impending cold. And he was calm and without any visible trace of worry, the events from the night before neatly taped-up in the back of his mind. As far as Freddie was concerned, in response to any police enquiries that came his way there was only the matter of showing some surprise, and perhaps even a little sorrow when he was told that his stepmother was dead, and of convincing his mother of his distress.

No one had seen him, and he had a clear alibi in his younger brother, whom he knew would never, ever let him down. He was waiting and watching for the local news on television to see if any bodies had been found that morning downriver, ending up at their usual resting place on the estuary or the beach. He had already spoken to his mother about his evening stroll with Anthony at around 5.30 pm to fetch some cans of beer, and his fall in the rain which meant that they had returned home without beer, and he with wet trousers, and how they'd then had a quiet evening in, just chatting and playing cards, as he was feeling slightly off colour.

June was already part of his story, and he had strategically set her up and ensured that she was listening and that she had absorbed the information, even though it had appeared to her to be a nonchalant chat. She could remember the washing machine running and the smell of toast cooking, just as Freddie said, so when the knock at the door came and the figure of Chester Bloomfield walked in without being asked, flashing an identity card at her so that she definitely could not read it, she was immediately on guard and fretful at the interruption of her routine. 'Who was it who was hurt?'

Chester did not say.

No, Freddie had been home early. She did not know what time. Her boys had been together that evening playing cards – they liked to play cards, her boys – and she was in bed early reading, with a headache.

Bloomfield told her there was no need to call her son Freddie down, he simply headed straight up the stairs, taking them two at a time with her protests ringing in his ears as to who he thought he was. He knew exactly who he thought he was. He opened what appeared to be a bedroom door, clearly the mother's room, with a tidy double bed – the pink quilt neatly and evenly spread and matching the open drapes – and women's clothes carefully folded on the armchair by the orderly dressing table.

The next door that he tried without knocking revealed Freddie, feigning relaxation on his bed, lying lengthwise and straight, straight as an ironing board, with his hands folded behind his head, propped up by two comfy feather pillows and watching day time TV, his dressing gown still carefully tied so that the folds lay neatly from his chest to his knees.

Bloomfield was surprised that Freddie expressed no surprise as he aggressively entered the room, but he simply smiled, and said, 'Good morning.' In the thirty seconds prior to his entry, Freddie had been listening at his door and had only just made the few yards back to the bed in time; he did not look convincingly relaxed, at least, not to a detective with Bloomfield's experience.

'Chester Bloomfield, Superintendent. Good morning, sir.' He flashed his identity card with his usual trick of flicking it away quickly so that nobody bothered to look. 'I'm here to make enquiries about an assault and attempted double murder on a woman last night down by the river, and you have been named as a suspect. Can I ask you where you were last night, sir?'

'What do you mean an attempted murder?'

'I mean we have a very sick woman in hospital who was picked up and thrown into the water last night, sir, and she tells us that it was you who did it.'

Freddie was shocked. She was not dead. She was not dead. She was not dead. Freddie would deal with this sickening surprise later by sitting for many hours with his head in his hands and being horrible to his brother, but meanwhile he had to front this one out and he knew he could do that. He did not shift his attention from the television, but asked to see the detective's identity card, his eyes visibly widened and his nostrils flaring somewhat.

Bloomfield noticed the body language, but he had no choice – if asked by a member of the public, he had to hand over his identity card.

Freddie's mother was standing at the door by now, remonstrating with Bloomfield to leave her house at once, but Freddie said 'It's alright, Mum, leave it,' as if he were calling off a pet retriever. He looked at the card, turning it over and checking the picture against Chester's face, offering it back only when he was ready, adding, 'Sorry, what was your question?' Freddie's eyes had returned to the television screen.

'Where were you last night?'

'I was at home, as always.'

'Did you go out at all?'

'Just for half an hour, in the early evening.'

'Where did you go?'

'Down to the shop for some beer, I usually have one in the evening.'

He was clearly lying, Bloomfield spotted the signs straightaway. Secretly, in the back of his mind, he was thinking this was an open-and-shut case, and that he would have it over as soon as he could. 'Can you verify that, sir?'

'My brother can – he came with me, but we didn't make it because of the rain. I slipped over and was soaked. Then we came in and played cards.'

'We'll speak to him, then, but meanwhile tell me where you got that scratch across your face?'

'What scratch?'

'The one running right across your left cheek.'

'Oh, yes, that one … yeah. Anthony did it … we were fooling around.'

'Does Anthony have long nails then?'

'Yeah, he plays the guitar.'

'Well that's fine, but I'm going to have to ask you to accompany me to the station for more questioning, and we'll have a doctor to look at that scratch, if you don't mind. You have been clearly identified and named by the victim of a serious crime that took place last night, and I am now arresting you on suspicion of the assault and attempted murder of Alicia Bradshaw down by the river in Loxley Meadow. You do not have to say anything unless you wish to do so, but anything you do say may be given in evidence.'

'No, no, it's not possible!' June, who had been listening outside the door, burst in and threw herself between Chester Bloomfield and her son. She had realised that he was being accused of attempting to murder

Alicia, and the very idea galvanised her energy so that she could fight this terrible shocking possibility, the truth of which was like lightning in her consciousness. In truth, the split second of realisation that took her breath away told her that of course her son would attempt to kill this woman – why wouldn't he?

'I'm not going anywhere. Mum, see him out.'

June pulled Mr Bloomfield by his coat sleeve imperiously. 'You're coming with me.'

Bloomfield almost laughed out loud at the ridiculous scenario of this mother attempting to arrest him, a police officer, while trying to obstruct him in the act of his own arrest of her son. Surely she wasn't going to respond to the boy's instructions, no. But yes, she did

'You'll have to go,' she said, and Chester Bloomfield thought that she might now be encouraging her son to go in peace. But no – she was talking to *him* and telling *him* to go. This turned his mild amusement into a pleasurable sense of farce.

'You're not taking my Freddie anywhere.' She squared up to him, placing her short build between him at six feet two inches, and her son of roughly the same height. Freddie watched his mother behaving like some feisty little terrier dog barking at an intruder, every sinew ready for action, her eyes glaring and nostrils flaring. She was formidable when provoked to protect her son, and she was brave in the way she stood up to this large man who was interrupting their world. Just the sight of her reassured Freddie and helped him to relax. She had him covered.

Bloomfield remained unsure whether to feel affronted, amused or annoyed by the crazy, and even comic, nature of the scenario playing out in front of him. He could hear the gossip down at the station in his head: 'Bloomfield dismissed from home by kid who calls his mother in to see him off.' He decided he would let this enhance his day rather than allow it to be a source of annoyance or the downfall of his reputation.

'That's alright, madam. If you would let go of my coat and stop pushing me, we can sort this out. Sir,' he addressed Freddie, 'we can do this in one of two ways. One way is for you to come with me quietly right now. The other is that I call in a team and we carry you out and put you in a nice cage in a large van, and that I charge you with resisting arrest. Your choice. Personally, I would prefer a more dignified approach and, of course, I can arrest your mother, too, if she continues to aid and abet you. Now, which is best for you?'

Freddie was resolute. Detective or not, he was used to getting his own way, and with his mother beside him in full flight he could not see why that would not be possible right now.

'I'm not going anywhere. Mum, see him out.'

Chester Bloomfield sat down on the armchair in Freddie's room and leaned back comfortably. He put his foot up on his knee and took his police radio out of his top right-hand jacket pocket. He didn't have to use it that frequently, being in plain clothes. 'Oh dear, I didn't really want to have to do this.' He called for assistance. 'No need to rush, boys, but I need a van and a few of the team to help with a gentleman resisting arrest, if you don't mind. No, no danger at all.' He clicked his radio shut, returned it to its resting place in his pocket, and leaned his head back into his cupped hands. This was a first for him, but he would complete the matter.

'Well, you relax and watch your programme, young man. I think I'll ask your mother for a cup of tea while I'm waiting for my boys, if you don't mind, madam? And meanwhile, you might want to get dressed, sir? It'll look a bit odd with you going out of the door in your pyjamas.'

June really had no choice but to go downstairs and produce a cup of tea. She was a bit confused as to who was winning this argument. Tea seemed like a good idea to create an interlude in proceedings. Chester Bloomfield followed behind her. When he asked for a biscuit she said she didn't have any, but she knew she did.

He sat in the lounge waiting patiently and looking relaxed, even though he had one ear out for what was happening upstairs, and he heard the television being turned up loud and could hear that the young man was talking to a younger male teenager whose voice had only just broken. This was noted, but was of little interest to him at that stage. He picked up June's *Daily Mail*, which he read while he waited.

Twenty minutes on, three uniformed officers in a police van parked themselves in the drive of June's home. She was mortified. What would the neighbours think? Bloomfield, though, was enjoying a pleasant cup of tea as he watched from the window, noticing the quietness of the road, the trimmed hedges and the postbox, and the pleasant-looking elderly lady enjoying the view from her lounge window a few doors down on the opposite side of the road. The only thing bothering him was the continuous and now tearful twittering of June as she protested his mistake.

He met his uniformed officers at the door, his tea in his hand. 'Upstairs, boys, second room on the left.' Another mouthful of tea and, refreshed from his moments of relaxation, he left the job upstairs to the professionals while he sat with his pencil and notebook to make a few more notes of the morning's events. As he scribbled and recorded he watched June's accusing face, which was turning now to look up the stairs, from where there could be heard the sounds of muffled scuffling.

'You have no right … Don't touch me! … Get your hands off me …' For the officers concerned this was simply a good sporting event, and they were delighted to flex their muscles with a young gentleman in pyjamas and a dressing gown. The bedroom door was shut, and their boss was downstairs and nobody was watching: they were having fun. Freddie was no match for their skills – they were trained to take people down.

Within less than a minute Freddie was carried downstairs in sausage fashion – because he had refused to walk – under the arms of two officers and with his hands cuffed behind his back, stiff as that ironing board again. There had been a few expletives and a little kicking of the feet at first, but he had soon learned who was in charge and resorted to determined silence. Possibly for the first time in his life, Freddie had been physically restrained and put in his place.

Chester drank the last mouthful of his tea, enjoying the sugar at the end. He handed his cup to June and thanked her for her hospitality, and then left to join his officers down at the station, explaining that he would be back later to talk to her son Anthony.

As the police van sped down the road, Freddie could be heard kicking against the door, June could be heard on the phone to her mother, and Gwen Knight's curtains were shamelessly pulled to one side as she examined the detail of the situation for her report to Angus. Chester Bloomfield had not been the only note taker and recorder of the morning. Gwen felt that the doctor should be prepared for the events that were about to unfold, although she did not yet know that the subject of this scene was lying in a hospital bed with her life, and the life of her unborn child, still in danger.

Chapter 42

What Doesn't Kill You Makes You Stronger

Chester sat at his desk contemplating the events of the morning, eating his lunchtime sandwich that he held in his left hand, while sketching notes with a pencil that he held in the right. While the notes did not necessarily add up very well yet, this act of making small sketches onto paper always helped him to think more clearly about what to do next. A criminal might have paid good money for the contents of his wastepaper basket – there was so much evidence there of his next move.

When he considered the scenario at the home of the suspect, he was mildly puzzled, though not troubled. Mrs Alicia Bradshaw had given him a clear and coherent picture of her assailant, and she had been specific about forensic evidence, like the scratch on the face, the red coat that had now been found, and the kicking she had given him. She was pregnant, and not prone to depression or despair and so he knew that this was not a failed suicide attempt. He had never really suspected the husband, but protocol dictated that he had to check him out as a possibility.

The suspect, whom she had named in person, had said that his brother, Anthony, aged fourteen, had put the scratch on his face, and Chester had yet to interview this young man. He had deliberately left that interview until now – it was tricky, as the boy was a minor and one could not just formally interview a minor without permission from both parents. That was next on his list of things to tackle. Unfortunately, his officers could not find evidence of any scuffle at the said location of the assault because the rain had washed away all trace of the evening's event.

A few more bites on the sandwich and a sip of hot tea helped his thinking process. The behaviour of Freddie Bradshaw was curious to him. He seemed totally nonchalant about the sudden appearance of a police officer in the home. It was as if he had been expecting him. The officer was more used to people being surprised and alert upon his appearance, but Freddie Bradshaw had not been so.

He had, however, noticed his face when he told him that Mrs Bradshaw was still alive, and try as he might the youth had not been able to cover his shock at this news. Now the question the detective had to ask himself was this: was he shocked because there had been an assault, or was he shocked because she was alive? He did not know yet.

The situation was a little less peaceful for Freddie once he was unpacked from the van at the station and delivered to a holding cell, still in his pyjamas and dressing gown. He was less sure of himself outside the comfort zone of his mother's home, although he tightened the dressing gown cord and stared them in the face, especially the one who had said they were sorry to have woken him.

Chester thought he would take his time over the whole thing, and had left Freddie to his colleagues for a little while to warm him up. 'Get him checked over,' he had instructed the custody officer, who, as he went past Freddie, brushed his coat uncomfortably close to his nose as he was held in an armlock by another officer, whose building muscles suggested that the pressure he was exerting might have been a little strenuous. This was all intended to show the young man who was in charge.

This kid will soon work it out, the custody officer thought. As a professional custodian he was aware of the impact of closed, locked doors on even the surest of criminals. Freddie had stumbled into the falsely lit temporary holding pen, and for once was speechless. All his defences had come to nothing for once in his life. There was no need for a custodian to clang a door behind such a prisoner when they were the only one with a key to the lock. This officer had no further point to make. He offered his young charge a mug of tea, but Freddie shook his head and so the officer returned to his desk, but made a note to observe the young man every fifteen minutes. Even those, he had learned, who demonstrated the strongest acts of bravado, may resort to acts of despair when faced with four walls and a locked door, symbolising the futility of defending oneself further from the truth of one's situation. The officer had read the young man's mind. This stage of his journey was particularly harrowing for him.

For now, Freddie only had the grey walls at which he could stare as he sat on the concrete plinth, which represented an indestructible place to rest and think, and so he sat quietly for an hour, staring into that colourless space.

By the time the duty doctor, a quiet and gentle man well past the age of retirement but with no tendency to give in to such a notion, arrived, Freddie had rested and recuperated and even accepted the tea mug and the cheapest brand of Osborne biscuit that Avon and Somerset Constabulary could offer him. Freddie would only concede to pulling his trouser legs up from the ankle to his knees. The face that the gentle doctor presented to Freddie belied the experienced rock-hard clinician beneath, who knew his job better than Freddie could ever have imagined, and whose pride in accurate diagnosis had never been known to be dismissed by court.

The doctor played along, always willing to make allowances for the callowness of youth, and examined the lower legs exposed by Freddie, on which there was some fresh moderate-to-heavy bruising that could have been incurred as a result of anything, but was unlikely to relate to the kicking that this sturdy young man had just been reported as giving the police van door. But he could see that something was being hidden and, not to be undermined in his quest for information, he quickly and deliberately pushed against Freddie's upper thigh, resulting in a knee-jerk reaction and a cry of pain from the prisoner before he realised he had been found out – again, that day.

The doctor had no idea what he was looking for, and he certainly had no idea about the circumstances of Freddie's activities the night before. He was, though, thorough enough to want to check out his patient for possible harm – he was not taking any chances. They had an unfortunate record in this custody suite, of injuries on arrival leading to problems; the trend had not yet been fully explained, but it would not be happening on his watch. There had been a death the previous year that started with a few minor symptoms, and had ended in catastrophe and an enquiry by the Police Complaints Commission. They had all learned from that. With this caution in mind, he pushed again at Freddie's thigh and Freddie growled and made a fist and all but hit him.

'I think I'd better look at that.'

'Get lost, you pervert,' was all that Freddie had to say, which did not affect the genteel doctor in the slightest. He simply continued with his duty and his oath to heal, and when he left he recorded his findings onto paper exactly as was required and delivered them to the custody officer, reporting: 'Some damage to the front of upper thigh. Suspect refused to let me examine directly. And a scratch across the left cheek, probably caused from fingernails, and bruising to shins, not because of arrest, possibly occurred more than twelve hours ago.'

Once Chester Bloomfield received the paperwork, he blustered without ceremony into the interview room where his suspect was now waiting for him, and told Freddie to remove his pyjama trousers.

'What is this place – full of perverts?'

'I'm not asking you, sir, this is not a medical examination. You are under arrest. It's the same routine as before, Mr Bradshaw – if you don't oblige to show me evidence then I'm at liberty to seize your trousers myself and will have to take the necessary action to do so. And my fellas aren't busy this morning, as you may have noticed.'

This was bluster. He could not actually seize anyone's trousers, but there was no camera in the suite and, as yet, they had not turned on the tape recorder for the interview, and the custody officer was an old friend who busied himself with some remembered task for a few seconds while Bloomfield conducted his preamble, because preambles were often more informative than the actual recorded interview – they all knew that.

Freddie realised that he could fight if he wanted, but he was not doing well that day at winning fights with this man, and he had the shocking and overwhelming sense that the world outside his mother's nest was not biased towards him. Instead he resorted to his next best defence, which was to make up brilliant and convincing lies. He tried to think quickly how to explain the bruising that had now come out on his thigh from the night before, where Alicia had kicked and kicked at his frontal femur and testicles. His leg was black, yellow and purple with severe bruising, and he knew it.

'Like I said, I was play-fighting with my brother. And I want my solicitor present first. I know my rights and you've not informed me of them yet.'

Bloomfield left the interview room without a response, temporarily thwarted, but only temporarily. 'Put him back in the cell until his solicitor gets here, and get the photographer over at the same time because I want pictures of that thigh.' Bloomfield knew this would give the suspect something to think about in the cell.

There was no record at the police station as to how the photographs of the bruised thigh and pelvis were actually achieved, but some hours later, on the basis of the pictures of said injuries – which were in the exact location described by the victim that morning – Bloomfield rang the Crown Prosecution Service to check if this was sufficient evidence for committal to proceedings, or whether he had temporarily to let Freddie go. He could not be held for more than twenty-four hours without good reason. While releasing him would be frustrating, Bloomfield was pretty sure that Freddie's mother would keep him safe at home for them, and that the young man would not be going anywhere if he did discharge him that day. Bloomfield had all the contacts at his fingertips and he spoke to his old friend in the CPS.

'No, that's not enough, Chester – I've had more than one suspect explain away bruising with the right barrister; we want it watertight. We need to be a lot more than fifty per cent sure of conviction these days, and we need to get past this alibi. I'm already in trouble for failed prosecutions this year. Get more interviews. Give it a few weeks. Make it watertight.'

The idea of watertight evidence, Bloomfield thought, was an ironic use of words considering the near-drowning of the victim. 'Oh, come on, give me a break, Matt. It's so obvious. The kid had every possible motive to want her dead. Even his dad is sure it was him. He's hated her for years, has a longstanding behavioural problem, poor attitude, and a bit of a personality disorder, if you ask me. Known to be aggressive and antisocial. Come on, let me bang him up.'

'No. I need more evidence, Chester. Watertight. Give me more. Come on, you know you can do it. It'll only take a few weeks.'

'Yeah, but I want him in today. He's given us no end of trouble. Teach him a lesson in respect, put the frighteners on him.'

'No, Chester.'

'Are you drinking on Friday down at The Oak?'

'Yeah.'

'You can buy me a pint for letting me down.'

'No, you can buy me one for being so stupid.'

He let Freddie go, with, he felt, some loss of face in front of his colleagues, but no matter: he would get him in the end, and there were no other suspects. He would follow through on all the investigations, but his nose told him what had happened here, and the truth would find itself, he knew. He warned Freddie not to get too comfortable, and that he had not yet completed his enquiries, telling him that they would be talking more.

Freddie, though, had not been idle throughout his incarceration, and had used up his excessive energy that morning by resorting to his next defence strategy in life, which was to make up stories about other people. His mother, he thought, would have been proud of him for resorting to his right to complain and for drawing up a claim of physical assault against the police officers who had arrested him. His solicitor explained to Freddie that the complaint was unlikely to hold water, as he had resisted arrest and had been fighting the officers concerned. Nonetheless, Freddie felt he had a claim, and his investment in his new defence brought him some consolation.

Chester Bloomfield was aware of the complaint as he went to notify Freddie that he could leave the station. He took great pleasure in leaving Freddie in reception in his pyjamas and dressing gown while the sergeant at the custody desk called him a taxi. 'Tell them not to rush to pick him up.' Bloomfield spoke to the custody officer out of the side of his mouth. 'I want to get to his house before he does and talk to that young kid.' He headed off for his final call of the day: to speak to Anthony.

One of his officers had already been despatched to Exmouth to pick up a red coat that had been found on the shoreline, a keen member of the public having reported the item as suspicious. The evidence was accruing, but still his officers could find no sign of a struggle down at the bridge, as had been reported by the victim. The rain had continued throughout that night, and any sign of attempted murder or any human activity at all had been washed away, just as Freddie had planned. The only interesting comment was from one officer, who had walked the pathway from the river back to town and found that some of the brambles had been freshly cut back. They vaguely wondered why, but were not yet able to explain it or give meaning to this slightly unusual occurrence. So, all was simply noted and held on file.

Neither the determined Chester Bloomfield nor Freddie in his pyjamas and dressing gown would make it to June's house before Charles Bradshaw, who left Alicia sleeping in the Intensive Care Unit of Taunton General Hospital with a promise from the duty sister that she would not take her eyes from her, and would call him if he was needed. He had given the sister June's number to call, as he knew that he would be there. He took the precaution of asking the sister to speak only to him, and not to say anything to anyone else about anything.

'Don't worry,' she had said, surprised at the idea that she might talk to anyone else. She knew he was troubled and had to get away.

Charles could not just sit there and do nothing while he watched Alicia struggle in pain and discomfort, wondering if their baby would survive any longer. They still had not had confirmation. He could not bear one more moment wondering what the hell would happen. The anguish tore at him and he had to do something.

All the energy that he would have liked to have put into stopping this event from occurring in the first place was now blasted at June as he stood in the dining room with her. 'Do you realise what all your years of parenting have led to?'

'Charles, I don't understand.' She held up one shoulder as if to protect herself from the pain of his onslaught, her bottom lip quivering, threatening the posture of complete composure that she had intended to portray that day.

'You don't "understand"? Of course you don't understand, you stupid, selfish woman. You've never bloody understood the part you've played in leading Freddie to believe that he can do anything he wants. You might have given him all your love, June, but the one thing you could never give him was reality. And now he thinks he is omnipotent, and is so lost in his own world and so riddled with anger towards anyone who goes against him, that he has tried to murder my wife and child!'

June was wearing a grey trouser suit that day, with a red polo neck underneath. It was an important suit for her, denoting her confidence in her position that her child was innocent. But the suit did not protect her from hearing what she did not want to hear, and she did not like hearing Charles refer to 'my wife and child'. *She* was his wife, and *they* had children.

Charles knew he would stop short of the physical shaking he wanted to give her. But all the shaking he would like to have given June was contained in his body, the pressure of the withheld energy making him quiver from shoulder to toe, visible only in the veins that stood out in his neck.

June had to work hard to hold onto her truth for her child, when every other part of her kept hitting against the facts that were to become increasingly obvious as the days went by. Every muscle in her body was holding this progress back, and finding its own way to suppress the relentless march of reality. She had been forced to change doctors in the past few weeks so that she could have stronger sleeping tablets, because somehow, with all her belief in her son, something kept waking her at night and tapping at the back of her mind. But Freddie? Freddie was fine and untroubled, and of course he would be: in her view he had nothing to fear.

'Well, *Freddie* is your child too, and I'm surprised that you are so quick to accuse him. He would never do a thing like that. It's understandable that he has hard feelings towards Alicia – she took you away from me and he feels that we should still be together. I think you should think about that, Charles, and show us more respect.'

He smashed his fist on the table, the closest he had ever come to violence towards anyone, let alone a woman. 'Why can't you see it? Why can't you face the facts?'

The gloves were off for once, and for the first time in his life Charles was on the attack. The past twenty-four hours had taught him all he needed to know about the reality of Freddie's mind, and he was not going to keep silent any longer. All those years of bullying that he endured at school, all the years that June had dominated and controlled him, his years of acceptance of Freddie as a bully, and he had kept quiet … but not this time. He was not going to stand by while his son became a murderer, and his ex-wife lived in denial of reality and supported him. He was beyond rage, and the words just tumbled out of his mouth like a river in full flow. He had no heed for how they landed, or of the fact that Anthony stood at the doorway, very pale and staring.

'You'd better be ready, you stupid, stupid woman, because your beloved one-and-only son is going to prison, and I'm going to make sure he gets a very long sentence. He's going to get put away for a very long time, and you're going to have that time to think about the part you've played in supporting him.'

Just for once, it was possible that June had a moment of doubt. She blinked away the tears that were welling in her eyes because she was hurt by this confrontation and genuinely wanted Charles to be on her side. She used her eyes to appeal to Charles to stop the deluge of words in which she was now drowning, and which she knew Anthony could hear.

Enough had been said, Charles knew.

The hope for her now, June considered in this moment, was in the form of Anthony providing a watertight alibi for Freddie. And now here was that detective again, knocking on the door. She had to answer. If Charles had not been there she might have ignored the knocking and not answered the door, but at least Charles would have to stop ranting if the police officer was present. She let Bloomfield in and she was ready, poised, the tears blinked back.

They sat in the lounge as Anthony, looking pale and very thin, presented his set piece. He appeared to Charles to have the silhouette of a cadaver, with dark rings under his eyes, and sunken cheeks. He had found eating and sleeping hard over the past forty-eight hours, bearing this burden for his brother. Charles was shocked to see the state of his son standing rigid as a post in neatly pressed jeans, his hair slicked back, reciting his lines as Chester Bloomfield took notes.

'We'd been playing cards together on the evening of this supposed attack, and we'd both set out for some beer, but Freddie slipped and hurt his leg, so we came home. I scratched Freddie's face and kicked him – we were fooling around and wrestling and things got out of hand. Freddie hurt me, and I kicked him back, hard.'

Charles drew in a sharp breath. His reflexes jolted him to intercede. He had to stop this. 'That's not true, Anthony, and you know it, you know it. You can't carry this for Freddie, you just can't. Don't do this, please, don't do this.'

'I'm sorry, Mr Bradshaw, you may not interrupt this young man's evidence; you must be quiet, or leave the room.'

Charles could not help himself. 'Son, please don't do this, don't put yourself in this position. You know what's happened.'

Anthony watched silently as his father wept passionate tears. He took out his handkerchief from his pocket. It had the initial A embroidered in the corner in blue silk. He passed it to his father, as if attempting an apology.

'I'm sorry, sir,' said Bloomfield, 'I can see this is upsetting, but it's probably best if you go and let me continue. I know you won't want to be seen to be interfering in proceedings.'

Charles, defeated, left the room and did not take a second look back. He had thought that the situation could not get worse for him, but these lies had sent him close to the edge of what he could possibly bear.

With the back door closed and his father driving away, Anthony finished his rehearsed statement; June was perfectly poised during this citation. She knew there had to be a completely believable explanation for everything, one that would resolve matters, and then things in her home could run smoothly again.

His story completed, Anthony asked, with perfect manners, if he could leave the room. His mother agreed, and there was a further affirmatory nod of the head from Bloomfield, who she felt was, at last, falling into line with her view. June's smile was interrupted as the phone rang. She hastened to answer, eager for a moment of respite: 'Mr Bradshaw? No, he's not here. Why would you call him here? Who is it calling, please? Oh, he's gone back to his other home. I expect you can contact him there.' She returned to Mr Bloomfield to refill his tea. 'It was the hospital for Charles. Would you like a biscuit, Mr Bloomfield?'

Anthony sat in his room, staring at the curtains with the moon and stars pattern as he had taken to doing in the past few weeks. He knew that he had just stabbed his father in the back, and that their relationship was dead. Behind the mask, he knew that he had lost his beloved dad from that moment onwards. While he had recited his lines perfectly, doing so had left him feeling like he had sold his soul, yet he had pleased his brother, and that felt more important than his father or his own soul. He had heard the phone ring and his mother answer it, but he continued to stare at his curtains, and the moon and stars, who were his parents now.

Charles drove back to Town End Cottage. As he made his journey he was not aware that the hospital had been trying to contact him. He drove slowly so that he could manage his thoughts. He had lost both his sons, and he damned well was not going to lose his wife. Not only had his oldest son just tried to murder her, but his youngest son had supported him totally, and without a blink had stared at the horizon and delivered his lines. Anthony had lied to the police and to him, while his mother stood beside him affirming his testimony. Charles had stared at his son's blank face, and the boy had stared at his mother's face, and his mother had smiled back at him, a soft comforting and reassuring smile. Charles had always imagined that there was some hope with Anthony, but this door of hope closed right then as he realised that the boy, too, had joined in the vendetta of hate against Alicia, by siding totally with his brother. So, he had to close his heart to his youngest child, deliberately and purposefully, just as the cell door had been closed on Freddie that morning.

***

Gwen sat in her mohair dressing gown, with her hands wrapped around the warmth of her evening beverage of cocoa, considering the comings and goings of the day as she observed Charles back his car out of the driveway of his former home. Things were coming to a head in that family, she thought, just as things always must come to a head eventually with every life event. Things had been brewing over there in that house for a long time.

Even with her octogenarian grasp on reality, Gwen could not have imagined the whole truth behind the events that were being played out before her. Freddie's story had meaning, she had no doubt, as did Alicia's. She was sure Freddie had done wrong, but she was equally sure that there was some meaning behind his behaviour: Freddie escorted from his home as if he were a rolled-up carpet, his mother screeching hysterically at the door with her youngest son looking blanker than usual, and Charles's face when he had arrived later that afternoon, full of a rage that she had never seen in him before. And then there was that nice police officer – Mr Bloomfield, whom she had known since he was a lad – going in and out. She watched him, and Charles, as they each left the house and turned right at the T-junction to head into town. Neither of them were heading for the river that evening.

***

Charles had retreated to the sanity of his own home for a few hours, where he had time to take a shower and change his clothes, and to think. He had a little piece of time in which to recover before he had to go back to hospital for visiting. He sat. He let his gaze catch on the fire grate, where cold ashes had spilled. Alicia had made up that fire and cleaned the grate only the morning before. She laid the fire with such neatness and accuracy, as if her life depended on her performance. The ashes were still in the pan, the ashes of all her efforts to gain the love of his sons … the ashes … the ashes … the ashes, powdery, soft and white, and an hour passed before his body jerked and he came back into his conscious mind. He realised that he had been staring at the ashes of his relationship with his sons.

Something had been broken that day, and of the two sons he realised that casting Anthony into the ashes was the most difficult, because he had held on to the boy with some hope that their relationship would be salvaged. He felt a sense of disgust at the way the brothers idolised each other, covering each other's backs. In another moment, as his thinking flowed, he knew that all Freddie had wanted was his father's undying presence in his life. This, Charles realised, was the thing that his son felt he had lost, and the void this had created in his world was what had driven him to such an act of terrorism. But whatever his unmet needs, whatever the reason for his behaviour, there was no excuse for what he had done, and there was no turning the clock back on what had just happened.

Charles went to the bathroom, took a very hot shower and scrubbed his skin with a rough flannel, trying to wash the horror away. The phone rang while he was in the shower. He had not heard from the hospital all day, he thought, as he dressed. He hoped that an absence of communication meant good news. If only it could be good news now, after the events of that day. The questions formed in his mind. Had they completed the scan to check the baby? He resolved that he would not move again from his wife's side until she was better.

When he arrived at the nurses' station, the same sister as on the previous night took him to that small room again. Alicia was struggling with a temperature of a hundred and two degrees Fahrenheit, and was fighting pneumonia. He had no control over events now whatsoever.

Chapter 43

A Time to Heal

Charles would spend another two days by Alicia's bedside as she struggled in and out of consciousness and fought off pneumonia. Those might be measured as two of the longest days of his life, but he would not remember them, his time delineated not by the ticking of the clock or the passing of day and night. Hospital time is not measured by these yardsticks but by something more intense than just hours and minutes, and that is the presence of life itself, manifested in the machinery and experts needed to maintain that life. In this case, the crude beep of the monitor that heralded every heartbeat demonstrated that her life was present, and that time was passing. The heart monitor was his clock and his master, dominating the square room with pastel pink walls and no window. This was a different world from the one he had known just two days before, when he'd had everything predictably under control.

She was in an oxygen tent to support her breathing, and Charles could not see her clearly through the crinkled plastic cover. He could only hold her hand by passing his own through a small aperture in the side. The opening sucked in his hand and sealed around his wrist with a cuff, so that none of the elements vital to her survival could escape. Whoever designed the apparatus, he thought, might have anticipated this human need to touch a loved one. He watched her face and stroked her forearm, which felt so frail under his large palm. She had not taken any solids since being found in the river, and had a drip for essential liquids. He observed with reverence the tube reaching into her arm, sustaining her life. He could do nothing now but survey all this unknown equipment until, he told himself, she was better, and so he was grateful for any interruptions to his bedside vigil that might give respite to the tension of not knowing what would happen next. The consultant, David Whitelaw, swept in on his rounds, and explained what would be happening and how they had given her antibiotics of a certain calibre so as not to affect the baby. Whitelaw knew to be direct with the man before him. 'If the baby is going to survive, I want it to be a perfect miracle, not an imperfect one.'

'Thank you.' Charles was grateful for crumbs of reassurance, and knew that the doctor had meant well. He held on to every piece of information and, like a child wondering when the journey is going to end, kept asking when they would monitor the baby. He had been told they still had to prioritise Alicia for now.

He clenched his fists against the waiting, but nothing, nothing would make time go faster or make anything change. What was happening was not going to occur within a time frame of his choosing.

Whitelaw, though, knew about waiting. He had watched people patiently and silently waiting for many years, and as a clinician he respected waiting. Nobody would ever know that in a quiet moment he had written a poem about waiting – such was his reverence for the art. Because of the waiting that he knew had to happen, he had told the staff to let Charles sleep in the chair by her bed.

'He's likely to lose her – you may as well let him stay. See if you can find him a blanket and make him comfortable.' This was his version of human compassion.

The nurses brought Charles food from the canteen, which they were not supposed to do: sandwiches that soon curled at the edges due to the warmth of the room, and chocolate Kit Kat bars that melted in the intense heat but were sweet to taste, and comforting. The nurses were kind and concerned, they, too, knowing how the healing process had to take its course, and that aside from good nursing, medicine and care, they could do nothing but let the patient fight the infection for themselves. So, while his wife and baby teetered on the brink of life and death, they did all they could to keep him comfortable and he was swept along with a plan over which he had no control, the outcome and the completion time of which he did not know. He was glad for every possible interruption: taking her vital signs, the door sweeping open. Every movement was full of possibility, even though she did not move.

Then there was a new moment – a moment when even he managed to take his attention off the heart monitor – heralded by the door being swept open and someone new, dressed in pink with a trolley and a monitor, breezing in with a cheery hello. He felt he should know what was happening, but he did not. He was momentarily distracted, trying to work out why her dress would be pink. Not until she was gone did he realise that all the nurses in the maternity unit wore pink dresses.

Her attention was given to his wife's pelvis through the gap in the other side of the oxygen tent; the bedclothes were turned down and clear gel was spread on her stomach. He asked if he should leave the room, and the nurse in the pink uniform finally explained her designated task: to check for a foetal heartbeat.

He would have much preferred to leave the room. He did not want to listen for a foetal heartbeat; maybe it would not be there, and he could not bear to hear nothing there.

The nurse in the pink dress read his face because she was used to reading faces, and encouraged him to stay. Always better that relatives knew everything, and this was her trade and so she was businesslike in her communications.

He stood childlike at her side as the monitor slid over the gel on her pale, rounded abdomen, with the nurse listening through the earphones so that she alone could hear. Like a child, he watched the face of the nurse, then watched Alicia's face, then the gel, and then returned his gaze to the nurse's face once more. He watched for every possible indication of news as she worked intensely, with the earphones in her ears, and then she stopped and held still for a moment … He knew this was it. He saw a smile, and before he could be hopeful at her smile she unplugged the earphones from the monitor and turned up the volume: 'There it is.'

Her triumphant nursery voice filled the moment, and he was lost in the sound of the cheerful and consistent little pip, swoosh, pip, swoosh, pip, swoosh of the baby's heartbeat through the amniotic fluid that had protected the little mite through everything that had happened. The nurse then wiped the gel away and covered Alicia up, and said, 'That's alright, then. I'll report back to Dr Whitelaw.' She took off the fibre covering from the earpiece, and started to put it away in the designated pouch.

Again, Charles had thought that there could be no more surprises, and again he had been wrong. Surely, out of everything, this news was most surprising of all, and he was left open-mouthed and incredulous that, despite all that had happened to Alicia, their baby had still lived inside her and had miraculously been protected from harm. Surely this was a sign of some strength in her that meant she could pull through, despite the setback of pneumonia. Surely this was a hopeful sign?

'Is this a hopeful sign?' he asked.

'Well it sounds jolly hopeful, doesn't it.' And the nurse swept out of the door with as little ceremony as when she had swept in, leaving Charles staring at his wife, and his vigil continuing. He began to will Alicia to open her eyes, because he knew this remarkable news would increase her impulse to get well. If he could only tell her right now. The impulse was too great, and he whispered through the plastic tent. 'You were right, the baby is alive, darling.'

Then all he could do was wait, half excited and elated, half despairing, and not knowing which emotion to rely on. He simply had to wait again, and leave all the work to everyone else: Chester Bloomfield to unravel the murder, David Whitelaw to oversee the care of his wife, the maternity consultant who would now be involved, and the ward nurses who would take care of the minute-by-minute monitoring of the pregnancy now, as well as of Alicia.

Despite his desolation, he could feel the support of the team in the Intensive Care Unit, and their ordinary kindness in contrast to the ruthless monitors, wires and oxygen tent which dominated the scene, doing a brilliant job – but without the human heart and flesh. He became a part of that environment, like a fish in a goldfish bowl. Every time Alicia's vital signs were checked by the nurses, he checked them, too. He even learned how to take her blood pressure. He knew exactly how to change a drip to rehydrate her, and when to notify the nurse that the catheter bag was full. He knew how often she should have an antibiotic injection, and was troubled if the procedure was even a few moments late.

He did not recall until much later that Angus Kennedy had called by to see how his patient was doing, and had spoken with him in detail about what had happened. He thought he might have dreamed this, but no, Angus did arrive to see him, his face appeared among the ocean of other faces of those who had visited – Ruby, Ryan and Gwen, but they were not allowed in and he spoke to them outside the room for a few moments at a time, accepting their good wishes and requests to help.

Many small momentos remained in his mind: Ryan held his hand and said he would take over at the office. He let Ryan hold his hand. Ruby sobbed her heart out and he had to hold her hand. Gwen placed her hand on his shoulder as they sat together, and spoke to him in soft words, a communication from which he only remembered the tone and not the sentiment, the chime of certainty in her voice that left him feeling confident. His father mumbled authoritatively with David Whitelaw at the end of Alicia's bed, and shook the consultant's hand. The old man raised his eyebrow when he was told that the pregnancy was still viable.

Of all the faces and sounds and smells, the one that would stay in his mind for days afterwards, and even months and years to come, was the sound of the lifeline: the beep, beep, beep, beep of the heart monitor attached to his wife. He held on to this sound like the ticking of no ordinary clock, but like the clock on a time bomb as he sweated every moment of the struggle with her and the baby. Forty-eight hours passed by as that heart monitor clock was ticking, and he was at one with the intensive care activity and lost himself in it to free his mind from worry. While he heard the monitor, he knew her heart was beating, and he was grateful for every stupid banal beep of every second of every moment that she fought her illness; and battle she did, just as she had fought everything difficult and dreadful that had ever happened to her. He knew, at least, that she could fight, and that was a comfort. And then the hour came when he could take the tension no more, and fell exhausted, unshaven and unkempt into the bedside chair with the blanket up to his neck covering a heart full of grief, aching with sadness and regret, and with his mind reverberating with thoughts of anger and revenge against his sons, which clashed violently with the tenderness and grief he felt for his wife.

He was a refugee and the chair had been his home for two days, the Intensive Care team his temporary adoptive family. He tried to be grateful, but it was all too much for him to bear, and he sank out of consciousness comforted only by the continuous beep, beep, beep of that heart monitor that had become his tyrannical, yet revered, companion. And, like most times in life when humans give in, this marked the point of change, whether for the worse or the better – giving in can often be the point at which things shift. He fell into a deep sleep, not knowing or caring any more what the world would be like when he awoke, and he dreamed he was in his garden rocking a baby girl in his arms, and he could hear her heartbeat – pip swoosh, pip swoosh, pip swoosh – and was kissing her soft forehead while he listened to her cooing, trying to show the baby something, something, they were trying to find something in the garden … and then he found what he was trying to show her. The mist cleared and there it was: he was trying to show her a tombstone, and he saw the name on that stone but could not remember it, but the pain of seeing the name shot across his heart and the fear made him struggle into consciousness. 'No, No, No!'

He checked the room to gather his bearings and settle himself. He wiped his eyes and sipped some water from the tumbler beside Alicia's bed. And when he regained his composure he resumed his vigil, noticing the curve in her stomach, her hands languid beside her body. When his eyes travelled upwards towards her chest he noticed her breathing and her neck, and her blonde hair tumbling over her shoulders, and then he could see her face and he found that she had her eyes open and had been watching him from inside her own goldfish bowl. 'What about the baby?' were her first words.

'The baby is fine, darling, you're both fine.'

And with this assurance she could attend to every other need in her body, and suddenly and remarkably she was feeling better and was hungry. Her temperature had dropped, her blood pressure was normal, and she could speak.

'I'm so thirsty, Charlie. Please can I have a drink? Why am I in this greenhouse, Charlie? Can I go home now?'

He had never been so glad to hear her moaning and complaining. He lunged at the buzzer for the nurse, who came sweeping in and retook her temperature and confirmed that it was dropping. Alicia complained about a drink again and, with the nurse's permission, he held her head through the aperture in the greenhouse and fed her the cup while she sipped at the water. At last he felt he could do something useful to help, his skills reduced to cup-holding, which he did as effectively as he could. And after her drink she continued to moan and complain again for some minutes before she fell back to sleep.

Although she was clearly bewildered, he knew from her sudden burst of activity that she had fought her battle. She had rekindled and found her will to live, and for the first time in days he slumped in the chair and could feel himself breathe, albeit shakily, with relief. He was overexcited, and asked if they could bring in the monitor so that she could hear her baby's heartbeat. Like a teenager replaying a record that he had loved, he wanted to hear it repeatedly, but the nurse advised him to let her sleep. Instead, in a manic reaction to two days of living on the edge of life and loss, he rang Ryan and cried incomprehensibly down the phone to him, such that his friend panicked and rushed to the hospital, terrified and ready for the worst. But by the time he arrived, he swung open the suction door to the picture of Alicia partially raised up in bed on a support of pillows, her skin flushed with pink, the oxygen tent cleared away, and the couple with their hands on her stomach, both smiling.

Chapter 44

A Time of Truth

Three months after lying for his brother to the police, Anthony sat on his bed and observed his curtains. It was all over for him now. He just had to wait for the train that would be coming to take him away, away from the lies, away from the trap he was in. He would miss his curtains and the pattern of the moon and stars on them, but it was time go. Freddie burst in the door.

'What the hell have you done?'

'What?'

'Mum's sleeping pills … I was looking for them.'

'You too?'

'Yes, me too. I'm not sleeping either. Freddie was struggling with his thoughts and he was struggling with his brother; watching him, he could see that Anthony was slipping, going downhill. He was going to tell someone, Freddie could sense it. He had to act. 'There are none left in there. What have you done with them? Have you taken them? Where are they?' He looked at Anthony's ashen face and the large pupils of his eyes and knew immediately.

Anthony could not respond. He felt sick and very sleepy. He had taken the entire thirty-day supply of pills about half an hour before, and now he was just waiting. His eyes were so heavy. He just needed to lie down. 'I'm very tired, Freddie, tired of it all.'

Freddie went to his side and helped him lie down. He pulled the shoes from his brother's feet and freed the blankets out from underneath him to cover him over. 'Just sleep then, Anthony. If you're tired, just sleep.'

Anthony, as always, obeyed his brother's comforting words, and closed his eyes to be swallowed by the all-consuming stupor that enfolded him; people were talking to him, his mind was thick with fog, he was thirsty, momentarily afraid, and then so, so tired of it all.

Freddie put on the radio beside his brother's bed, closed his door and, with a last glance, quietly left the room. He sped downstairs to his mother, who was watching television, and smiled to her from the door. 'Anthony's feeling a bit queasy. He's having a rest, said he didn't want any dinner tonight, OK?'

'OK, darling, I'll look in on him shortly.'

'No, he didn't want to be disturbed, Mum, leave him.' And, obedient as she was to her oldest son, she smiled, and did exactly as he had told her.

It was not until the next morning that she went up to Anthony's room, after getting no response when she called him for breakfast. Freddie was at the table eating toast. He had said nothing when Anthony did not come down to eat. He delayed her further, by saying 'Let him sleep in, Mum,' but eventually she was compelled to go up. Freddie was putting more butter on his toast when he heard her make her way down the stairs and pick up the phone. 'I don't think he's well, Freddie. I can't wake him up. I'm just going to phone the doctor.'

'No, don't, Mum, leave it. I had a word with him this morning. He's fine. He's just tired, and to be honest, we had a few drinks last night. He's just sleeping it off. Leave it.' He took the phone from his mother. 'Look, Mum, I really fancy some egg on toast this morning, and there are no eggs. Could you get some? Seriously, I'll keep an eye on Anthony, don't worry.' He got his mother's coat and bag from the peg and passed them to her. Of course she would go to the shops and get what he needed, he knew that.

It was about midday when June finally called Angus Kennedy, who was on the phone within seconds of seeing Anthony at their home, calling an ambulance to get him to hospital. 'How long has he been like that? Has he taken something?'

Freddie answered. 'No, he's been fine, just a bit tired recently. What's the problem?'

'He looks like he's in a coma, that's what the problem is. You should have called me when you first noticed. His mother said he was ill last night. Why didn't you call me then? We've lost vital hours.'

Freddie said nothing.

At Taunton General, Anthony was rushed from accident and emergency to the Intensive Care Unit. It would be another twenty-four hours before his kidneys, heart and liver failed, and his body went into shutdown and he was pronounced dead, his mother and Freddie sitting at his bedside.

Prior to his death, a young psychiatric registrar sat by his side to assess the boy's mental state. His notes indicated that the patient was constantly trying to speak about something, and that he had wondered if he would break through into consciousness during this time when he was constantly jabbering and thrashing around in a painful toxic stupor that was clearly affecting his brain. The boy seemed to be trying to respond to the registrar's questions, but it became a pointless exercise. The only thing the registrar had written on his page were some unmistakable words that represented a simple exchange that had occurred:

'It was Freddie. It was Freddie.'

'What was Freddie, Anthony?'

'He killed Alicia. Freddie killed Alicia. I lied. Covered it up. Can't live with it. Help Freddie, please, help my Freddie.'

The young doctor took not much notice of these words, and dismissed them to be the ramblings of a boy struggling between life and death, and with the toxicity of some substance or other, but he did write them down on his pad before moving on to the next admission, which was of much more interest to him than a boy who was not long for this world. The information might have been consigned to the shredder, except that the registrar did mention it to his senior consultant, who told him he would have to report it to the police. 'Really, sir? It was nothing but rambling. I really don't think its relevant.'

'Do it,' responded the consultant. 'It's a reported homicide, mentioned in a formal assessment and recorded on paper. We have to report it. Not for us to judge whether it's relevant or not. The boy clearly died of some distress or other. He may have been holding on to something in his mind that is relevant to a crime. Get it done immediately.'

The young registrar was brought up sharp, and picked up the phone and spoke to the local police desk sergeant about a crime that had been reported on the deathbed of a young teenager called Anthony Bradshaw.

'Bradshaw … Bradshaw … that name rings a bell,' said the desk sergeant. 'Bradshaw. I think that's Chester Bloomfield's case.'

And when Chester Bloomfield picked up the note from the desk sergeant he was unmoved, simply because the information fitted perfectly with the emerging picture of what had been happening in the Bradshaw home. For two days he had been sitting on a further piece of evidence that Freddie had attempted to murder Alicia Bradshaw, and that his brother, Anthony, had lied and been made to keep the matter a secret.

Chester Bloomfield would never know the whole truth of how Freddie had delayed help for Anthony after his overdose; had it come to light, it would have made him culpable for his brother's manslaughter as well as for the attempted murder of Alicia. It would be recorded at the coroner's court that Freddie and his mother had not realised that Anthony had taken an overdose, and had left him to sleep. The secret truth would go with very few people to their graves and Bloomfield would not be one of them, but this did not matter: he had more to think about. The something that had been on his mind for a few days was just a small snippet of information, but one which also fitted perfectly into the jigsaw.

Bloomfield had been approached by the general practitioner for Blessingham, who seemed to be concerned about a conversation he'd had with two older ladies living in the community. Dr Angus Kennedy had called him and asked for a meeting, at which he said that Gwen Knight had come to him because she had been reading through the notebook of her close friend, Abigail. In an entry from some three months previously, her friend had made a clear note that she had seen Freddie Bradshaw go past their home one the evening, heading for the river, and then returning less than an hour later, looking very wet and in a great hurry. There was nothing unusual in this, because Freddie lived in the road and would often be seen going by. The significance was in the date. The ladies had been chatting, and it had dawned on them that Abigail had seen the young man in question at around six in the evening, the very time of the alleged attempt on Alicia Bradshaw's life. He had been recorded as being in the vicinity of the murder at the time it was committed. They had also recorded his regular walks up and down the lane at around the same time for some months before. They were, admittedly, slow to come forward with this information, but nonetheless it was there, written down and corroborated by the two of them.

This time, Chester did not even check with his friend in the Crown Prosecution Service. He knew that the case was solved, and that there would be enough evidence for arrest and prosecution. Anthony had finally admitted that he had been an accessory to the crime, and had told the truth about what he knew. The tragedy was that he had killed himself because he could not continue lie any longer. Later, in court, his words would be dismissed by Freddie's defence team as the incoherent mumblings of a boy as he lay dying, but the young psychiatric registrar gave a good account of the event, produced the notes written at the time – that were corroborated by his senior consultant – and his report was eventually accepted by the judge as admissible evidence. The jury believed what Anthony had said.

A car sped Chester Bloomfield to Didcot Lane, where Freddie had just arrived home with his distraught mother from the hospital. He was arrested, without a word of argument, for the attempted murder of Alicia Bradshaw; his mother called her parents. In one single day, two of her sons had been cruelly dragged from her life for no reason that she could think of. At least her parents would understand.

Chapter 45

A Time to Know

His phone at home had rung the previous day and Charles had ignored it, taking it off the hook. He was engrossed in preparing for the future: his return to full-time work, decorating the nursery and organising the garden. Someone had tried to call, and had tried again that morning – twice in fifteen minutes. When he tested for the callback number, he recognised the numerals, which were scored deep inside his memory – they were from his former home with June.

He unplugged the phone. He did not want to be disturbed for the next forty-eight hours. He had become ruthless about protecting their time. He did not want to speak to his ex-wife about her children; whatever she wanted, he told himself, he was neither bothered nor interested, and the call was hardly likely to be a matter of life and death. It was probably June still trying to convince him of Freddie's innocence. He pulled the cord out from the socket with such force that he felt guilty that he might have broken it, and immediately plugged it back in again. He had no wish for Alicia to see his rage at this stage of her pregnancy. The dialling tone was still consistent, and so he pulled the plug out gently the second time, as if he was perfectly in control. He justified his actions in his mind; they had tried to ruin his life, and had nearly murdered his wife and baby to take them away from him, so he now had the right to look to his future and to ignore them.

He distracted himself from the thought that kept coming into his mind that it might be something important, by digging deep into the compost in his garden at Town End Cottage. He had a plan, and it was a beautiful plan, and today it would stay a beautiful plan. Nothing was going to interrupt that. He would fill Town End's little walled garden with cottage garden flowers, to attract bees and butterflies in the spring and summer, after the baby was born. His vision was of buddleia, marshmallow, lavender, honeysuckle and roses. These were flowers that were easy to raise and which would proliferate. Buddleia, he thought, can even grow out of a wall on a railway siding; he had seen it when sitting on a train recently. Surely, then, he could grow it in his garden, even if he were a clumsy beginner. Of late, he had begun noticing more signs in nature of how life survived against the greatest odds, and buddleia, it seemed, was one species that could do just that, growing out of concrete with apparently no soil whatsoever.

This was a parallel to what had happened in his life, with his wife refusing to lay down and die, and their baby girl – they had found out the gender in a recent scan – surviving and growing well, and to be born in early March, just over three months away. No, he would not answer that phone, instead he concentrated on his digging. His spade split the tough damp autumn turf into a precise segment which he then turned over and broke up. Every now and then he checked on the whereabouts of his wife with a smile – every moment with her was now precious.

She sat resting on the wooden swing seat that he had put up for her under an old spreading lilac tree that was now bereft of all but a few leaves. She was wrapped in her warmest baby-pink cashmere jumper, with a blue tartan rug draped over her legs, catching the late autumn sun on her face, and alternating between watching his display of heroic digging and enjoying the sight of some hardy roses that were holding onto their blooms. She was sleepy and relaxed, and the sharp smell of autumnal decay and sweet twittering of garden songbirds filled her senses and uplifted her spirits. She was alive, her baby was alive, she felt life was healing her, and her husband loved her and had not left her side for weeks as he nursed her back to health – as if she were his only child. Nearly three months after the terrible trauma of the attack and it was all finally starting to come together. They were creating a new normal for themselves. Her broken femur – out of plaster now – was healing, and that leg rested along the swing seat, while the other was firmly placed on the ground, pushing the seat lazily backwards and forwards. Her forearm had also been relieved of its plaster, and her collarbone had knitted back together, although they both gave her pain at times.

Fixing her broken bones had not been the most difficult part of the healing process after the attack. Bones were easy to re-form; the healing of the mind was more complex, and subject to ups and downs, but she was managing, and had so much to look forward to that she was determined not to let any creeping doubts about what Freddie might do in the future undermine her progress. They had no news of any arrest or prosecution and this had caused much concern and anxious discussion between them. Chester Bloomfield had told them: 'It's got to be watertight … the case has to be watertight.'

She couldn't see how much more evidence was needed – she had stared Freddie in the face while he pushed her in the water. She stopped her thoughts immediately. She did not like to relive that moment, and again reminded herself that she had to think of her baby. But her mind always came back to Freddie, and she could not help but wonder what he was doing with his time, and whether he might be watching her. Every now and then she found herself glancing down the path towards the river, wondering if he might be there.

The previous week she had walked down there with Charlie, and defiantly stared at that bridge. She had wanted to get over this hurdle before the baby was born. They stared for many moments at the scene of the crime, the river flowing and babbling in all innocence as she showed her husband, in detail, exactly what had happened. The trauma psychologist had told her to do this, and she boldly struck out down that river path facing the haunting sense that Freddie may be lurking still. While her body was healing, her mind was slower to be convinced of her own safety, and they both remained vigilant following the assault. And Freddie remained, some three months after the event, completely free.

Alicia's pregnancy, and all the hormones coursing through her system, were a protective blessing that kept her buoyant and prevented her from continuously revisiting the horror in her mind. She told herself all the time that she had many good things to look forward to, and did not want to spoil the birth of what clearly would, at her age, be her only child. That the pregnancy had not aborted or miscarried due to her near-drowning and the attack on her, was her very own personal miracle. She believed that the power of nature's determination to help her survive, combined with her own fearlessness, were the reasons why she now rested with a well-rounded stomach and felt her baby girl kicking her from inside.

She also believed that she had been subject to mercy – God's mercy on this occasion. The very concept that a God existed who took pity on her plight and showed her mercy brought her comfort, and helped to give her hope and ameliorate the dread that she felt when she thought of the attack. Every kick from her baby was welcome and a joy, even though her broken ribs – discovered later than all the other breaks in her body – were most painful to manage as her stomach grew larger. Medics and psychologists agreed that her recovery had been spectacular, but she knew exactly why this had been – she had everything to live for once she knew that the baby was safe, and Charlie was glued to her side. Freddie had not rent them apart, but had bound them closer together. She remembered parts of their wedding vows: 'until death us do part'; and 'let no man put asunder'. She repeated them to herself as her antidote to thoughts about Freddie, when they made unwelcome visits in her mind.

As they were peacefully lost in this idyll together, they did not notice a vehicle that quietly negotiated their drive, softly and slowly creeping along and crunching on the gravel as it parked outside their home, until Charles put his hand on the base of his spine and stood up from his digging with a nervous jump as he heard a car door slam; and then he saw Chester Bloomfield walking across the lawn towards them.

'Oh, Christ, what now.' His heart sank into his boots as he sliced the spade one more time into the earth, and he left it standing there on guard while he went to attend to his visitor.

He immediately assumed the worst simply from the look on the police officer's face, which was grim: the grey temples exaggerated, the lines in his forehead deep, and his mouth set straight.

'Good afternoon, sir. Have you not been answering your phone?'

'I turned it off. I didn't want to be disturbed.'

'OK. Well, we've been trying to get in touch. I wonder if I could have a quiet word with you on your own. I'm afraid I have some difficult news for you and I don't want to upset your wife – I know how much she's been through.' Chester looked over to Alicia and waved, forcing a half-smile onto his face. 'How are you, ma'am? Any better?'

'We'd better go in,' said Charles, softly. 'I'll make some tea.'

'I'm coming, too, Charlie. I want to know what's happening.'

'No, darling, you'd better sit there for a bit – the sun's lovely, and it's good for you.'

'No, I'm coming.'

He looked helplessly at Chester Bloomfield, and shrugged his shoulders. His wife was, without doubt, back on her horse; while this was something to celebrate, she was still fragile, but it was becoming clear that there was something of great importance about this moment, and that she would have to be included.

'It's OK. She's on top of things. There's nothing that can surprise us now … I don't think. *Is* there something that's going to surprise us?'

Chester sunk into himself. 'Let's go inside.'

Chapter 46

The Time to Mourn

When Charles returned from seeing Chester out, Alicia was staring at the fire grate, their point of stability and focus during many discussions of the events that had happened during their life at the cottage together; the freshly made-up fire was ready for the evening, laid with newspaper and kindling, but unlit. He didn't interrupt her train of thought, but just sat with her. They were both comfortable to sit in this silence – so important to the conversation they were about to have. She glanced to her side and considered his distraught face, her eyes soft against his startled stare.

'I am so sorry, my darling. I would never have wanted this … never, whatever has happened. You mustn't blame yourself. Really. You were pushed to your limits when Anthony lied for Freddie – you're only human. You couldn't have done more to try to understand Anthony.'

'I know. I know nobody would have wanted this. None of us, not June or Freddie or you or me … none of us could imagine this. You weren't the only victim, my love; there was Anthony, struggling away in the background, hidden behind Freddie, and very gradually losing his mind. And I couldn't be there for him. I couldn't reach him any longer.'

Alicia knew that Freddie would not have considered this at all. But this was not the time for her husband to have to think about the possibility that Freddie had deliberately held back on an emergency response to Anthony just to meet his own ends. She, though, had been sure in a flash that this is what had happened. For now, she could only rock her husband in her arms while his tears soaked into her dress as he rested his head on her large stomach. She stared on, into the fireplace. Somehow, at this terrible moment, the worst was over for her.

But they both knew that their grief had not even begun yet, and that, by some terrible twist of fate, Anthony had solved this crime for them only minutes before he died. He had been helpless against the onslaught of Freddie's insistence, he was forced into the lies about the murder, and he had not the strength to rise against his mother and Freddie; but in the end, his last gesture had been to save Alicia from the danger that Freddie may never have been found guilty. Anthony had shown immense loyalty to his father as he sacrificed his own life.

Alicia was filled with hope at this enormous last gesture, but weighed down with the secret she was holding that Anthony's brother was very likely responsible for his death; but her overriding thought was to protect her baby from the emotional turmoil of the next few weeks, and she determined that this would be her priority, and that she was ready.

***

It was a foggy mid November morning ten days later when the funeral party arrived at the crematorium in Taunton. The beautifully clipped grass and gardens seemed to be laid out in compensation for, and recognition of, human suffering, as if defying by their very precision the lack of control that we have over anybody leaving this world. The deciduous trees looked as if their outer leaves had been dipped in orange paint, with the inner green still holding on, and were rustling and whispering as quietly as the mournful group that was gathered there. This included many young people from Anthony's school, all in their uniforms, looking polished and stiff but forlorn, wondering and whispering quietly to each other about what might happen at funerals. Would they see him get cremated? In contrast to this civilised setting, the crows, always dressed for a funeral, cawed out their primitive call, oblivious to human pain, proclaiming the death and loss of a fourteen-year-old child. These sights and sounds were to be remembered by many of the people there, who took in the calm images of a day ravaged by the choking stab of grief and loss.

Freddie's was an absence that somehow marked his presence; he was detained now without bail in preparation for trial. Alicia, at nearly seven months pregnant, stood alone in a loose, black, crepe maternity dress, and a hat with a large brim; her pregnancy was obvious to all who were present: the growing baby girl a stark contrast to the dead son.

She watched her husband, as with five other bearers he bore his son's coffin on his shoulder, moving slowly down the aisle of the multi-denominational chapel. They laid the light-oak, brass-handled casket on the curtained plinth, Charles with his face set firm against his agony. They had said that he did not have to carry the casket, but he wanted to. Alicia understood. He had to carry his son to make up for the way he had not understood his plight.

June stood between her parents, who held her up between them offering encouraging words. She stared at the elegant coffin, the last resting place of her youngest child, and she was staring at reality: the loss of both her boys – one was to be buried, the other already incarcerated at Her Majesty's pleasure. She wore the look of a broken woman. She did not glance at Alicia or Charles. She thought that Alicia should not be there, and felt that she was the cause of all this. She'd had deranged telephone exchanges with Charles just the day before the funeral, in which she'd expressed her protests, and arguments for excluding Alicia from the burial, which she said was 'for family only'. But Charles would not have it. Anthony was his son, and his wife would be at his funeral. She was his family. He felt she deserved this sense of closure, and a last goodbye, and Alicia, anyway, was determined to be there, and told him that she would stand outside the door if they would not let her in. She had always tried with Anthony, and she owned a little piece of him in her heart. Not the least for the sake of her husband, she would hold that piece for the rest of her life as an acknowledgement of Anthony's last nod to her – telling the whole truth – and of the secret that she held about his death at the hands of his brother. She held on to Charles when he came to stand beside her. He was beyond grief on the day, and could not deliver even the small speech that he had prepared about his son. The paper remained in his pocket. The lines he had scrawled just did not do justice to his passion for his child:

He was a good boy and I loved him, and I was proud of him. We had a special bond. He always tried hard to please … was loyal to his brother … loved his mother … loved cricket, golf and football, and he liked to cook.

Instead, Anthony's grandfather, June's father, said grandfatherly things about the boy, and assiduously sidestepped and avoided any mention of his collusion with Freddie in a murder attempt, or the mental anguish and desperation that he must have felt before he died. Instead, he spoke about his grandson's love of sport, and love of his family and how well he did at school, which was all perfectly acceptable and all true, but only ringing one of the bells about Anthony's life.

We never tell the truth at funerals. The best that Charles could do was simply give his son a respectable send-off, as would be expected of a father like him. He paid for tea for the congregation, at a nearby hotel where they gathered after the service, nibbling at tiny sandwiches, and sweet, iced cakes – which were a pleasing distraction – slurping tea, and speaking in reverential tones, only the quietest few talking about 'what on earth happened?' Charles saved the sharp pain of grief that was bursting in his heart for later. He did not speak to June or her parents. There was little that could be said that would not set him screaming beyond all reason, and it was therefore better that nothing was said. When the curtain was drawn around the coffin at the end of the service, the congregation sang the solemn and final hymn of the child's life:

'Abide with me; fast falls the eventide;
The darkness deepens; Lord, with me abide;
When other helpers fail, and comforts flee,
Help of the helpless, oh, abide with me.'

Charles thought how perfectly the words of the antique hymn matched his feelings, especially the line 'When other helpers fail, and comforts flee,' and he hoped beyond measure, as he sang, that his child had found the help of great Comforter in his hour of need. This idea, the solemnity of the hour, and the solidarity of purpose in the people around him, brought relief and a moment of balm. But they had not sung the second verse before his peace was shattered, by the image of June rushing forward to stop the curtain around the coffin from closing to cover her son's casket, shutting him off from everyone forever. Rather than experiencing a soothing moment of goodbye, she was deeply disturbed by the reality of what she had to accept. Her parents tried to pull her away, to stop this ungainly spectacle from happening, but it made her more determined in her efforts and, as her parents tried to hold her back, she struggled against them. Amid this commotion the congregation continued to sing, undeterred in their focus and final goodbye:

'Swift to its close ebbs out life's little day;
Earth's joys grow dim, its glories pass away;
Change and decay in all around I see;
O Thou who changest not, abide with me.'

The hymn completed, the congregation heard the final blessing, and the closing curtains were wrenched from June's hands. Charles and Alicia walked out with everybody else. Despite the display and loss of control, Charles felt for June at that moment, but he left her to her parents. And Alicia, too, felt for the woman who had lost her child. But she wondered how June could have been so stupid as to fall for Freddie's stories. Today, at Anthony's funeral, there were no winners, least of all Freddie. Alicia could only wonder at what stories he would tell himself now, but she did not dwell on it. Everyone tried not to think about Freddie that day, and this collective effort made it feel strangely as if he were present, and as if he were running the proceedings.

Charles was to spend several more weeks in a state of anguish before he recovered sufficiently from the indigestible hammer blow of loss that would never leave him. After a few weeks he felt well enough to return to work, where he was treated with kindness by his team, who gently encouraged him back into life, and with due decency signposted the way back into the office normality that they all needed. They had covered for him for weeks, and it was becoming imperative to the business that he returned, and began to take back the helm.

Time is not necessarily a healer; some pain just has to be borne and cannot be cured. Grief is just such a pain, remaining in the heart as if the deceased person themselves existed inside of the griever. Various emotions crashed together for Charles at times, like the trucks on a train that is slowing, bumping into each other in a chain reaction: the shock of what had happened to Alicia, the grief of the loss of Anthony, the disgust at Freddie, and the impending joy of the new life that was due to arrive in early March, which would change everything about the future but nothing about the past. He had the rest of his life to recover.

When he became a parent, he had never envisaged having to say goodbye to both of his sons at the same time in such tragic ways. He could never have imagined such a possibility – ever. There was some small compensation that he could find in Anthony's death. Whereas before this event he would never have been able to forgive the boy, now that he was dead it was perfectly possible to fully let go of what he had done. Both he and Alicia agreed upon that, as they sat in front of the fire the evening after the funeral; it was their joint decision at the end of that terrible day, and the banner that they carried into the future. It is so much easier to forgive the dead than the living. His son had suffered, and paid the price that no fourteen-year-old should ever have to pay. And so, by some terrible twist of tragic fate, Charles could love his son again, and hold him in his heart in a sacred and comfortable place. This was the only consolation left to him. At the end of all of this, they had become the family that he wanted them to be.

Chapter 47

I Am Mercy

My name is Mercy. I am Mercy Marina Bradshaw, born to a mother whose bones were mending as I grew inside her, floating in my cosy velvet world. I have no conscious knowledge of what she went through when Freddie, my half-brother, tried to murder her, but the event has run through my life like a river from even before the day I was born.

I did not feel her nearly dying from cold and drowning, or from the pneumonia – all her energy was directed to put me first, and to keep the sanctity of the little life that she bore. That is why she called me Mercy. She felt that it was through God's mercy that she was alive and that I was born. She had no other explanation for her survival. And my dad chose the middle name, and called me Mercy Marina because he felt that my very existence should mark the water that had upheld my life. He was like that, my dad, especially towards the end of his life: filled with irony about how we survive, filled with gratitude for every moment, and yet living with the loss of both his sons, a burden scored deep across his heart.

He never really recovered from Anthony's suicide and, in my view, he was broken, and the shock heralded the onset of the heart disease that killed him. He always partially blamed himself, but Mum thought differently; she told me that Freddie alone set up the whole thing, and that Anthony was as much a victim of his plans as she might have been. She was sure that Freddie had watched Anthony grow closer and closer to death for twenty-four hours, before calling a doctor. She was convinced of this, even though it was never formally understood by anyone. Mum never got over this secret and never shared a word of it, except with me, when I was older. I think she thought that I should know just to what extent my half-brother could act without mercy, although I would eventually find that out for myself.

I put my mother's survival down to a series of fortunate events that day, a chain reaction that, once set off, would not stop. How else would you explain a farmer losing his cow, and accidentally finding her and pulling her from the water? Somehow, it was a day of perfect timing, of which she was only a part. But I'm trained as a psychologist, and I suppose I think about things in a certain way. I did not have to call on mercy to help me, and I did not have the same mind as my mother, and I was not the one who had to struggle through Freddie's attack on her. There was no struggle at all on my part. Life simply upheld me. Perhaps Jung would have called it synchronicity, or a scientist might opine that it was a perfect symmetry of events. Either way, the events weighed heavily in my mother's favour on the day. I am twenty-five years old now, and I live with Mum here at Town End Cottage. Dad died five years ago of a sudden heart attack. The pain finally got to him.

Freddie Bradshaw was considered culpable as an adult, having committed the crime when he was just a few months over the age of eighteen. He was sentenced to twenty years in gaol for the attempted double murder of my mother and me. He was released on licence after ten years, for good behaviour. He blamed his father for his brother's death, and therefore felt no guilt whatsoever about what had happened. He felt sad at the loss of Anthony, but this sadness never surpassed the anger at his father for leaving them both, which he continued to feel was the entire cause of the problem.

But there was an upside to his incarceration – his time in prison was his first experience of people telling him exactly what he had to do, and when he had to do it, and this, he loved. It was what he had always wanted in his life: rules and limits. I feel sure that he would have been a different person had he had this guidance in his childhood. In prison, he found himself feeling at peace. During that period of containment he trained in woodwork, and left prison with a City and Guilds qualification in carpentry, which enabled him at least to work for his living in something that he enjoyed. He lived with his mother, never married and never saw his father again.

Mum and Dad told me the full story about Freddie after I saw him in town when I was about ten years old. I was drawn to a young man who looked strangely haggard. I sensed immediately that the person I had seen was him, and I went straight to my parents and told them. Dad thought that I should know what he looked like, but he was just a stranger to me, and I did not live with the same fear as they did about him being anywhere near me. In the end, though, I made a detailed study of this phantom figure, in the shadow of whom I was born and brought up. I was compelled to know more about him and what he had done. I was raised with love and attention and warmth, but there was always the spectre of Freddie at the back of our lives. I had to hunt this down, hunt down all the unknowns and find out about myself, and so I wrote this book to try and explain it all.

When I did my research, I wrote and asked the criminal court for the narrative of the judge at the end of Freddie's trial. Judge Coulson, with many years of experience as a Crown Court Recorder, was sitting at the time. I had to pay for the copy of the transcription, and it took many months to retrieve, but it was worth the effort in the end. It changed things for me, and really gave the events some roots. Here is what Judge Coulson said in his summing up:

'The jury have made a unanimous decision and found you guilty. They have clearly been swayed by the information put before them, despite your continued refusal to make an admission in the face of mounting evidence to the contrary. I have no doubt in my mind of your guilt. Sadly, Mr Bradshaw, there is no excuse for what you have done. I can find nothing that will mitigate your sentence. Nothing whatsoever. Psychiatric reporting shows no mental syndrome that would account for your actions, except that you struggle with symptoms of Antisocial Personality Disorder and have always tended to erratic behaviour and the breaking of rules, although the report stops short of diagnosing this disorder. This personality tendency no doubt has contributed something to your decision to try and murder your stepmother and her baby, but the psychiatric report also refers to you as having misogynistic thoughts that would account for your gross behaviour. Your demeanour continues to justify this assertion.

It is clear to me, that you wilfully and consciously planned this murder, that you deliberately cut a path to the scene of the crime and spent several weeks stalking the victim. You knew exactly what you would do, and you tried to cover your tracks by making your brother lie for you, and by making it look as if Alicia Bradshaw had tried to drown herself, or that she had been subject to an accident. The ruthless act of pushing her over that bridge when she was three and a half months pregnant, can only be described as a determined act of cruelty. You appear to have no conscience, and no shame about the outcome of your actions, and I therefore consider you to be a danger to the public in the future, and particularly a danger to women.

You have never admitted your guilt, you have shown no remorse, and you have ignored the impact statement of the victim that has been put before you, saying that you have no comment. It is only because vigilant and responsible members of the public came forward that you were ultimately found out. You might have got away with your crime had it not been for these individuals, and for this I commend the two ladies who live opposite you for their diary-keeping and their reports to their general practitioner, as well as the psychiatrist who reported his notes to the police. I also must commend the farmer Jed Cooper, who saved this woman's life by pulling her out of that river and resuscitating her. Without his presence of mind and bravery, she and her baby would undoubtedly have perished, and you would have gone to prison for a lot longer, young man. Fortunately, there are plenty of decent people in this community who have contributed to putting right the evil that you committed, and you now have many years to consider this.

We will return to the court for sentencing tomorrow, when I have had time to consider the technicalities of exactly how long a sentence can be allowed in matters such as this. But I must warn you, since you seem to find it so hard to accept reality, you must expect to spend a long time in prison.'

The story was in the local and the national newspapers the following day: *Stepson Tries to Murder Stepmother and Her Child.*

We have all the clippings in a file that Mum has always kept, because she knew that she would have to tell me about it one day, and she wanted me to have evidence of the facts. Fortunately, by the time I was at school it was all blown over, and so nobody ever knew that I was 'that' child, and I lived in relative obscurity. Mum was offered a large sum of money by a popular magazine for her story, but she would not give it. I was the only person who had a right to the story as far as she was concerned. The press tried to get it out of everybody. Mum said that they got short shrift when they turned up in front of Gwen's picture window, thinking that she would give them something. She absolutely would not, and she and Abigail threatened to turn their garden hosepipe onto the throng of reporters, who soon ran.

I know that Dad was very worried that the adverse publicity would affect his business, but it never did. Within a year it was all blown over, although I know he always was grateful to Uncle Ryan, who was the one who ran the company with strength and charisma – and remained a loyal friend – at a difficult time for Dad. Ruby was another anchor for the company, and her influence among the farming community – along with that of her father Jed, who saved Mum's life – was more powerful in Somerset than any morning newspaper. The Coopers put out the word to leave well alone, and so it was the case that any curiosity that arose was soon eroded.

Freddie's grandfather Dick, and his grandmother Brenda said that they would appeal against the verdict, but the appeal was denied, with it being said that there was no evidence that would merit such a procedure from the court, and that the jury had made a unanimous decision.

I never had sight of Freddie until the time he came back to live with his mother on the other side of Blessingham. June felt that Freddie was back where he belonged, and they re-entered their *folie à deux* where the death of Anthony could be blamed on Charles, and would be nothing to do with her son's intentions. His mother's innocent denial of his guilt continued to support him, and she never did recognise the manipulation and cover-up that had taken place under her very nose.

There was always a picture of Anthony on the sideboard in our front room, and there was also one of Harry, my other half-brother brought up by Katrina and Gordon, but there was never one of Freddie. I had dreams of him: dreams of thunderstorms, and dreams of being washed away on torrents of rushing water, and dreams of hanging in a tree, and I would wake up shouting. Dad would come and cuddle and soothe me and put me back to bed, but I would dream again. I never knew why I dreamed such frightening things, when I was brought up in such a safe and loving household with more than enough of everything, including love and affection. When Mum sat me down with all the papers and told me the whole series of events, it came as no surprise. It was as if my brain knew all of it already.

Dad got to be the hero he wanted to be in the end, but it was not in the manner of his childhood imaginings, by winning the battle in a suit of shining armour, or by being superman, or even by getting everything right. He became the hero in Mum's eyes by coping with humility and acceptance with the hand that was dealt to him, and thinking through every minute as it came, and caring deeply for us both. That's what made him her hero. And he was always my hero. And what a hand he was dealt. He was young to die at seventy, and had a sudden massive heart attack that took him out in a few breathless moments. Mum found him in the garden one sunny afternoon after he had been digging. He had been dead, they said, for about half an hour, lying there on the grass. When the ambulance came, his head was in Mum's lap and she was stroking his hair and weeping.

I stood at my father's funeral, the darkest of days for my mother and me, and, at a time when I could have been filled with grief and longing for him, I was instead occupied with a deep-seated disgust for Freddie Bradshaw, who arrived at the ceremony unannounced, sweeping in at the last moment so that nobody could protest. He placed himself strategically so that he could see us. He was not there because he loved my father. He was there because he hated him. I looked up from my mother, who was sobbing into my shoulder, and saw his face. He was smirking a contented and comfortable smile. This was his moment of payback to the wife who had taken his father away from him. He had finally won. The angel of death on this day was on his side, and his story was complete.

The End.

Dr. Joanna North is a psychotherapist, psychologist and author. She loves to weave her professional knowledge and personal imagination into life stories that speak to us of both our deepest and darkest as well as our lightest and most exhilarating emotions. She believes that stories are a pathway for human salvation bringing us back from the brink of our existential despair and deepest fears. Whilst she has written many professional papers and publications, this is her first novel.

Lightning Source UK Ltd.
Milton Keynes UK
UKHW012221030620
364156UK00008B/19